GABRIEL'S REDEMPTION

Gabriel's Redemption

Peter Schmitt

St. Ambrose Press
WHITE POST, VIRGINIA

For Reba Barley—
friend, confidant,
erstwhile editor and
primary reader.

Contents

Acknowledgments

This book is dedicated to my dear friend Reba Barley who has doggedly encouraged my writing. It was Reba who first told me the story that inspired this novel and was my sounding board throughout the creative process.

I would like to thank retired Clerk of the Court, Mike Foreman for his direction and help with the legal system of the time, also retired police officer Fred Hildebrand for guiding me through police procedure. I would also like to mention the members of the "No-Name Writers Group of the Northern Shenandoah," primarily Peter Mowett, Bob Flanagan and Bob Riggs for their input and patience. I will be forever grateful to Joan Vannorsdall, my first writing instructor and talented author for instilling in me a passion to write. Thanks also goes out to my writing coach David Hazard who helped turn an interesting narrative into something much deeper and meaningful.

I would be remiss if I did not mention my three sons, Sam, Andrew and Paul for their continued interest and encouragement and the long suffering Hope who put up with my insanity for twenty-seven years before finally seeing the light, but who never once doubted my ability to write. I am also thankful for the kindness and support of my sister, Otti, my brother Joe, and my parents all of whom have always been there for me when I needed them.

I would also like to thank my friends Ashley and Steve "Hawk" Hawkins for being my safety net, providing a safe haven, a ride, and even bail money should I ever need it. Thanks to Alice Irvan and her husband Bruce who have advised me and supported me in so many ways.

Finally I want to thank Rebecca Gail Heflin, my muse and reason for waking each day, who always makes me strive to be a better person than I am, no matter how often I fail at it.

P. S.
White Post, VA, 2012

PROLOGUE

Fog and Snow

An arctic clipper bullied its way into the Shenandoah's weather system, a cold-blooded pugilist challenging, sparring and defeating an unseasonably warm opponent. Canadian lumberjack versus tropical beach bum, both weather patterns aberrant meteorological events for the first of December in the Valley of the Shenandoah. The result was fog, the moist dust-up of a bare-knuckled bout of weather fronts.

The old man awoke to the fog, the ache in his arthritic joints announcing the drop in barometric pressure long before his eyes opened. When he did open his eyes, the bright pale glow seeping around the drawn curtains, deep forest green curtains, transported him some three thousand miles away and fifty years into the past. He blinked several times at the greenish cast of the room, sat up slowly, and swung his legs out of bed, placing his feet in carefully positioned carpet slippers. His joints crackled and clicked like a pinewood fire, and he groaned as he leaned forward shifting the curtain an inch to see snow covered ground. The whiteness deflated him in body and spirit. Sighing inwardly he rubbed his eyes with the palms of his hands as if to erase what he had just seen.

In the frowzy warmth of the bedroom he begged and cajoled the inaudible voice to forgo the cemetery today. His back and knees invited him to rest, his eyes to read a good book, and his soul to take several naps.

The voice that guided him his entire life was no longer a voice at all. At one time it used conversational mind-speak but long ago evolved into something much different, first metamorphosing into habit and then mutating into obsession.

The inner debate continued, thrust and counter-thrust, as the old man completed his morning ablutions and carefully dressed for the day. Making his way down the hall to the kitchen, his mind's polemic escalating as it had a thousand times before.

Can't go out into the cold. Why do I have to risk pneumonia or a broken hip? To what end? This is crazy, what do I really accomplish? Who am I fooling? What's the point then. I'm coming apart at the seams. How much longer can I do this?

Standing at the kitchen window, he saw his backyard had turned to cloud. The winter fog was a talisman to the past, transcending his pain. He prepared his single cup of coffee for the day and customary breakfast of toast, peanut butter and banana. Before he knew it, and unable to stop himself had he recognized what he was doing, he committed the unnatural act of taking two analgesic tablets. It was something he did not want to do, but this day the voice was not to be denied, certainly not in the presence of snow and fog. What needed to be done was something only he could do, it was his redemption, it was his reason for being, his reason for waking each morning.

He paused at his front gate to appreciate the stillness before starting off on the four blocks to the cemetery. The uneven rough bricks proved a blessing this morning, tree root induced obstacles providing traction and toe holds against the ice that was beginning to form on the streets and sidewalks of New Surrey. Anyone gazing out of a window would have seen an apparition suspended in the fog, the long woolen overcoat, timeless fedora, fingerless gloves and cane, a spirit levitating through the mist, unaware that the old man's mind was fifty years away.

"Bernie, I don't believe it, I just can't imagine . . ."

"What's that, dear?"

"That silly old man is heading out in this weather. I'll bet you he's off to the cemetery."

"Gertie, why should that surprise you? He's been doing this nearly everyday for as long as we've lived here. Would you pour me another cup of coffee while you're up?"

"I'd give anything to know why he does that. I mean how many times can a person go to the cemetery?"

"Why don't you just ask him then?"

"I've tried, Lord knows I've tried. He'll barely say a word when you talk to him, and any time you try to ask him something the tiniest bit personal he changes the subject to the weather or baseball or something else." Gertie said as she turned from the window to retrieve the coffee pot.

"They say he was in the war."

"So was my Uncle Jimmy, but he doesn't visit a graveyard everyday."

"Pour me just a little more, thanks. I imagine it affected everyone differently and some men more than others."

The medieval limestone gatehouse, wanting a portcullis but possessing a wrought iron gate, appeared suddenly and dramatically in front of the elderly man. He passed through the eye of the needle, the smaller gate within a gate to the side of the structure. The cold contracted the metal so that the latch gave easily and the door swung lightly, only the slightest grating of metal announcing his arrival. This morning the cemetery was otherworldly. With absolute determination, he took up where he had left off the morning before, having made the habitual but careful point of memorizing the section, row, and grave.

Something caught his eye just inside the gate. The shifting mist created an illusion of movement. Like a soldier walking point he stood stock still, checked his breathing and carefully studied his surroundings. Then he saw it. A stone the size of a bread loaf had fallen out of the wall. The old man had known the wall for twenty years, while the stone had rested in its spot for more than two hundred. Fulfilling its destiny until today. He went over to the stone, slowly and painfully replacing it to its proper place. The old man knew about stone walls. That night he would dream about one.

For twenty years, since returning from self imposed exile, he had made the daily walk to Nineveh Cemetery and methodically worked his way through the various sections of Confederate graves, through the Union dead and the casualties and veterans of other wars, through family plots, past mausoleums, the columbarium and into the loose rows of individual graves, which appeared haphazard due to the wide variety of headstones and statuary. In the fog the tops of the markers, a collection of spires and crosses, stone tablets, angels and arches, had the appearance of a fairytale city nestled in a sacred kingdom.

He stood stiffly on the first grave of the day and with a clear voice read from the stone, "Calvin C. Carlyle," no dates, no epitaph, just the name. Retrieving a small notebook and pencil stub from his coat pocket, he hung the cane over his arm and made a notation. So began the sacrament known only to the old man.

The lace formed by the ice, dirt and brown grass crackled and hissed under his high-topped shoes whispering a persistent invocation...dust to dust. "Margaret Marie Becker".

"Infant Juliana Becker," again his clear voice spoke out into the mist, an archangel reading names from the Book of Life, and each time a penciled notation made with wizened fingers. "John H. Becker."

"Kenneth Scott Fitzroy." In parts of the cemetery he skipped most of the graves, but then he would happen upon a different section of the hallowed ground and read every tombstone. The old man only read the names of those who had been dead seventy-five years or more, for they surely would have no one left to speak their names, keeping them alive. "Elijah G. Phipps."

"William R. Walters." Other stones were also passed by, thin stones of white-gray marble and umber sandstone, too weather and timeworn to read. Sometimes the moss would grow in a cooperative way, or the soot would have outlined the letters, but not very often. "Donald Warren Kelly".

"Frances A. Sonntag." When he was a younger man, he would produce a piece of rice paper and a thick black crayon from a pocket and coax the name from the age-old stone, the name, date and an occasional epitaph miraculously appearing on the paper shroud. "Thomas T. Tulle."

"James Parker Franklin, Jr." Some days he would spend as long as two hours speaking the forgotten names back to life. For many, it was the first time the name had been invoked in generations, and for most, probably the last time they would be spoken out loud. "Flora C. Franklin."

"Charles D. Spellman." He wondered who these people were, what they looked like, who had loved them and a hundred other questions as he shuffled from grave to grave, the mist parting before him and drawing closed again behind him.

"Miles Jonah Harper."

"Catherine J. Hoffman." After the first half hour of resurrecting the dead, the old man would enter into a state of beatitude, a grace-filled calm, a place of purpose and destiny that was both spiritual and physical. Neural pathways formed by the rivulets of memory and habit caused an endorphin release in his brain that was his due reward and appeasement. "Heinz P. Hoffman."

Nonetheless, after an hour he was beginning to get cold. The temperature had dropped, and the act of breathing became an exercise in self-awareness. The fog was beginning to move from the ethereal to the material, and he felt its resistance as he walked, stood, and spoke. He felt its weight on his hat and coat, but more so, the weight of his age, and the immensity of the task his conscience had placed on his stooped shoulders. He was tired. He needed to sit down. The old man made his way to the end of the row where a marble bench stood in a small alcove of venerable boxwood. On the bench's edge was inscribed into the marble, IN MEMORY OF ELIZABETH REED. He dutifully spoke the name aloud but made no notation in his notebook and sat down.

The contact with the damp marble hastened the penetrating cold as it assaulted his joints and made forays into the visceral core of his body. After several minutes of rest, the anomalous weather pattern asserted itself. It began to snow. The old man noted the first flakes, tiny spheres of ice, more like hail than snow, but soon the hexagram harbingers of winter were dancing on the dark wool of his overcoat.

Snow and fog. He had not witnessed the phenomenon for fifty years and could not remember if he had ever seen it before then. The acuity of his senses was the one thing that age had not stolen from him; his body might be enfeebled, but his hearing and vision were those of a man in his prime. He held his breath for a moment and heard the faint but persistent hiss of the snow falling on the boxwood. It was the sound that whispered in his nightmares. He was immeasurably grateful his hearing had been spared.

His resumed breathing had slowed, his formed breath adding to the cumulus surroundings of the cemetery at less regular, ragged intervals. He looked down the row of headstones and began to see movement. Men appeared moving across the path at the edge of his vision. They advanced slowly, carefully, crouched over, weapons at the ready, in olive drab greatcoats and helmets, others draped in white, with white covers on the helmets, camouflaged in the winter field and forest. In an instant they had moved into the mist. Then there were others, in bloused white tunics and field-gray coats, different weapons, machine pistols, lighter rifles, the coal-shuttle helmets of the Third Reich. He wanted to shout a warning but had no breath. The words would not come, and then they, too, were gone. The only sound was the crystalline whisper of the falling snow, and he became aware that the light was changing as if it was leaving his eyes. In the gloaming before him, he saw a solitary figure approaching. The man wore the vaguely familiar clothes of a different time, a slouch cap clenched in his hands. As he approached, the old man looked into the hardened face of a well muscled, fit, young black man and closed his eyes.

When the old man, the warrior of long ago opened his eyes and looked up, no one was there. He shook the snowflakes from his fedora, clapped his hands and blew warm breath into them. He would not abandon his post, he would not leave the dead to be covered in fog and snow. To be again forgotten. His only choice was to carry on. It was his duty, his fate . . . his redemption. No one would ever say he didn't work hard enough to save those around him. No one... except the old man could level that charge against himself.

CHAPTER I

Schlacht im Hürtgenwald

His eyes opened abruptly as if operated by a spring-loaded mechanism. His body was stiff with cold, filth and fatigue, and so the electrical movement of his eyelids was almost jarring as he lay against the frozen dirt. Sleep had only come in twenty to thirty minute increments as it had for the last couple of weeks. It was a shame because sleep was sanctuary from the misery of the body, soul and spirit. A refuge against the dreariness of the routine and the horror of the extraordinary. It took a monumental act of concentration to detect the presence of his feet. All he could feel was a small patch of warmth on his back where he was leaning against the curve of Garrison's shoulder. They shared blankets and body warmth, and that was all that mattered. Private First Class Mike Garrison had purposely dug his foxhole wider and deeper knowing that he would invite Gabe to share it. Garrison figured sharing the hole with the platoon medic was a good thing, especially a medic who had made the landing in the first wave on D-Day. Normandy gave the medic his bona fides; for Garrison, Gabe was a good-luck charm, a walking, breathing rabbit's foot, a four-leaf clover, a sentient Rosary.

Gabe looked up and saw through the pine bows covering the shelter that the surrounding darkness had slightly altered. With a practiced eye he could tell that somewhere beyond the Huertgen daylight was returning. He shifted his weight eliciting a muffled cough and a groan from Garrison and fished his lighter from his coat pocket. The metallic click that initiated the small light by which he could read his watch was greatly exaggerated in the primeval stillness. The watch read six o'clock, six hundred hours; he hated military time.

The watch was a Hamilton, given to him by his father just before he shipped overseas. It was a little fancy for a G.I. but kept good time in spite of the abuse it had suffered. When his father gave it to him during a family dinner, the elderly Mr. Gabriel reminded Gabe of his sacred duty. A duty to his country, a duty to his fellow soldiers and most importantly duty to himself, and if he did not betray the latter, it would always serve him well. There is nothing, nothing a man can't accomplish if he sets his mind to it and works hard enough. No excuses, no failure. And a real man takes responsibility for everyone and everything in his life. No excuses, no failure. Gabe had wondered if this would be the last time he'd hear the speech intoned all through his life. His father's axiom was like a leap year or solar eclipse occurring just often enough for the words to be carved on his heart and mind, more in granite than flesh and blood. Gabe accepted the watch and then observed that it would look good on the wrist of some German. His gallows humor had brought conversation to an abrupt halt. The memory of that small incident filled him with regret numerous times since his arrival in Europe.

He unbuckled the watch from his wrist and wound it, a ritual by which each day began. Again the tiny sound of winding gears and springs roared in his mind, and he involuntarily stopped and listened for a response to the noise. Of course there was none. Gabe credited his hyperesthesia with keeping him alive these last six months. He nestled back against Garrison, whose breathing had returned to a nocturnal rhythm. Gabe knew that it wouldn't be long before his bladder or second squad's NCO would force the issue and he would have to be up and about.

But until then his mind slipped back into the comfort of the twilight world between sleep and where-with-all. It was the place thoughts and dreams melded seamlessly. For Gabe it had always been the most pleasurable time of the day, all the more so since joining the army. But of late the pleasure of the moment had been greatly diminished. The cold, the dirt, bloody bandages and gaping wounds, the screams of the wounded along with the staccato bursts of German MG 42s now haunted his half-sleep. He could no longer contemplate elaborate meals or conjure get-rich-quick schemes for after the war. The intricate sexual fantasies that had kept his mind entertained during the first few months of separation from his wife eluded him. Snow and sleet, vigilance and luck had replaced thoughts of his Norma's athletic thighs and the angle of her breasts as their bodies intertwined and engaged. All levels of Gabe's consciousness were now focused on a few basic questions: exactly when would he be warm again? Exactly when would be the next time he'd be able to sleep in a bed? When and where will he be able to shower and change clothes? And the pressing question: how many more men were going to die because he was so damn ignorant, helpless and unable to do anything for them? There's nothing you can't do if you put your mind to it and work hard enough. A real man . . .

Finally it was his bladder that made it impossible to prolong semi-consciousness on that morning in late November. His ears detected the normal sounds of an infantry company waking up, muffled voices, some coughing and spitting, the rustle of branches and even the crackle of pine branches being consumed by fire. All was well with his soul, for there were no sounds of combat, no orders or shouts of "Medic!".

Once, when he was helping out at the Battalion Field Hospital waiting to be assigned, he spoke with a wounded sergeant. The man had just been evacuated from the Huertgen, and he just shook his head and said over and over again "Wild and weird, wild and weird". It didn't take Gabe long to figure out what he meant; the sergeant's words visited him regularly now. One of the wild and weird characteristics of the forest was the way sound carried. Sounds traveled over great distances and with the utmost clarity. He could hear the constant drip of water from the branches, the sounds of tin cans being opened, the crackle of radios and clicking of weapons being disassembled and cleaned. There were even times when he could hear German being spoken as if they were in the next foxhole. If the perfect transmission of sounds in this dense, gloomy nightmare of a forest were not eerie enough, what was truly unnerving was that Gabe could never tell from which direction the sound came. Countless times he had closed his eyes and tried to determine the bearing of the reverberations, and time and again he was unable to detect their direction. This was particularly disturbing to a man who believed that his five senses and hard work created his good luck.

"C'mon Mike, up and at 'em, welcome to another day in paradise."

"Go to hell Gabe, ya damned sadist."

Gabe mentally shrugged and used Garrison's shoulder to push himself up out of the hole. He inhaled the smell of fresh cut pine as he moved the branches away and climbed out. The scent was a pleasant change from Garrison's stink and his own had he still possessed the ability to smell himself. Wood smoke was also in the air and wood smoke meant warmth.

Once out of the foxhole he had to maneuver bent over like an old man. It was another of the hateful peculiarities of the Huertgen. The forest was endless miles of hundred-foot tall conifers. With branches reaching so low that men had to stoop to move through it. The interlocking boughs formed an impenetrable canopy that kept the forest floor in half-light like living in a green cave. There was no undergrowth, only mud, pine straw and sap-oozing tree trunks. Oversized drops of freezing water fell from the treetops, and men gazing upward unable to see the sky, wondered if it always rained in Belgium. On this morning, the forest was enshrouded in cloud, the fog adding a haunted presence to the forest. Gabe walked a few yards and found a place next to a four foot in diameter pine trunk where he could stand up straight to relieve himself With steam rising from the bundle of roots at his feet, he buttoned himself back up against the damp and extracted a compass from his shoulder bag. He had made a mental note last night, that they had dug in about sixty yards North-by-Northeast of the firebreak the company had been following.

"Hey Doc, are ya lost or are ya going to stand there with your pecker in your hand for the rest of the day?"

Gabe heard laughter but never got a clear view of where the voices were coming from. Orienting himself with the compass he began making his way towards the firebreak. Hunchbacked shadows were moving in the same direction, shuffling sounds whirling around him and the smell of wood smoke and cigarettes leading him on.

Visibility was no more than ten yards, and after walking for several minutes he realized the firebreak was getting close. The sounds of men preparing for the day were being played out against a backdrop of sound he could not place. It was a soft hiss and while he knew he had heard the sound before, he could not remember where or when. As Gabe approached the road the source became clear. The light just ahead had grown significantly brighter. It was snowing. The earth and sky were indistinguishable.

He couldn't remember ever seeing snow and fog at the same time. Not in Virginia, not anywhere. He thought maybe he liked it. Hell, if it was going to snow anyway, why not throw in some fog to make it interesting, could make walking around these God-forsaken woods a little safer. Maybe.

The firebreak was just wide enough for a couple of Jeeps and half-ton trucks parked at fifty-foot intervals. If one of them broke down or was destroyed by enemy fire, getting past it would be almost impossible, and turning around only slightly easier. The snow, mud, the deep road ruts and arboreal density saw to that. The trucks towed small trailers, one of them a field kitchen.

Smoke was rising from the black metal chimney disappearing into and enhancing the fog and falling snow along the rough-cut road. Snow was dusting the flat surfaces of the vehicles and the shoulders, helmets and hats of the men standing in line for powdered eggs, a chunk of fat passing for bacon, a lump of dough not passing for a biscuit and coffee. It started out being hot but was just beyond being warm by the time the men were able to sit and eat. Some ate back in their foxholes, some in the improvised shelters that had been prepared along the dirt road, shelters rigged by cutting branches, tying ropes, and slinging tents and tarpaulins over them. It was a makeshift cantonment complete with company headquarters, sickbay and mess tent, hardly Fort Dix, but it would do.

Good old Yankee know-how. Gabe smiled to himself as he headed towards one of the tents. Too bad there aren't a couple of doughnut dollies, Tommy Dorsey's band, and Betty Grable throwing kisses.

Gabe entered one of the shelters with a mess kit filled with rapidly cooling provender and his tin cup of coffee not faring much better. A group of ten or fifteen men were standing, sitting or gathering around a small fire burning in an old metal drum, issuing the black greasy smell of motor-oil-laced wood smoke. Some of the men acknowledged him, others didn't, either lost in their thoughts, rumors or powdered eggs.

Ben Schwarz had thrown his ground cloth over a rock outcropping and was sitting cross-legged, unshaved and dirty. He looked like a hobo on a picnic. Ben usually had a good word for Gabe and this morning was no different.

"Jeez Doc, ever see fog in a snowstorm?"

"Not that I can remember, kind of like it though, means nobody'll be movin' round much, neither the krauts or us."

"Yeah, let's hope not anyway." Ben replied through a mouthful of egg.

The canvas tarp afforded some protection from the weather but not much else. The men were a study in dogface wretchedness; low on supplies, low on morale, sick, wounded or about to become one or both. They were stretched to their limit. The atmosphere in the tent mostly reflected it. The scraping of spoons on aluminum mess kits, coughs and sneezes, the lighting of cigarettes, more coughs, a few words, but mostly brooding silence and the barely audible but persistent hiss of falling snow brushing the canvas filled the air inside the tarp.

Finishing breakfast Gabe walked over to a virgin patch of snow and quickly cleaned his kit. Reentering the tent and stamping his feet, he noted a new vacancy next to the fire. He occupied it with extended hands, savoring the warmth and wishing he could stay in that exact spot for a week. His reverie was short lived.

Paul Juergens, first platoon's medic, entered the tent and tapped Gabe on the shoulder. He gave a start that surprised both Juergens and himself. "Captain wants to see us in a half hour, didn't say what was up, but wanted to see you, me and Steibel together." Without waiting for a response Juergens ducked back out of the shelter.

Captain Goodman wants to see the company medics, means we're either in for a fight or we're being pulled out of the line.

Gabe spent the few minutes before he was due at the C.O.'s tent walking the line and checking on the twenty-two remaining men in his platoon. Over the past two months since being assigned as second platoon's medic, replacing Doc Foster, Gabe had come to know his charges as a school master knows a group of rowdy boys, or the way a shepherd knows his flock. It was the same with Doc Foster, he knew the men as well as anyone could and better than most, and he was well liked and respected by them. That seems to be the nature of the relationship between foot soldiers and their medics, a symbiotic relationship whose main purpose was to keep one another alive, an often hopelessly difficult task. Indeed, an impossible task as a splinter of shrapnel from an 81mm mortar round eviscerated Foster while he was carrying a wounded man out of harm's way. Foster's death came as no real surprise to the men. Since the company had entered the forest, the Huertgen had devoured men in the blind feeding frenzy that is twentieth century warfare. Also, Foster's death was a self-fulfilling prophecy; the men considered him unlucky, and there is nothing more important to a foot slogger than luck. Two of the enduring truths of the infantryman are that there are no atheists in foxholes and bad luck is contagious.

Foster's aura of ill fortune and eventually his fate were sealed through an unfortunate string of coincidences involving mail. Every time Doc Foster returned from a supply run to battalion HQ with the mailbag he would inevitably be the bearer of bad news. The post he delivered generally contained at least one or two Dear Johns, perhaps a note announcing the death of a parent or sibling, news of foreclosures or business failures, job losses or any other string of calamities. In the ancient tradition of shooting the messenger Foster was branded as unlucky, well liked, a good medic, but unlucky. In the end they were right.

For Gabe the exact opposite was true. He had been a talisman of good fortune from the moment the men set eyes on him. It happened when he stepped in a large pile of dog shit while reporting for duty to Lt. Brownlee at battalion headquarters. A couple of the men witnessed the incident, and the myth was born. Just as Foster was the bearer of disaster and mayhem, Gabe's mail call always brought wonderful news, packages of cookies, socks and hometown newspapers, perfumed letters, birth announcements and other tidings of joy. This alone made him a hero in the men's eyes, and from the time that he brought a small box to Corporal O'Hara that carried the well-worn Rosary of his sainted grandmother, Gabe's status was confirmed. For unbeknownst to him three hours before he handed the package over, Donald O'Hara had had the left temple of his eyeglasses shot off by a German sniper without so much as a scratch to his face, scalp or ear. It was nothing short of a miracle, a miracle credited to Gabe's account with the soldiers of second platoon.

Gabe's contemplative state lasted through small talk with two G.I.s. It was only broken when he came upon Private Snyder. Phil Snyder suffered with trenchfoot as did many others mired in the Huertgen that late fall of 1944, but Snyder was either too lazy or too stupid to prevent it.

"Snyder, how're your feet?"

"'Bout the same Doc, they hurt like hell."

"Let me see."

Snyder painfully climbed up on a log next to his foxhole and removed his boots and socks.

"Aw hell, Phil, your socks are disgusting. What'd I tell you about that? How many pairs you got?"

"Three, the two I got on and another in my pack."

"Let me see the ones in your pack."

Snyder called to Kohl, his foxhole buddy, to toss him his pack. He rooted around inside the small bag and removed a balled-up, wet, pair of dirty wool socks, identical to those he had just removed from his feet.

"Jesus, Snyder, you dumb-shit, how many times do I need to tell you to keep your socks dry and change them every chance you get? As soon as you're done I want you to take two pairs over to a fire and get them dry, then keep them inside your shirt until you need em, and rotate them around to keep at least one pair dry. I don't care about them being clean, nothing you can do about that, but they gotta be dry. Got it? I see you with wet feet again and I'm going to the lieutenant and he'll have your balls."

The Private's face was the picture of despair. Gabe cradled each foot in his hands and rested them on his knee. He trimmed away pieces of dead chalk-white skin, massaged Snyder's feet as gently as possible, and then dusted them with sulfa-powder. When he looked up, the young soldier was crying. Gabe couldn't figure out why, the reasons were too numerous to decipher. The only thing to be sure of was that whatever the cause of Snyder's distress, he had caused it, and that pierced him. Gabe dug down into the pockets of his greatcoat and extracted a pair of clean, dry wool socks and carefully slipped them onto Snyder's feet.

"There you go kiddo, Phil, it'll be all right. Go over and dry those socks. You gotta take care of your feet; they'll kill you sure as a Nazi bullet. O.K.? I'll check back with you later." Gabe stood and walked away shaking his head. Great medic, nothing like kicking 'em when they're down.

He talked with a few other men, dispensing advice and nostrums until finally reaching the lean-to serving as Company HQ. By the time Gabe reached company command, all the officers as well as Juergens and Steibel, the other two medics, were gathered around a large folding-table studying several maps. The men, each in turn, shuffled over to a small improvised stove and poured themselves tin cups of steaming black coffee, the only guaranteed positive aspect of being called to Company HQ.

Everyone turned and looked at Gabe as he entered the shelter, stamping his feet to knock off the mud and snow. Captain Goodman made a show of looking at his watch. Gabe ignored him with a purpose. Damn military time.

Shifting his weight from foot to foot, blowing on his hands and rotating back and forth refilling his coffee-cup, the captain brought the platoon leaders up to speed on the new orders that had arrived at daybreak.

"This is it, this is as far as we can move with supplies. The Division G3 is reporting that all roads and firebreaks east of here have not been cleared for mines and roadblocks. From here on we move by foot, and the weather forecast for the next few days is more of the same, which should work for us since air support is out of the question anyway, and the weather may, just may, blind their artillery observers. We are the far left flank of a general advance slated to move out at 0600 tomorrow after a day of rest and resupply. We are establishing this spot as a jump off point."

The officers began raising objections immediately and with good reason. The condition of the men and their equipment was approaching critical. The Captain parried each thrust, and in the end it was the old saw "that orders were orders" that sealed D company's fate.

Through most of the thirty-minute briefing, Gabe, Juergans, and Steibel positioned themselves as near to the stove and coffee as possible without blocking egress to the officers. They were surprised by the fact that they had been called to the briefing. While each of the men knew there were other things to do, tending to their men, they were loathe to leave the fire and coffee, and any guilt attached to their current state of comfort was assuaged by the knowledge that not a man in the company would have begrudged them staying put as long as possible.

When the Captain finally did motion for them to join the others, they were questioned about the overall status of the men, first in gener-alities, then in specifics. The platoon leaders had already given their reports, but the Captain had risen through the ranks and wanted the unvarnished truth.

"So let me get this straight, and any of you platoon leaders jump in here, what you're saying is that somewhere between thirty-five and forty percent of the men have some kind of medical issue."

"That's correct, sir." Juergens acknowledged.

"And of those, how many are you actively treating?"

"I'd estimate about around twenty-seven or twenty-eight percent, sir, depending on the day."

"Bottom line?" Captain Goodman took a cigarette from a green pack of Luckys sitting on the table.

Gabe spoke up. "Bottom line, sir, is that we've got about a dozen men between the three of us over in our aid station that need more than we can provide for them. Even if we were flush with supplies, and we're not, they're in pretty rough shape."

"Wounded?"

"Not really, the wounded are tagged and taken back to battalion pretty quickly. Our problem, sir, is that the men are sick. Influenza, pneu-monia, trench foot, dysentery and a couple we're not sure of, typhus maybe, somethin' bad. We're low on supplies across the board and all but out of paregoric, but as far as I know it should be no problem re-supply-ing, at least from Battalion's end.

"Yeah, disease'll kill more men than the Germans. Saw the same thing in seventeen. So with battle casualties, sick call and taking replacements into account the Company is at about seventy percent effectiveness. Rest of you concur with these figures?"

There was general agreement around the table.

The Captain continued. "I feel for those guys with dysentery. I had it myself once or twice, sitting in your own shit, cold, slimy, stinking to high heaven. Let's get em outta here."

"You know I once knew a medic that was so afraid of catching dysentery he started taking paregoric to prevent it, and then got hooked on it. He didn't shit for three months and when he did it was a god damned work of art." Lt. Brownlee added.

"O.K. here's the thing. I'm sending one of you back to HQ with the sick. You'll re-supply and bring back any replacements assigned to D Company. Juergens, you're ranking medic, who accompanies the men?" Captain Goodman interjected, dismissing Brownlee with the tone of his voice.

Now it was Steibel's turn to enter into the discussion. "That's easy, it's gotta be Gabe. Most of the men are from second platoon, there's nobody better at scrounging supplies, and we all know he's the luckiest son-of-a-bitch in D company."

"Brownlee, you all right with that?" The Captain asked, turning to refill his coffee cup.

"Yes sir, most of those men are mine."

"Corporal Juergens?"

"It's fine sir. Me and Steibel will cover second platoon until Gabe gets back."

It took a little more than an hour for all the preparations. The Captain wrote up orders and assembled reports for the dispatch bag being taken to battalion HQ. Gabe attended the sick, dispensing the last of the paregoric to the dysentery cases, seeing everyone was given plenty of liquids, hot tea, and the few extra blankets he could cadge. Fortunately, all but two of the men were able to climb into the truck on their own. Steibel and Juergens loaded the other two on stretchers while Gabe gathered a couple of things for the trip. Lt. Brownlee had given him a packet of letters to be posted, mail being crucial to men in combat.

Gabe also grabbed his Thompson submachine gun and strapped on a .45, a habit ingrained from his initial training as a combat scout. Something that occurred long before the need to become a medic surfaced within him. Whispered tales and raised eyebrows were never far from Gabe, he was a walking, talking paradox, and rumored to be the most heavily armed medic in the division, probably in the whole army. This caused Gabe to smile inwardly, and he never really tried to quench the stories; his men found it a source of comfort. Medics were hardly ever armed.

Corporal Ralph Parker, Captain Goodman's clerk/valet/confidant was sent along with Gabe. He was a short, square man in his early twenties who could be spared for the day and could knowledgeably conduct the Capt.'s business at HQ. More importantly, he could drive. He could drive anything, anywhere, anytime. It was part of growing up a farm boy in rural Virginia.

The distance to Battalion was about three miles, not very far by most standards. But over coarse, rutted, unmarked fire trails, during a snowstorm shrouded in fog, through a forest held by a determined enemy, it might as well have been three hundred miles. The last bit of preparation that needed tending before leaving was to tie a piece of canvas painted white with a large red cross in the center to each side of the truck's covering tarpaulin. It provided little enough protection to the wounded inside the truck, but everyone who saw it was reminded of the vestiges of civilization, mercy and honor, and hoped the enemy would feel the same.

"You ready to go, Doc?" Parker asked as he started the truck and watched Gabe settle onto the seat next to him.

"Yeah, I'm ready, how about you and Willy?"

"Don't worry about Willy. He starts, stops, has fuel, oil, water and good tires."

"O.K., Ralph, then let's hit the road. Take it slow; those guys are sick as dogs."

Parker threw the truck into gear and began the difficult task of turning the truck around on the tight dirt road, bumping trees, revving the engine and grinding gears. Like a mechanized contortionist the truck turned around as Gabe peeked through the small opening into the back of the truck. There was no grousing or swearing, only pale and drawn silence as the men patiently waited for clean clothes, medicine and warmth. The truck moved forward barely quicker than a walk due to the condition of the road, the steadily increasing snowfall, and to spare the men additional discomfort. While both Gabe and Parker were concentrating on the job at hand, shepherding the men to safety, they could not help but be pleased at the prospect of a change in routine and the possibility of some creature comforts at battalion headquarters.

"Looks like the fog is lifting a little. Fog and snow, don't think I've ever seen that before coming to these god-damned woods." Parker wrestled the wheel.

"Yeah me either, fog may be lifting, but it's starting to snow like hell." Gabe replied.

"I'm glad it's a straight shot to battalion. A fella could get lost in these woods and end up at kraut central, if ya know what I mean."

"You mean ya haven't been leaving a trail of bread crumbs?"

"Hell no, none of that Hansel and Gretel shit for me, too hungry, besides the god-damn snow'd cover em up before the birds could eat em." Parker laughed.

Parker and Gabe lapsed into silence as the 4X4 carefully made it's way down an incline. The trees were spaced a little further off to the sides, opening the snow covered shoulders. They passed a burned out German halftrack, the snow piling up on it and the charred remains of its driver and passengers in a stark contrast of black and white. Both men gazed at it in passing, their faces expressionless; the grisly had become commonplace. Gabe turned in the seat and looked back at the men. They were huddled on the benches, their heads down and rocking with the motions of the truck.

Instinctually Gabe's senses had again sharpened to the point of displacing words and thoughts. Observation was all and everything. Passing

the German wreck had triggered the reaction. It was about self-preservation, it was about preserving the lives of those around him. A real man is
responsible for everyone . . . The ability to draw on his senses and be
immersed in his surroundings without any internal distraction was itself
a sixth sense.

Parker broke the silence first. "I'm freezing my ass off in this god
damn worthless piece of shit sorry excuse of a truck. The heater barely
works, the defroster ain't worth shit, and the wiper on your side is so
caked with snow and ice it's all but quit workin'."

Gabe grunted from deep in his throat to acknowledge Parker, his
mind too busy processing sensory input. His ears heard a myriad of
sounds, the growl of the engine, the sound of the tires digging into the
snow, the whir of the inadequate heater fan, the rhythmic beating of the
windshield wipers, the crystalline tap of snow against the windscreen
and a hundred different rattles and clanks as the 4X4 crept along the firebreak. His body felt each bump and sway as tires careened in and out of
ruts and over hidden rocks. His body was a collection of warm and cold
spots, aches, cramps and the distinct possibility he might have to relieve
himself before they reached their destination. Mercifully his nose could
only detect the faint mixture of engine exhaust and Parker's cigarette
smoke, not bad considering they were ferrying a bunch of guys soiling
their clothes with blood-tinged diarrhea. Gabe's eyes flitted to and fro
looking for movement in the trees and trying not to marvel at the beauty
of the falling snow as it lined and laced the pine branches.

"I gotta do something about this wiper, it's driving me crazy not
being able to see what's in front of me." Gabe replied, the restricted vision
a direct threat to his personal safety and sense of well-being.

"Don't worry about it, I can see all right and we're about half way,
so there's no point in stopping. Besides, if we stop going up this hill I may
not be able to get this heap going again."

"You don't have to stop. I can reach around and knock the ice off
the wiper blades from here." And with that Gabe rolled down his window and reached his arm around the front of the windshield to knock
away the snow and ice. It didn't work. He closed the window, blowing

on his exposed fingers poking out of woolen gloves. "Man, it's colder than a well digger's ass out there."

"You mean a witch's tit, which everybody knows is colder than a well digger's ass. It'll be another six weeks before it's this cold at home, and I'll bet they haven't gotten the first snow yet." Parker replied as Gabe removed his medical bag, Thompson, cartridge belt and holster, carefully stowing them at his feet. "What are ya doin' now?"

"I've got to be able to see out the windshield. We're moving slow enough, I'm going to get out on the running board and clear off the ice. Keep her slow and steady, okay?" and with that Gabe rolled down the window, opened the door just enough to squeeze out onto the running board and with one arm securing himself inside the vehicle began cleaning off the windscreen and wiper.

Again, conscious thought receded to the back of his mind as he became absorbed by the task at hand and the tableau of sensory input his brain sorted and analyzed. He could feel each individual snowflake as it struck his face and could feel and hear tiny fluctuations in the wind as the Willy's crept along. His eyes were fascinated by the infinite crystalline shapes presented by each six-pointed star as it settled on his coat sleeve for the briefest moment. He felt the small bump as the driver-side tire rode over the manmade bulge and forever after wondered if he imagined or really heard the small click of the trigger apparatus a fraction of a second later.

CHAPTER 2

The Waking Wounded

Gabe slowly became aware. He performed mental triage, prioritizing the immediate circumstances as he experienced them. First was the headache, so severe it assured him he was still alive, but wishing he were dead, with its attendant blurred vision, nausea and the rushing oceanic sound in his ears. An ether-induced hangover? The result of a large dose of morphine bidding him farewell, its artificial opiate peace and harmony giving way to reality? A concussion? Yeah, my head is sure as shit bandaged.

Next, the burning and stinging sensation from his legs, back and buttocks. As he shifted his weight, a crystalline shard of pain stabbed behind his eyes, and he was convinced that the skin of his back was tearing loose. Shit. My legs are bandaged too, and it hurts too much to roll onto my back. The surge of pain cleared away the lingering fog of morphine with hurricane ferocity. Instantly his mouth filled with the bitterness of bile as panic welled-up from the primal depths. He carefully eased his hand down his abdomen, making a palsied effort at undoing the drawstring on his pants. He felt down between his legs. He was able to breath again. Oh thank God, there's no pain, no sutures, everything's still there. Gabe would have laughed if it didn't hurt so much; his discovery went a long way towards easing his mind. As he relaxed, he wondered if that was the great fear every wounded soldier had endured down through the ages.

Gabe took stock of his surroundings. He was lying on a cot with an IV line connecting his arm to a bottle of plasma hanging next to him. The room was large with whitewashed walls, a beamed ceiling and windows

22

at the roofline allowing in the weak winter light. There were several crucifixes on the walls and other saint-someone inspired objects he didn't recognize. Bare light bulbs were strung over the beams, despairing to provide what light they could. The room held a dozen or so other cots comforting or torturing men, casualties in various states of disrepair, the spilth of the Huertgen Forest. The acrid smell of carbolic disinfectant, alcohol and the organic mixture of blood, excrement, urine and infected wounds was itself a presence in the room. Apron-clad nuns in blue and white, orderlies in green fatigues and an occasional white-coated doctor hovered at the edges of his vision. Somewhere in the room a man was crying for his mother and babbling in German, someone else telling him to shut the fuck up.

When he awoke, Gabe had no concept of time other than the room had grown dim. The light bulbs flickered with a pitiful ochre light casting shadows, halos and auras that were no doubt drug and head injury induced. When he stirred, a nun brought him a cup of water; he drank gratefully, not realizing how thirsty he was. He asked some questions, but when she answered him in thick-tongued Flemish, he realized it wasn't worth the effort and lay back on the pillow. Mercifully, the headache had begun its retreat and, filling the vacuum it left, came reason. He began to piece together the events that landed him here.

He closed his eyes and began to concentrate, seeking the most elemental aspects of those fateful seconds: the smell of Parker's cheap cigar, the sudden rush of cold, the sensation of the small no-nonsense snowflakes striking his face, how he had to squint to see what he was doing, the literal white noise of the wintry forest beyond the sounds of the truck engine, how quickly his feet and fingers began to go numb. The morning's events came rushing back to him. It was an avalanche of terror, helplessness, frustration, and then the guilt. Why did I survive? Surely there were better men in that truck than me. His body trembled involuntarily, his bladder letting go, and just that quickly he was back in the Huertgen.

Gabe realized exactly what was happening as he struggled to clean his side of the windshield. His per acute senses, experience and combat intuition already had him turning to jump off the truck when the five kilograms of TNT inside the Tellermine 42 exploded.

The shock wave caused by twelve pounds of tightly-packed dynamite igniting threw him nearly thirty feet, with pieces of rubber, steel, glass and human tissue flying by him. He bounced and slid across the ice-crusted snow, coming to an abrupt stop when his head made contact with the trunk of a pine tree. Were it not for his helmet, he would have died there and then. Lying on his side, with his head bent at an unnatural angle, he was able to see the large and small pieces of the 4X4 and its passengers falling into the snow as if dropped from a great height. The chassis of the truck shuddered as it settled back onto the rutted road, its skeletal remains twisted in corkscrew destruction, with debris shed in a perfect circle around it; the cab looked like a can of beans blown open in a campfire.

The adrenaline, released and coursing through him, brought Gabe to his feet but was immediately overruled by his drive for self-preservation; he threw himself to the ground again, waiting for a German patrol to open fire. There was only silence, save for the clicking and tapping of the rapidly cooling, useless metal and the sounds of weather. No screams, no cries for help. He made two unsteady attempts to get back on his feet. With the third try, he was able to stand and take slow, mincing steps towards the truck. It was only when he felt the cold air on his legs and backside and the startling wet chill of snow and ice on bare skin that he checked himself over, reaching around and feeling his shredded clothes. When he looked down at his hands, they were bloody. In shock, and in the absence of rational thought, he tried to look at his wounds turning several times in place like a dog chasing his tail. His eyes did not register the trail of blood leading back to the indentation in the snow near the towering conifer. Blood from the struggle to gain his legs had left a demonic snow angel.

In his delirium he began to pull men from the truck, fifty, sixty men, dragging and carrying them to the embankment, thanking God out loud the Willy's wasn't burning.

Where did they all come from? There couldn't have been that many guys in the truck. How the hell am I going to put these guys back together with a half dozen bandage rolls, a tin of sulfa, scissors and five morphine syrettes? Where the fuck is my bag? I can do this, I can save them, only need to concentrate, only need to push harder.

Finally overcome by exhaustion, the loss of blood, hypothermia and shock, he sank to his knees amidst the dead. Gabe wept.

The night nurse, one of The Sisters of Mercy, heard the sobs coming from cot number six and mistakenly assumed the patient was in corporeal pain. She went for the orderly on duty. He injected the painkiller into the muscle of Gabe's upper left arm, and after ten minutes, Morpheus, god of dreams, beckoned Gabe to follow.

It was well into the next day before Gabe awoke. It was difficult for him to alert his mind, but making the effort, he was surprised at how easily his mind and body began to engage his surroundings. The angle of the light, the cup of water, bowl of tepid soup and chunk of coarse bread on the small table gave him a point of reference for guessing the time. He could tell it was shortly after noon; what he couldn't tell was what day of the week it was. His bandages were freshly changed, he felt clean and dry and was clean-shaven, all of which had been accomplished without his cooperation, consent or consciousness. When a nurse came by to take his pulse and temperature, he thanked her in French. "Merci" he whispered as she held his wrist and hand. She smiled, not bothering to correct him, and answered in Flemish, "graag gedaan".

As the sister withdrew from his side, Gabe was surprised to see Ben Schwarz standing at the foot of his bed, wool cap folded in his hands, dispatch bag over his shoulder, his coat mud-spattered and stained with his last meal and other less savory items. The sight of Ben cleared his mind instantly.

Ben grinned broadly. "How the hell are ya, Doc?"

"Kind of a dumb question."

"Yeah, I guess so." Ben said.

"Good to see you. So what are you doing here? Besides checking on me? Need a couple of bucks 'til payday?"

"Ha-Ha. Good old Doc Gabriel, still a funny-guy even after he's been sliced and diced. You know, just thought I'd come to town, buy a couple of cases of champagne, couple pounds of caviar, maybe get laid by a French contessa, the usual shit. Now whose turn is it to ask dumb questions?"

"Touché." Gabe acknowledged.

"So, Doc, you're never gonna believe this, but the head saw-bones here is a Captain Stanley Buchinski. Well, I knew a square-headed Pollock back in Cleveland named Stanley Buchinski, dated his sister for a while."

"You've dated everybody's sister."

"Yeah. Can I help it if the broads find me irresistible?"

"Yeah, and a snappy dresser too." Gabe said.

Ben continued. "Well, sure enough, it's him. It was like old home week, meeting him here. So I got the skinny. He said you have a pretty bad concussion, and that he picked a bunch of shrapnel out of your butt, sewed you up and you should be good as new in a couple more days."

"Great. Ya mean I'm not going home?"

"I was lookin' out for your best interests and told him you'd give him a case of scotch for a ticket home. You know those ass wounds can be pretty nasty."

Gabe just smiled. "Two. Two cases of scotch."

"No such luck. Stan said he was a Bushmill's kind of guy. It'd have to be a case of Irish whisky and a stack of polka records. Any idea how hard it is to find polka records in Belgium? And besides, it's not like the company is exactly flush with medics. Oh, yeah, and one more thing. He said you were the luckiest son-of-a-bitch in this man's army, but everybody already knows that." Ben shook a Lucky Strike out and lit it. "Smoke?"

Gabe ignored the offer. "Yeah, Lucky. Ben, tell me something. How did they find me? How did I get here? Did anybody else make it?"

Ben turned and walked across the room, bringing back a wooden stool and sat down on it heavily. His demeanor had changed, and all humor left his face. "You sure you wanna hear this?"

"Yeah, I have to."

"Okay, if you say so, you remember the damn weather, fog and snow, really unnatural if you ask me. Everybody figured we'd take it easy for a change; you know, hold the line, try and stay warm and dry. Lieutenant Brownlee had other plans, though. He rousted first squad and ordered them out on patrol. Guess he didn't want the krauts blindsiding us in that godforsaken fog. Well, we, that is first squad, were standing around, bitching and moaning, checking weapons, ammo, when we heard the bang. Everybody heard the bang. In our guts everybody knew what it was, knew it had to be you and Parker, single explosion, no artillery, no small arms, had to be a mine. Brownlee knew it, too. So he sent first squad down the road to check it out and sent third squad out on patrol." Ben paused; he wasn't quite sure how to continue.

"Go on."

"Iverson was point and visibility was about twenty yards or so when we came upon the truck." Again Ben paused, looking down and wringing his wool cap in his hands.

"Go on, Ben, it's okay." Gabe repeated.

"The truck was completely destroyed, twisted up, bits and pieces all over the place, just about blown in half. And then there was you."

"What about me?"

"Well Doc, I gotta tell ya, it was about the weirdest thing any of us had ever seen."

"What was? Come on, just get to the point."

"All right, all right. You were lying curled up on your side, gray, no, almost blue, the side of your helmet flattened, your uniform shredded. You were barely breathing. Doc, here's the weird part— lying next to you, in a near perfect row, were, uh, were body parts. All put together, trying to match up legs, with torsos, with hands, bits of guts, like you had somehow tried to reassemble them. You were caked with near frozen blood, lots of your own, but mostly from the others. Couple of the guys, and not rookies, a couple of the guys upchucked, and everybody just stood there staring. Finally, like something clicked inside of them, a couple guys took off their coats and wrapped you up in them. DeAngelo, that big guinea from Jersey, picked you up in a fireman's carry and double-timed you back to company HQ. Never seen that big pisano son-of-a-bitch move so fast. Doc? You okay?"

"Yeah, I'm okay. I don't remember much, but that clears up some things. I can't believe I made it. I'm the only one?"

"The only one. You always been this lucky? A couple of us are playing your birthday and serial number in the Irish sweepstakes when we get home."

"All right, long as I get a piece of the action."

"Ten percent, no sweat." Ben had lightened up again. "Oh, hey, I almost forgot." He began rummaging around in the dispatch bag, as chips and flakes of dried mud fell to the floor, "This was waiting for you when I grabbed the company mail this morning." He handed Gabe a letter, his name and address written in the familiar handwriting of his wife. "I figured it'd cheer you up."

Gabe fumbled with the envelope, and with some effort opened it and extracted the neatly folded letter, holding it up to his nose for the scent of perfume and Norma's touch. He stared at the page for a moment, a slight frown passing over his face and handed the letter to Ben. "My vision is still a little blurry. Mind reading it to me?"

"You sure? It might be kind of personal."

"It's okay. If it is, and you tell anybody, I'll kill you in your sleep." Gabe said with a menacing look.

"Okay, here goes." Ben automatically brought the paper to his nose and breathed deeply. "Hey…she's spending all your money on the good stuff. That ain't no cheap-ass French-whore toilette water."

"Yeah, yeah, just read it, will ya?"

"Okay, okay, here goes:

Nov. 7, 1944

Hello Sweetheart,

How are you? I hope you are taking care of yourself and keeping safe and warm. Sometimes we read such dreadful things in the newspapers, and then other times it sounds like the war will be over in a week or two. I hope so. I really hate this war, and I hate the Germans and Japs for

taking you away from me. You'll be glad to know I have
moved in with your mother. I guess you noticed the return
address on the envelope. It's been three weeks now, but so
far everything is going well. With my work at the mill and
her keeping the books for old Doctor Morris, we barely see
each other. We're like ships passing in the night. We have
decided, though, to have dinner together one night a week.
Your mom sure can cook, even with the rationing, but you
already know that. I've decided to learn as much as I can
about cooking, so that once you're back home, you'll never
want to leave again. Of course, there'll be something else to
keep you home, Darling. I miss you so much. I'm lonely
for you in the worst way, so please come home soon! Things
haven't changed too much around here, like I said. There's
the rationing, and there's a star in almost every window in
town. I used to cry every time I saw a gold one, but now I
just worry about you. Is that terrible of me? The harvest
came in pretty good this year, and that certainly helps make
the food rationing easier to take. Annie and I get together
all the time, going to the movies or out for a drink. It's nice
to have a good friend, with you not being here! The house
looks good, your mother has moved her bedroom down to
the old study on the first floor, and I'm sleeping in your old
bedroom. I think we will be pretty good roommates, and
I'm trying to save money so we can have our own place to
fill up with kids when you get back. We've decided its time
to fix the place up a little. You know nothing much has been
done since your Daddy passed. We're painting and scrubbing and moving furniture around all weekend long, which
helps the time pass by. Did I tell you I miss you? For the
heavy work, your mother has hired a man to help out.
Remember that colored boy, Enoch Baker? We all call
him Knock-knock Baker. You remember him, the football
player, he's strong as a mule and pretty good at fixing

things. So this place should be in tip-top shape by the time you get home. Well, I'm rambling on, and it's late. I'm off to bed to dream about you. I love you the most.

Your loving wife,

Norma

"Wow, she sounds like a sweetheart of a gal."

"Thanks, I think so too, but you know we were only married a couple three months before I left, and we only dated a couple of months before that. Sometimes I think we barely know each other."

"Yeah, well, that's all right. When this damn war is over, you'll have all the time in the world to get to know each other, and I mean that in the Biblical sense, if ya know what I mean." Both men laughed. "Well, Doc, I better be getting back."

"Okay, give my regards to the guys and tell them I'll be back saving lives and stamping out disease before they know it. Unless I can find a stack of Polka records."

"Take care, Doc. I'll try and stop by again in a couple of days if you're not back by then." Ben Schwarz turned and left, leaving a small trail of dirt and other detritus behind him on the floor. Gabe was glad, so very glad, Ben stopped by, a friendly familiar unwashed face.

Gabe grew stronger each day, his vision improved, his headaches and nausea subsided and soon he was carefully walking around the ancient cloister serving as the regimental hospital. He healed physically, but inside he was convinced more than ever, that no matter how much he fooled himself or bullshitted Ben and the others, he couldn't save lives or stamp-out disease. Hell, he couldn't even keep a bunch of G.I.s with flu and dysentery alive.

The main portion of his recovery and subsequent return to the line took just a little over two weeks. When he caught back up with his platoon, he was still sore, but in a new uniform and freshly resupplied. His reputation as the luckiest dogface in this man's army was galvanized.

Gabe tried to argue repeatedly, if being lucky was true he'd be on board ship heading for New York right about now, or at least he would have stumbled onto a stack of polka records. His arguments didn't hold up, mainly because the men wanted to believe, no, needed to believe his was an act of providence in the hell of the Huertgen forest.

CHAPTER 3

Mrs. Thomas Jonathan Gabriel

T he late autumn rains of the Valley had stripped most of the trees down to bare branches with the notable exception of the oaks, which held on to their brittle brown leaves with that enduring strength that mankind holds in awe. The magnolias, pine and holly stood as a constant reminder that winter does not mean the death of all things. An occasional hardwood still defiantly flashed its golden leaves as a torch weakly flickering to hold off the darkness. The streets of New Surrey were more often wet than dry in late November. Fallen leaves lay plastered against the pavement like wet hair on a child's forehead. The dampness gave the air an edge that belied the true temperature, and at night and early in the morning people's breath took form.

In a little more than a week, December 7th 1944, the United States would mark its third year at war, and her people were growing tired. Grim determination, sacrifice and duty had replaced the bravado of honor, glory and patriotism as the warp and weave of society's fabric. As with weather and seasons, the war affected all things, touching the lives of everyone in New Surrey and the surrounding county. Blue and gold stars hung in the windows of homes and restaurants, offices and shops with such frequency that a casual observer would believe that every home had sent a son. The gold stars hung in the windows of homes to which loved ones would not be returning. The rationing of sugar, butter and gasoline, among other staples, scrap metal drives, victory gardens and U.S. war bonds were now all part of the day-to-day routine. The gold stars helped to put things in the proper perspective; the sacrifice of some was far greater than that of others.

But in spite of it all, in spite of an entire nation going onto a war footing, the people of New Surrey, Virginia had the advantage of populating the seat of an agrarian county, a county that had been feeding the people and animals of the Shenandoah for more than two hundred years. The pastures, gardens and orchards had seen the passing of British dragoons and Daniel Morgan's Rifles, the "foot cavalry" of Stonewall Jackson and the blue coated cavalry of Philip Sheridan and the ravages of "Black" Dave Hunter. The farms had sent off their horses, crops and sons with Blackjack Pershing to Flanders' fields and the hell that was Passchendaele and again twenty-something years later to Bataan and then Normandy, yet local farms continued to feed their own, government rationing not withstanding.

Norma Marie Gabriel, nee Bittner, was twenty-six years old that November. She, too, sacrificed towards the war effort; she bought war bonds and could not buy silk stockings or decent coffee. More so, almost a year earlier she had seen her husband off to Fort A.P. Hill for basic training and subsequent deployment to England and later France, all after only ninety days of marriage. They had barely gotten to know one another as husband and wife. On Gabe's last leave before shipping out to England they had tried desperately to conceive a child, a baby to keep Norma occupied and fight the loneliness while Gabe was away, and for the unspoken possibility that he might not return. The timing was not right and there was no pregnancy, but not for want of trying.

Once his orders had come through, Gabe had decided it would be best if they gave up their apartment over the shoe store downtown. Norma could then move in with her mother-in-law, Dorothy, to save money and help the old woman around the house. Norma acquiesced to Gabe's wishes and plans. It was not an argument she wished to pursue, especially with him going off to war. Jokes regarding the great lessons Norma would learn about patience repeatedly danced through the pillow talk during their last night together. In the familiar darkness of their bedroom Gabe could not see her face as he teased her about his mother.

Many months passed before Norma could bring herself to fulfill the request her husband had made their last night together. The pending move was a frequent topic of conversation with her best friend Anne and an occasional topic for lunchtime banter with the other secretaries at work. In time, the tone of Gabe's letters became more insistent, and he clearly began making mention of it in letters he wrote to his mother. The elder Mrs. Gabriel, much to her credit, did not push the issue, but gently and firmly would choose her moments to make her son's wishes known to the younger Mrs. Gabriel. In recent weeks, as summer gave way to autumn and autumn marched headlong towards winter, even Anne took Gabe's side. Her persuasive points were honed by the logic of practicality, the war effort and patriotism. Norma suspected Gabe was writing Anne as well, of course she knew that wasn't true. Correspondence was not Gabe's forte.

Since Gabe's departure, Norma and Anne breakfasted together three days a week. It was a standing appointment, 6:30 a.m. at Elvira's Country Kitchen and one of the small self-indulgences others may have frowned upon. The women always sat at the same table but varied their choices of breakfast and fruit juice. Coffee, hot and black, like their choice of seating never varied or faltered. The friends' conversation flowed in a great continuum, picking up where it had last concluded, often circling back to cover ground already traversed like a hunter lost in a wood realizing a tree or rock looked familiar.

"So, are you ever going to move in with Dorothy? You made a promise." Anne spoke the words while absently fumbling in her purse for a cigarette and not finding one.

"I did no such thing. I never promised; I just told Gabe I would."

"Same thing."

"Not really."

Anne took a sip from the heavy white cup, leaving a Tahitian Rose lipstick smudge and dabbed at her lips with a napkin. "What are you afraid of? Dorothy is a sweet old thing, and think of all the money you'll save not paying rent and halving the groceries."

"Oh, dear Lord, Annie, let's not flog that dead horse again. I know you're right and there's every reason in the world to move in. It's just hard. You know? It took me so long to finally move away from home and get a place of my own. Heck, I had to go get married to do it, and now I have to move back into somebody's house. It's like taking one step forward and two steps back."

"But think of the money. With what Gabe sends home you'll save enough for a down payment on a house, or buy a car, and some nice clothes."

Norma saw her chance to redirect the conversation to more comfortable and equally familiar terrain. She and Anne were soon discussing fashion, critiquing how mutual friends and acquaintances dressed. They approved of some, and sharpened their claws on the fashion sense of others. Norma was able to finish her creamed-chipped-beef-on-toast with some small inner peace, until breakfast the day after tomorrow would see the conversation coming full circle, both women never realizing they were lost in a forest of thoughts and ideas.

As the women parted ways on the street, Annie turned and, walking backwards a few steps, called back to Norma, "Hey, want to go out Friday night, maybe to a movie or dance or club or something?"

"Maybe. I'll let you know. Bye."

Eleven months after Gabe went to boot camp, Norma moved in with her mother-in-law. She was no better prepared for battle than her husband had been when he enlisted for combat. It would not be a physically taxing move. The couple's sole worldly possessions filled two oversized suitcases, which she struggled and strained to place next to the door and then telephoned for a cab. The dispatcher said it would be twenty or thirty minutes as it was Tuesday and he only had one driver taking fares. Norma draped her coat, hat and gloves over the suitcases, sat at the small writing table in the living room and lit a Chesterfield. She watched absently as the smoke displaced the dust motes in the hard winter light. The light angled in sharply, slanting through the front windows staking claim to a faded place on the carpet. Collecting her thoughts, she gazed around the room seeing it as she had the first time the landlord had shown it to the newlyweds. Norma slowly acknowledged to herself that the three months she had shared this apartment with Gabe had given her some of the best days of her life, and as the smoke swirled and danced in the light she wondered what the coming days would bring.

She turned to the desk, and to pass the time took a writing tablet and freshly sharpened pencil out of the drawer to begin a letter to Gabe. She was smoking her third cigarette and had not gotten beyond Hello

Sweetheart and the date when a knock on the door gave her a start. She snubbed the cigarette in the ashtray, crumpled the unwritten letter into her hand and answered the door.

"Well, good morning Norma, where you off to? Going on a trip?" Charlie Townsend smiled as he waited for Norma to don her coat, hat and gloves.

"Charlie, you're still driving a cab?" Norma said returning his smile.

"Yes indeed, been at it thirty years now, should start getting pretty good at it sooner or later." He grabbed one suitcase and was caught up short as he tried to lift the heavy bag. "Good Lord. What have you got in here, the kitchen sink, or did you find bars of rebel gold in the cellar?"

"Neither, Charlie, that's everything we own, so be careful lugging them down the stairs. My Grandma's dishes are in there."

"And so where we going with this precious cargo?"

"God help me, I'm moving in with my mother-in-law. Take me over to the Gabriel house on Pritchard Street."

"Know it well. I grew up there, you know, and your husband's daddy was one of my best friends. I watched that family grow up, and I was the first one there when John collapsed on the kitchen floor, guess it was about three years ago. It was his heart, was nothing anybody could do about it, suspect he was dead before he hit the ground." The rotund balding man loosened his muffler and unbuttoned his jacket before lifting the bag a second time and carefully easing it down the stairs. "You wait here, Norma, and I'll be back for the other bag. It's colder than a witch's...uh, it's cold out there this morning."

But Norma followed Charlie out of the apartment, having left two sets of keys on the kitchen counter and closed the door firmly. The glass doorknob had always been loose and nearly came off in her hand. Norma then stepped in front of Charlie and led him down the stairs, holding the building's door open.

Once the bags had been gently situated in the trunk, she climbed into the front passenger seat of the dark blue Packard, and as Charlie took the wheel asked, "You don't mind if I sit up front do you? It feels funny sitting in the back all by myself."

"No, I don't mind. Suit yourself."

"Mind if I smoke?"

"No, course not, just open the window a crack." He reached forward and snapped open the ashtray on the dashboard. Norma opened the small triangular vent window, lit her cigarette and dropped the match out onto the pavement.

"I see you have a "B" sticker. At least you get a little more gas than everyone else."

"Yes, well, you know, taxies, busses and the like, and what with New Surrey being just a small city, it works out fine, especially if I keep it to the thirty-five speed limit. Course, I have to anyway here in town, but even when I get a fare out to the county, I keep it to thirty-five. Helps save gas, but more importantly, the rubber, got to save rubber, tires are fiercely expensive now and becoming scarce." Charlie had warmed to the subject, but Norma was now just staring out of the window, and Charlie took the cue.

Except for Charlie's quiet, tuneless whistling of dissected Christmas carols, the rest of the short trip passed in contemplative silence. As the cab turned onto Pritchard Street, tentative flakes of snow began to fall. The finely wrought, wind driven flakes portended the season's first snow could be a big one. The street was lined on both sides by large working class homes, mostly of brick, some framed, with postage-stamp front yards, commodious front porches and wrought-iron fences and gates. The houses on the North side of the street were uphill where stone and brick retaining walls replaced the iron fences. Mature sycamore trees stood as mottled sentinels on both sides of the street, their roots buckling and undermining the brick sidewalks and their branches forming a protective canopy over the street.

"Here we are, Norma, the Gabriel house." Charlie announced as he pulled up in front of number four-twenty-seven. "I grew up right over there in four-twenty."

"That's nice, looks like a nice place." She handed him the fare plus a little extra. "Keep the change, and thanks."

"Oh thank you, and a Merry Christmas to you, Norma."

Charlie once again gingerly handled the large suitcases, and as he was climbing the porch stairs the door opened and Dorothy motioned for them to bring the bags and themselves in from the cold. Charlie removed his hat and exchanged pleasantries with Dorothy, who then asked if he would mind taking the bags upstairs. He didn't mind, and again loosening his muffler and unbuttoning his jacket got more exercise that morning than he had in a long time. He refused the money Dorothy held out to him as he was leaving and wished both Mrs. Gabriels the best of the season.

Dorothy took Norma's hat and coat and hung them in the hall closet. She then turned and engulfed Norma in her strong arms and hugged her to her matronly bosom, kissing her on the cheek. Norma returned the perfunctory hug and kiss and then, with some embarrassment, took her thumb and rubbed the lipstick smudge from Dorothy's cheek.

"Welcome, Dear, I've waited so long for this day, and Gabe will be so happy to hear the news."

"Thank you, Mrs. Gabriel, I'm sure he will. It was one of the last things we talked about before he left."

"I know, Dear, and please call me 'Dot', everyone else does. Now you can go and settle in to any of those bedrooms upstairs. After John passed, I moved into the downstairs study. It just made more sense living here by myself, and besides our old bedroom just didn't feel right anymore. The bath is upstairs and the kitchen is down here, so we can be like ships passing in the night."

Norma smiled at the image.

Dot took Norma on a quick tour of the house, pointing out the small peculiarities present in every home, showed her how to manage the heat, what to do if she ran out of hot water and where the fuse box and spare fuses were. Norma then went upstairs to unpack.

She had first considered occupying the master bedroom since it was the largest and most nicely appointed, but then thought it might prove a little awkward. So she moved into Gabe's old room, which was much the way he had left it. She was surprised at how large and comfortable it was. He had lived there up until the time they were married.

Norma had fully intended on going back to work that afternoon, but as she gazed out of the window into the backyard, the snow was falling steadily and the ground was turning white. She rang the office and asked if they were busy. Of course they were not, and so she took the afternoon off. She brewed some tea, unpacked, and with uninterrupted and unrestricted curiosity explored Gabe's belongings embarking on the journey to know her husband. On that winter afternoon it seemed like an odyssey of mythic proportions.

As weeks passed and the ebb and flow of daily life established itself, the two women managed for the most part to stay out of each other's way. Norma's fears and concerns never materialized, which came as a subtle surprise.

The fact was that the two women were more alike than either had suspected or admitted. Both worked. Norma because she had little choice in the matter; she liked nice clothes, wanted a car, and hoped that she and Gabe would one day own a home, reasonable expectations. Dorothy, on the other hand, did not need to work. Her expenses were minimal, and she and her husband had saved for retirement through the years. She was wise with money, so Dorothy worked to get out of the house, to not lose touch with people and to remain an active member of the community. Both women were confident and competent and managed their bosses' affairs in ways that made them indispensable. In many ways, they were the powers behind the thrones.

Dorothy kept the books of Dr. Morris P. Franklin, a septuagenarian physician who had birthed and buried generations of New Surrey and county citizens.

Dorothy had free reign over Dr. Franklin's books. She forgave and forgot the bills of people who were barely getting by and just couldn't afford to pay, and she padded the bills of those who were bothersome, obnoxious or took advantage of the good doctor's grace and could, of course, afford to pay a few extra dollars. In the end it averaged out, and Dr. Franklin never knew the difference. Dorothy truly loved dispensing justice this way. With the wisdom of Solomon and the guile of Robin Hood, she was doing her small part to set things right in the world meting out social justice as she saw fit.

Norma worked at the McDermott woolen mill in a large room with tall windows looking out into a courtyard. The brick buildings that held the looms and machinery that had lined the McDermott family's pockets for more than eighty years surrounded the manicured square. The business office was the heart, mind and soul of the factory complex, and Norma along with three other secretaries were the ipso facto rulers. Appointments could be made and cancelled, documents lost and found. In addition, the orders, supplies, wages and sick pay all passed through the women's hands and were tacitly approved or disapproved. They were the narrow gate to upper echelon management, indeed to Archibald McDermott III, himself. The women often proved themselves more competent than their bosses and certainly were better time managers.

Dorothy's words to Norma had proven right; the two women were like ships on opposite tacks except for Thursday nights. Thursday nights had started early on in their cohabitation to be an evening meal together and a chance to catch up with one another. The Thursday suppers became a tour de force of Dorothy's cooking skills. It was the main meal of the week and provided leftovers for several more suppers. It was the focus of rationed sugar, butter and other foodstuffs. Norma appreciated the good food and Dorothy's labor of love. Dorothy appreciated the company. Their relationship progressed from the obligatory position ordained by marriage to an actual friendship stripped of its social shackles.

Dinner began promptly at seven and progressed with a time keeper's precision, soup, main course, dessert and coffee or tea, accompanied by war news, local news, gossip, letters from Gabe and finally household necessities.

"Why do you always stop halfway through the letter? I always read you the whole thing." Dorothy smiled knowingly at Norma through the rising steam of her tea.

"Because maybe the rest of it isn't any of your business." Norma smiled back sweetly as she felt her cheeks flush.

"I know, Dear. I used to get those letters from Gabe's daddy when he went to France in nineteen and eighteen. Some of the things he wrote me would make a whore blush, and he made me burn up those letters when he got home."

"It's not like that, Dot. Gabe's not much for talking dirty. It's not like he's a pansy or anything. He just doesn't talk dirty, at least never has to me. But sometimes, I swear he gets so mushy sweet, I begin to wonder who it is he's writing to."

Dorothy nodded and looked at Norma over her glasses. "Yes, he always was a sensitive boy. He was a moody teenager, going off by himself and writing in a notebook. His brother took it from him once, and his father beat that Andy within an inch of his life and then handed the book back to Gabe. It was the strangest thing. Gabe got so mad that he took the book and marched himself out back to where trash was burning in a barrel and tossed it in. When he came back in the house I asked him why he did that. Know what he said?"

"I can't imagine." Norma answered.

"He said his father had no business fighting his battles for him, he could take care of himself."

"So why did he burn his journal?"

"I really don't know; I guess just to make a point, Gabe was always big on making a point about something, always standing on one principle or another. He was a strong willed child."

The proscribed sequence of Thursday night dinners was that the evening end on a pragmatic note, for these two women were indeed pragmatic. It was another of the unspoken things they had come to like about one another. Laundry, cleaning, shopping and cooking, the daily routines usually took care of themselves with each Mrs. Gabriel fending for herself or taking care of the task with silent equanimity. The problem was the heavier, more complicated and specialized work that needed doing, the projects in which the absence of a man in the house was acutely felt.

An ice jam had caused the guttering around the back of the house to pull away from the roof. The street level cast iron door to the coal chute had come off its hinge and was stuck. A huge dead branch, a widow-maker, had crashed down and destroyed a section of picket fence, and the handrail up the front steps was quickly becoming a safety hazard. The "to do" list had been steadily growing since late summer and was becoming worrisome.

"The mailman almost jerked the handrail off the porch this morning. I swear this place is falling down around our ears." Dorothy lamented, idly pushing the remains of her apple cobbler around the dessert bowl.

"Think we can fix it ourselves?" Norma asked, reaching for the cream.

"I doubt it; it needs cement. You have any idea how to do that?"

Norma grinned. "I could probably figure it out, but I'd be afraid of making a mess of the front steps. Besides, I'll bet cement plays holy Hannah on your hands and nails."

"I swear, Norma, you're too much, hands and nails. There's too much around here that needs fixing. I'm going to have to hire a man."

"Where are you going to find a man? The only men left around here are too old, too dumb or too crippled up to do any heavy work."

"I was going to stop by Blanche Turner's house and ask Missy Baker to send Knock-knock around to see about work." Dorothy continued.

"Knock-knock Baker? I thought all he was good for was playing football, singing in church and washing Judge Colson's Hudson. How long has his momma been working for Blanche Turner?" Norma took another sip of coffee.

"About six months."

"Really? Six months? My, my, that must have stuck in the judge's craw since nobody can cook like Missy. But Knock-knock? Everyone around here says that colored boy is a retard, dumb as a stump."

Dorothy's face hardened. "That boy is no retard, and he's done some good work for folks around town. He built that stonewall for the Gouldings and painted old Roscoe Kent's house. He's a hard worker and always ready to make a little extra money on the side."

The next day Dorothy stopped by Blanche Turner's house on Wellington Street and had a word with Missy.

CHAPTER 4

Simon of Cyrene
and the Tablets
of Moses

December the third was the first Sunday of Advent in the year of our Lord, 1944, and despite the war, joy seemed to outweigh sorrow. The Advent: an approaching light shining in the darkness. The Church on Hiram Street was filled to capacity that Sunday morning, ostensibly due to the season, the state of the world, and a covered-dish dinner scheduled for the afternoon. If the women of the church indulged in a little sinful pride, it was due to covered-dish dinners. A love feast at Simon of Cyrene was not something to be missed.

The pock marked brick building with its stone foundation and metal roof had been built ninety years before and except for a few short periods between 1861 and 1864, had been in constant use as a house of worship. During the War Between the States, as the conflict was known in New Surrey, the building had been commandeered in turn by both sides because of its proximity to the railroad. Opposing combatants had treated the sanctuary roughly, but it was Union Cavalry that heaped filth and indignity on the altar and tried its best to desecrate the structure. Thankfully, the building was only brick and mortar, while the church was, and is, a living, breathing congregation, who came back and made repairs. After eighty years the wounds were still apparent, indelible bloodstains on the wooden floors, charred ceiling beams and patches of soot as well as initials and dates carved into the wood of the pews and altar. The brick edifice proudly displayed its scars like campaign ribbons on an old soldier's lapel.

The congregation of Simon of Cyrene Freewill Baptist church had begun using the structure for its services in the mid 1890's. Its parishioners comprised the oldest Negro body of believers in the city; freemen and the sons and daughters of slaves had established it shortly after the war's end. Changing politics and demographics made the building available for a nominal rent, its white parishioners having literally moved to the other side of the tracks. The wealthy and poor alike sacrificed, each according to his or her measure, and the building was purchased in 1911. It was a great day.

The Reverend John Crenshaw was preaching the first of his series of Christmas messages. The choir and children's Sunday school class primed the congregation with a powerful chorus of *Joy To The World*, a soulful rendition of *Go Tell It On The Mountain* and a majestic refrain of *Adeste Fidelis*, the choir having painstakingly learned the Latin words to *O Come All Ye Faithful*. If any of the older folks that made up the backbone of the congregation, and held the purse strings, had a problem with Latin being sung out loud in a Baptist church, they made no mention of it.

Pastor Crenshaw ended the service with a long prayer, one in which he thanked God for the birth of the baby Jesus, the shepherds, the animals, the innkeeper, the place in the stable, the manger, swaddling clothes and every other aspect of St. Luke's narrative he could call to mind. His closing prayer was a lengthy summation of the Christmas story in the unlikely event that anyone in the pews wasn't familiar with it. The voices of the saints punctuated his prayer with outbursts of "Amen", "Yes Lord", "Uh-huh, thank you Jesus" which rose into the rafters like sweet smelling incense. When Reverend Crenshaw's booming "And Amen" came, more than a few folks were ready to stretch their legs and get a little fresh air. The men quickly filed outside, while boys and girls moved chairs and helped set up tables under the supervision of the women who had begun to prepare the food. Tight little circles of friends and neighbors formed on the sidewalk and front steps, making small talk and enjoying the crisp air.

"The Reverend Crenshaw sure enough can preach. I do believe he talked more than all three them wise men put together." Brady Jack smiled, his gold tooth flashing as he spit out a piece of tobacco from his hand rolled cigarette.

"Hush up, boy, you got no call to show disrespect to the preacher." Kenneth Windham said as he exhaled cigar smoke that joined the blue cloud rising above the group of men standing at the front corner of the church.

"What'd you say 'bout it, Knock-knock? You think preacher's message was extra special long today?" Brady continued, trying to drive home his point.

"Yes sir, Knock-knock what you think? Seeing as everybody in that church thought your snoring was going to raise the dead." another voice chimed in.

"Least ways till his mama poked him in the ribs and stomped down on his foot." Kenneth said, giving Knock-knock a playful prod to his side.

Enoch Baker was a head taller than the rest of the men, his broad chest and shoulders strained the worn gabardine of his Sunday coat. "I wasn't sleeping, or snoring or nothing. I just shut my eyes and was thinking real hard on what the preacher was talking about." He spoke gently, looking down and tugging at a thread on his jacket.

"Sure 'nough you was, Knock-knock, we all knows how good you are at thinking real hard. You thought so hard it took you three tries to get through the second grade." Brady said half in jest.

"Brady Jack, Knock-knock may not be able to read or write so good, but he sure enough could whip your sorry ass." The others all nodded in agreement with Kenneth.

"I believe I'd like to see that one of these days." Sam Tatum chimed in.

Enoch looked up knowingly, smiling, but with eyes hard as ebony. "Like Kenneth said, maybe I can't read or write so good, but I can work with my hands, I'm smart enough to measure twice and cut once, and there ain't nothing made of wood I can't fix. And another thing, Brady, leastways I got me a good job down at the fiber plant. I'm a getting plenty overtime, too, what with war contracts and all. Brady, you don't know shit, maybe you got through the second grade in only two tries, but you ain't held a job long as I known you."

"Okay, okay, man, I'm just pulling your leg a little, don't mean nothing by it."

"Go ahead, Knock-knock, go ahead and whip his sorry ass here and now. " Sam whinnied.

"Mind yourself, boys, this here is the Lord's day and we're standing in front of the church. There ain't gonna be any ass whipping here." Kenneth said, his deep voice speaking plainly.

"Yessir, you're right about that." Enoch mumbled as he turned away and started making his way across the crowded sidewalk, heading for the outhouses around the back of the church.

Brady Jack is an asshole, no doubt about it, a bona fide asshole. Enoch's mood deteriorated as he became the third man in the queue for the little house of comfort.

Enoch shifted his weight from leg to leg, impatient to empty his bladder, and starting to get a little cold as the small barrel of a man in front of him turned and smiled, "Well, hello there, Knock-knock. How you doing this fine Lord's day?"

Enoch grunted in reply, not as an act of rudeness, but the result of being distracted by a fine looking woman who had gotten into line for the women's privy. But even the sight of a beautiful woman did nothing to raise his flagging spirit. That Brady Jack don't know shit about me, he had no call to say those things, asshole, one hundred percent genuine asshole.

He no longer felt like talking to anyone. He was always surprised at how quickly his mood could shift from light to dark. He no longer wanted to be there, no longer gave a rat's ass about the covered-dish dinner and certainly didn't want to make small talk with some fool cobbler.

"You okay, Knock? You lookin' a little hangdog this morning."

"I'm fine, Joe, just a little tired, and I really needs to pee."

"You sure enough picked the right time a day to go to the stall."

"How's that?" Enoch could feel the layers of his patience peeling away.

"Cause everybody knows that dinner time all the flies are in the kitchen." Joe guffawed as he entered the outhouse tugging at the buttons on his pants.

Finally Enoch's turn came, and as he was stepping out of the privy, grateful that the cold had helped to mollify the smell, he decided to leave the church grounds. He did not consider himself fit for civil company, so he turned towards the street and decided to just take a walk.

Maybe that son-a-bitch Brady is right. Maybe I am just a big dumb no account nigger. Playing step-n-fetch-it at work, step-n-fetch it for Mama at home, step-n-fetch it for the white folks who give me a little work now and again, tossin' me a pork chop bone like I'm some kinda dog. What the hell am I doin' here? End up marryin' some fat-ass nappy headed church girl, havin a passle of nappy headed children, playin' football til my knees give out and then tellin' lies about the good old days down at the barbershop, or Tap Room. Shit.

As he turned onto Buford Street, he walked past the Sinclair filling station and paused staring at the white sandwich board sign, it's large black lettering neatly stating Clean Restrooms. Whites Only. The jumble of letters in and of themselves did not mean much to Enoch, but through the years his mother had pointed out the sign, and its meaning to him numerous times. It was part of the survival skills she had taught her son to stay alive in New Surrey. It served as one of many reminders to him of his rightful status in this Southern town. Most days, he would not have even noticed it, an invisible part of the background, just like he himself was invisible, but today it fed the worm of unfathomable rage and discontentment that churned through his insides. Shit.

It soon dawned on him that his mother was going to be madder than a wet hen when she discovered he had left church. Damn. I don't care what she thinks. I don't give a damn about anything round here. 'Sides, I'll just tell her I felt like I was coming down with a touch of the flu and didn't want anyone else to catch it.

Missy Baker had lost friends and relatives in the influenza pandemic of nineteen-eighteen, and the memory of that year was etched stone-hard in her mind. Enoch or his sister needed only to invoke they were coming down with a touch of flu and it was like having a amulet that would rescue them from whatever their mother expected of them. A touch of flu, yeah, that's what I'll say, a touch of flu, Mama, I opened the window and influenza. Shit, I'm a growed man, why I got to say anything? Can't even go for a walk without getting' somebody's permission.

As he turned the corner onto Market Street, a sharp North wind struck him head on and momentarily stole his breath away. He relished the sensation for it reminded him that he was alive physically, despite the contrary track his mind was stuck on. His pace slowed as he passed the plate glass windows of the closed shops. It didn't much matter that they were closed. These were stores he had never been inside, and the shopkeepers were not likely to ever serve the likes of Enoch Baker, or any other colored man or woman for that matter.

As he stood staring into the glass his eyes gradually shifted focus from the radios and kitchen appliances to the ethereal and transparent reflection of him. Yeah, that's you all right, Enoch Baker. People just see right through you 'cept maybe on the football field, they sees me then.

When Enoch came to the manicured lawn in front of the county courthouse he sat down on a park bench, looking around and waiting for someone to tell him to move along. His eyes saw, but didn't see the now winter-deadened drinking fountain with it's small neatly lettered metal sign standing guard and announcing, as he had been told, "Whites Only." His gaze settled on the granite obelisk that memorialized New Surrey's Confederate dead. The names and inscriptions were meaningless to him, but there was no mistaking the dates on the stone's base, 1861-1865. You poor sorry ass cracker sons a bitches, what you have to die for anyway, maybe you lost the battle, but you done won the war. This still be the South, there still chains, even if you can't see 'em, even if they be of my own making. Shit. I gotta get away from here, Mama says she got a cousin in Chicago. Can't leave her though, bein' the last one home and all, needed to help with the chores and the bills and what-not. Can't go to the army for the same reason, shit, who want to be a cook or dig ditches in a war anyway? Can't be no proper soldier no how."

Enoch put his hands into the pockets of his jacket to warm them a little. After a moment he extracted a watch cap from the right pocket and pulled it down over his short cropped hair and small ears, the tips of which had begun to sting from the cold. From his left pocket he pulled out a small linen pouch of Bull Durham and a pack of Bugler rolling papers. He rolled a near perfect cigarette, collecting the stray bits of tobacco off of his pant leg and carefully dropping them back into the bag. Waste not, want not. Cupping his hand against the wind he lit the cigarette and inhaled deeply.

In his heart of hearts he derived a terrible comfort from his melancholia. Melancholia, that's what mama calls it, I just calls it being pissed off. When Enoch was in one of his foul moods, he at least knew what to expect, and that was to expect nothing. To just be left alone, his mind trudging a well-worn track of circular thoughts, his depression a black dog that kept him company and ambled along at his side, sometimes for hours and sometimes for days at a time. A terrible comfort.

"Hey there, Knock-knock. What you doin' on my park bench? Just loafin"?

Enoch snapped pine board straight on the bench, the inch and a half ash from his forgotten cigarette tumbled to the ground as he looked over his shoulder. Standing there, rocking on his heels, was Deputy Sanders with an empty smile on his face. "Yessir, yes sir, just loafin' a little, enjoying a Sunday afternoon smoke and taking the air."

"Well, don't be loafin' round here too long, boy. Shouldn't you be getting in shape for next season? A star quarterback can't start practicing too early, can he?"

"Yessir, you right about that. I was just getting' up anyway. Thank you, sir." Enoch pulled his cap down further on his head and started walking in the opposite direction. What you doing, fool? If you want to sit on your sorry ass and smoke a cigarette in the cold, you just go ahead and sit on your own stoop. That way, only one tellin' you to move is your mama. Enoch was about ready to head back home, but his feet were not, nor was the black dog nipping at his heels.

He turned left at the next corner onto Winslow and slowly proceeded up the street, tripping on a root heaved section of sidewalk and very nearly falling. Fool. Anybody seeing you trip like that gonna think you a drunk nigger in the wrong part of town. Just then, regaining his footing, he looked up to see a man, woman and two children walking towards him. A primordial instinct carried him to the other side of the street. Two hundred years of social mores summed up in crossing the street. Laws carved into the stone tablets that were New Surrey society, as familiar to Enoch as the stone tablets of Moses. Thou shall not kill...thou shall not commit adultery...thou shall not steal...thou shall not bear false witness...thou shall not walk on the same side of the street as respectable white folks. Shit. Enoch continued walking on the other side of the street until he again came to a corner. He turned east onto Pritchard Street heading in the general direction of home and his, no doubt, furious mother.

Leathery, dry sycamore leaves scratched along the pavement in the breeze as the sun disappeared behind low hanging clouds only to reappear again a few seconds later. The bare branches over the street accentuated the changing light and gave the street the grainy appearance of a newspaper photograph. Enoch stopped and turned as he heard a raspy mewing sound behind him. A long thick-necked cat had padded up behind him demanding attention, then rubbing his face and shoulders on Enoch's pant leg. The cat brought a smile to his face as he squatted down and rubbed its ear. The cat tilted his scarred gray head and leaned into Enoch's fingers, squinting his yellow eyes in ecstasy. Enoch liked animals in general and cats in particular. He envied their independence and appreciated how their every movement was that of a finely tuned athlete. Well, hello there, Mr. Tom. You jus' trying to cheer me up? It's okay, I'll feel better shortly. Always do. Me and you are just a couple of strays out takin' the air, ain't we? The cat looked up at Enoch and abruptly scurried back under the porch from where he had probably come. You catch a mouse for me, Mr. Tom.

Enoch straightened up and saw that he was across the street from number two hundred twenty four Pritchard Street. He reached into his rear pocket and took out his billfold, removing a piece of paper that when unfolded had the number two-hundred-twenty-four written on it in his mother's handwriting. She had written the number down on a scrap of paper several days before and told him that Mrs. Gabriel had some work for him to do around her house. At the time he had thought that maybe Sunday afternoon would be a good time to stop by and see what needed to be done. But like all of his dealings with white folks, he could never be sure of the timing. His decision was to not make a decision, and he gave the matter little more thought. However, even today, when he left the church in a huff through his self-acknowledged bleak mood, he allowed the possibility that he would drop by and speak with the woman. Now he stood across the street from Mrs. Gabriel's house, the moment forcing a decision.

What the hell you doin' here? I can't go knocking on some old white woman's door on a Sunday afternoon, like as not I'll scare the livin' daylights outta her, give her a heart attack or conniption or some such. She might call the police, and I can't be talkin' to the police twice in the same day. 'Sides she probably napping or listenin' to a radio program or catching up on her mending or somethin'. He turned and started briskly walking up the street, knowing that it was definitely time to be heading home. He had walked about a hundred yards when he stopped in his tracks.

Shit. Why can't I go knock on that door. I ain't no criminal and she's the one who wants the work done. I ain't got the time to be traipsing back and forth like this, and Lord knows we needs the money. We always needs the money.

Soon he again stood in front of the house, now trying to decide whether to go to the front door or around the side to the kitchen door. Common sense and just about every part of his being told him that he should go around to the kitchen. Honor your mother and father that your days may be long...thou shall not kill...thou shall not steal...thou shall not go to the front door of a respectable white woman's house. On any other day, that's what he would have done, the kitchen door, but today on the first Sunday of Advent, he was under the melancholia, today he was pissed off and with a foolhardiness bred from righteous indignation, he decided it would be the front door.

His hand reached out to open the latch of the wrought iron gate when the front door opened. Standing there was a sturdy older woman in a blue flower-print house dress, her hands smoothing her apron, and with one fluid movement, then pushing back the steel gray strands of hair that had run away from the tight bun on the back of her head.

"Knock-knock...Knock-knock Baker is that you?" she asked smiling broadly.

"Yes ma'am, it's me all right."

"Well, what a pleasant surprise. I was hoping you'd come around so I could show you what needs fixing. How's your mother?"

"Yes ma'am, she's just fine. I decided to take a little air after church and well, you know, thought maybe I would stop by. But if this be a bad time and all, I can come back another time." Enoch had removed his hat and was wringing it in his hands like a guilty schoolboy. His oaken-hearted resolve of just moments before evaporated; authoritative women, colored or white, had that effect on him.

"Nonsense. Knock-knock, do you mind if I call you Knock-knock? You're here now, and I'm glad to see you."

"Knock-knock be fine, ma'am."

"Well, good. Then please come in before you catch your death." Dorothy turned sideways in the doorway and beckoned him in.

"Yes ma'am, thank you ma'am, I'll just go ahead and meet you around the side at the kitchen door."

"Don't be ridiculous, Knock-knock Baker. Come into this house here and now. I can't afford to heat the great outdoors you know."

Enoch stood in the warm foyer, a set of stairs to his left and a door to the living room, which was cluttered with Victorian furniture and a decorated Christmas tree. Feeling awkward, he stammered, "You sure do have a pretty house m'aam, deed you do, and I believe that's as fine a Christmas tree as I've ever seen, yes it is ma'am."

Sensing his discomfort, Dorothy spoke warmly, "Why, thank you. I didn't put up a tree last year, but now that my daughter-in-law, Norma, has moved in, well, I thought I'd spruce up the place a little for the holidays. My son is serving overseas, and I thought the tree would lift our spirits."

"Yes ma'am, I seen the blue star in the window, you must be powerfully proud."

"Yes, we are, we surely are. Let's go back to the kitchen. I was just going to fix myself a cup of tea. You can join me, and I'll tell you what needs to be done."

They walked back to the kitchen where Dorothy motioned for Enoch to have a seat. She lit a burner on the stove and put a kettle on to boil. Enoch sat ramrod straight on the edge of the chair, his hands folded in front of him, "Knock-knock, make yourself comfortable. Let me find paper and pencil, and we can write the list of jobs and figure things out."

"That's fine, Missus Gabriel, you just go ahead and write down a list, I'll see to it." Enoch, through the years had become adept at disguising his weakness when it came to reading and writing. Contrary to so many other aspects of his life, no amount of hard work and perseverance allowed him to hurdle his functional illiteracy. "It's busy down at the plant. What with the war and all, but maybe some evenings and Saturdays be all right with you? No more football for now, and baseball don't start til springtime."

Dorothy sat down across from Enoch and began listing the projects she envisioned him undertaking. She commented and briefly explained each one before assigning it a number, in order of priority, on the sheet of paper. Enoch nodded and asked a question here, and a further explanation there, as Dorothy continued her list.

After several minutes the kettle emitted its shrill whistle announcing it was at a full boil. Dorothy walked over to the stove, turned off the gas and prepared a pot of tea. She set cups and saucers, spoons, milk and sugar on the table, adding to Enoch's discomfiture. He observed Missus Gabriel closely, mimicking her preparations, adding milk and sugar and gently stirring the tea just as she was doing. Having a proper Sunday afternoon cup of tea in a warm well-appointed kitchen was a new experience for him. Sharing a cup of tea with a muscular young colored man in her kitchen was a new experience for Dorothy as well. To her credit, she treated Enoch with kindness and respect, well aware of how strange this must have been for him.

They had picked up their conversation again when Norma suddenly appeared at the door. "Oh my..." escaping from her lips, unable to hide her surprise.

Already nervous, Enoch jumped to his feet as if stuck by a hat pin, nearly upsetting his chair and spilling tea into his saucer. His clumsiness embarrassed him and only served to further the fact that he was out of his depth. Norma just stood there for an instant, her eyes widening and then narrowing again. She then brought her hand to her mouth and started to laugh, nervously at first and then escalating into uncontrollable mirth. Enoch stood there looking at her in undisguised horror, until he saw that the contagion of laughter had spread to Dorothy, who had begun a gentle laugh. A deep guffaw erupted from deep in his belly and diaphragm. Much like seeing someone yawn, the urge was impossible to stifle or resist. Nor did he want to. The laughter diffused his tension and was just what he needed. Just what he needed that particular Sunday afternoon.

"Oh...oh, oh my." Norma managed between breaths, "I didn't mean to scare you. It's just, just that I heard voices and then the kettle boiling and decided to come and see who was here."

"It's all right, dear, we all needed a good laugh, didn't we Knock-knock? This is my daughter-in-law, Norma. Norma, this is Knock-knock, uh, Enoch Baker. He's come to see about the work we talked about last week."

"Oh, yes, I remember, and I know Knock-knock Baker. I was in the crowd when you scored the winning touchdown against the Stanley Boilermakers; that was really something. Pleased to meet you." Norma held out her hand to shake.

Enoch just stood there a moment, unsure of what to do. He then took her hand and shook it, subconsciously taking note of her firm grip and warm soft skin.

"Thank you, m'aam. It's nice to meet you, too."

"Well, excuse me, don't let me interrupt you two. I'll just grab a cup of tea and get out of your hair and don't I look a fright? It's no wonder I gave you a scare." Norma was dressed in old dungarees, a too large man's cardigan, and her hair tied up in a red bandana like a field hand. As she turned to get a cup from the cabinet, Enoch could not help but notice the curve of her hips moving under the sweater and blue jeans. He was not immune to the charms of young women.

As Norma turned back around she caught his gaze, and he quickly looked down. "Well, it's back to laundry and mending. Nice to meet you Knock-knock, and I'm sure I'll see you around here again."

"Yes m'aam, there's lots of jobs round here need doing." Norma left the room.

"Well, I guess that's about it then, Knock-knock. You just come by when you're ready to get started, and let me know what money you need to get supplies." That had been the first mention of money, not that Enoch was too worried about it. Missus Gabriel was a good and decent woman, and she'd pay a fair wage for an honest day's work.

"Thank you, ma'am, and thank you for the tea. I'll be by before long." Enoch left by the kitchen door at the side of the house, the list shoved into his pocket.

A few minutes later Norma came back into the kitchen, "Well, that was different. I didn't expect to come around the corner and find a big colored man sitting in our kitchen sipping tea like a lord."

"Oh, he's a nice boy, and he does good work. I've known his mama for years."

"Dot, he's a big strapping colored man. I'd hardly call him a boy."

"You know what I mean. I just can't get away from calling 'em boy."

As Enoch walked down Pritchard, the clouds had left the sky and the afternoon sun flooded the street in crystalline light. The sky had turned Maxfield Parrish blue, and he looked back for the cat he had met earlier. Yessir, Mr. Tom, I'm feelin better now, always do, always do. He made excellent time walking home.

"Enoch Franklin Baker, where have you been? What's the matter with you, just up and leaving church like that? You outta your mind? Don't expect me to fix you any dinner, you coulda ate with the rest of us at church." His mother was every bit as angry as he expected.

"Sorry, Mama, I think I got a touch of the flu or something."

"The flu, the flu? Then why in heavens name you go walking around in the cold for? Here, let me fix you some warm milk and honey, and you go in and sit by the fire."

It was the first time all day Enoch smiled sincerely and was truly at ease.

CHAPTER 5

Old Times and Old Friends

Norma slept in that Saturday morning. It had been a late night out dancing and carrying-on with a couple of girlfriends from the office. Her mouth was cotton ball dry, and her head held on to a dull throb in spite of the bromo-seltzer she had forced down a half-hour earlier. Now she needed something to settle her stomach, maybe some coffee and a bowl of oatmeal, or better yet, some tea and toast. She padded down to the kitchen put on the kettle and took the toaster from the cabinet, plugging it in. She shook her head imperceptibly at the ancient appliance. Norma had always been a little afraid of the metal box with the frayed electrical cord and cracked bakelite plug; she knew it was only a matter of time before it electrocuted her or gave her a third degree burn or started a fire. You're a silly thing, Norma Marie.

She snapped the toaster shut and stood there mesmerized for a full two minutes as the metal coils changed from black to red-hot. I wonder if watching bread toast is more fun than watching paint dry? Better safe than sorry. Wouldn't want to tell Gabe I burned down his mother's house. A sharp rap sounded on the glass pane of the kitchen door. It nearly stopped her heart just as if current from the toaster had surged up her arm. She gave a little cry, turned and clutched her chest in a single movement.

Opening the door she caught her breath, "Knock-knock Baker, are you crazy? Don't you know you just scared the living daylights out of me? I'm a little fuzzy-headed this morning, and you just about killed me." Then she smiled at him.

Enoch looked at the floor, "Sorry Miss Norma, uh, I mean Missus Gabriel, didn't mean no harm. Is the other Missus Gabriel here? I wanted to start working, get an idea what I need, see what I can get done today and such."

"Dorothy is at church working the Christmas bazaar. She must have left right early."

"Well, I can come back another time then."

"Don't be silly, you're here now, and there's lots of work to be done around this old place." Norma walked over to Enoch, stood squarely in front of him and took both of his hands in hers. "Enoch Franklin Baker, how have you been? Last Sunday when I came into the kitchen and saw you sitting there at my kitchen table, well, you could have knocked me over with a feather."

Enoch stumbled back, bumping into the counter and knocking the newspaper and several letters to the floor. Stooping to pick them up and regain his composure, he said, "I felt the same way Miss Norma, imagine me sittin' at a white lady's kitchen table sippin' tea from a cup and saucer and then you come traipsin' in. I had me no idea you was livin' on Pritchard Street."

"Life is full of surprises. I guess I owe you an apology, though. I'm sorry I acted like I didn't know you. It's just that you really did take me by surprise and it was just easier, you know . . . less complicated, than having to explain everything to my mother-in-law."

"You did right, girl. I'm not sure Missus would have understood too good."

"Oh, she'd understand all right. She's basically a good woman, but she does like to go on so, and she would have kept us all day asking questions and wanting to know…"

Norma's thoughts were disrupted when the kettle began piping like the wreck of the old Ninety-seven. Just then, gray smoke and then small flames erupted from the toaster. Norma cried out, "Oh, oh no. Fire!"

Enoch yanked the cord out of the wall, juggled the burning toaster in his calloused hands and threw the antique into the sink and turned on the water; the toaster hissed and steamed before it died. Norma rushed to take the kettle off the stove, the high-pitched whistle having renewed the throbbing in her head. She opened the door and each of them grabbed a kitchen towel and fanned the smoke out of the door. Then absurdity of the scene hit them and they began to laugh. Enoch felt a little less awkward.

"Well, I sure am sorry I ruined that fine old toaster, but I 'spect that's a sight better than a house fire. You can just have Missus Gabriel take it out of my wages."

"Don't worry about it, I'll tell her I did it. The only thing is, she's going to accuse me of murdering that old thing. She knows I've hated it from the get-go. Darn thing is older than I am."

"Norma, girl, you haven't changed a bit, have you? Just like when we were little, you still gettin' into mischief and still needin' me to get you out of it."

"Get outta town. I remember it just the other way around. One thing has changed though."

"What's that?"

"We're not children anymore." Their eyes met and dropped.

"You remember that time you had the big idea to make popcorn balls and go and sell them to the neighbors for a penny a piece? What were we, seven or eight? You told me there was nothin' to it, but we made a powerful mess of your mama's kitchen."

Norma rolled her eyes, "Well it seemed like a good idea, and I had seen her make them lots of times. We had butter and popcorn and molasses covering every square inch of that kitchen, on our clothes, in our hair and even on the cat."

"Oh yeah, deed I remember, it looked like a popcorn tornado done had its way with us." Enoch said it with the sincerity she remembered from her childhood.

"And then when my mother came in and pitched a fit, you went and told her the whole thing was your idea, you had a powerful hankerin' for popcorn balls. You bailed me out that time."

"Sure did, and then when your mama done told my mama what happened, I got a tongue lashin' that still gives me night sweats. She came over and cleaned your mama's kitchen top to bottom just to make amends. My, my."

Norma fixed herself a cup of tea and offered one to Enoch, which he refused. "Remember that other time when I got a brand new bicycle for my eleventh birthday?"

"Now that you mention it I do remember somethin' about that, but I'd sooner forget it."

"Well, I remember it perfectly. You talked me into letting you take it apart so you could make an invention, and then you couldn't put it back together again."

"That invention making was always gettin' me in a heap of trouble. Then you went and lied to your Daddy and told him you broke it and I was just tryin' to fix it right again."

"He bought it hook, line and sinker. You have to admit it saved both of us a trip to the wood shed."

"It did, Norma girl, it surely did."

"The funny thing is my Daddy had a hard time getting the bicycle back together. I don't think it was ever quite right after your invention making."

"We had some big times, didn't we?"

"Yes we did, those were fun days, Enoch." A silence fell between them with only the sound of her spoon stirring in the china cup marking time.

"Well, I best be going down to the cellar to look at those old rickety stairs. Thought I'd start with the indoor work while the weather's so cold."

"Yes, I have some chores that need to get done too, It was good to see you again."

"It is nice to see you again, Norma Bittner. You sure are a sight for sore eyes if there ever was one."

"Gabriel, now it's Norma Gabriel."

"Sorry, jus' forgot."

"That's okay."

"Norma girl, that ol' Tom Gabriel is a lucky man, deed he is."

CHAPTER 6

Do the Right Thing

*Consider your origin; you were not born to live
like brutes, but to follow virtue and knowledge.*
DANTE ALIGHIERI

It seemed to Gabe that in the short time he was away recuperating from his wounds, much had changed. It should not have surprised him. But it did. It would not have been as obvious in the day-to-day grind of soldiering, but after three weeks absence, he felt like a stranger in the company. A great deal really had changed. For one thing, geographically they had advanced deeper into the Huertgen and were now solidly fighting on German ground. Resistance had stiffened; the men simply attributed it to the enemy fighting on his own soil. That was certainly true, but years later military historians would describe how the Germans were defending their staging areas for the Ardennes offensive. The Germans dubbed it "Operation Wacht am Rhine", in the West it became known as the Battle of the Bulge.

Mostly though, the changes in personnel are what disturbed him. The unending stream of new faces disturbed everyone. Replacements. Replacements of replacements. Unlike the other veterans of D Company, he tried to learn their names and occasionally tried to initiate human contact with them, but it was difficult. The Huertgen devoured the fresh and inexperienced with malignant ferocity, and to invest the emotions and energy into men who would not likely survive a week was more than most could bear.

When Gabe began making supply runs again and transporting wounded back to battalion, he usually was the first to meet the raw, green troops, ferrying them forward to D Company. Each fresh new face served as a reminder of some other soldier he had failed. He stood accused by the small voice that did not speak with words: a man dead because he did not work hard enough to save him. Replacements. He would likely fail these men as well, and still they came, and still he tried to preserve their lives.

In dark moments he wondered if he was responsible for more deaths than the Germans. It was an irrational line of reasoning, one he recognized as unhealthy and patently false. These thoughts overwhelmed him with waves of futility eroding a bulwark constructed over a lifetime; a citadel that both protected him and held him captive. In a place within too deep to recognize, a stone tumbled from the walls. A real man could accomplish anything with hard work. A real man was responsible for . . .

He knew the feeling of someone's life slipping through his fingers, the look on the face, the emptying of the eyes, a ragged breath, a shudder, the momentary lightening of the body as life left it and the immediate heaviness as a human being became just so much organic matter. He once considered keeping a list, a written record of the names that ceased to exist under his ministrations, but he knew he would remember them. He couldn't, of course. How many had there been? Twenty or thirty? Fifty or sixty? Hundreds? Too many.

During the weeks before Christmas, German activity in D Company's sector markedly increased. Gabe went out on two combat patrols, and second platoon took several casualties that he treated, tagged and evacuated. The severely wounded and the dead sapped the company medic's energy and emotions, but it was the walking-wounded that accounted for the daily routine; men with minor wounds and injuries and/or illness that remained in the line. A few did so by choice, but all of them did so by the weight of circumstance. There would be few medals or promotions for this kind of bravery and precious little recognition, but bravery it was. Gabe and Juergens and Steibel did their best to alleviate the suffering, but really, there was little they could do to lessen the misery.

So the routine continued. It was a Wednesday afternoon, though most of the men did not know the name or number of the day. They only knew that they were over the hump and with any luck at all, there would be warmth and better food, maybe even a shower in the very near future.

D Company had spent the morning moving east, leap-frogging from position to position, while rumors buzzed around like corpse-blown flies. Only the new guys paid them heed. The afternoon proved to be a respite, the infantrymen occupying foxholes dug by others days before. By soldier's standards, sleeping and taking watch in two hour increments was not a bad way to spend an afternoon.

Gabe sat by a small fire with the squad leaders and their seconds who had been called together for a short briefing by Lieutenant Brownlee. He had dozed off and was startled when the lieutenant started speaking. Brownlee wasn't there a minute before.

"All right, listen up. We're going to hold here for the rest of the day and into tonight. I want the men fed and well rested, weapons and ammo seen to, and for God's sake, tell them to try to keep warm and dry."

"I don't think we need to tell them that, sir." Sergeant Manning interrupted.

"Right. At twenty-three hundred we're going to move out and occupy that small ridge over there." Brownlee pointed towards a low wooded elevation eight hundred yards from where the company rested.

"You know, I thought I'd be really happy to see those God forsaken woods thin out a little, but now we've got open ground to cross, ain't that some shit?" Corporal Slater said attempting to light a cigarette with trembling hands, the breeze making it nigh impossible.

"Aw hell, Art, you're never satisfied, are you?" Manning replied handing Slater a lit cigarette to help him out.

"We're going to relieve I Company, occupy their position, and we're going to do it as silent as the grave. No talking, helmets strapped, buckles, dog tags, ammo belts, everything taped and tied. I want them rigged for silence. You know the drill." Brownlee was emphatic. "There's just about a full moon tonight, so with the snow, the going shouldn't be too bad, at least until we're in the trees anyway. Of course if we can see, so can the krauts, so silence is everything. Any questions?"

"Yeah, then what?" Sergeant Rickert asked.

"Don't worry, there's more, and it gets better." Brownlee stifled a yawn, which spread around the circle of men with easy contagion. He extracted a map from an inner pocket of his greatcoat and unfolded it over a fallen log. "That little bump over there is called hill two-forty-seven and overlooks a crossroad, the east side of which leads to Blaufels. Our final objective." The wind whipped at the corners of the map as Lieutenant Brownlee fingers stabbed the points of interest and the men sank deeper into their coats.

"So, come daylight, second platoon is just going to walk into Blaufels?" Rickert broke in again.

"Why don't you let me finish?" Brownlee snarled, redirecting everyone's attention to the map. "There's a small rise about two hundred yards up the east road, here. At the top is a farmhof. There's a stone two-story house and some out-buildings. The krauts have fortified the whole place with wire, trenches and a pillbox. We're talking Siegfried line stuff here."

The sun passed behind the clouds with a perceptible drop in temperature coinciding with a perceptible drop in the men's spirit. "Okay, here's how this is going to work. Well, hold on a second, this'll make more sense if I lay it out for you." And with that he scuffed the powdery snow away from a three by three foot area and conducted an impromptu scavenger hunt, picking up a few sticks, stones, k-ration cans and candy bar wrappers. Brownlee then fished a small spiral pad from his coat pocket, checked his notes, and began laying out the next day's battle on the makeshift sand table. He scratched in the roads, placed sticks marking lines and arranging cans, wrappers and stones. "Okay, here we go. This is the tree line halfway down the eastern slope of hill 247; this is the cross road. These are pretty substantial roads, so there are drainage ditches on each side. Here's the farm, the main house, the pillbox, this is a line of wire, and over here a hundred and fifty yards to the right is a small swale with a wet weather stream. You follow me so far? Any questions?"

"Yes sir, why do the Germans get to be the Hershey bar? Can't we be the Hershey bar?" Manning asked smiling broadly.

"Shut up, asshole, and pay attention. Sir, how far is it from the trees to the farm?" Sergeant Rickert asked, giving Manning a hard shove.

"It's about a half mile all told, three hundred yards to the road and about another two hundred up to the farm. The ground is pretty rough, potato and winter wheat fields, that will slow the men down a little, but if they have to go to ground there'll be some small cover in the furrows." Lieutenant Brownlee continued.

"Sir, if this is a prepared position, those fields are probably mined." Sergeant Manning interjected, trying to make up for his previous gaffe.

"The G3 report says it's not likely. Apparently it's a low priority area for the krauts, and the fields look to be recently worked, whatever that means. While we're on the subject of G3 reports, word has it Blaufels and this portion of the line is held by Volksstrum . . . old men, young kids and the infirm; the krauts call them stomach troops."

"Yeah, yeah, heard that before, the check is in the mail, and I'll respect you in the morning." Corporal Swinburne shook his head.

"You're one cynical S.O.B., aren't ya? Manning shot back.

"Maybe so, but it's kept me alive so far." Swinburne answered flatly.

"All right, all right, let's get on with this, I want to get some rest before tonight." The lieutenant continued. "At o-seven thirty, with first light, battalion arty is going to open up on the farm with their one-o-fives for fifteen minutes; during the confusion first and third squads are going to haul ass down to the drainage ditch on the near side of the north-south road taking positions on either side of the intersection, here." Brownlee scratched another line in the dirt for emphasis. "Soon as the one-o-fives finish dropping H.E., they're going to lay down smoke. When you see the first smoke rounds hit, I want third squad to lay down suppressing fire; first squad is going to advance towards the far left of the enemy's position and get into that house; second squad is going to work it's way up the swale, here. Sergeant Rickert, I want you to assign a couple, three, four men, to assault the pillbox with satchel-charges and cover the rear to bring down anyone leaving the bunker. And Rickert, it goes without saying you're going to have to task this to a couple of guys who know what they're doing. This whole shootin' match is going to depend on taking out that pillbox, that and the one-o-fives cutting the wire and hopefully flattening the stone house. Questions?" There were none spoken aloud. "Okay then, we'll meet again here, at twenty-one hundred for a final run-through. You're dismissed."

As the men stood and walked back to their squads, Lieutenant Brownlee stepped over to Gabe who was stretching his legs, "What do you think, Doc?"

"Does it matter? It's not my job to think; it's my job to get these guys through this in one piece."

"I'm not asking you as a tactician. I'm asking you as a friend."

"Well, in that case, Ted, here's what I think. We gotta do what we gotta do."

"Right answer. Thanks." Ted Brownlee turned and started back towards his foxhole and the prospect of a couple of hours of sleep.

It took nearly an hour and a half before Gabe finally made it back to his foxhole. He made the rounds, checking on the men of second platoon. He was not an officer, nor the platoon leader, but these men belonged to him every bit as much as they did to Lieutenant Brownlee. He dispensed aspirin and paragoric, changed bandages, checked feet, passing on a good word and a modicum of encouragement where he could. A friendly face, a sympathetic ear and a little moral support being the most effective medicines he had.

"Where ya been, Doc?" Briscoe asked as Gabe slid down into their shared accommodation and pulled some fresh-cut pine boughs back over the hole.

"I was just checking on the guys, and before that I happened to be over with the N.C.O.'s when Brownlee briefed them."

"Anything I want to know about?"

"Probably not."

"Yeah, you're right. Why spoil a quiet afternoon? Truly, ignorance is bliss." Jake agreed.

"Well then, I ought to be the happiest son-of-a-bitch in this man's army." Gabe chuckled, shaking his head. "So how are you doing, Jake, my friend?"

"Other than the blisters on my feet and these damn cracks and fissures in my hands, okay I guess."

As Gabe rifled through his shoulder bag for a tin of petroleum jelly, the muted light filtering into the foxhole brightened. Gabe handed Jake the tin, "Here, work some of this into your hands, it should help a little. Hey push the branches over and let's see if we can warm up a little. Sun's out."

"Actually Doc, um, actually that was a lie. I'm not okay, not okay at all."

"What d'ya mean?"

"I been thinking about this for about a week now. This is a big mistake, a big fucking mistake."

"What is? The war?" Gabe took off his helmet and wool cap, allowing the sun to bathe his bare head.

"No, not the war, at least I don't think so, not at the moment, anyway. The mistake is me being in the war."

"Shit, Jake, nobody in their right mind wants to be in a war. Hell, I want to be home bedding down my wife, drinking mulled cider, eating turkey with all the trimmings. Besides, you're a replacement in a U.S. Army rifle company. It's a little late to reconsider your options now."

"That's just it. I didn't have to be here. I didn't have to be in this stinkin' hole in the ground waiting to be killed or worse, maimed, blinded, my balls blown off. Hell, I didn't even have to be in France . . . or Belgium . . . or Germany."

"Well, it's too late to be second guessing. You are here. You did the right thing." Gabe fished around under his coat, took out a couple of pairs of dirty socks and spread them on a rock to dry. Briscoe, seeing the wisdom in it, did the same.

"Yeah, the right thing for the wrong motives. Do you know why I joined up?"

"Uh . . . to travel to far away places and see the world courtesy of Uncle Sam?" Gabe said.

"Get this, because my old man said it would look good on my résumé. There I was, in my third year at U.Va., my last name a guaranteed acceptance to Law School, my own car, nice clothes, president of my fraternity, I was the consummate 'big man on campus', and the women, my God, the women. Cheerleaders, debutants, sorority gals, English majors, hell, even the librarian, all throwing themselves at me. Every Friday night, I was off to Mary Washington or Longwood, a mass exodus to the girl's schools. My God, the women, I had to beat them off with a stick."

"Sounds rough." Gabe stifled a yawn.

"Yeah." Jake gave a short bitter laugh. "So I enlisted at the end of the school year, June 1941. The old man said he'd pull some strings and get me posted to Washington. A pencil pusher at the Department of the Army, or playing Cornet in the Army Band, or any one of a dozen other cushy jobs. Then just about the time I was getting over my guilt at sitting out the war stateside, he changes his mind. Says he went overseas in nineteen and eighteen with Blackjack Pershing, and it did him a world of good. Made a man out of him. So the next thing I know, I'm in France and he's arranged for me to be a clerk typist for Colonel Whitehead at Regimental."

"Wow, some story. So how did you end up here as bait, uh, as a replacement?"

Jake lowered himself deeper into the foxhole and lit a cigarette, inhaled deeply and moved back to the edge inclining his face towards the sun. "That's when I made my next mistake. For some reason I started thinking that I should probably see some combat before it was too late, before the whole damn thing was over. Shit, I thought it might even be a good thing to get a medal or two. So one afternoon I went in to see the Colonel, laid my cards on the table and asked for a transfer to a rifle platoon. And here's the irony, don't let the fucking irony get lost on you . . . he transferred me because he liked me. Hell, imagine where I'd be if he didn't like me. What the hell was I thinking?"

Gabe leaned back and closed his eyes soaking up the weak warmth of the winter sun. "You know Jake, you're one of those guys who manages to do the right thing in spite of yourself. I'm proud to know you. Hell, at least you're honest with yourself and with me. I think you're giving this way too much thought. Just do what you gotta do and you'll be fine. There's nothing you can't do or get through if you're willing to work hard enough."

"That's just it Doc. I won't be fine, because I can't, I can't do it. I've been in this platoon for a month now and I haven't fired my weapon one time. I try, then I swear I will the next time, but I don't. I can't."

Gabe sat up and opened his eyes. "Hey, do you think you're the only guy not firing your weapon? Hell, in any firefight half the guys there on both sides aren't shooting. They're either too scared, too amazed or too busy keeping their heads down. It happens all the time. Shit, if every dogface in the platoon would just shoot when he's supposed to, the war would be over in a week. You're going to be fine, you're going to do your job, and you're going to make it through this. Just do it, just do what needs to be done. Do what you're told and work it hard. Hell, you might even win a medal or two."

"I don't know, I'll give it some more thought. I have to piss like a racehorse, be right back." Not believing a word of Gabe's entreaties, Jake made his way deeper into the trees and relieved himself. When he got back, Gabe was sound asleep.

Second platoon, together with a handful of supernumeraries, executed the night maneuver with textbook precision. The cold was unforgiving, but the air was still and rarefied, invigorating the men, the cold becoming a dangerous backdrop they had grown accustomed to. The waxing moon, the glory of the constellations and the faint smudge of the Milky Way allowed the men to gain the tree line of hill two-forty-seven with nothing more than the sound of boots biting into the ice-encrusted snow.

Each man's universe contracted to the immediate ten yards around him, and his sole contact with the human race consisted of the G.I. on either side of him. Similarly their objective had been parceled out into a series of miniaturized tasks: cross the field in line abreast, at the trees form in column on Lieutenant Brownlee, occupy the foxholes on the far side of the hill, see to the emplacement of the attached machine gun crews, get some rest. A soldier's world is a small one.

Had he given the matter any thought, Gabe would have been glad to note that his five physical senses and the sixth sense imbued to combat veterans had not diminished in the least. Instead, they remained razor sharp, just below the surface of his conscious mind. On that mid-December night that conscious mind was trapped and then held captive by the words and melody of a nineteenth century Christmas carol. Over and over again, Silent night, Holy night skipped through his brain like a scratched seventy-eight. He could not rid himself of it, nor did he really desire to. It was an annoyance, a pebble in his boot . . . it was a comfort, a mother's caress.

With the night's objective successfully achieved, Gabe settled into his foxhole, huddling against Briscoe for warmth. His raptor-sharp vision could make out faint lights glowing from the imperfect shuttered windows of the stone house across the valley, and he envied the faint wisp of smoke rising vertically from its chimney, Silent night, Holy night all is well, all is bright . . . his only thought as sleep carried him away.

At o-six hundred the NCOs, wraithlike in the predawn darkness, began moving among their squads. At each foxhole whispering the sign and receiving the countersign, they roused the men and reiterated the need for silence. After giving them a few minutes to clear the sleep from their minds and eyes, they returned to each entrenchment. In turn, briefing the men on the next phase of the mission, on what was expected of them and how it was to be carried out. In the ensuing hour and a half each soldier prepared himself for the coming fight. Singly and in pairs the men crawled from their holes and made their way deeper into the trees to relieve themselves, stretch their legs and work the cold from their joints. Most of second platoon found discarded ration cans as well as small to medium sized stones to cobble together diminutive cook-stoves in the very bottoms of their foxholes. With the small fuel tablets in their k-ration boxes they warmed food and water for coffee, although warm over represented the nature of their breakfast. Some of the men smoked cigarettes with cupped hands huddled well below ground, others closed their eyes in restless meditation, others prayed, while still others wished they could. Like their fathers' generation in the Great War, they waited for the signal. They were waiting to go over the top.

As the low sky paled to whitish gray and the shadows retreated, men checked their watches, tightened straps, checked and rechecked weapons, rearranged pockets, fingered rosary beads and performed any of a thousand small individual preparations for the assault. The NCOs moved among their squads telling them to be ready to move on the signal.

The thump of a solitary one-o-five howitzer broke the morning stillness. All heads turned to the east as every set of eyes watched for the fall of the spotting round. Interminable seconds later a flash, a crash, and a geyser of smoke, dirt and snow erupted forty yards short and twenty yards north of the German position. Thirty-seconds later a second thump and then another eruption of fire and dirt as a corrected round exploded in the center of the compound, smoke billowing from what had to be a large crater. D-Company saw the frantic movement of the Volkstrum running for cover, taking up firing positions and milling about. To Gabe and the others it was like watching an anthill that being kicked by a mean spirited boy.

Before the dirt and rocks had fallen back to the ground, the forward observer uttered three of the deadliest words in the military lexicon into his radio . . . FIRE FOR EFFECT. Seconds later, the fury of battalion artillery batteries was unleashed, and to second platoon it sounded and felt as if the end of the world had begun two miles to their rear and was rolling towards them in a great wave. The opposite rise disappeared in a holocaust of fire, smoke, earth and sound. The ground trembled, the concussion of the high explosive ordnance detonating drove the breath from each man's lungs and jarred his entrails. But all they noticed and all they could hear was the shrill whistle emitting from a small silver cylinder at Lieutenant Brownlee's lips.

The three squads of second platoon, Company D poured out of their foxholes and wordlessly ran towards the drainage ditch and stream bed. Some of the men ran crouched, leaning in, as if advancing into the teeth of a hurricane. Others sprinted, their legs carrying them inexorably forward with the piston-like pumping of an overwrought steam engine. Forward . . . Dammit . . .Forward. No thought of the cold, no thought of mines, no thoughts at all, just make the drainage ditch before the krauts realize what's happening.

Gabe advanced with the third squad so that he would be positioned in the center of the line. The men were more than halfway to the road before the first tiny flashes of small arms fire appeared. A few steps later tracers began arcing towards them, signaling the krauts had manned their machine guns. The German fire appeared ineffectual, until out of the corner of his eye, Gabe saw the first man go down thirty feet to his left. He threw himself down and assessed whether the ground around him was being raked by fire. Satisfied it was not, he rose and ran over to the fallen man, who was already getting to his feet, spitting out dirt and ice, with no dark patches of blood or obvious wounds evident.

"Stepped in a fucking hole, Doc. C'mon let's go."

The entire line gained the drainage ditch at about the same time, the men flinging themselves into it's frozen bottom. Each man conducted an instantaneous assessment, checking for wounds and double-checking his weapon. Gabe looked back across the field up towards hill two-forty seven and was incredulous to see no dead or wounded lying shattered in the field.

Lieutenant Brownlee was lying prone several paces from Gabe and signaling first squad to move left and get ready to make for the stone house. He turned and looked right to see second squad disappearing up the swale towards the pillbox. Third squad had crawled to the edge of the ditch and were training their weapons on the German line. They watched in terrible fascination as round after round fell on the farmhof, creating a manmade Götterdamerung. The force of the explosions moved the cold air against their faces as each man's mouth gaped either from experience or reflex to keep eardrums intact. In the gaps between the fall of the shell and their attendant explosions, the men could still see movement on the top of the hill and muzzle flashes that corresponded to the hiss of bullets above their heads or thumping into the dirt of the embankment, raising puffs of dirt and snow with ominous thuds.

As the line hunkered down against the Germans' return fire, the air was rent by a massive blast greater in magnitude than previously felt and heard. All eyes went to the top of the hill in spite of the small arms fire. The second story of the farm house had vanished and the remaining timbers were ablaze. A cheer arose from the American line as the artillery barrage came to an abrupt halt. Brownlee then gave the order for third squad to return fire. The crack of rifles along with the metallic ping as clips emptied their last rounds and the staccato tear of the squad's BAR replaced the crash of artillery fire.

Moments later came the impact of the first smoke rounds and the hilltop was engulfed in an acrid artificial fog bank. Lieutenant Brownlee signaled first squad to begin its advance. Simultaneously Gabe heard the first frantic screams of "Medic!" from the far right of the line. He scrambled over to where he found Pete Arbutus already dead, his throat half torn away and the men on either side of him splattered in blood and still firing away. Gabe tore the bloody dog tags from under the dead mans uniform, pocketing one and shoving the other into Pete's lifeless gaping mouth.

"Anyone else hit?" and barely waiting for the grunted response he made for the swale to join second squad moving towards the still-firing pillbox.

Second squad's luck had held. They had worked their way to within twenty yards of the concrete fortification and had not drawn any fire. The ten men were formed in a short line along the bank of the stream. Sergeant Manning tapped four of them to move to the head of the position.

"Schwarz, Tyler, you take the satchel charges and knock out that God damn pillbox. Mancini, you and Briscoe work your way around to cover the back door. Go . . . Go . . . Go! The rest of you assholes cover fire, Now!"

The breeze had picked up and the smoke was dissipating almost as quickly as it was being laid down. At the center of the line Brownlee watched first squad through his field glasses as they gained the farmhouse, entered it and began pouring a flanking fire into the German entrenchments. The one-o-fives had done their job, the wire had been breached, the farm house taken a direct hit and German resistance was faltering as old men and boys began throwing down their rifles and raising their hands, surrendering to the men in the wrecked main house.

Near the swale it had seemed like only seconds before Schwarz and Tyler had scrabbled crab-like to the blind side of the pillbox. Gabe heard the calls for medic coming from the center squad and began moving down the streambed. Before taking a half dozen steps he heard Briscoe's

voice screaming for help from over his shoulder. Making the snap decision he turned and began running towards the closer screams. Sixty yards
up the stream bed Gabe found Briscoe cradling Mancini in his arms.
Mancini's shattered right arm was hanging unnaturally, attached by
strands of cloth and a few quivering strings of tissue. Blood was spurting
obscenely from the gaping hole at his shoulder, and Briscoe was trying to
cram his gloves into the wound to staunch the flow.

"Thank God, thank God." Briscoe rasped as he eased his wounded
mate down, picked up his rifle and turned to continue towards the pillbox. He stopped and turned to look at Gabe.

"Go . . . Go . . . do what you have to do . . . Go . . . now!" Gabe shouted as he jabbed a morphine syrette into Mancini's thigh and began pack-
ing the wound with field dressings.

Briscoe was surprised to find himself crouching behind a low stone
wall with a clear view of the rear of the bunker not fifty feet away. He had
no sooner gained the position than two hollow metallic explosions rang
out, and smoke began pouring from the front of the pillbox. The steel
door directly in front of him was thrown open, and a thin bald-headed
man staggered out of the blinding black smoke, his uniform smoldering
and blood pouring from his ears. Oh shit . . . oh shit . . . Briscoe watched
in paralytic wonder as the man collapsed and began convulsing on the
ground and then seemed to deflate before his eyes.

In his inexperience, Briscoe hurtled over the wall and ran to the
steel door. Through the thinning smoke he entered the pillbox, not sure of
what to expect and sure as hell, not knowing what to do. The concrete
room was a tangle of destruction. The machine guns were twisted into
useless cylinders of metal, every piece of equipment, supply box, furniture and communications gear was destroyed. There was a dead body in
the center of the room, and various body parts and bits of uniform were
strewn around the walls. Briscoe's university-educated mind immediately went to the seventh ring of hell, whispering Dante's immortal words,
"Abandon Hope all ye who enter." He heard a low moan, and turning in
the semi-darkness, saw a pair of legs protruding from a splintered
upturned table. He shoved the table aside to see a blond headed boy, who
couldn't have been more than fifteen years old propped against the wall.
Blood and tears were streaming from his eyes, and blood was pouring

from his ears and mouth. His lips were working wordlessly, and his head was slowly moving from side to side.

As the boy's eyes focused and beheld the heavily armed enemy standing in front of him, he let out a piercing child-like shriek that bounced around the cement walls like one of Dante's demons.

In the minute after the satchel charges had detonated, Ben Schwarz and Otis Tyler were sitting against the blind side of the pillbox. They had already noted that for the most part silence had fallen over the battle zone. Ben lit a cigarette, and both men were about to congratulate themselves on a job well done and, more importantly, they were still in one piece. The shriek caused them both to jump, Schwarz burning himself with the cigarette. In one reflexive motion, Tyler ripped a hand grenade from his belt, pulled the pin, flipped the spoon and swung around violently pitching the smoking grenade into the pillbox aperture.

Inside, Briscoe was standing in front of the screaming child in mute horror when he heard the metallic ping of the hand grenade bouncing onto the floor. He didn't have time to think, he didn't have time to leave, all that he had time to do was hurl his body protectively over the hysterical boy. It was the last right thing he would ever do.

Tyler and Schwarz entered the again smoke filled chamber. They saw Briscoe's shredded body lying rolled off across the boy's legs. "Son of a Bitch . . . son of a bitch, he killed Briscoe." And with that Tyler fired two rounds into the boy's chest.

Neither man ever acknowledged the truth of what happened that day on the outskirts of Blaufels. They couldn't; they, too, had to somehow survive the war and they, too, knew mistakes were made in combat situations. If a mistake had indeed been made, and who was to say?

The G3 report had been correct. The crossroad garrison were second line troops and conscripts, and to a man the company was pleased and amazed that the entire action had taken less than half an hour. They were also pleased that casualties were remarkably light, four dead, Tompkins, Smith, Mancini and Briscoe, and four wounded, none seriously.

Gabe had seen to the wounded and was standing next to the four dead covered by rubberized canvas sheets when the truck pulled up to take them back to graves registration. He knelt down and pulled the sheet back from Briscoe's ashen face. "You did the right thing, Jake, I was wrong, everything was not going to be all right . . . but you did the right thing." Another rock tumbled to the ground.

That evening, he asked the Lieutenant if he could write the letter to Briscoe's parents. Afterwards he dreamt about a wall.

CHAPTER 7

Winter of Their Discontent

Gabe commandeered the largest stall as a makeshift sick ward. He shoveled out the dried horse manure, laid down fresh straw, and constructed a crude table from boards, crates and a stepladder. Candles on the table supplemented the anemic flickering of an oil lantern hanging from the rafters. Gratefully, Gabe found himself alone, a rare occurrence. For the moment, the men were bedded down or playing cards, waiting for their stretch of guard duty. Sitting at the table staring into a candle flame, he wondered why it was so difficult to write Norma a letter. There seemed so much to say, but then again, he had written the same things over and over, until the thoughts didn't seem as important as they once did. He couldn't seem to get past the small talk, and it wasn't as if she would ever understand life as a GI. He had recently begun to wonder if small talk wasn't all there was to their relationship and marriage.

"Hey, Doc, what'ya doin' here sitting by yourself?" Ben Schwarz sat down heavily on a milking stool across the table from Gabe. Then realizing he was seated too low, he pulled over a bale of straw.

"Trying to write a letter, but you know, just don't have anything to say."

"Writing Norma?" Ben asked, shaking a Lucky Strike out of its pack and lighting it with a candle.

"Yeah. Only it's more like not writing Norma."

"Hell, you're writing your wife, tell her you're going to screw her until the cows come home once this war is over. You know, when in doubt, write smut."

"Yeah, I guess, but that's all I ever seem to write, and you know, I'm beginning to wonder if that isn't one of the only things we got going for us." Gabe reached beneath the table and brought up a bottle of Cognac and two enameled metal cups, placing them on the table, pouring a splash in each.

"Feeling sorry for ourselves, are we?" Ben tipped the cup at Gabe, a mock toast, and drank down the brandy in one pull.

"So Ben, tell me, do you believe in love at first sight?"

"Huh? Uh, yeah, I guess so, don't you? Hey, you wanna . . ." he motioned towards the bottle with his cup. Gabe obliged Schwarz, pouring himself some more as well.

"You know, I used to, but now I'm not so sure."

Ben sipped his second cup of brandy with more deliberation. "Actually, now that I think about it, I do believe in love at first sight. See, there was this time I was down in Richmond visiting my mother's grave when I saw this girl. She was placing flowers by a headstone, and the sight of her stopped me cold. Gabe, she actually took my breath away."

"Was she beautiful?"

"Is the pope Catholic? She had long dark brown, almost black hair, green eyes, and the face of an angel, all the right parts and long tapered fingers. You can tell a lot about a woman by her hands. I truly believe that, Gabe."

"Hmmm, sounds more like lust at first sight to me."

"No, really, it was way more than just her looks, she exuded something, grace, charm, class. She moved like water, like raindrops flowing down a pane of glass. She was peaceful. I don't know, I can't explain it, but you know, if she'd have asked me to die for her right then and there, I would have, in a cotton pickin' minute, I swear I would have."

"You could tell all that in one glance?" Gabe smirked.

"Absolutely."

"Schwarz, I never figured you for a romantic. So did you ask her out?"

"Nope, I was frozen in place. She turned around, gave me a sad smile and walked away. You know, I went back to that cemetery the same time every day for a week and never saw her again. One of the great regrets of my life. And you know, from time to time I still think of that girl. Yeah, I believe in love at first sight, all right."

"Probably worked out for the best. I'll bet she was a bitch, probably a real ball buster."

"No way. Man, not only are you feeling sorry for yourself, but now you're trying to make me miserable too. You're a cynical son of a bitch, you know that, Doc?"

"Thanks, I love you too."

"Hand me that bottle. Raining on my parade. You owe me another drink."

"Yeah, I guess I do." Gabe shoved the bottle across the rough boards.

"So was it love at first sight with Norma?"

"Truthfully?"

"Of course." Ben lit another cigarette, passing the pack across the table to Gabe, who ignored it.

"Truthfully, no."

"So why'd you marry her then?"

"I didn't say I didn't love her, it just wasn't, you know, fireworks. Funny thing though, when I was a kid I always thought that's how it would be. Wham. Like a bolt of lightning. You know, there was a girl like that once, in high school. We were in storybook love, but then she went off to college and met some guy a lot smarter and richer than I was. Maybe that's when I stopped believing in love at first sight, or whatever you want to call it."

"That's sad, Doc. Really sad."

"Nah, just realistic. Guess I've gotten practical in my old age. See, it's like this, I married Norma because she has potential. A good family, a good heart, and I know that over time I'll be crazy in love with her. You know the old folks married by mail order, and then learned to love one another, I figured why should I be any different.? You gotta put in effort to make love and marriage work, make a decision to fall in love. It'll come, but for now, it sure makes letter writing hard. What d'ya write someone you don't really know that well?"

"So, you married her because you thought she might make a good wife?" Ben shook his head as he shifted the bale of straw so he could lean against the wall.

Gabe ruminated on Ben's question for a long minute. "Yeah, that and well, it was time. I wasn't getting any younger, and I was tired of tom-cattin' around. I needed some stability in my life." A white picket fence, two chickens in the pot, kids, a dog, you know. The whole nine yards."

Gabe paused, and in the dim light realized Schwarz had fallen asleep.

Enoch had banked the coal in the furnace and tossed on an extra shovelful. He knew that made his mama mad, but if there was ever a night that needed a few extra chunks of coal, it was this one. It was the coldest January anyone in New Surrey could remember, and this was the coldest night of the winter so far. The wind whistled through the clapboard siding on the little house on Ogden Street. The windows rattled, and the curtains moved with each gust while the tin roof rumbled to wake the dead.

It had been a long day. He had worked his regular shift at the plant and then put in a couple of hours doing odds and ends for Mrs. Gabriel and Norma. He never stopped being thankful for having a good job and for being able to pick up a couple of extra dollars on the side. He was proud of having a defense job, putting in an effort for the war. But in the moment, he was grateful for the three quilts on his bed, his flannel union suit, striped pajamas and tattered robe, all of which kept him in a cocoon of warmth waiting for the sleep that would shortly arrive.

Ever since puberty, when true desire had kindled into flame, he had fallen into the habit of lulling himself to sleep by thinking about women. Women he'd had and women he'd wished he had. Lately, he fell asleep thinking about Phoebe, the waitress down at Huckleberry's who took him home once in a while. He recalled the amazing way she could work her pelvis against his and how her breasts swayed and shook to the rhythm of their coupling. Before that, it was Ruby, that mulatto girl down at the plant who would meet him in a janitor's closet on their lunch break doing good things for him, and he for her. Until she got fired, that is, for expanding her horizons with Melvin on coffee breaks and then getting caught at it. Melvin got fired, too.

But on this cold winter's night, beneath three quilts and amidst the fluttering curtains, interspersed between recalling Phoebe's ecstatic groans and cries, another woman began to take shape.

He made a conscious effort to dismiss her from his mind, but like all men, the greater he tried not to think of her, the more he did think about her. Norma had gone from being a girl who climbed trees and played kick-the-can with him to a handsome full blooded woman. He found himself thinking about the curve of her ass under a tight skirt, the shape of her calves, the way she smelled, clean and of expensive perfume when she walked into a room. The fact that they went way back only made it worse.

He threw back the covers and went down to the kitchen for a glass of milk, anything to clear the fantasy out of his mind. But when he crawled back into bed, it all started again. The way she laughed, admitting to himself he had tried to look down her blouse, the curve of her neck—a hundred pictures flooded his mind.

When it started over, Enoch got up again and kneeled next to his bed, praying the way he had as a small boy. He asked God to remove all thoughts of Norma from his mind, to not make him suffer an impossible situation. He felt the weight of three hundred years of social and cultural taboo resting on his shoulders, and a sense of self preservation allowed him to rest easier when he went back to bed. It scared the hell out of him, but called to him at the same time.

But deep in his heart of hearts, in the place he chose to ignore and pretended didn't exist, he knew. He knew that if the chance ever came his way, he wouldn't be able to say no. He knew.

Norma had arrived at the roller rink a half hour early. She needed to get out of the house and thought that watching the skaters, the gliders and bumblers alike, listening to the Wurlitzer and having an orange pop and a hot dog might cheer her up, might lift her out of the post-holiday doldrums. She always got blue this time of year when the festive season gave way to dreary long winter nights, and this year was worse than most. Gabe was overseas, and her three girlfriends had decided to go to New York City for New Year's Eve, so she spent the holidays with her parents and with the Gabriels. Christmas morning with Dot and her son and his family was pleasant enough, but somehow she felt like Scrooge and the ghost watching from outside the window. It made her feel dull, bored and a little resentful. Finally she felt guilty for experiencing those very emotions. She thought she was missing out on something and couldn't figure out what it was, some elusive happiness and some exotic form of excitement. Perhaps it was the sense that life was passing her by; she couldn't put her finger on it. But one thing was certain, without Gabe and her friends, and in spite of her older family members, she was lonely.

"Hey, sweetie, have you been here long? I thought we said seven; did I get it wrong again? You know what a feather-brain I am." Norma's reverie was broken by Anne's voice, as she took her uncomprehending eyes off the circling skaters. Anne was dressed beautifully in white stretch pants, a white fur-rimmed sweater, gold pendant and was carrying skates with matching white fur pom-poms on the lace's aglets. She belonged in a Sonja Henie movie. Norma felt suitably frumpy in her gray wool slacks and old green sweater.

"Wow, look at you. Aren't you something? That outfit is the cat's pajamas, it's gorgeous.

"Thanks." Anne purred.

"Where did you get it?"

"Oh, it's just a little something I picked up in New York. I bought it to go ice-skating in Central Park."

"Now I get it. That's why you wanted to go roller skating, to show off your new outfit." Norma smiled.

"Well, maybe that was a teeny part of it, but I wanted to see you, and I remembered how much we used to love the roller rink. We have lots of catching up to do. How were your holidays?"

"Not as exciting as yours. You've got to tell me every last detail."

"Oh, Norma, it was fabulous. It was out of this world, I've never had so much fun in my life. Let's see, we arrived at Grand Central Station early Tuesday morning, took a taxi to the Marlboro Hotel and checked in. I can tell you one thing, taxies are a lot more expensive in New York, and the hotel wasn't as nice as we thought it would be, but those were the only disappointments for the whole trip."

"Was the hotel shabby?"

"No, I guess we were expecting the Waldorf-Astoria, that's all. But we got to see the Waldorf anyway, but I'll get to that later."

"Okay, so you got settled in, then what?" Norma lit a Chesterfield and blew out the match.

"Shopping, that's what. We went to Sak's Fifth Avenue, that's where I got this little number. We took the subway there because none of us had ever been on one and it was cheaper than a taxi. We walked up and down Fifth Avenue a hundred times, going in and out of the stores and fingering every bit of clothing that caught our eyes. Betty bought shoes at Bloomingdales."

"Sak's? Bloomingdales? I am so jealous, Annie, I could just scratch your eyes out." Norma laughed.

"You should have come along. I asked you to, you know I did."

"I know you did, sweetheart, but I would have just been a millstone 'round your neck. It wouldn't be fair to you girls, dragging an old married lady along. And besides, who could afford it; it must have cost y'all a fortune." Norma got up and walked over to the snack counter and came back with two bottles of orange pop.

"Oh…No…it didn't at all; here comes the best part."

"It gets better?" Norma's mouth smiled, but her eyes did not.

"Oh yeah, Tuesday night we decided to take in a show at Radio City Music Hall. I've always wanted to see the Rockettes, and believe you me, they're everything I thought they would be. Anyway, during intermission we were out in the lobby, went to the little girl's room and then came back and just watched the crowd. Then, all of a sudden out of the wild blue yonder came these three handsome boys in Army Air Corp uniforms, and each one had a cup of Coca-cola and a box of candy in his hands." Anne sipped her soda.

"Yeah, yeah, go on."

"Well, they told us they were in town on leave before shipping out overseas and asked if we would do them the honor of showing them the sights. They were real gentlemen, and they were officers, too."

"Gentlemen? Yeah, I'll just bet they were."

Ignoring Norma's remark, Anne continued, "I was going to go along and let them think we were from New York, but you know Betty and Margie, neither one of them is too quick on their feet, and before I could open my mouth they already told them we were from out of town too."

"I swear, Annie, some girls have all the luck." Norma's voice was flat.

"Oh, don't say that. You're the lucky one, a ring, a husband, a nice place to live, family, you've got everything the rest of us wants."

"I don't know, the grass is always greener on the other side. So did they take you out on the town?"

"Take us out on the town? My dear, we painted the town red for the next three days. Let me see . . . we went to the Copacabana, The Stork Club, El Morocco, the Four Seasons, ate lunch at the Waldorf, went to the Metropolitan Museum of Art, rode a Hansom Cab around Central Park, went skating, I told you that already, and then we spent New Year's Eve in Times Square. That's the most exciting place in the world to spend New Year's Eve. I'm sure I left some places out. My beau is named Lawrence and he's from Iowa, has the cutest little Mid-West accent. He said he'd write me every week and look me up in New Surrey after the war. Maybe we can double date, me and Lawrence and you and Gabe."

"You left out a part."

"What's that, Norma?"

"You know, did you, uh, did you do it?"

Anne's face blushed deep red in contrast to her white ensemble, and that was all the answer Norma needed.

"You know, I really don't feel like skating anymore, I think I better go."

"Go? Norma Marie you just got here, what's wrong? Did I upset you? Make you mad?"

"Don't be ridiculous, I'm thrilled for you. You had a wonderful trip to New York, and you met someone wonderful; I'm so happy for you, I really am. It's just that I'm starting to get a migraine and if I don't get home and take something for it, I'll be worthless for the next two or three days."

"All right then, I'm sorry you're not feeling well. Maybe we can try again next week. You're sure you're not upset?"

"No, really, I'm not." Norma stood and put on her coat as the Wurlitzer began another round of The Beer Barrel Polka.

"O.K., then, take care, call me."

"Sure, bye."

"Bye."

Norma cried herself to sleep that night.

CHAPTER 8

"What We Gonna Do?"

Over the course of two and a half months Enoch Baker had managed to make himself an indispensable part of the Gabriel household. Partly because a somewhat neglected sixty-year-old house needed much repair and maintenance, and partly because he was dependable and did good work. Enoch managed to put in between eight and twelve hours a week, and his duties were expanded to running errands for the two Mrs. Gabriels besides making repairs, cleaning out the furnace, painting, replacing storm windows. . . He would go to the market and hardware store, post office and anywhere else he was asked to go. The two women paid him for piece work; each time he finished a job or ran an errand they would ask him how much they owed him, and he would always answer the same way: "Ma'am, you jus' pay me what you think its worth."

Inevitably they paid him more than he expected, which never failed to bolster his tenuous self-esteem.

He began holding back a little spending money for himself. He couldn't remember the last time he had a couple of dollars of his own, and he still managed to give his mother extra. When he was given a house key, Enoch was humbled and proud at the same time. It was not unusual; most of the colored cooks, maids and housekeepers had keys to their employer's houses. Their honesty was never questioned, and it didn't need to be. In a Southern town the stakes were too high. But for Enoch Baker it was a new experience and instilled in him a sense of responsibility and importance he had not known before. Four twenty-seven Pritchard Street was now his house to take care of.

Of course, he was the brunt of some jokes and ribbing by the boys down at Huckleberry's Tavern, going on about being Missus Gabriel's "Step 'n' Fetchit" and taking good care of those two white women, especially that young one with the fine ass. There was more of the same from the other janitors and stock boys down at the plant, but Knock-knock never answered any of them. He just smiled; it tickled him to let them think what they wanted to. Even his mother cautiously teased him, good-naturedly reminding him of his newfound responsibility and maintaining a sense of propriety working for two white women with no man around. It was especially important since Missy was starting a new job cooking and keeping house for Judge Barstow.

The February blizzard was the kind of snowstorm that happened once in a decade. Enoch remembered a storm like this when he was a boy, except then, his only responsibility was to throw snowballs, build snowmen and forts, and slide down Cannonball Hill on flattened trash can lids or a piece of cardboard. Down at the plant they drew straws to see who would stay as part of the skeleton crew keeping the boilers stoked and the pipes from freezing. Thankfully he drew a long straw because likely as not, the skeleton crew was going to be stuck there for a couple of days.

"My, my, you're a sight for sore eyes," his mother announced when he came in the front door, stamping his feet, blowing on his hands and brushing the snow from his hair and shoulders. "I was hoping they'd let you home early. The Judge sent me home early too; he allowed as how we might get as much as eighteen inches."

"I believe it, Mama. It's comin' down somethin' fierce out there."

"I stopped by Peabody's and got some milk, bread, and toilet tissue. I don't 'spect we'll need anything else." She sighed. "Now you go upstairs and put on some warm, dry clothes and I'll fix us some hot cocoa. I don't want you catch the influenza."

When he had emptied his mug and wiped the froth mustache away, he thanked his mama, kissed her on top of her head, and went to the hallway closet. After rooting around in the closet for a few minutes he found his old pair of galoshes, the left foot having only one metal buckle;

then he found the scarf his grandmother had made for him, a pair of brown cotton work gloves and a wool hat.

"Where do you think you're going in this storm?" His mother asked, concerned.

"Mama, I'm just going out to sweep the steps and get a start on shoveling the sidewalk, then I'm headin over to the Missus Gabriels' and doin' the same, make sure they got heat and water an' all."

"You must be crazy, boy, it'll cover up as fast as you shovel it. Just wait 'til it's done snowin'."

"If I start on it now, that'll be that much less work later. I'll be fine Mama, snow shovelin' keeps you warm."

Enoch did not consider the walk over to Pritchard Street a chore, but more like an adventure. He liked the idea of braving the elements. He liked the feel of the snowflakes striking his cheeks and falling into his eyelashes. He liked that hardly anyone was on the streets and that the snow made New Surrey look like a picture on a Christmas card. He savored the boyhood wonder of it all.

When he arrived at the Gabriel house, he swung the long-handled coal shovel from his shoulder and began digging into the accumulating snow. It was more difficult than he had anticipated. The rough, irregular brick paved sidewalk did not allow him to easily push the snow aside. It was much easier to clear the hard packed dirt in front of his mother's house.

Enoch had worked halfway across the front of the house when the glass-paned door opened and Norma, standing with her arms wrapped around herself against the cold, called "Knock-knock, what are you doing out there in this weather? Leave that walk alone until it's done snowing."

"You sound just like my Mama, but you womenfolk won't be the ones out here shovelin when it's up over your knees." He called back to her.

"Suit yourself, but you come in and warm up when you're done, I'll put a kettle on."

"No need for that."

"Nonsense, you come in when you're ready."

A half hour later he had finished the length of sidewalk only to look back and see that nearly another inch had fallen since he had started. He straightened up, stretched and just shook his head. Leastways that's a start. This is gonna a be a bigger job than I thought.

Ignoring his better judgment, he walked around the side of the house, leaned the shovel against the wall, pulled off a glove, and rapped on the glass. Norma opened the door with a towel in her hand and a pair of slippers she dropped onto the floor. "Here, give me your coat, dry yourself off. Take off those nasty old galoshes and step into these."

"Norma, I can't, I shouldn't, I needs to go, Mama's specting me home for supper."

"Will you stop being so contrary and just do as I say? She won't expect you to come home without warming up first, you'll catch your death."

"Or worse, the influenza."

"Oh, I forgot about that. Does she still carry on about the influenza?"

"Sure does, she surely does."

"Well, here have a seat while I fix us a hot toddy."

"A what?"

"A hot toddy, it's what Daddy always drinks to warm up after he's been out shoveling snow. It's delicious, and you're going to love it." Having said that she brought a teapot to the table and half filled the two mugs she had set out, put an overflowing tablespoon of honey in each, a pat of butter and filled the mugs the rest of the way with Jamaican rum. "Here, try that." Enoch obediently took the mug and carefully sipped it.

"Oh my, that is good."

"See, I told you so."

"Deed, you did. Where's Missus Dorothy? She still at Doc Morris's?" Enoch took another drink from the hot toddy he cupped in his cold hands.

"Oh, she went over to Harmon Falls to visit her cousin who's been feeling poorly. She called and said she was just going to stay there until the roads are cleared."

With that, he stood up and nervously put the mug down. "Norma, girl, I needs to go. I can't be sittin' here getting liquored up; Mama's gonna be worried, she's waitin' on me."

"Then just call her and tell her you're fine."

"We ain't got no telephone."

"Well, she'll be all right. Good Lord, Knock-knock, you're a grown man, she'll be fine."

"She'll be fine all right, she'll be fit to be tied is what she'll be."

"Sit down and stop worrying. I already told you once not to be so contrary." Norma reached over and squeezed his hand; he reflexively pulled it away as if he had been scalded. Norma ignored it.

"You always was a bossy thing."

"Still am." And with that, she poured each one of them another toddy, this time with more honey and rum than tea.

With the second drink, Enoch started to relax. The light outside faded as the afternoon disappeared, and Norma turned on the kitchen light. He had long stopped protesting that he had to leave. They drank, smoked Chesterfields, laughed and talked, sharing memories. The syrupy warmth of the honey and rum flowed over them, and they exulted in each other's company that snowy evening. Neither one of them felt the burden of maintaining a facade. It was reminiscent of when they were children sitting by the town run pitching in stones and sharing heartfelt secrets.

"Enoch, do you like music? Funny, I don't remember us ever listening to music or even talking about it."

"Course I like music, who don't like music?"

"Well, then come listen to this new Benny Goodman record I just bought, it's the living end." She stood and walked to the parlor with Enoch obediently following her. She pulled the shades down, switched on the light and put the record on the Victrola. She sat down on the sofa and Enoch settled into a comfortable chair. They both tapped their feet and bobbed their heads to the sound of Goodman's Clarinet taking the A train. When the 78' finished, she immediately flipped it over and swayed in place to a slower melody.

She walked to the chair, grabbed Enoch's hand. "Dance with me."

He stood and instinctually took her in his arms, the Jamaican rum having worked it's magic. She leaned into him, resting her head on his shoulder. They breathed in each other deeply and held one another tight against the raging storm, against the whole world.

"Enoch, do you know what day it is?"

"I do. It's Valentine's Day."

"Yes it is. Happy Valentine's Day." She tilted her head up and kissed him. They looked into each other's eyes and kissed again. They were overpowered. They were overwhelmed by the momentary torrent and surrendered to it completely. The music stopped, the needle repetitively hissing as they explored one another in playful nibbles, pecks and passionate discovery. Their hands moved over each other's bodies, he cupped her breasts in his hands and she moved her hands down his back and pulled him into her. She broke away, took his hand and wordlessly led him upstairs to her bedroom. They made love ferociously, without guilt, without any thought at all, only in the animal pleasure of the moment. When they finished, they held on to one another again until their breathing had slowed and kept time with one another.

"Now what we gonna do?" Enoch whispered.

"What do you mean, what are we going to do? Are you ready to go at it again?"

"You know that's not what I mean, I mean, what we gonna do?"

"I know what you mean. We're going to live for the moment and take things day by day." With that Enoch kissed her lightly on the forehead, got dressed, went downstairs, and left by the back door.

"Enoch Baker, where have you been? I have done worried myself sick, you bein' out in that snow."

"I'm sorry, Mama When I came by Hard Corner I saw that Huckleberry's was open, so I stopped in for a little nip against the cold. Well, Marvin, Robert and the boys were in there and one thing lead to 'nother and befores I know it, it's dark and all."

"I shoulda figured that. Well, I kept your supper warm in the oven, it's probably spoilt by now."

"Thanks, Mama." He went to the hall closet, hung up his coat and put away his gloves, cap and scarf and reached up far onto the shelf and pulled out a small box wrapped in red cellophane.

"Here, Mama, I got you a little surprise."

"Enoch! Oh, you know how much I love those chocolate cherries." She hugged him and then stepped back, "You smell like perfume. Who else was over there at Huckleberry's?"

"Oh, that was Phoebe, she jus' was wishin' me a happy Valentine day."

"Hmmm, I see."

"Happy Valentine's Day, Mama."

"Thank you, baby."

CHAPTER 9

Rumors

Ill deeds are doubled by an evil tongue.
WILLIAM SHAKESPEARE

"Blanche, I declare, you have absolutely outdone yourself. What a lovely afternoon." Marge sighed, getting up from the card table and making herself comfortable in a blue silk covered wingback.

"Thank you, dear, it was lovely wasn't it? It seems like forever since the bridge club met. I hope we can start getting together again regularly. I've surely missed it."

"Well, if you believe the papers, and according to what everyone's saying, Germany is all but finished. The last letter I got from Robbie said he expected to be in Berlin any day now."

Blanche stood and stepped over to the sideboard, "Can I interest you in something else to eat? There's still plenty of Waldorf Salad left, or how about another small piece of pie?"

"Oh,no, I've already eaten much too much. I'll bet you thank your lucky stars everyday that Missy Baker came to work for you. I've never known a cook to be able to do so much with so little, I swear a body would hardly know there was a war on."

"'deed, I am lucky. Betty Colson hasn't given me the time of day since Missy started. The Judge is still cordial though; he's a true gentleman if there ever was one."

Marge nodded in agreement and continued, "Of course, it is a little easier living in the valley, what with farms, gardens and the way people can and put up preserves. I can't imagine laying out a spread like this if we lived in Washington or Richmond. But still and all, Missy works her magic."

Life on the home front did seem to be getting better. The days were getting longer and the weather warmer. Jonquil and tulip buds were showing color and the forsythia bushes loitering at the corners of every other house on the block brought smiles to people's faces. There had been minimal frost damage to the apple and peach orchards, and all the war news was good. The Allies had captured the Remagen Bridge over the Rhine and taken Cologne, and in the Pacific, Manila was back in American hands and the Marines had invaded Japanese soil, storming and dying on the volcanic sand of Iwo Jima. The hopes and dreams of the people at home were growing more optimistic by the day.

"Marge, I believe it's time for a drink, I'm going to fix myself a bourbon and branch. Care to join me?"

"Well, all right, just a small one though. The sun is over the yardarm as Robbie used to say."

Blanche sat down in the matching chair next to Marge, placing the glasses and napkins on the round pedestal table between them. She then opened a silver box and removed two cigarettes, handing one to Marge. Lighting them with the matching seashell shaped lighter, the women sipped their bourbon, exhaled rich Virginia smoke and appeared to be the very picture of genteel relaxation.

"My, my, what do you think the poor people are doing right about now?" Blanche smiled.

"Oh, you're terrible. You ought to be ashamed of yourself." Marge grinned, winked and clicked her glass on Blanche's. Then she leaned forward and looked from side to side conspiratorially and lowering her voice said, "But I bet I know what one of 'em's doing."

Blanche sipped her drink and looked at Marge from over her glasses. "What's that?"

Marge looked around again and said, "Well, I'm not one to gossip, but I've heard that Missy's boy Knock-knock started making pretty regular visits to Dorothy Gabriel's house, once her daughter-in-law moved in."

Blanche emptied her glass, and as the warmth of the expensive corn whisky spread through her she let out a laugh. "Oh my, people do talk. Missy told me herself that the boy was doing repairs and odd jobs around the house. I'm sure there's nothing to it."

Blanche lit a second Raleigh with the stub of her first, blinking as the smoke curled into her eyes, "Well, he is a fine looking, handsome young buck, as my daddy used to call them, good looking for a colored boy that is. But like I said, he's just helping out doing some man's work around the house."

"Man's work indeed." Marge winked. "Then why has Ida Jean seen him coming and going on Wednesday nights when Dorothy is at church?"

"Ida Jean, that old biddy? The truth's not in her; she's the biggest gossip in New Surrey." Blanche frowned.

"Gossip or not, she lives across the street. She only has to look out her window to see what's going on. And another thing, I've heard from other folks that he's been dressing mighty nice. Nancy Brewster said she saw him in a tweed jacket she knows belonged to Tom Gabriel. How do you explain that?"

"I don't know how to explain it, and I'm not sure why anyone would need to. I'm sure it's all innocent, a colored boy and a white woman, surely that Gabriel girl has more sense than that."

"Well, as my Daddy used to say, where there's smoke, there's fire." Marge reached for a second cigarette.

The pocket French doors behind the women suddenly slid open and Missy Baker stood in the opening, "Will there be anything else, Miss Blanche? I have the kitchen cleaned up."

The women turned with a start. Blanche answered, "No Missy, that'll be all, I'll get the things from in here." Missy turned and left wordlessly, sliding the door closed behind her. Blanche looked at Marge, "How long do you suppose she was standing there?"

"Hard to tell, that's the thing I hate about colored help, they're always padding around like, like . . . spooks"

Both women flushed red, but not from the bourbon.

When the first few warm days of spring arrived, life reappeared not only from the soil, but from the front doors of houses all along Ogden and Hiram streets. In the working class neighborhoods on both sides of town, men, and in lesser numbers women, would sit on front door and porch steps enjoying the evening air and one another's society. At the end of the work day, during the relaxed hours on either side of supper, before it got too cool and dark. Before a favorite program started on the radio, if they owned one, people would trade stories, catch up on the news of the day or week, and pass around jokes along with a bottle openly hidden in a brown paper sack.

John Winslow and Roscoe Hill were local landmarks, parked on John's narrow steps from six to eight p.m. every night. John's wife swore they had worn two shiny buttock-shaped indentations in the cement of the stairs.

Roscoe removed the ever-present cigar from his mouth, spit into the dirt and reached down for a pint-sized paper bag and took a pull. The wrinkles around his eyes deepened as he squeezed them shut, grimaced and gave a quick shake of his head. He passed the bottle to John and re-lit his cigar. A moment later, he chased the whisky with another, longer pull from the quart bottle of Miller Highlife that had been sitting between them. He handed it to John to do the same. John pushed back his slouch cap and scratched at the silver stubble on the dark skin of his chin while Roscoe began cleaning his fingernails with a penknife. On most nights, passing a bottle, smoking, and spitting took precedence over conversation, which suited the two old friends just fine.

Both men looked up when they heard the friendly voice of Knock-knock Baker calling out to them. "Evenin' Roscoe, evenin' John, been a long time since I saw you two sippin' and spittin' " he laughed, "Spring has surely arrived and summer ain't far behind."

"You right 'bout that, c'mon over and have a snort with us." Roscoe called back, not bothering to remove his cigar.

"Can't, Mama's got supper on, maybe later." Enoch waved as he hurried up the street.

John took a sip of beer. "You hear 'bout that boy bird-dogging some white girl up on Pritchard Street?"

"Course I heard 'bout it; who ain't? But more like tom-cattin' than bird-dogging, I expect."

John set down the bottle of beer, fished a small cloth bag and pad of Bugler papers from his pants pocket and deftly began rolling a cigarette. "You ever had a white woman?"

"Me? Nooo, Lord, I stay away from that stuff. How 'bout you?"

"I almost did once, overseas in the last war, but I didn't have the two dollars she was chargin'." Both men started laughing.

"Yes sir, but this here ain't nothing to laugh about. Ol' Knock-knock headin' for a world of trouble, and we all watchin' him go to hell in a hand-basket." Roscoe lamented.

"He's a growed man, what'd you want to do? Hell, he's gonna have to learn. He may have a little pussy now, but he gonna end up with a tiger by the tail." John stood and stretched.

"You got that right."

Gabe and the rest of second platoon were billeted for the night in a comfortable stone building that had once served as a carriage house and stable. It stood two streets away from the town square. The company had secured the insignificant German town earlier that afternoon and was pleased to find it largely unscathed by war. Gabe staked a claim to one of the small rooms upstairs, the one time living quarters of the coachmen. He tightly closed the window shutters and built a small fire in the hearth to take out the chill. Having gotten himself settled in, he sat at a small table and began writing letters.

He had only been writing fifteen minutes when the door silently opened and Private Jerry Morgan stuck his head into the room. "Hey Doc, I need a favor."

Gabe jumped and looked up scowling, "What's that?"

"I found a bottle of wine this morning and been carrying it all day. You got a clamp or scissors or something I can get the cork out with?"

"Aw hell, Jerry, just come in and break the neck off on the edge of the fireplace. You scared the shit out of me."

"No way, this is a bottle of good wine; it deserves better," and with that the private stepped into the room and presented the bottle to Gabe as if he were the sommelier at the Ritz.

Gabe took the bottle and read the label by the firelight, "Hmm. 1936 Riesling. Don't know much about wine, but it's old enough, must be good."

"Trust me, it's good." Jerry smiled.

With that, Gabe turned the brown bottle over and began thumping the bottom with the heel of his palm. "Hey, what're ya doin'?" Jerry said as he took half a step towards Gabe.

"Watch and learn, my young friend, watch and learn." Gabe grinned, and after a few more thumps the cork began to slide, and with a steady rapping on the bottle the cork moved enough for Gabe's fingers to gain purchase on it and extract it.

Jerry couldn't hide the amazement on his face. "Wow, where did you learn to do that? It's like a magic trick or something."

"Yeah, well, I may not know much about wine, but I know a whole lot about opening bottles." Gabe then raised the bottle to his lips to take the first sip.

"Whoa, whoa, whoa, we've got to let it breath a little."

Now Gabe was the one with arched eyebrows. "Breathe?"

"Yeah, breathe."

"Okay, if you say so."

"I do, Doc. Lets have a smoke and give it a couple of minutes."

"Whatever you say, it's your wine."

Gabe plucked a burning splinter from the fireplace and lit a cigarette, then handed it to the private to do the same. "So what do you know good?" Gabe watched Jerry's adam's apple bob up and down as he blew a couple of perfect smoke rings.

"Don't know anything, but sure as shit hear a lot."

"Yeah? So what have you heard?"

Jerry lowered his voice, "Well, Morrison in first platoon has a buddy in the motor pool who knows another guy who's a clerk typist at regimental H.Q., who says—now get this—who says the war ended a week ago, and they're not telling the dogfaces because they don't want a riot on their hands. They think we'll all go nuts and discipline will all go to hell."

A look of condescension passed over Gabe's face as he ran his hand through his hair. "Jerry, I do believe that's the dumbest thing I've ever heard, and I'm from the South, so I've heard plenty of dumb stuff. Shit, they could never keep a secret like that. The word would be out in the blink of an eye. Is that wine done breathing yet?"

The private handed Gabe the bottle, and tilting his head back he took a long satisfying drink, while Jerry continued his explanation. "What'd ya mean they couldn't keep a secret like that? You know as well as I do, we're the last to know anything. Hell, we don't even know where we're going in the morning. You ever hear of the fog of war?"

"Never heard of it. The only fog around here is the fog between your ears. You know, that's the kind of rumor that can get a man killed."

"Doc, I'm tellin' ya, the war is over. Ain't nobody going to get killed anymore, leastways not by the Krauts. If anybody buys the farm from here on out, it's going to be from pneumonia, or dysentery, or a truck wreck. Mark my words on that."

"No, man, you mark my words, that crazy idea is going to get you or somebody else killed. Listen to me, it's a rumor and rumors are dangerous."

As Jerry pushed his chair back from the table, the wooden legs of his chair scraped loudly across the rough floorboards. He set the empty bottle of wine on the mantle. "I'll be right back."

He soon reappeared with two more bottles. In turn, he opened each bottle, using the technique Gabe had taught him. He couldn't wait to show off his new-found skill the first opportunity. As the bottles were slowly drained and the fire slowly burned down to embers, the atmosphere in the room turned jovial, then nostalgic and finally contemplative.

The two men joked, reminisced and finally drifted off into fitful sleep. Jerry's supposition about the war's end long forgotten.

Gabe awoke to the gray light filtering in through an open shutter. For the life of him, he couldn't remember how the shutter came to be open. A sharp pain shot across his shoulders and neck as he raised his head off of the table. He looked down to see the ink smeared on the page he had written. He had drooled in his sleep. A dull ache began to throb in his head in lock-step with the beating of his heart. He let out a low groan and sincerely hoped that Jerry was in worse shape than he was.

Ben Schwarz burst into the room, "Hey Doc, c'mon, shake a leg, the Lieutenant is downstairs grousing about what a lazy bunch of bastards we've turned . . . " Ben paused in mid-sentence as he looked down at Gabe, whose head was again resting on the table. "Man, oh man, you look like shit; you look like death warmed over." He then spotted the three empty bottles of wine and gave a wicked smile. "Well, lookee here, serves you right you selfish son-of-a-bitch, polishing off three bottles of wine all by your lonesome."

"I had help." Gabe rasped.

"That makes it worse. You were up here diddling a fraulein, while I was downstairs listening to snoring and farting G.I.s."

"Yeah, right. Jerry came in for a corkscrew, and one thing lead to another, and now I've got one hell of a hangover. I feel like the wrath of God."

"Jerry? Jerry Morgan?" Ben scratched under his chin.

"Yeah."

"That explains it then."

"Explains what?" Gabe asked as he rose unsteadily to his feet.

"Well, Doc, you're not gonna believe this. At the crack of dawn, Morgan gets up and announces to no one in particular that he's going to take a stroll around town, maybe take a dip in the fountain over in the square, and before anyone has a chance to stop him he's gone. That dumb son-of-a-bitch acted like there wasn't a war going on."

"The dumb shit, bet he was still half drunk." Gabe held his head in his hands.

"You're probably right. He came back an hour or so later, covered in puke and he had shit himself. Literally, he stunk to high heaven and was offering twenty bucks for a clean pair of drawers." Schwarz chuckled.

"Did he say what happened?"

"Oh yeah."

"What?"

"He made it to the fountain all right, but then had his helmet creased by a sniper, kept him pinned down for the better part of half an hour before he was able to get away. Brownlee sent a squad over to take care of the goddamn sniper. Don't know what got into Jerry."

Gabe allowed, "I do."

"Must have been the wine."

"Worse. A stupid ass rumor he'd heard."

CHAPTER 10

Small Talk

Dorothy called from the hall as she pushed the carpet sweeper back and forth. "Norma honey, would you go downstairs and tell Knock-knock that when he's finished with the basement steps he can start out back."

"Sure thing." Norma answered, draining her cup of coffee. She pushed away from the table, smoothed her clothes, and ran her fingers through her hair. She walked over to the basement door, opened it and descended the stairs to the sound of a banging hammer and Enoch's deep voice singing 'It is Well with my Soul'.

Enoch stopped, looked up and smiled broadly. "Well, hello Miss Norma. How are you this fine Saturday mornin'?"

"Fine, I guess. I'm supposed to tell you to start cleaning up the yard when you're finished down here." Norma sat down on the step next to where Enoch worked and looked up at him with expressionless eyes.

"I hope that's all you down here for and ain't got no other plans, 'cause I'm busier than a one armed paper hanger." Enoch smiled reaching over and stroking the inside of Norma's thigh.

Norma exploded into movement, slapping his hand away, scrambling off the stairs and looking around to make sure the door was still closed. "What are you crazy?" she hissed, her lips and jaw tight with malice.

"Oh, I was just fooling around. Nobody down here but me an' you. 'Sides, old Missus Gabriel don't 'spect a thing between us." Enoch hissed back trying to imitate Norma's voice and tone.

"I know, I'm just a little on edge and cranky." Norma relaxed her grip on the handrail.

"We still on for our regular Wednesday night, uh . . . date?"

"I don't think so, not this week." She whispered.

"Girl, don't be like that, now you're mad at me." Enoch reached to touch her arm.

Norma twisted away again, "It's not that, I started my monthly this morning."

"Oh, I see." Enoch paused for a moment, then leered, "Well, you know there are other ways to take care of a man, and I knows you know how."

"Sex, sex, sex. Is that all you ever think about? Because that's all you ever talk about. I've got to tell you, Enoch, it's getting a little bit boring, don't you ever have anything else to say for yourself?" Norma's voice became a little more shrill with each word.

Enoch straightened up to his full height, his eyes flashed than narrowed and the muscles of his jaw tightened as he rasped. "What the hell you want to talk about girl? Want me to tell you how wonderful it is to be colored in New Surrey? Maybe you want to talk about your husband? You want to discuss me an' you runnin' away to Chicago or New York? How 'bout that? That be a good thing to talk about. You wanna talk 'bout that? Nah, didn't think so."

Norma stood there silently, her eyes downcast and her cheeks flushing red. Enoch's tone softened, "You jus' tell me, I'll talk about anything you want." Norma turned and walked back up the stairs, neither saying a word nor looking back. Enoch did not move for several moments, staring ahead, feeling empty.

The young Mrs. Gabriel was quiet and circumspect the rest of the day. She spent the afternoon and evening in her room, telling Dorothy she was cramping. The whole time Enoch's words repeated themselves like a skip on a scratched seventy-eight. Norma's finely honed emotions moved irrationally from rage to apathy, from guilt to righteous indignation, until in the end she was sorry for what she had said. Thus began several hours of self-loathing through which sleep eluded her. She knew he would come over Wednesday night, she knew she would do whatever he wanted. She knew she couldn't refuse her own needs. She never could. Things would continue as they had for the previous weeks and would for the foreseeable future. She got word to Enoch the next day, and he was glad things were back to normal.

CHAPTER II

A Forgotten
Dog Tag

Victory belongs to the most persevering.
NAPOLEON BONAPARTE

April twenty-ninth, nineteen hundred forty-five dawned bright and clear, the sky a mild yellow-orange with no trace of red whatever. Gabe was thinking the sky foretold the arrival of a perfect day and in fact, it matured into the spring day of poets' inspiration.

Second platoon, D company, had taken up positions on the outskirts of Würtzheim, a small Bavarian market town. In the next few days they would be among the first units to enter Munich, the birthplace of Adolf Hitler's National Socialist Party. But before that, Würtzheim had to be cleared of enemy combatants and secured.

By midmorning in the crystalline light and soft breeze of that penultimate spring day the men were already congratulating themselves on a job well done. The day's Mission already accomplished and without taking casualties. The men of second platoon had hardly fired a shot. Their presence was enough to defeat the demoralized, frightened old men and boys ordered to defend the town. Those that didn't rout away at the sight of the unshaven, dirty, heavily armed G.I.s had simply dropped their weapons and surrendered.

Now they were at rest. Lieutenant Brownlee walked over to Gabe half-joking that Hitler's thousand year Reich had lasted slightly less than twelve years and was in its death throws, not with the rictus of a defiant howl, but with an exhausted groan.

Gabe watched the group of young men, most in their late teens, listening to their talk which was flush with the hubris of victory. He understood they couldn't be blamed for assuming the war was all but over and that they would soon be home safe, sound and ready to populate the world with tow-headed babies. He also understood that a number of them would die believing that. He'd seen it before—The relief of surviving a battle, the youthful belief in good luck and, even one's own mortality; especially one's own mortality.

And so, first and second squads were now at ease, resting and refitting in one of the covered open-air market stalls lining the town square. Opposite them on the east side of the square Sergeant Manning and third squad were doing the same in a matching set of stalls. Despite their appearance and war weariness the men of second platoon were in an exhilarated frame of mind, the result of the morning's easy work and the glory of sublime spring weather.

Gabe stared out across the square, observing the dance of light and shadow peculiar to the time of day. He felt satisfied that for the most part he had performed his duty, his personal duty ingrained in him by his father. He was responsible for these men, and as for the ones he had failed, and for the ones he would fail in the future, well, he would figure out a way. Figure out a way to make it up to them.

Walter Pomeroy, one of second platoon's replacements who had learned the survival skills of an infantryman pulled out a thin bundle of letters. He took the top envelope, placed the others on his lap and began to examine it. He ran his fingers over the written address, sniffed the back of it, shook it and finally opened it with deference. A few of the other men taking the cue from Pomeroy began to pull out letters and read and reread them. Walter looked up from his mail and made eye contact with Gabe.

"Letters from home, Doc. First chance I've had to look at them."

"Yeah, nice to get a letter now and then." Gabe answered, not wishing to dwell on the subject.

"So what'd ya hear from home, Doc, anything good? Look at Morris over there, his old lady sends him her panties once a week." Pomeroy said laughing and tossing a pebble at Morris.

Screw you, Walt, can't you mind your own damn business? I haven't heard from Norma in months and even my mother barely writes anymore. Something's wrong, maybe she realizes we rushed into things too. Gabe didn't answer Pomeroy's question, instead he stood up, and walked over to the next stall where the lieutenant and a few other men had gathered to relax and take stock of things.

Lieutenant Brownlee resting on one knee stubbed out his cigarette and fingered the worn leather case hanging around his neck. He looked out towards the North side of the square studying his surroundings. Brownlee saw the random buildings flattened and charred by Allied bombers, the fronts of other buildings pockmarked by bullets and the buff colored stucco chipped away between the timbers by the same bullets. He noted the old stone church standing untouched as if protected by the provident hand of God.

Gabe too stared out into the market square, seeing, but not seeing the damaged buildings, saddened a little by the broken statuary around the fountain in the middle of the square. One small detail in the tableau troubled him beyond the general destruction. In a strange way ancient granite cobblestones stones had been crushed, broken and torn out of their rightful place by the passing treads of heavy panzers and halftracks, the tires of a myriad of vehicles and the hooves of horses pulling wagons. The havoc wrought upon such good and practical stonework offended a deep sensibility in Gabe's nature. He knew that soon the advance of American armor would only worsen it. The destruction of someone's hard work and perfection struck a deep chord in Gabe. It was something he understood all too well.

"I think I'm going up that bell tower and take a look around." Brownlee said to no one in particular.

"Perfect day for it." Sergeant Rickert said, leaning against a post also gazing into the bright light.

"Yeah, that's what I was thinking. A spectacular view and hopefully some recon." Brownlee answered.

"Hey L.T. mind if I join you? I'd love a bird's eye view of some of this prime farmland. The fields and orchards kind of remind me of home." Gabe said.

"Don't mind at all."

"Hey, you guys be careful. There might still be snipers out there. It'd be goddamn stupid to get killed now, when the krauts are about to go tits up. Sir, I'd like to at least send a man along with you in case of trouble." Sergeant Rickert said with obvious concern.

"Sure. Thanks, Sarge. Good idea."

The Sergeant's eyes moved immediately to Private Menendez. The Private sat leaning against the wall trying to pitch playing cards into his helmet set out in front of him. The corners of Rickert's eyes crinkled into deep crow's feet as a smile flickered across his lips and disappeared as quickly.

"Menendez."

The young soldier nearly jumped out of his skin and scrambled to his feet at disheveled attention, leaving a rocking helmet and scattered cards at his feet.

"Manny I want you to go with the Lieutenant and Doc up that church tower. Keep your eyes and ears open."

"Yes. Sir." The Private picked up his helmet and rifle and walked over to where Brownlee and Gabe were standing.

"You ready?" Brownlee said, turning towards the square not waiting for an answer. He led the two men out into the square. Crouching, they double-timed along the buildings skirting the square until they reached the stone church seventy-five yards away. The Lieutenant's movements were meant more as a nod of respect to Sergeant Rickert and as an example to the men than for caution.

Entering the old stone church, they let their eyes adjust to the dim light filtering in through the still intact stained glass—blue, red, and golden light bathing the marble-tiled floors and the dark wooden pews. They noticed they weren't alone. Stationed every ten feet or so along the walls stood a small pantheon of Catholic saints, some in the suffering of martyrdom, others in the exultation of Divine revelation. Menendez dipped his fingers in the small marble font of holy water near the doors and made the sign of the cross. He removed his helmet and tucked it under his arm. Brownlee and Gabe looked at one another, shrugged and did the same. Gabe thought Menendez was a good man for showing the respect and conviction the place required. The Lieutenant made his way to the right side of the sanctuary, Gabe moved to the left and Menendez stood in the center aisle. Each man slowly moved to the front of the church in the quiet reverie the cool dim space inspired. Off to each side of the altar was a stone alcove, one nestling a statue of Christ, his hands outstretched and a flaming heart centered on his white tunic, the other held the Virgin Mary in a blue robe and a golden halo rising from behind her head.

Manny dropped one knee to the tiled floor, then slid into a pew to his right. In the muted light Gabe and Brownlee looked at one another across the church, shrugged again and sat at the ends of the same row. While Manny knelt with his head bowed, his lips moved slightly as he prayed. Brownlee closed his eyes and rested. Gabe sat studying the magnificence of the intricately carved wooden altar. His eyes slowly looked up to behold the grace and artistry of the heroic sized crucifix hanging over the altar, suspended just below the Rose window.

In those quiet moments he thought about how commonplace such masterworks and cultural heritage were. He marveled at the hard work and dedication that must have driven those artists. The idea comforted him. Every village, every town as well as large city was full of objects and structures of unimaginable beauty that were being destroyed daily. How was it possible that a people who created these things, the people of Beethoven, Bach, Mozart and Schiller were capable of such evil and such cruelty? Such madness?

Brownlee's voice broke into Gabe's thoughts, and he saw Manny's head raise up from his prayers. "Okay, let's check out behind that door and find the stairs to the belfry."

The men replaced their helmets, grabbed their weapons and passed through the heavy door into the wood-paneled vestry. Another door stood off to the right. Entering it, they found themselves at the foot of rough-hewn wooden stairs leading steeply upward. A long thick rope, knotted at the end, hung next to the stairs. Manny and Gabe stood like two awestruck little boys, craning their necks so their eyes could measure the ropes ascent.

"Either one of you jokers even think about ringing those bells and you'll be pulling shit duty for the rest of the war."

The two just smiled at the Lieutenant. They began climbing the stairs with Manny taking the lead. The stairs creaked but were surprisingly solid as the three men climbed ever higher. As the stairs snaked around the four walls of the towers they passed long thin windows allowing them to gauge their progress. The Sun filtering in highlighted the swirling dust disturbed by the heavy footfalls on wooden planks. The structure only stood six or seven stories tall, not particularly imposing as church spires go. But as it happened, none of the three men were particularly comfortable with heights. Reaching the top each man found a wall or banister post to lean against. As they caught their breath each took a turn at pulling a swig water from the canteen Gabe offered. Then, trying not to be obvious, propped themselves against the brick and stone corner posts of the belfry to look out across the village and surrounding environs. Caught up in the moment, the light, and the long vistas, Gabe began to relax, allowing himself to get comfortable with the high perch they occupied.

Below them, stretching to the horizon, the miniaturized landscape before them still had wisps of smoke rising in the still, warm air. The thin gray smoke the last exhalation of dying embers from burned out buildings and vehicles destroyed in the previous night's air raid. Off to their right, around the corner from the market square and not far from the church, stood a ruined factory and complex of warehouses. Two brick smokestacks and a water tower were the only structures still standing among the tumbled down walls. To the left, laid out before them was a residential section with some trees splintered around the skeletal remains of several houses.

Manny had moved to the center of the opening next to where the lieutenant was sweeping the town with his field glasses. Gabe stood behind Menendez waiting to get a chance to look through Brownlee's glasses.

Manny could no longer bridle his enthusiasm. He cupped his hands to the sides of his mouth and in full voice bellowed, "HEY . . . HEY YOU GUYS . . . UP HERE . . . LOOK UP HERE . . . YOU DON'T KNOW WHAT YOU'RE MISSING . . . THERE'S, THERE'S A . . ."

The impact of the first bullet caused Manny's face to vaporize in red and gray mist. His helmet and the top of his head smashed back and caught Gabe square in the face. The G.I. was lifted off his feet, knocking Gabe down as the lifeless body was hurled back, spilling down the stairs and coming to rest on the first landing below them. Menendez's helmet spun like a top and careened off the edge of the platform, a moment later the clang of metal hitting stone reverberated from six stories below. Gabe wiped the blood and brain tissue from his face, realizing that the front edge of his own helmet had kept the cannonball sized projectile of Manny's forehead and helmet from breaking his nose and jaw.

The second round hit Brownlee as he turned to see if Gabe was all right. Gabe saw the bullet tear through Brownlee the same moment he heard the crack of the sniper's rifle. Brownlee's face contorted as the bullet entered his lower back, and exited between his upper ribs, dropping him in place.

Gabe's only thought was to get Brownlee out of the line of fire. He grabbed his wounded friend under the arms and dragged him away from the opening lowering him onto the rough oaken floorboards. Knowing that Menendez was dead he focused all of his attention on Brownlee. A small dark stain was spreading around the torn cloth of Brownlee's field jacket just below his left collar bone. Clearly one lung had been punctured and collapsed. He began gasping for breath. In his controlled panic, Gabe could hear the sound of men running and then gunfire. It was coming from the direction of the burnt out factory.

Brownlee's eyes were wide open in horror, his visage gray-white and his mouth working like a huge fish out of water. His body spasmed as he sprayed Gabe's face, chest and arms with more gore. In a moment, he settled back as a blood-tinged foam began bubbling from his mouth. Gabe tore Brownlee's field jacket open, and in one fluid motion unsheathed his knife, inserted it between the top two buttons of his friend's shirt and slice downward sending buttons skipping across the dusty oaken planks. He then bunched the Lieutenant's undershirt, pierced it with his knife and tore it away from Brownlee's heaving chest. The exit wound was an almost perfect circle the size of a Liberty dollar. Bits of mottled pink lung tissue protruded from the wound, with surprisingly little blood.

Gabe's reflexes gave way to reasoning, logically thinking through what just happened and how he was going to save his officer and friend.

Damn . . . Damn . . . Damn . . . How could I have left my bag down below . . . We did all the exact things we told the men not to . . .

Gabe's mind worked with astonishing clarity. No blood, either it didn't hit a major vessel or he's bleeding into his chest. The edges around the wound were torn ragged, the muscle and skin like so much damaged cloth or paper. The tags of skin, muscle and shreds of lung moved in and out as Brownlee struggled to breathe, a gruesome low rasping sound emitting from the wound. Shit, a sucking wound to the chest...have to seal it . . . don't have much time . . .

Gabe rolled the Lieutenant up onto his side to examine the entrance wound. It was a small neat hole about an inch or so in diameter, its edges were neatly cut and pushed inward. Again the bleeding was minimal, but large reddish-purple bruising surrounded the wound like gathering storm clouds.

"I got it now L.T., I got it. Just hang on, I'll help you breathe, I got it. Just hang on. We can do this, we can work it hard and do it. Just hang on, hang on. You're mine, I got ya."

Gabe tore Brownlee's undershirt into two pieces and soaked both pieces with the contents of his canteen. "This is gonna hurt some. Just hang on. We can do this. I'm gonna keep you alive, by God I'll keep you alive. I know I can. Ted, look at me. You're not going to die, look at me."

Brownlee tried to focus on Gabe's face, but his eyeballs kept threatening to roll up under his lids. Gabe took the wet pieces of Brownlee's undershirt, one in each hand and compressed them tightly over the two wounds. Ted's eyes flashed, his back arched and an unearthly sound bubbled out of his mouth spraying more bloody froth. Gabe then positioned himself over Brownlee lying across him and using the weight of his upper torso to seal the makeshift dressings over the wounds. With his left hand he held the jaw and with two fingers of his right he cleared, serous foam, saliva and clotted blood from the Lieutenant's mouth. Gabe clamped his mouth over his friend's and blew as hard as he could, insufflating the lungs to allow something like normal breathing. It took three attempts before the Lieutenant took a ragged breath. Thank God . . .

Time had slowed, minutes turning to hours. Gabe discovered that after every four or five breaths he had to again move a large amount of air into Brownlee's lungs, in effect sighing for him. This meant he could not leave Ted for even a few minutes and that by sheer force of will and endurance he could keep him alive.

The gunfire from down below became sporadic and then ceased, an explosion serving as the crescendo and coda. Piecing together a scenario from what he'd been hearing, a rifle-grenade must have scored a direct hit. Gabe did not know the details, but knew the sniper was dead when the gunfire didn't reassert itself.

It was not long before Gabe's hands were tingling, then falling asleep at regular intervals and his back and neck ached from the contorted positions he was forced into. He would continue for hours and days, if necessary, with grim determination. Over the years his father's voice had diminished to a whisper, but as the voice grew weaker, its influence grew stronger. It was the guidepost, a North Star, the moons of Jupiter by which he navigated through hard times and good times alike.

After an interminable period of time Gabe heard movement in the church below. He had been too involved in the immediacy of Lieutenant Brownlee's wounds to call out for help above the gunfire.

"Lieutenant . . . Doc. . . you up there?" Someone shouted. "Menendez . . . Hey you guys all right . . . sound off." Gabe recognized the voice of Ben Schwarz, followed by the vibrations and sound of infantry boots on the staircase.

"Get . . . my . . . bag." was all Gabe could manage to say or think about. His concentration and awkward position over Brownlee's body telling on him. He heard a set of footsteps rapidly descending the tower stairs. A moment later the heavy footfall of three other men halted ten or fifteen feet below him, to where Menendez' body had tumbled.

"Oh Christ, oh no. Menedez. You two take him downstairs. I'm going up to check on Doc and the Lieutenant." There was no mistaking Corporal Ben Schwarz's nasal Jersey accent. Thirty seconds later he topped the stairs. He saw Gabe sprawled across Lieutenant Brownlee's still body. When he saw Gabe's blood splattered face and blood caked hands, he knelt down next to the prostrate medic. "Doc, Gabe, where're you hit?"

"I'm okay, I'm not hit." He paused to shift his hands and body and blew a long hard breath into Brownlee's mouth. "It's . . . L.T., two sucking chest wounds, he's in shock. I need plasma and an I.V. line. Tell Rickert to radio Battalion Aid for an ambulance or a jeep, and we'll need a litter to get him down."

Ben stepped over to the opening, bent over the ledge and shouted Gabe's orders down with cupped hands. He screamed the message three times, the second and third attempts ending in spasms of smoker's cough. It was on the third try that one of the men of first squad made it to the foot of the tower and understood what Schwarz was saying. Ben watched the man turn and run back to where Sergeant Rickert was waiting. Still looking down he saw Max Palmer running back across the square with Gabe's medical kit. Thankfully Palmer was the fastest runner in the platoon. Ben watched Gabe go through fifteen breathing cycles before Palmer crested the stairs, sweating and panting like a marathon runner. Palmer handed the medical bag to Schwarz and then doubled over trying to catch his breath. When he saw Gabe sprawled over the Lieutenant, bloodied and struggling, Palmer staggered over opposite Schwarz and vomited out the window.

Gabe instructed Schwarz to pull field dressings, sulfa-powder and gauze wrapping out of the bag. He continued tightly clamping the wounds and shifting to fill Brownlee's lungs every thirty-seconds or so. Gabe and Ben made two awkward attempts at wrapping the wounds tight enough to adequately seal them. It was clear they did not have enough bandage material or expertise to bind Brownlee's chest, and each attempt wracked the Lieutenant in pain. Gabe knew he would have to continue his lifesaving contortions for hours. He truly wondered if he had the strength to do it. His father's voice assured him he did.

The two enlisted men plead, begged and finally demanded that Gabe allow them to take over breathing for the Lieutenant. Gabe obviously needed to be spelled, but they could not topple the stonewall of his obsession. With Schwarz's help, he established two I.V. lines, instructing the men to suspend the bottles of plasma from the stairway railing.

It was an hour before the jeep with its litter and two bearers arrived, but it was much longer in Gabe's exponentially expanded sense of time. When the lieutenant was finally strapped onto the stretcher for the trip down the stairs Gabe had to make a difficult decision. Moving Brownlee had caused him a great groundswell of pain. He broke into a cold sweat and blanched white as death. Gabe knew his patient could lose consciousness or worse while being jostled down to the waiting jeep. Up to now he had resisted giving the Lieutenant morphine. He knew the drug could cause respiratory suppression, and although he couldn't be sure, he figured that was something to be avoided. Now there was no choice in the matter. He stuck the syrette into the wounded man's thigh and squeezed the contents into its large muscle. Wetting his finger with thick half-congealed blood from a puddle on the floor he drew a large purplish "M" on Brownlee's forehead.

While waiting for the opiate to perform its act of mercy, Gabe instructed the litter bearers how they were going to get the officer downstairs. Namely he would walk next to the litter keeping the chest wounds sealed and on every count of one hundred they would stop for him to move air into the wounded man's lungs.

After turning his patient over to the doctors he staggered to an ancient oak standing in the yard of the old stone school house that had been converted to a hospital. With adrenaline no longer coursing through his veins, he felt like an old man. The muscles of his back were stiff from the tension of the moment and the exertion of keeping Brownlee alive. He sat down heavily against the trunk, removed his sweat soaked shirt, enjoying the feel of the rough bark scratching his back.

Lieutenant Theodore Richard Brownlee survived the arduous rocking, thumping trip down the stairs followed by the equally rough rutted bumpy ride to the battalion aid station. Gabe never once let go of the two wounds or stopped moving lifesaving air into Ted's body; it had been almost six hours since the Lieutenant had been wounded. Now Gabe unlaced his boots, drained the contents of his second canteen, lit a cigarette. He leaned his head back and closed his eyes. He had saved a life. Job well done.

It had been a long time since such a profound sense of self-affirmation surrounded and protected him. The numbing and exhausting experience had served to ground him in who he was, and who he would always be. He had done the right thing, by his father's exacting standards, by anyone's standards he had worked hard and accomplished the near impossible. As he sat there in his self-congratulatory respite, some tiny uneasy feeling was at work in his psyche like a pebble in a shoe or seed stuck between teeth. He couldn't identify or verbalize the feeling. He couldn't dislodge the seed, he couldn't find the pebble, but knew in time he would figure out what it was.

In the gloaming of half-sleep he detected a presence and when a shadow passed across the light under his eyelids. He opened his eyes. Standing before him was a tall square built man, his large bald-head encircled by a clipped salt-n-pepper fringe. The man wore thick black glasses, had thick lips and thick fingers on a baseball mitt hand, which was outstretched to Gabe. On the breast of his dingy white coat was the symbol of the Army Medical Corps and his shirt collar bore the gold bars of a Captain. When Gabe's eyes focused on the symbol of rank he quickly rose to his feet and standing shirtless and shoeless saluted, trying for some small semblance of military dignity and decorum.

"Relax soldier. I should be saluting you. I'm not regular Army. I'm just an old guy doing the only thing he knows how to do. They gave me these silver bars so I wouldn't go near a gun and hurt myself. Anyway, this is my aid station." The man said his hand still outstretched. Gabe did not move or say anything.

"Are you the medic that brought the officer in with the chest wound?"

"Yes, sir. Lieutenant Brownlee, that was me. How is he?" Gabe answered.

"Thought it was you. Well, I just wanted to shake your hand. You single handedly saved that man's life. In two and a half years of patching up and putting G.I.s back together, I can count on one hand the number of chest wounds we've pulled through. You did everything just right, and for once in a blue moon everything around here worked just right, not the usual snafu. So Lord willing and the creek don't rise Lieutenant Brownlee will be around to tell his grandkids about the man who saved his life." The doctor stepped forward and took Gabe's hand in both of his. "What's your name?"

"Gabe, sir. Actually, Tom Gabriel, but everybody calls me Gabe."

"Actually, they told me that, but I just wanted to introduce myself. It's an honor to know you, and I'm not a sir. I'm Don Forrester. Everybody around here calls me Dr. Don, not exactly Army regulations, but I'm not exactly regular Army. My good friends call me 'Cue', lost my hair before I turned twenty-one. I'd be much obliged if you called me 'Cue'."

"Yes. sir." The Captain tilted his head and his bushy eyebrows arched above his glasses. "Oh, sorry. Force of habit. Glad to meet you Cue." Gabe said visibly relaxing.

"Gabe, there's one more thing."

"Yes sir. . . Cue?" Gabe said, thinking some other shoe was about to drop, unable to relax and enjoy the moment.

"Well, I thought I'd like to do something for you. You know, for making my day, and certainly for making your Lieutenant's day."

"What's that?"

Cue continued, "I've arranged a three day 'medical' pass for you. Officer's quarters are in a big half-timbered house just before you get to town square. It was the bürgermeister's house, it's nicely furnished, has a good wine cellar and great big old bathtubs with lots of hot water. Oh, and by the way, apparently the mayor must have been something of an Anglophile. There's an English style garden behind the house that's worth enjoying. Hit the wine cellar, pick something nice, there's a '34 Piesporter you should try. Help yourself, my clerks will be expecting you. I kind of think of it as the spoils of war. I figure the krauts owe us that much. Anyhow, I want you to be my guest, clean up relax. Eat and drink like a king for a couple of days. God knows you deserve it. You play cards?"

"I don't know what to say. You've got it all arranged?" Gabe said.

"The order is on its way to your C.O. even as we speak. So head on over, clean up, there'll be a fresh uniform waiting, wander around, sleep, whatever you feel like doing. I'll see you over there when I get off duty."

It was a short and easy walk to find the officer quarters. The entrance hall of the imposing house had been turned into a makeshift administrative office. It was large enough to fit two desks and several stacks of boxes and a bookshelf. Two men were seated at the desks, both in crisp clean uniforms, the badge of the Army Medical Corps on their collars, and sergeant stripes on their arms. They looked up at the mud and blood splattered G.I. standing in front of them; the scratched and faded red cross on white painted on his helmet told them everything they needed to know. One of them took a hastily written note off of his desk.

"You're, uh, let me see here, you must be Private Gabriel. You're the medic from D Company that brought in the lieutenant with the chest wounds."

"That's right." Gabe said removing his helmet, coming to an approximation of attention.

"You're a lucky guy. Doc said to give you the red carpet treatment. Give us a little time to get your room ready and round up a clean new uniform. Why don't you go out and relax in the garden. I'll have the housekeeper bring you a bottle of wine. Her name is Maria, and by the way don't get any ideas, she's Doc's main squeeze. Oh yeah, one more thing, I'm Gil and this is Pat, we're pretty relaxed around here. Welcome to Doctor Don's army, and whatever you do, don't salute." Gil said with a broad smile spreading across his face and gesturing towards the back of the house.

Gabe removed his shoulder bag and stripped off his cartridge belt and sidearm and left it all with Pat and Gil. Then he walked casually from the front room, down a corridor to the back of the house where he found a glass atrium and a set of French doors leading into the garden. There was not a cracked pane of glass or potted plant out of place. Though Gabe had observed such scenes time and again he couldn't easily accept what they represented. The paradoxes of war. Each time it gave him pause and made him wonder, why this place and not that, why is that man dead and I'm alive?

The lot behind the house was much larger than expected. Its plants, shrubbery and trees had a sense of manicured chaos that made English country gardens so charming. Had Gabe been familiar with English gardens, however, he would have seen small touches here and there that were more in keeping with Bavaria. At the back of the yard was a small open area of crushed gravel on which a weathered wooden bench sat positioned to be shaded from the afternoon sun. Ten feet across the small patch of gravel positioned to catch sunlight all day long stood a dark thick pole. Atop it was a small covered box that reminded Gabe of the nativity creche his mother put out every Christmas. Inside of it was a beautifully carved Crucifix perhaps two feet tall. Gabe walked over and looked up at it marveling over the exquisite detailing of the carving. Seems not even God, your own father could keep you alive. But you showed them three days later, didn't ya J.C.? You sure showed 'em three days later.

Sitting down on the bench in the shade of an oak tree he allowed himself to float again in the satisfaction of a job well done, a good day's work and its subsequent just rewards, something he could rarely indulge in. Gabe couldn't believe his luck this time. He tilted his head back and allowed the kaleidoscope of shade and brilliance to caper across his face. It wasn't long before the crunch of footsteps on the gravel brought him back into the moment. Bending down to set something before him was one of the most beautiful women he had ever seen—a woman with the porcelain skin, golden blonde hair and ice-blue eyes of an Aryan goddess. Now he understood Gil's admonishment; this was Maria. She placed a small wooden tray bearing a bottle of wine, the sun glancing off its green glass, a stemmed wine glass, a corkscrew, hunk of coarse black bread and thick slice of cheese next to him on the bench. She smiled, wordlessly turning, and walked back towards the house. Gabe watched the fluid feline movement of her body as she disappeared behind a tall hedge. Ahh, I wonder if it gets any better than this? Today, life is good.

Gabe opened the bottle and remembering a previous lesson allowed a few minutes for the bottle to breathe. The pale yellow-golden wine was liquid sunlight and the nutty flavors of the black-bread and cheese were transcendent. For the second time in almost as many minutes Gabe couldn't believe his good fortune. Sometimes, hard work is its own reward and at other times it reaps additional benefits. This was one of those times.

As he took a sip of his second glass of the excellent Moselle wine, he began fumbling with his shirt pocket for a pack of cigarettes. Shaking out a cigarette, he began tapping it on the bench surface to pack down the tobacco. He then fished into the same shirt pocket for his lighter, but the Zippo wasn't there. Gabe tried to think where he might have dropped it, but to no avail. He patted down all of his pockets but there was no sign of the lighter.

But Gabe was nothing if not persistent. He began systematically turning his pockets inside out. He found the Zippo in the small breast pocket of his field jacket. That was not all he found there.

Feeling the thin sliver of metal he knew what it was without looking at it, and suddenly it felt as if it weighed twenty pounds. The uneasy feeling that had haunted him earlier suddenly made itself plain. Menendez's dog tag should have been turned in with a report, but somehow it had remained in his coat pocket. Gabe scratched away the dried blood and sat there staring at it for several long moments. Suddenly he had no taste for the wine and cheese and the urge to smoke disappeared as the unlit cigarette fell to the ground. Menendez, Christ Manny, I'm so sorry I almost forgot you… thinking of food, showers and a clean bed I just got caught off guard. Christ, as if it wasn't bad enough not being able to save you, I've already forgot you. Man, I'm so sorry . . . I don't deserve this place . . . you do.

The hand that held the dog-tag had started to tremble. Try as he might, Gabe was unable to picture Menendez's face which only fueled the immolation of his conscience, as the flames of self recrimination kindled into a great blaze; the blaze forging the guilt and blame solidly in his mind. Gabe stood and slowly made his way along the winding garden path, his face a *tabula rasa* with eyes moist and unfocused.

A black bird of uncertainty lighted on a precariously balanced stone, its tiny weight causing a section of wall to collapse.

When he entered the front hallway the two sergeants were still at their desks shuffling papers. Without looking up from his paperwork Gil spoke. "Hey buddy. Beautiful garden, ain't it?" So listen, you're gonna need to give us another half hour or so. Is there anything I can get you?" When the sergeant finally did look up he dropped a stack of papers on his desk and stepped over towards Gabe. "What happened buddy? Are you ok? You look like you've seen a ghost or someone walked over your grave. Here, have a seat, let me get a glass of water." He returned in less than a minute with a tall cool glass of water and handed it to Gabe., who set it on the table.

"I need to go." Was Gabe's only reply.

"What're ya crazy? You just got here. There are guys out there that would give their left nut to spend a weekend here. Especially with all expenses paid and no strings attached." Gil said, trying to appeal Gabe's decision.

"I need to go." Gabe said, retieving his bag and webbing from the floor.

"Sorry to here that, guy. This is a limited time offer, and it doesn't come around too often. Sure you don't want to reconsider? Doc Don is going to be really disappointed." Pat added.

"I need to go." Gabe said one final time as he left the house.

"Do you believe that guy? What is he nuts or something?" Gil said posing the obvious question to his comrade.

"Man, oh man is that guy ever the definition of FUBAR." Pat said.

"Yeah, fucked up beyond all recognition, you got that right."

"Mus Be Fool Crazy"

But whoso committeth adultery with a woman lacketh understanding: he that doeth it destroyeth his own soul.
PROVERBS 6:32

Enoch stood in front of the bathroom mirror over the sink and wiped away the remnants of shaving cream. He smacked his face with Bay Rum and the alcohol sting made him feel alive with anticipation. He had timed things just right, lingering at the Huckleberry after work for a beer and a bump to ensure that his Mama would not be home, this being Wednesday night prayer meeting. He knew in his heart of hearts that if he wasn't fooling her, at least he could avoid the disapproving expression on her face for the time being.

He stepped into his bedroom and pulled out the bottom drawer of the scarred oak armoire and found a fresh pair of underwear and socks. He paused there as his thoughts raced in a dozen different directions. Desire, guilt, fear, elation and empowerment hurdled across his mind towards a destination he refused to contemplate. He willed the more complicated and difficult thoughts to fade into the background like the dull and peeling floral wallpaper that surrounded him.

What do I wear? Important to choose right. She said she liked me in my work clothes, but that part don't matter none, I be taking them clothes off right quick, he smiled inwardly. Course work clothes better if'n somebody stop and ask me what I'm doin' on that street after dark. But that don't matter none either, been usin' back alleys, garages and backyards to get around town since I was little. Got to remember to take some bacon and biscuits to keep the dogs quiet.

Don't know. Them clothes from her old man are mighty nice. Had to lie to mama 'bout them. Seems I'm lying to mama a whole lot these

121

days. That white woman somethin' else, she surely is, tellin' me I look better in those clothes than her husband do. Probably better I don't wear them clothes, don't want either of us thinkin' about that man. I only want her thinkin' 'bout me.

What're you doin' boy? I mus' be fool crazy, messin' with a married woman, that's against every law ever was. Then there be mixin' of the races, that against the law too. This is the mos' dangerous thing I ever done, expect mos' excitin' too. Havin' me a white woman to do with what I want, and she beggin' for it and all. My, my, ought to have my head examined, this gonna put me in a world a hurt if'n I'm not careful. Enoch was absently shaking his head from side to side. Jus' a couple more times, that's all, then we got it out of our sytems, it be okay jus' a couple more times.

Enoch decided on work clothes. He drew on a clean white undershirt and on a whim he dropped his boxer shorts and stepped out of them, pulling on a clean pair of coveralls over his naked bottom. He smiled wickedly at himself in the mirror and felt himself hardening.

Norma straightened her leg and rested her foot on the edge of the tub, watching the soapy water drain off of her red polished toenails. Cupping a small amount of baby oil in her hand, she began working it down the length of her leg. She picked up the safety razor from the tub's edge and started the careful process of shaving her legs. She completed the task, and in the steam filled confines of the pink and gray tiled bathroom she lay back against the end of the tub, dried her hands and lit a Chesterfield. She induced her body to relax and as she became heavy in the water, her mind bobbed and swayed from thought to thought.

She gradually came to the realization that this hour of self-indulgence was perhaps the best part of the evening. She also began to wonder if the anticipation of coupling with Enoch wasn't better than the act itself. She skillfully pushed those thoughts aside and began visualizing and fantasizing about how the evening would play out. She smiled inwardly, marveling at the total control she could exercise over such a physically powerful man, marveling at what simple creatures men were, and a colored man all the more. A light touch, a suggestive word or two, and the subtle loosening and shifting of her lingerie and he would do anything for her. Anything.

She snubbed out the half smoked cigarette in the souvenir ashtray, dwelling for a second on when she and Gabe visited Natural Bridge and had stolen the ashtray from the cafeteria. Lowering herself deeper into the water and moving her hands to and fro causing small waves of warm soapy water to flow over her breasts and throat she closed her eyes and tried to empty her mind and cast adrift. But in the calm sea of thoughts, there were thermals and undercurrents of emotion, and obscured moving shadows of rationalization and justification, plans and contingency plans, and the hubris of a seductress; some thoughts and feelings so far below the surface that her inner conversation did not verbalize them. And still, like dangerous leviathan they would occasionally breach the surface and she would find herself face to face with a monster of her own making.

Won't be long now, the damn war has got be over any day now. And then what? Then Gabe gets home and we begin our life again. Oh Gabe, what have I done? What am I doing? It's nothing, really, nothing at all. There's no love, just sex, pure animal sex. Just a little dilly-dallying to pass the time, and besides, it's nothing husband dear wasn't doing with every French whore and farm girl all across France. I don't know, maybe Gabe coming back doesn't matter, I don't think I was ready to get married. Maybe I just fell in love with the idea of falling in love . . . and marrying. Maybe we should a never gotten married. Norma Marie, you've really made a mess of things, one man you probably don't love and another you really can't love.

Well, it'll end soon. One way or another, it'll end. He's just a man, but my, my, what a man he is. After last week, I didn't think I could walk for two days. But that's it then. After tonight it's finished, I'll tell him it's over. If he gives me any trouble, well, there's ways to handle him. Who're people going to believe, a white woman or a black man? It won't come to that, but if it does...

CHAPTER 13

The Best
Laid Plans

Man plans, God laughs.
YIDDISH PROVERB

For the people of Munich, the war ended on Monday the 30th of April, 1945. Two events occurred on that day ending the city's long nightmare. One was painfully obvious, the American army had entered the city and all organized resistance had ended, the other would not be known for another week or two, as there were no longer radio broadcasts or newspapers. At five-fifteen that morning, Adolph Hitler and his new bride of several hours, Eva Braun, committed suicide; he by way of a 9mm bullet through the brain, she by biting down on a capsule of cyanide.

For Gabe, and the men of second platoon, the war ended the following Tuesday, eight days later, when they were given the word that Germany had unconditionally surrendered. The news exploded over and around them with the concussive force of a near-miss artillery shell. Some men were dazed and stunned, others experienced the relief of having survived. A few were felled, falling to their knees or on their ass right where they stood. Intermingled among the men was the occasional skeptic, thinking it was a rumor and that the news was too good to be true. In a way, it was.

The three squads of second platoon assembled a hundred yards up the street from where they had been billeted the night before. The men crouched and sat against the wall of a heavily damaged bookshop. A few had gone inside and were making themselves comfortable on the piles of books strewn across the floor, all of them moved about or rested with caution, snipers were still believed to be active in the area, and it would be a singular piece of bad luck to be wounded or killed hours after the war had ended.

The shop stood on a corner that formed part of a fifty-yard square courtyard. In its center stood a fountain that was miraculously unscathed with water flowing from four bronze spigots into a round stone basin. Perched on top of it, the brown green bust of a man stared out across the square in resolute defiance; the encrusted pigeon droppings covering his pate only slightly diminished his dignity. Lines of threadbare, demoralized civilians carrying a haphazard assortment of containers lead away from each spigot. The queue silently parted whenever a pair of G.I.s stepped to the front of the line to fill canteens. A luxury they performed quickly not wanting to tempt fate in a sniper's crosshairs.

As Gabe looked out across the courtyard he marveled at the scene before him. A three-hundred-year-old fountain carrying on its duty as if the war had never occurred, while all around it fully one-third of the city had been flattened and burned by Allied bombers. It was the random survival of buildings and objects amidst the unexpected precision and totality of destruction that amazed him. How a perfect line of charred rubble could extend for three city blocks, while right across the street buildings stood untouched except for shattered windows. Sometimes it worked the opposite way.

Once on patrol, Gabe and a half dozen men from third squad came upon a village house where what had once been the garden was now a deep crater, but the stucco and half-timber building walls did not bear a scratch or mark. When they entered the house, sitting around a table, upright and in repose sat a family of four, their heads slumped forward as if in prayer. Congealed blood trailed from their eyes, ears, noses and mouths. The explosion outside of their kitchen window had killed them, the shock waves bursting lungs and other organs in a fraction of a second. They were probably dead before the roar of the explosion ruptured their eardrums. On the table, not a single dish or glass was disturbed. Of all the horrors Gabe had witnessed, this was the scene that kept returning to his mind.

The voice of the platoon sergeant broke Gabe's reverie. He turned to see Lieutenant Devlin, Brownlee's replacement, disappear into the ruined bookshop.

"Fall in men, the lieutenant wants to have a word. Gather up, everybody inside. Corporal Haines, post two men from third squad at the front, Klemmer, two from your squad around back." Sergeant Tompkins growled the words without removing the dangling cigarette from his lips.

As the members of second platoon filed into the room, Gabe watched the lieutenant make his way towards the back of the room, stopping when something on the floor caught his eye. He bent over and picked up a reading lectern, stood it up, removed his helmet and placed it on the stand. This guy sure has a flare for the dramatic, reminds me a little of Ted, must come with being an officer. Gabe thought to himself as he watched the lieutenant prepare to address the men posturing himself like class valedictorian.

"All right men, listen up. First of all, congratulations, we won the war." The men let loose a roar of affirmation.

"You're probably wondering what comes next." The lieutenant paused for dramatic effect.

"Home, lieutenant, home is what's next!" A voice shouted across the room.

"Yes that's true, at least for some of you, the ones with enough points to get discharged. Captain Williams will be putting the word out in a couple of days and those of you with enough will muster at Battalion HQ for demobilization." An unnatural silence fell over the room.

"For the rest of you, for the time being we'll stay here in Munich to help keep things in order, round up prisoners and help process refugees and so forth." He paused again shifting his weight to his other foot.

"We are also...we are also going to continue training. We will be setting up a shooting range, just out of town and we will be drilling, the whole company, and my platoon in particular is going to stay in top form. Is that understood.?" the men responded with good-natured groans and boos.

The lieutenant raised both hands, palms outward, and gestured to the men, "Settle down, settle down, I'm not finished yet. As you know the United States is still at war with Japan." The atmosphere in the ruined book shop changed palpably. "Ike, er, General Eisenhower that is, has already tapped a handful of divisions to be transferred to the Pacific, A.S.A.P., and you guessed it, we're one of them."

The men released a string of obscenities that would have toppled the books off their shelves, had Allied bombers not already done so. "Hey Lieutenant, why the fuck do we have to go and fight the nips, ain't we done enough? We don't know nothin' from fighting no Nips, or fightin' in no Jungle, it ain't fair." One of the men from first squad called out in a grating New York accent. The rest of the men barked out ragged agreement.

"Have you guys had your heads in the sand? Look around you, do you still think life is fair? We're going. We'll learn how to fight the Japs and we'll be damned good at it. We'll learn how to fight in the jungle and we'll finish the job, just like we done here. I'll keep you posted as best I can. You're dismissed."

Euphoria and optimism gave way to depression and fatalism as if some giant cosmic pendulum had swung in ten minute's time. Gabe went back outside, squatted in his previous spot and again contemplated the fountain. "Ain't that some shit, Doc?" Sam Stout rasped at Gabe, cupping his hands to light a cigarette.

"Yeah, that's some shit all right." Gabe said only half listening and replying mechanically. Gabe knew he had enough points accumulated to go home, but he struggled with whether he could or should leave the men. Too many had died in and at his hands and he knew that he owed them something. He owed both the living and the dead. Then there was Norma and his mother, didn't he owe them something too? Every bone in my body is screaming go home, but how can I? The jobs not done and I can't shirk off my duty, the work, just like that. I saved Brownlee by force of will. I know I can do the same for others. Besides, Norma probably couldn't care less, and after these last months . . . neither do I.

"Doc, you surely have enough points to go home don't ya?"

"I'm not really sure. Hope so." Gabe lied, trying to keep his options open and not plunge Sam into deeper despair.

"Maybe it won't be so bad, I got a brother-in-law in the First Marines, and he was writin' home that he sure was glad he wasn't in the

'Big War', ain't that a hoot, they call this "The Big War". So maybe, it ain't so bad after all, who knows?"

"Who knows?" Gabe stared out across the square.

CHAPTER 14

The War Ends, the Battle Rages

A time to love, and a time to hate;
a time of war and a time of peace.
ECCLESIASTES 3:8

I t had been a long time since Gabe had spent a sleepless night. Of course there had been nights when he was too wretched, too cold and wet to drift off. There were nights he had to tend to the sick and wounded, and nights when enemy patrols were probing the lines. Eventually massive exhaustion won out, even if it was for just a few minutes before the first fingers of light flexed over the horizon.

Gabe's head formed a trough in the feather pillow and as he turned his face slightly he inhaled deeply and savored the smell of the wind, sun and cleanliness of the linen pillowcase. He shifted his head and pillow slightly so that he could watch the curtains flutter in the slight breeze that carried a new dispensation, a time of peace and uncertainty for Germany, Europe and the entire world. The ethereal light of the full moon softly illuminated the room through the wide-open window and except for the windowpanes having been replaced by cardboard and tarpaper; it was as if there had never been a war at all. Insomnia moved his eyes systematically around the room, past the armoire, past clothing hanging on wallpegs and on to the dresser. Atop the dresser were a few bottles, some nondescript shapes and a picture frame. In the abbreviated light he could not make out the photograph, but the strip of black fabric crossing its upper right corner identified it all too clearly. There had been a war all right.

Gabe clamped his eyes shut, arched his back and neck, made his arms and legs rigid, and stretched. Irmgard stirred and pushed her back against him, falling back into rhythmic breathing. Gabe opened his eyes to look straight up the whitewashed wall as the top of his head pressed against its cool hard surface. He found himself at the foot of the Cross. The Crucifix was centered on the wall a few feet above his head and Gabe was staring at the shadows made by the bottom of Christ's feet, and outstretched arms, and in the semi-darkness he could just make out the shape of His face angled down in death. Gabe stared intensely trying to make out the crown of thorns.

Oh God. What I have done? We're going to have to deal with this some other time you and I. But not now.

Gabe once again closed his eyes and in that moment the weight of his life began to crush him. The lapses of judgment, the lies, the crimes great and small, the failures of duty, the cowardice and all matter of shortcomings common to man. The litany culminated with the breaking of the vow. He had set a new personal low and had transgressed into a virgin territory within the borderlands of sin. The double *entendre* was not lost upon him. While he could have plead the war and the nature of men and their needs, he didn't. Maybe I just shouldn't have married her, maybe this is just the proof I needed. Ahh, bullshit. I don't know anything except it's over with Norma, and should have never happened in the first place.

Gabe happened upon the thin, angular woman on his second day in Munich during an early morning patrol. Her nearly white blonde hair and deep brown-black eyes provided contrast worthy of a renaissance painting. Despite the physical, mental and spiritual scars she bore as the result of almost six years of war, she was beautiful. She was helping a wizened farmer unload milk cans and paper-wrapped packages off of an ancient farm wagon drawn by a single haggard gelding. They were carrying the items into a shop with boarded up display windows. "Milch und Lebensmittel" had been hastily painted across the wooden planks that replaced the shattered glass.

At the time it wasn't the woman that captured Gabe's attention, but the normalcy of the scene before him. He fell out of the loose formation on the pretext of checking his medical kit and observed the commonplace tableau. The farmer wiped his hands on his shiny leather apron, adjusted his green felt Tyrol hat and handed the shopkeeper a bill. She studied the invoice before fishing into an apron pocket, extracting a small packet of bills and counting the Reich Marks into the farmer's hand. Life goes on. Gabe thought to himself. Thank God.

The day before he could never have imagined it, at least not in the city of Munich, the cradle of National Socialism and birthplace of the Nazi party. Gabe's company had entered the outlying residential district, or what was left of it, to the cacophony of air raid sirens, the rumble of trucks and tanks, and the occasional distant sound of small arm's and artillery fire. The air was thick with the dust of rubbled buildings and smoke of a hundred fires. Except for the American military, there was no one to be seen, it was as if they had passed through the gates of hell to find it unpopulated.

After a time, but before the men noticed the sirens had stopped they began to wail again. Instinctively they all looked up to see a cloudless blue sky, empty of aircraft of any kind. The sirens ceased to scream as abruptly as they had just started. The men of D Company neither knew nor cared what the sirens meant. In a moment their meaning became clear.

All along the streets, in twos and threes they began appearing, Teuton troglodytes emerging into the light from warrens of air raid shelters and cellars. Women, girls, boys less than twelve, old men over sixty, blinking and rubbing their eyes and congregating in small groups on either side of the street.

To a man, the G.I.s didn't know what to expect and brought their weapons to the ready clicking off safeties. Some soldiers abruptly stopped and stared, others bumping into them as they did. Derision, pity, loathing, revulsion, hubris and a dozen other emotions passed through the American's minds and across their faces. Would the Germans hurl stones at them? Curse them? Scream? Weep? In the end they did nothing, standing in utter silence staring in wide-eyed disbelief. It proved to be an anticlimax to the triumphant entrance into the city.

Later, some of the men mentioned they would rather have withstood the German's anger than their apathy. It wasn't apathy. When Gabe asked Irmgard about that day, long after the fact, she told them it was relief; relief that there would be no more bombs, no more anonymous death raining down on their heads. No more notifications from the Deutsche Dienststelle of the death of a husband, father, son or brother.

A few days after Gabe's platoon was billeted in a bomb damaged townhouse and he had fallen into the routine of continued training, patrols and medical duties, Gabe found himself furtively wandering the two blocks to the shop advertising Milch and Lebensmittel. It wasn't the blonde shopkeeper that drew him to Nr. Sieben Bockenheimer Strasse, it was something far less glamorous. Gabe's rudimentary German had told him that Milch and Lebensmittel translated to milk and groceries. He had seen the cans of fresh milk off loaded by the farmer with his own eyes. Of all the things that Gabe missed, fresh milk ranked near the top, and he couldn't believe his good fortune that he had stumbled on the lone shop in the district that had an arrangement with a local farmer.

Soon the visits were the highlight of Gabe's day. The same became true for her. The woman's face would light up when he entered the store and she would involuntarily run her fingers through her hair and her hands down the front of her clothing. Gabe began mentally rehearsing some clever quip or greeting on the way over to see her. Between her broken, square English and his broken, square German, they were able to communicate surprisingly well.

Early on, he learned her name was Irmgard and her three-year-old son was Karl. She was a war-widow. Her husband had been a Wehrmacht Feldwebel and had been killed at Stalingrad. The letter from the Deutsche Dienststelle had stated he had died heroically. Gabe came to admire her philosophical attitude towards the death of her husband. He also admired her common sense and intelligent survival instincts. Gabe had always enjoyed the company of intelligent women.

Without fail after each visit to the shop, Gabe's mind raced and he would feel as if he were walking on air. Each time the same humorous thought would enter his mind, I feel like I'm Fred Astaire in a movie musical. Many times he would arrive back at his quarters and not remember how he got there. He remembered leaving the shop, but not what or whom he saw on the way back, or if he had seen or greeted anyone he knew.

When the small brass bell jingled as the shop door closed behind him it was as if the bell served as a signal for his thoughts to take flight.

Boy oh boy, she looked good today. What a stroke of luck to get to see her everyday. Her hand was really soft, thought it would be a rough working hand. She's touching me when she talks. I do believe she's flirting. I think she likes me, she's a doll all right, can't help it, might as well admit it, I'd like get her in bed one night. Hell, I need to get some gal in bed, I'm going nuts here. Aw hell, Norma, what's keeping your letters? Well, I don't write worth a damn either. Something's not right, she must be having the same feelings I am. I guess they'll give us leave before we're shipped out to Japan. but hell, I don't have the energy to start things over with her. Don't even think I want to. Aw hell, Japan, Japan, what a meat grinder that's going to be. I've made it this far by the skin of my teeth, I won't make it back from a frontline unit in the Pacific. They showed that stupid bullshit film last night, 'Two Down, One to Go.' What Hollywood bull-shit, suppose to make us feel great about beating Germany and Italy and just dying to beat Japan. Just dying, that's about right. Well, can't be wor-rying about that right now, got to take things day to day, hell, hour to hour. Seen too many guys with big plans shot to pieces, who's to say they weren't having the exact same thoughts as me and wham, it's all over, never saw it coming. The lucky ones were dead before they hit the ground. I wonder if that big jerk of a supply sergeant over at battalion still has parachute silk to trade. Said he'd let it go for a couple of bottles of good scotch. Watkins owes me a favor, he'd find some scotch for a couple of cartons of smokes and a Nazi flag. Yeah this'll work, I'll make it work, Irmgard will love some silk, maybe she'll make a teddy or something to model for me. Aw shit, there I go again. Just gotta go day by day, nothin's going to happen, we're just friends, I'm married, just want to do some-thing nice, just be a nice guy. Hey, I'm lucky to be alive, lots of dumb ass unlucky bastards aren't, what ever happens, happens. Let the chips fall where they may. Boy, oh boy, she looked good today.

But deep inside, where the voice without words dwelled, he knew that if he worked at it, if he was persistent, but subtle, clever, but self-effacing, kind, but not overbearing, he could have her. He also did not put much stock in the idea of luck, Sure, there were random events that shaped one's existence, but why was it that the people who work the hardest and pay the most attention have the best luck? There's nothing you can't have or do if . . .

Again, Gabe was a little surprised to find himself in his room. He untied his boots, kicked them off and stretched out. He was asleep in minutes. Later that evening, when Ben Schwartz came back to the room, Gabe was sound asleep and smiling.

Saturday the twenty-seventh of May, 1944 was another of those perfect Spring days. The cloudless sky was a rich blue, the temperature warm with a slight breeze and the light had gem-like clarity. Gabe spent the day resting, talking, drinking beer and smoking. He also found himself filling a wooden apple crate with scrounged and purloined items he thought Irmgard and Karl might enjoy: chocolate, chewing gum, coffee, medicines, a flashlight, sewing kit and various other small items including a baseball he had "borrowed" from crazy Doug Dugan in third platoon. Gabe was particularly delighted with the ball.

"Tomas, Guten Tag. Is a herrliche Tag, no? I love Spring better than all other times." Irmgard continued sweeping the shop floor.

Gabe looked at her quizzically, "Herrliche?"

"Oh sorry, wunderbar, very nice, oh yes, magnificent I think is best word." Gabe smiled inwardly at her inability to pronounce the "th" sound, making an "s" sound instead. He also didn't bother correcting her when she called him "Thomas". Thomas was indeed his first name, but no one had called him that since grammar school.

"Here. I brought some things for you and the boy." Gabe said as he carried the crate past sparsely stocked shelves and placed it on the counter in the back of the store.

Irmgard had leaned her broom against the wall and followed him, wiping her hands on her apron and straightening her hair. She stepped around the counter and began looking through the items in the box.

"Tomas, you are very good to us. Thank you, but you don't need to do this. We can manage." Irmgard cheeks flushed slightly and she cast down her eyes a little embarrassed.

"I know you can manage. That's not the point. I want to do this because I can. Don't give it a second thought."

"Well then, vielen dank Tomas. Now you must let me do something. Please come back in two hours, I will close shop early and we will go on Spring afternoon picnic. Is O.K.?"

Gabe smiled. "O.K."

It was a magical afternoon. It was dark by the time Irmgard and Gabe returned to the shop; she and Karl lived in the apartment upstairs. They had gotten back later than expected for several reasons. Foremost was that they had enjoyed each other's company and the beautiful day so much they were loathe to have it end. Secondly, they had dropped Karl off at his aunt's house on the way home.

"Karl spends every Saturday night und Sonntag with my sister and her Kinder. That way he goes to mass and then can play with other Kinder." Irmgard explained on the way there.

"Don't you go to mass?" Gabe inquired.

"Nein. Gott and I have not been speaking since 1940. Maybe again some day, but I am still mad about some things."

"I see." Gabe said, and left it at that.

Irmgard picked up the pace and slipped her arm into Gabe's. Gabe squeezed her hand with his other and a cascade of emotions tore through his mind.

Upon arriving at the shop they went immediately upstairs and settled into the small sitting area. Gabe melted into a well-worn overstuffed chair. Irmgard excused herself for a moment and returned with a bottle of white wine and two crystal glasses.

Gabe admired the topaz colored wine as it swirled in the fine crystal stemmed glass. Irmgard sat on the arm of the chair and clinked his glass with her's and offered a toast. "To the best afternoon I have had since 1940."

She then stood in front of him, took his glass, placed their glasses on a low table and took both of his hands in hers pulling him to his feet. She kissed him on the cheek and looking up into his face whispered, "I want to thank you for today, and for everything you've done for us. You are a very kind man." She then took his hand and brought it to her breast, he instinctively squeezed it gently and brushed his thumb across her nipple before pulling his hand away. She pushed his hand back and stepped into him rubbing her leg inside his thigh, they kissed a kiss that would haunt Gabe the rest of his life.

"We shouldn't do this, I'm a married man. You don't need to do this to repay me." Gabe sighed into her ear his cheek pressed against the side of her head, his face buried in her hair and inhaling deeply. It was the most wonderful of fragrances and as he savored it his resolve melted away like a late spring snow.

Irmgard abruptly stepped away from him, her eyebrows forming a chevron of righteous indignation. "What do you mean? Do you think I am a prostitute? Do you think I invite every man into my bed?"

"Oh no, oh no Irmgard not at all. I'm sorry if you thought..." He enfolded her into his arms and held her firmly against his chest. To his surprise, she began to weep, not the quiet crying of anger or frustration, but the great heaving and weeping of mourning, death and loss. He tilted her head up and kissed the tears from her cheek, wiped her nose with his thumb and kissed her sad, trembling lips.

"Don't make love to me as a payment, or from pity, or as a kindness to a lonely widow. Make love to me as a man to a woman, two people who need one another, here, now." She took him by the hand and led him into her bedroom.

CHAPTER 15

Blue

Enoch traveled with silent grace through alleys and backyards, like a warrior brave covering this exact ground two centuries ago. A time when New Surrey was the frontier. Both men, generations and cultures apart, separated by two hundred years but gliding along on the same mission: to take a white woman, one woman, a farmer's daughter, unwilling, kicking and screaming, the other a lonely wife, seductive, needful and hungry. As Enoch moved with stealth and purpose through the deepening shadows, he thought about his boyhood. He loved playing cowboys and Indians. He was always the Indian.

Enoch vaulted over the picket fence into the Gabriel back yard. A light, muted by a drawn shade in the upstairs bedroom filled him with anticipation. The difficult part was over, if anyone saw him now, he was simply doing some outside chores for the Mrs. Gabriels. The bottom floor of the house was unlit and still, and as Enoch stepped towards the slanted basement doors, he saw what he was looking for. The prearranged signal was in place, a box of Rinso laundry soap sat prominently in the bathroom window. The small window was just above the double doors leading down to the cellar. A sense of familiarity and routine had grown with each nocturnal visit. Enoch carefully lifted the doors and disappeared into the cellar, closing the doors behind him. The clicking of the doors was barely audible. Enoch's breathing slowed, knowing the rest of the evening would play out like a twice-told story. Although he knew he could figure it out, Enoch had lost count of how many times he had spied the box of Rinso and climbed the stairs to the kitchen and then on to Norma's bedroom. He figured it was somewhere between ten and fifteen. Every once ina while I feel like the luckiest man alive. Leastways on Wednesday nights I do.

Norma had left the bathroom and bedroom doors open so that she could hear when he entered the house and made his way to her room. Her movements were deliberate and her breathing close-mouthed and slow so that her senses would be heightened. As she looked at herself one last time in the bathroom mirror, her patience was rewarded with Enoch's footfalls on the stairs. A second later the regulator clock hanging in the hall began chiming, tolling seven o'clock, as she remembered it doing each other time Enoch had come to her. She was amazed that a man who didn't own a wristwatch could be so perfectly on time. She smiled slyly at herself in the mirror and gave a tiny wink.

Well, he is highly motivated . . . thank goodness for that.

She lightly touched her hardening nipples through the silk of her camisole and smiled again. She slipped on her pale blue dressing gown and loosely tied its sash. In her peripheral vision she saw the lighting in the hallway change and knew he had turned off the bedroom's overhead light, and switched on the small table lamp next to the upholstered chair she never sat in. But he would be sitting in it. He always did. Like a well-rehearsed staged play they would begin their lovemaking at the chair and then move to the bed or floor. She entered the bedroom, Gabe's old bedroom, and as expected saw Enoch sitting in the chair, having kicked off his shoes to the side, leaning forward and smiling.

"Well, hello Sugar, come over here gal. I got somethin' for ya." Enoch slid to the edge of the chair spread his legs and beckoned her over.

"I'll bet you do." She walked over to the chair, stood between his legs bent over and kissed him several times on his upturned face.

"You had a good day? You been a good girl?"

"I'm never a good girl, Knock Knock Baker, you know that better than anybody."

"Deed I do girl, deed I do, and glad 'bout that too, I needs a bad girl tonight, a really bad girl . . .you that girl, Norma. . . you that bad girl tonight?"

Norma formed her most wanton smile, narrowed her eyes, straightened to her full height, undid the sash and let the gown drop to the floor, standing before Enoch in only a white silk camisole, its laced hem resting just above her navel.

Enoch's eyes caressed the contour of her pelvic bones and traveled down the length of her legs. He slowly closed his eyes and inhaled deeply; the smell of freshly scrubbed and perfumed flesh mingling with the unmistakable scent of a woman's growing desire. He loved the smell of women, and savored their scent on his fingers as a reminder of his pleasure. The first moments of lovemaking were always an exalted experience for Enoch. He had been with numerous women and each time marveled at how each one's body was different yet the same. How each one smelled and tasted different and yet the same, how each moved and responded to his touch the same and yet differently.

Up until these past few months he had only ever enjoyed the pleasures of colored women, all shapes and shades, from the blue-black working girl in a cat-house in Baltimore, with her white teeth and island lilt in her voice to the high yellow school teacher that had sent him a note after a football game. A note he couldn't read, but its meaning perfectly clear. All shades of honey, coffee and mahogany, and now a vision of pink, peach and lily white, each entirely different, but so much alike. Enoch knew women, but he didn't know the love of a woman. He never would.

As if remembering some unattended errand, Norma turned from him, walked across the room and firmly closed the door. "There, that's better." She returned to Enoch and stood before him once again.

"What'd you do that for? Aint nobody here, and won't nobody be here for two hours."

"I don't know, it's just the way I am I guess. I can't even pee with the door open in an empty house. It doesn't matter. Now, where were we?"

With that Enoch reached forward, placed his hands behind her knees and slowly moved them up her thighs until he cupped and gently kneaded her rounded bottom. She closed her eyes, inhaled sharply and locked her hands behind his head. She pulled him to her, leaned into him and placed one foot up on the pillow of the chair. After several minutes her hips began working in syncopation with Enoch's ministrations. She felt the familiar warmth as her breasts, then neck, then cheeks flushed.

Norma wanted and needed to prolong the inevitable, the night was young and she was a greedy, determined lover. She knew that she could keep him under her control and that she was the master of every aspect of Enoch Baker. She enjoyed the strength, possibilities and the power. To her, it had become the all-consuming *raison d' être*.

She stepped away from him and took both of his rough hands in hers. With her legs straight and stiff she leaned back as if taking a pratfall and pulled him to his feet. She locked her eyes on his with serpentine intensity. The cobra ready to strike. She began undressing him.

In a thick voice he whispered, "Good God girl, you the best, the best I ever had. Here, let me help you with that."

"Shhh." Norma pressed a finger to his lips. "Be still now Enoch Baker, now it's my turn." She pulled his unbuttoned coveralls off of his shoulder and slid them down his torso as she lowered to her knees before him. "Why Enoch Baker you nasty boy, where are your underpants?"

"Didn't put any on." He laughed, "Knew you'd like that, went free-ballin' for ya darlin'." He gently brushed the hair away from the sides of her face, then grabbed some between his fingers and guided her to him. He was now the one who felt in control and she allowed him to think so.

When she judged that he was rapidly approaching the summit of passion, she rose to her feet, took him by the hand and motioned for him to step out of the bunched coveralls. She wiped her hand across her chin and lips and began to laugh. "Take off your socks, there's nothing sillier than a naked man in socks." He wordlessly did as he was told. She again took his hand and led him to the bed, making him lie on his back.

Norma walked back to the chair and picked up Enoch's coveralls. She began rifling through the pockets. In her haste a curved wooden handled knife and some change fell to the floor, as she found what she was looking for. She tore open the cardboard packet and shook out the condom as she walked back to the bed. She tossed a second boxed condom onto the nightstand. She pulled the condom onto him, slipped her camisole over her head, climbed onto the bed and mounted him.

For the first and only time during their affair the lovers shuddered and groaned within a split second of one another. She had no idea how long it had taken as she had trained herself to never look at the alarm-clock on the night-table during sex. To Norma, the simultaneous orgasms were a pleasant surprise, that happened from time to time. For Enoch, who had never experienced such, it was the apogee, the true zenith of their relationship. He knew that it would never get better than this. He was right.

Norma nestled into the crook of his left arm, resting her head on his chest and straddling a leg over his. When she had climbed off of him she allowed herself a glance at the clock. It had been a half hour since he had arrived. They laid together in post-coital tenderness for several minutes until their breathing had slowed to quiet symmetry.

Norma propped her head up on one elbow, and with the fingers of her other hand began lightly brushing back and forth across the tightly coiled hairs on his chest. "You know, Enoch, there's something we need to talk about."

"What's that, girl?"

"I think you know."

"Yes'm, I think I do. I was jus' hopin' it would be a while before we had to."

"It's time."

"Yeah, I know." Enoch sighed.

"The war's over and everything is going to be different now."

"Know that too."

"So I think it's time we stopped doing this. It's been exciting and fun, and I love not feeling so lonely, and you're great in the sack, but I think it's time to bring it to a friendly end. Don't you, Enoch?" She caressed his cheek with her open hand. "I'll never forget you, and you've made me realize that Gabe, well, Gabe isn't the one for me. You've showed me that, but there's no future for us either. you and I are both trapped. Me, in this stillborn marriage and you, you by the accident of birth, born the wrong color in a place like New Surrey."

"What's the hurry then? You don't want to be with your husband and I don't want to be with anybody but you. I know what you're saying is right, even thought about it myself, but now when I'm with you, and you making me see stars tonight an' all, well, now it's not so clear to me. I heard it going to be a couple a months before they get home, ain't that true?"

Norma sat up onto the edge of the bed, reached for her pack of Chesterfields and lit one for each of them. "There's that other part, you know, what we never talk about."

"What're you saying, if we don't ever talk about it, how am I s'pposed to know what you're trying to say?"

"Don't act stupid Enoch, you're pretending to be stupid again. It's the danger Enoch, the danger. You know what'll happen if we ever got caught? And each time we do this it gets more dangerous, you've got to know that."

"Danger? You think I don't know the danger? You ain't the one that's gonna be strung up on some cracker's tree out in the county. Don't tell me about danger. Fact is, I think the danger is parta what makes this so good, so special. I knows you think the same way, I can feel it when we at it, can see it in your eyes when you first comes in the room."

Norma stubbed out her half smoked cigarette and moved the ash-tray away from the edge of the night-table. "Let's dance, let's put on some music and dance." She crossed to the small table radio she had brought with her from the apartment. After switching it on, the dial slowly lit up and she began spinning it across miles of static until she found a dance band. She turned up the music, began swaying gently and took Enoch by the hand. The two of them, naked and still shiny with sweat danced slowly, song after song, never moving out of one another's arms.

Norma pressed her head against his shoulder and whispered, "We danced the first time we were together, do you remember?"

"Course I remember, man got to be a fool to forget somethin' like that. I remember it was Valentine's day, and I got to say, you gave me the best valentine present I ever got."

Norma just smiled and reached down between his legs. He responded immediately. She stepped back from him, took a pillow from the bed and kneeling on the floor next to the radio, rested her head and arms on the pillow. He took the small cardboard packet from the night-table, opened it and slid on the condom. He knelt on the floor and took her from behind, slowly at first but with rising speed and intensity. Norma pushed back against him and would teasingly move her hips to the beat of the music, until Enoch began moving with such force, that she could concentrate on nothing but her rapidly approaching climax. For the second time that night, they came together, and with that, their world came to a crashing end.

They both felt and knew there was something horribly wrong, before they saw or heard anything. Terror turned their insides to water as the looked round to the presence in the doorway. The door had opened silently and Dorothy was standing there, holding on to a door jam for support.

"Oh my God, my God, what have you two done? Norma, what have you done? What are you doing here? Just answer me, what have you done?"

In terror and shock, Enoch stood before Dorothy, the condom falling to the floor. Norma began to vomit on the pillow.

CHAPTER 16

Fury
Brings Evil

I know indeed what evil I intend to do, but
stronger than all my afterthoughts is my fury,
fury that brings upon mortals the greatest evils.

EURIPIDES

A second passed and it was as if all the air had been sucked out of the room. An eerie calmness settled over the place like the respite in the eye of a storm. Dorothy regained her balance and stepped into the room. Her movement broke the spell, triggering Enoch's cyclonic scrambling to pick up his clothes, shoes and toolbox.

A low growl ascended from deep within Dorothy. Her face went pale, and then flushed several sanguine shades until blossoming crimson. Her eyes flashed with the incandescence of an Old Testament prophet. She raged with an epic anger and swift, sure judgment. Enoch, nude and clutching most of his belongings crouched over and pushed past Dorothy as if advancing into a typhoon. Her hands pummeled his head and shoulders; the blows raining down on him like fist-sized pieces of hail. Two words snarled from her lips over and over. They followed him into the hall, down the stairs and into his soul. "You bastard, you bastard, you bastard . . ."

Dorothy then turned her terrible presence on Norma, who had pushed the vomit-soiled pillow aside and was curled on the floor naked and helpless as a fetus. She moaned in fear and anguish. The moan robbed Dorothy of whatever self-control she still possessed. Stepping towards where Norma lay, Dorothy looked around the room and saw what she was looking for. Standing on the floor, leaning against the bookshelf was Gabe's Louisville slugger. In 1926, he had hit the home run that won the state championship. In 1945, it was about to become a lethal weapon in the hands of his mother. She had never felt anything like this before. She was incapable of rational thought, white hot fury reigned; a blast furnace fueled by righteous indignation, embarrassment, shame, shattered social mores and profound violation. It was anger capable of killing someone.

"You bitch. You whore. Jezebel, Jezebel. How dare you? How dare you? You whore, you cheating nigger-loving bitch, you whore . . ."

Dorothy stepped forward and stood over the nude, prostrate woman. Norma covered her head and neck with her arms. She peered at Dorothy from behind the protection of her arm, her eyes beseeching the older woman for mercy and forgiveness. Norma did not speak a word, but upon seeing the woman standing with the baseball bat raised above her head, a large dark spot spread across the carpet beneath her; she lost control of her bladder.

Dorothy stormed on. "How could you? How could you do this to my son? You whore. With that nigger, in my son's bed, in my house. I'll kill you, you whore, you-good-for-nothing worthless bitch. I'll teach you. I'll teach you to cheat on my boy."

Norma began to wail with an otherworldly resonance. She emitted a sound of suffering that women had known since the exile from Eden, and still, she lay there, never once trying to rise.

But Dorothy's anger was not be assuaged. She turned her wrath on the room. She kicked over the nightstand, the lamp crashed to the floor, it's bulb and glass chimney shattering, it's shade bending and careening off of Norma's back. "How dare you? How dare you? I take you into my house, I take you into my family and this is how you repay me? This is how you repay my son, who risks his life every day for us?" Dorothy pulled books off of the shelves Gabe had built in high school woodshop. She swept her arm across the top of the dresser sending Norma's perfume bottles and costume jewelry flying through the air like glittering shrapnel.

Norma was suspended in time. Seconds and minutes became meaningless and unrecognizable. Dorothy's words covered her like a mudslide, burying her deep in a place of misery.

Norma did not realize the cataclysm had ceased until she felt Dorothy's strong fingers wrapping around the flesh of her upper arm. "Get up, get up, what have you done, you whore?"

Norma sat on the edge of the bed, staring straight ahead, her eyes unfocused, peering into the coming darkness. Tears streamed down her cheeks, her hair was bedraggled and her whole body shook, the tremors vibrating the bed. Dorothy ranted on several more sentences until the words ceased abruptly and a clenched-jaw silence enveloped the room. With the stillness, Norma's eyes came into focus upon her mother-in-law standing before her, her arms down at her sides, the baseball bat rolling across the floor. Dorothy's face was wet with sweat and tears, wisps of iron gray hair had worked themselves free and she breathed heavily through flared nostrils. Norma saw her tormentor's jaw working; the old woman was grinding her teeth.

Dorothy turned on her heels and surveyed the detritus strewn about her. Seeing the wreckage of her son's room and her son's life over-whelmed her. Her eyes stopped and rested on the wooden handled knife lying next to the chair amongst the spilt change. Not far from the knife she saw the two discarded condoms lying limp and obscene on the floor. A wave of nausea rose in her, quickly fading. Her emotions rekindled. A conflagration exploded yet again.

In a single motion she turned back towards Norma and with her extended left arm she grabbed a handful of Norma's lank hair. With her open right hand she slapped Norma across her face, with an audible crack. The skin turned the color of old roses, the sting and heat served to bring Norma back into the moment. Though on in years, Dorothy was surprisingly strong. Years of farm work, her thick frame and the surge of adrenaline allowed her to pull Norma again to the floor with a movement as smooth as swinging a scythe. Norma broke her fall with her hands and was able to tuck herself into a roll to escape Dorothy's grasp. Dorothy shook the loose hairs from her hand.

Dorothy visibly deflated and pressed her right hand to her bosom and staggered backwards to the chair. The tightness in her chest and shortness of breathe warned her against much more agitation. She dropped heavily into the worn upholstery, covered her face and began to weep inconsolably. In a matter of five minutes, the world had changed and their lives would never be the same again.

It took several minutes before Dorothy stopped crying. For several more minutes she sat staring coldly across the room. Norma had also stopped her keening and lay silently on the bed, having turned her back to her mother-in-law, her shoulders still heaving. Dorothy rose and stepped over to the bed.

"No, please don't touch me, I'll pack and leave right now, just don't hit me." Norma sobbed.

Dorothy gently but firmly placed her hand on Norma's shoulder. Norma flinched and shrunk away from the touch. Dorothy spoke cold and calmly. "You'll do no such thing child. Go and clean yourself up, but on a robe and come down to the kitchen. We need to talk. No woman is going to make a fool of me and my boy. And one more thing, don't touch a thing in this room, leave it as it is."

By the time Norma came downstairs Dorothy had brewed a pot of chamomile tea. The well-lit kitchen appeared as usual, a sanctuary of domestic tranquility and Dorothy appeared as its high priestess. The scene was a model of normalcy. Dorothy poured two cups of tea, and then motioned Norma to sit down. The distraught young woman complied wordlessly, pulled her robe tighter staring blankly through the steam rising from her cup.

Dorothy had always been a plainspoken woman. "It must be a terrible thing." Norma did not acknowledge the comment. "I said it must be a terrible thing."

In a soft, exhausted voice Norma locked her eyes on Dorothy's, "I'm sorry, I'm so very sorry . . ."

"Stop it. You just stop it. The only thing you're sorry about is being caught, that's what you're sorry about." Dorothy hissed.

"That's not true."

"Shut your mouth and listen carefully, I said, it must be a terrible thing."

Norma finally caught on; it was as if Dorothy was telling some horrible profane joke, she took the bait, "I know it's a terrible thing, what are you trying to say?"

"I'm saying it must be a terrible thing . . . being raped by a nigger."

"I wasn't raped. It was stupid and wrong, but I wasn't raped."

Norma's voice was flat, not comprehending the implication of Dorothy's words.

Dorothy reached over and grabbed Norma's wrist, spilling tea and sending a spoon careening across the table to the floor. "Now you listen to me, and you listen to me good, you whore. I said it's a terrible thing being raped by a nigra. You were raped. I don't care what happens to that black son-of-a-bitch, and for all I care you should be whipped and run out of town on a rail. But I do care about my son, his good name, my good name and this family's good name. So you were raped, there's no other way around it. Doesn't matter what happened, what happened is what you say happened. Whose word are they going to take? Some nigger's or two upstanding white women in the community? Do you understand?" Norma did not answer. "I said, do you understand?"

Norma still did not answer, she fumbled for a cigarette from a crumpled pack in her robe pocket, with shaking hands lit it and blew the smoke out across the table. Finally she answered. Her answer sealed the fate of many. "I understand."

CHAPTER 17

La Collaboration Horizontale

Guilt upon the conscience, like rust upon iron, both defiles and consumes it, gnawing and creeping into it, as that does which at last eats out the very heart and substance of the metal.

ANONYMOUS

For many people, morning's light resolves a problem, or at least puts it into perspective. For Gabe, the opposite was true. His nights were full of wonder and fantasy, reflecting on what his life and love could be like. The morning wakeup call snapped him into harsh reality. A reality that he tried to work out, gloss over or patently ignore.

In Gabe's mind, the past weeks in Munich had been the happiest of his life. But he was old enough and wise enough to know that his bliss was a house of cards and that it could collapse in a heartbeat. Therefore he questioned the veracity of his bliss. Was he just euphoric at having come through the war unscathed when so many thousands had died or been maimed in titanic struggle? Was he thrilled at having a clean, dry place to sleep and three square meals a day in relative safety? Was he elated at having found love? Drop dead, head over heels, storybook, Hollywood movie love? Was he overjoyed at feeling like a teenager again? Was he just ecstatic about regular and meaningful sex? Was he joyous at having a small boy look up to him? Was he exhilarated at being needed by someone other than a wounded or dying G.I.? He was intelligent enough to ask the questions. He was, however, not old or wise enough to comprehend his emotional state. The dynamics and combined effects of stress, relief, sudden safety, newfound idleness and loneliness confounded him. He had been blindsided. He was covering new ground and the rules had changed.

You know, it really doesn't much matter why I'm so happy, it only matters that I am this happy. I can't wait to see her again, can't wait to eat and get a shower, don't even mind the stale hashed over training exercises.

What I can't stand is the thought of leaving Irmgard and the boy. Not sure if I even want to leave Germany if that's what it means. 'Course, don't want to go to Japan no matter what. What about Norma? What the hell am I gonna do about Norma? Is it fair to string somebody along if you're not sure you love 'em? Hell, we barely knew one another and don't know each other at all anymore. Really, probably never did. Can't remember the last time I got a letter from her, or wrote her one for that matter. Maybe I should just go ahead and write her a Dear John letter in reverse. Bet that doesn't happen too often, guess it would be a Dear Joan letter. Everything's changed. Going to have to do something . . .

Gradually Gabe became aware of movement in the room. He opened his eyes and as they began to focus he saw his longtime friend Ben dressing.

"Rise and shine, up and at 'em guy. You plan on wastin' a Sunday in your bunk?" Ben called out good naturedly once he noticed Gabe's open eyes. "C'mon, I'll wait for ya downstairs and we'll go over to Hartmann's for some breakfast."

Café Hartmann was a ten-minute walk from Gabe's billet, situated in a mostly undamaged building. It was a café and konditerei, a pastry bakery, as opposed to a bread bakery, both of which were taken very seriously in German culture. Larger than most cafés it had been essentially commandeered by the American occupiers as an oasis of good coffee and better food. US Army patronage and the owner's attractive daughters ensured that it was a well-stocked and thriving enterprise. On Sunday mornings business boomed.

Small brass bells tinkled as Gabe and Ben pushed open the door, but it was barely audible above the rumble and laughter of masculine conversation. The air was thick with tobacco smoke and redolent with the aromas of coffee and baking. The men made their way to the glass showcase and surveyed the magnificent array of tortes and pastries. Just two months ago they could not have conceived of food like this, and now, thanks to Frau Hartmann, and a couple of sweet toothed general staff officers, it had become almost commonplace. Both men marveled at what scrounging, black-marketeering and having friends in the right places could accomplish. The men placed their orders and turned to find a table.

From halfway across the room a familiar face stood and called out above the din, "Hey Doc, hey Schwarz, come on over and take a load off." The soldier motioned to two recently vacated chairs at the linen covered table. Of the four men seated there, Gabe knew three of them by sight, Barnette, Evans and Rezabek from D company's third platoon.

Barnette, who had called them over, slapped Ben on the shoulder, "Hey guys, how's it goin?"

"Not bad." Both men answered in unison and laughed. "You owe me a coke, Doc."

"No, I believe you're the one who owes me a coke." Gabe replied.

"No way." Ben said.

"Bullshit. I outrank you. You owe me the coke and that's an order." Gabe good-naturedly wagged his finger at Ben.

Barnette raised his hand, "Okay, okay, Let me introduce you guys. You know Rez and Evans." They nodded and shook hands all around. "And this is an old buddy of mine, Lefty Finch, from back in Scranton. He's motor pool from over at regimental."

Both men nodded again to Lefty, "Regimental, huh? Boy you're really slumming it today, ain't ya?" Ben quipped.

Finch laughed and looked around the room, at the empty plates and coffee cups on the table and overflowing ashtray. "Yeah, you guys got it rough all right. Wait til I tell the guys over at H.Q. about this place, there gonna knock twenty points off of each of you. Shit, you won't get discharged til nineteen sixty-two." Now, all four men were laughing.

"We were just catching up, and getting the skinny on things. You know how it is." Barnette said, lighting a Lucky Strike. "Lefty was just telling us about when he had to drive a staff officer over to Versailles a couple of days after the krauts surrendered."

Lefty was interrupted by a freckled-faced red-headed girl with a laden tray. It was Gabe and Ben's order. Her wholesome beauty and grace brought conversation to a halt and each of the men instinctively smiled at her. The nineteen-year-old girl smiled back at them knowing she generally had that effect on female-starved soldiers.

Rez broke the spell. "Say, shatzi, could you refill these cups of joe and bring us each one of them special brandies you brought us last night? I forget what you called it."

"Asbach Uralt?" she asked in plain German.

"Yup, that's it, a round of Ass-Bock for each of us." Rez answered, full of himself. The girl gave a mock curtsy, giggled, and headed back to the kitchen.

"Aw, what the hell, it's Sunday, and the sun is over the yard-arm somewhere." Lefty said, lighting a cigarette.

"Can't dance and it's too wet to plough, that's what the old-timers used to say." Barnette added.

"Yeah, yeah, yeah, can we get on with the story already. You were about to tell us about Paris. Ooh-la-la, I'd give my left nut to get to gay Pariee." Evans chimed in.

"Yeah, but only if you had one in the first place." Rez added.

"Wise ass." Evans said, draining his cup of coffee.

"Yeah, well, like I was saying, Versailles is only 10 miles from Paris, so once I dropped the Major off, I had some time on my hands. So I hitched a ride." Lefty spit a bit of tobacco leaf onto the floor.

As Gabe and Ben started eating, Lefty began a long-winded travelogue about the sights and delights of liberated Paris. Ben and the others inserted an occasional comment and question. Gabe's mind wandered. He allowed his senses free reign. The coffee and torte proved to be transcendent. Enjoying them, his eyes wandered around the room. The whitewashed walls, dark wooden floors and furniture, glass cases of baked goods, bottles of liqueur and brandy. A set of stag horn spikes over the door to the kitchen, a crucifix, cuckoo clock and various alpine scenes rendered in watercolor were distributed around the other walls. Uniformed men and elderly civilians sat around enjoying mid-morning coffee and cake. How could this be? How could everything be so normal, when only weeks ago war raged across the continent? How can people be so resilient? Is this how it's going to be from now on? Happy days are here again? God, I hope so . . .

It was only when the conversation turned to sex that Gabe's mind came back into the moment. "So Lefty, we get that you saw the sights, but did you, you know see the sights?" Barnette interrupted.

"Yeah, we've all seen French postcards, did you get to be in one? Man o' man, those French mademoiselles know what they're doin' all right, and the hookers are even better." Evans said, leaning forward.

"Oh, so you guys want to know if I dipped my wick, of course I did, what kind of red-blooded American boy goes to Paris and doesn't get his ashes hauled?" Lefty leered.

"How was it?" Evans asked.

"How was it? What kind a question is that? How was it? It was great, it was fantastic, like sleeping with a gunny sack full of wildcats." Lefty lit another cigarette as if just thinking about it made him crave a post-coital smoke.

"And even if it wasn't great, what the hell do you think he's going to tell us? Ever known a guy tellin' his buddies he was a disaster in the sack?" Rezabek chimed in.

"You got that right, about not telling, that is, not about bein' a disaster." Lefty guffawed and then continued, "Speaking of French women, the nice and the not-so-nice, I did see one pretty weird thing."

"Finally." Evans leaned forward again, "I once heard about a girly show at the carnie where a naked dancer could squat over a roll of quarters, pick 'em up and make change, you seen somethin' like that?"

Rezabek smacked the younger man across the top of the head, "C'mon, ya pervert, let the guy finish will ya?"

"Like I was saying, on the second day I was there, guess it was around lunch time I came outta the pension and heard a big hullabaloo up at the corner and saw a buncha people yellin' at something. So I made my way up into the crowd and what a sight."

"What was it?" Evans eagerly interrupted again.

"It was ten or fifteen women being herded down the street by some French cops."

"That's it?" Evans spoke again.

"For cryin' out loud, if you don't let him finish I'm going knock you upside of the head and not even Doc here'll be able to put you right." Rezabek intoned.

"So these women had their heads shaved and swastikas painted on their foreheads, and it was a pretty rough job of it, some had cuts with blood running down their scalp and others had tufts of hair here and there. But that's only part of it. Their clothes were torn up and a couple were half naked and a couple were completely naked, trying to cover themselves with their arms and hands. The crowd was screaming at them and spitting at them and trying to hit'em, if those cops weren't there who the hell knows what mighta happened. That crowd was out for blood. And ya know what? Not a one of those women looked like they were crying, guess maybe they didn't have any tears left. They just walked along with their heads down, staring at the ground like it was just something they had to get over with. Pretty strange."

"So did you ever figure out what was going on?" Barnette asked.

"Yeah, when I was standing there this old lady must have seen the look on my face, she tugged at my sleeve and pointing at the women said, '*la collaboration horizontale, la collaboration horizontale!*' Well my French wasn't that good, but after I asked around a little, I found out it meant those women had sex with the Nazis."

"No shit." Evans seemed breathless.

"Yeah, and ya know what else was weird, after I found out what that whole thing was about, well, I felt kinda bad for 'em, or at least part of me did. I mean, that stuff just happens, you put men and women together, and well, it just happens, of course it happens with the whores, but it happens to regular gals too, just happens, that's all. But then another part of me completely understands why everybody was so pissed off, hell, they were aiding and abetting the enemy, what did they expect? Hell, they might have been screwing the very krauts that killed our buddies and tried to kill us. I don't know, it's just hard to figure out, see what I mean?"

The table fell silent, as if, with Lefty's story complete, they were waiting for someone else to pick up the narrative. The ironies of war no longer surprised them, but they sat in silence none-the-less.

Lefty's story had touched something in Gabe. Suddenly Gabe did not want to be inside this pleasant café and did not want to be around these men. The sky had clouded over and everything had turned to shit.

"Sorry guys, I gotta head out. I've got some things to take care of and I need to get some fresh air." Gabe said, standing abruptly and fishing some bills out of his pocket.

"Doc, you o.k.? What's the rush? You just got here. C'mon, sit down, that shatzi is comin' back with some brandy." Evans spoke with concern in his voice.

"Nah, really I gotta go." Gabe put some script on the table.

"I got this, keep your money, you can get it next time. See ya later." Ben said, as Gabe nodded, turned and made his way out of the crowded café.

"Jeez, was it somethin' I said?" Lefty asked as the waitress arrived with five small snifters, each a third full with rich amber Asbach Uralt.

"I've been with him for close on two years, going back to basic training. He just gets that way sometimes, somethin' set him off, must've been your story. Don't take it personally, he's been getting' the blue devils a lot lately, he's either high or low, not much in between. The good news is: somebody's gonna have to drink that extra brandy, so I guess I will. It's a tough job, but somebody's gotta do it." Ben moved Gabe's glass in front of him, swirling it and contemplating its color and legs. He lit a cigarette.

Gabe left Hartmann's walking along briskly, his hands shoved in his pockets and looking down at the ground. He marched along like an automaton, his legs and body habitually falling into the rhythmic shuffle of an infantryman on the move. He had to resist the urge of going to see her, of making a beeline directly to the grocery store apartment. And so, he walked in the opposite direction. He found himself following the route by which he had entered the city as conqueror nearly two months before.

It was a byway that required no thought or navigation and that would take him to a place outside of the city environs.

Gabe walked for nearly two hours, working up a sweat and considerable thirst. He was no longer in the city, the signs of war were still around him, but less obvious. He started looking for a place to rest, not knowing what else to do or where else to go. Leaving the dirt road, he cut through a pasture towards a copse of trees several hundred yards away. The sky had literally clouded over and the air had become humid and cloying. Gabe was relieved to enter the coolness of the trees and more relieved to happen upon a stream running through the patch of forest. He took a long drink and gave brief thought to other places he had slaked his thirst. Places far less pleasant than this.

In near despair he sat down on a bed of moss and leaned back against the trunk of an oak tree not far from the stream. Drawing up his knees he buried his face in his hands.

A darkness, a deep sense of shame and guilt enveloped him like a moonless night.

What have I done? Broken vows . . .cheated on my wife . . . Fallen in love . . . recognized the truth about my marriage . . . Will they do the same thing to Irmgard if I leave her, shave her head and paint an American star on her forehead?

The thoughts repeated themselves, word for word, over and over, lapping one another like the chariots in Circus Maximus. With each obsessive lap the thoughts wore deeper ruts and with each cycle of self-incrimination new thoughts edged into position and entered the fray.

Why did I make it? Why couldn't I save those guys? Why couldn't I help them? I'm a fraud, a fake, a coward. I thought if I came through the war I'd be a better man, and now I'm this. Did I come through it all to be this?

Hours passed as Gabe wrestled and raced the demons endlessly in the arena of his mind. He would occasionally walk to the stream, drink, come back to the tree and start all over. Night fell and nothing changed. The same patterns, the same inner words tirelessly running laps.

Will they shave her head and paint an American star on her forehead?

Gabe spent the night in a Gethsemane of his own making. When the false dawn appeared he stood one last time and took another drink and began the long walk back. Nothing had changed, and nothing had been resolved.

"Good, so we understand one another?" Norma did not answer. "I said do we understand one another?"

Something changed in Norma. Her eyes narrowed and through clenched teeth she hissed, "Yes, we understand one another."

Dorothy stood, went to the icebox and meticulously chipped a corner from the ice block and wrapped it into a dishrag. Handing it to Norma she ordered: "Tilt your head back and put this on your forehead, it'll help you feel better and calm down. I'm going back upstairs to get everything ready."

"Ready for what?" Norma puzzled.

"For the police of course."

"Oh God." Norma whimpered, beginning to cry quietly into the cold dishrag, in abject, helpless despondency.

Dorothy ascended the stairs with world-weary heavy footfalls. She was emotionally and physically exhausted. She entered her son's room and surveyed the wreckage. Unwittingly her convulsive anger had set the stage. With growing satisfaction she kicked the wood-handled knife towards the bed. She then tugged and arranged the chenille bedspread into a disheveled heap. The old woman then steeled herself to attend to one final detail. With farmhand pragmatism and set-jaw resolve she picked up the two condoms being careful not to spill their loathsome contents. Feeling bile rising in her throat she milked semen onto the bed sheets, carefully emptying both condoms. She took them across the hall and flushed them down the toilet. She then washed her hands with obsessive thoroughness. Twice.

Back down stairs, Dorothy again sat across from Norma. "You been thinking about what happened?"

Norma answered with resignation, "Dumb question, don't ya think?"

"Don't get smart with me. I mean, you been thinking about what you're going to tell the police?"

"Yes." Norma answered, her voice in resignation as she pushed herself away from the table and stood.

"Where do you think you're going?"

"I'm going to call Annie and go over to her apartment. I need to get away from here and I need to get away from you. What we're doing is wrong. It's just plain wrong."

Dorothy stepped in front of her and growled, "What's wrong is what you did upstairs. What's wrong, is what that black son of a bitch did, that's what's wrong. And if you had even a shred of decency in you or gave a tinker's cuss about my boy, your husband, you'd see that.

Norma looked down at the floor. "I need to go." And stepped past Dorothy.

CHAPTER 18

Serious
Trouble

Double, double toil and trouble;
Fire burn, and cauldron bubble.
WILLIAM SHAKESPEARE, *Macbeth*, Act 4 scene 1

The ladder-back chair scraped across the worn linoleum as Enoch pushed himself away from the table. For the past ten minutes he had maneuvered a mound of heavily peppered scrambled eggs around his plate and had taken only a single bite from a biscuit the size of a cat's head his mother had set before him. He took a final sip of black coffee and stood. "I gotta go momma."

"What's the matter with you? You haven't touched a bite. You can't go and work all day without breakfast."

"It's o.k. momma, I just don't feel a hundred percent. That's all."

"You sick? Got a runny nose and grip in your chest?"

"No, nothin' like that."

"Your bowels runnin'?"

"No momma, didn't sleep well, just tired that's all."

"You comin' down with somethin'? You getting' a touch of the influenza?"

"No momma." Enoch sighed.

"Well, little wonder, you tom-cattin all night and hanging around with them good-for-nothin's down at the Huckleberry. You come home and stay home tonight. You need some rest, you hear me?"

"Yes momma. I really got to go. See you tonight." He kissed her on the forehead, turned and walked out the back door, leaving his lunch bucket on the counter. Missy Baker stood there for a moment just shaking her head.

It was a forty-five minute bus ride up the valley, three towns away, to the American Synthetic Fibers plant where Enoch had been employed, having toiled as a cutter and maintenance man for the past three years. War production ensured him a good paycheck and until a few hours ago the future appeared brighter than ever. Seated at the back of the bus, he closed his eyes and leaned his head against the cool window. Ignoring the jarring vibrations, and the buses' starts and stops, his mind worked through the events of last night.

Knew this was gonna happen. Just knew it. Shoulda stopped it 'fore it happened, ain't no piece worth this trouble. My own worse enemy, yes sir, everytime, jus' my own worse enemy. Nothin' I can do now, can't run away, can't leave momma, no use cryin over spilt milk. Nothin'll happen, maybe nothin'll happen. I just got to lay low and stay away from Pritchard Street, lay low and stay home for awhile. Nothin'll happen, nobody knows 'bout it 'cept old Missus Gabriel, and she sure don't want it getting' out. Nope, don't thin k anybody'll say a thing. Jus' need to lay low, that's all. Norma sure don't want it getting out either, just give it a little time. Nothin'll happen, maybe nothin'll happen.

It was eleven A.M. before the two patrolmen returned to the station house and reported to Police Chief, Hiram P. Delaney. It was another twenty minutes before Chief Delaney, having been briefed and his questions satisfied, called detectives Dan Hopkins and Jim Little into his office. The detectives were veteran police officers that had risen through the ranks to become the city's sole detectives. They began formulating a plan before the chief finished his dissertation of the facts.

"Chief, you said that Charlie recognized the knife?"

"Yes, that's right. You know, Charlie is one of the best men I got. He said he's seen one of those hooked knives before, said it was a knife for cutting leather, but that his father had one just like it back when he worked down at the fiber plant as a cutter."

"Let me see that thing." Dan held his hand out towards the chief. "Guess, no one thought about fingerprinting the knife?"

"Yeah I asked them about that, but Charlie and Pete said there was no point in it, since the old lady handed it to them the minute they were in the front door." The Chief continued. "So that's it then, you've read the report, it's dirty business, and I want it cleared up as fast as we can."

"I agree, once the county boys, and town rowdies get wind of a white woman being raped by a nigra, all hell could break loose." Jim Little intoned while lighting a cigarette.

"The way I see it Chief, we need to get every man we got mobilized on this. Tonight, shortly after supper time, say six, six-thirty you send em out and gather up every young buck they can find, say between twenty and thirty years old, and take em in for questioning. Jim and I will head down to the plant, see how many of em work there and bring em in for the same. Then we'll bring this Norma Gabriel in and see if she can identify her assailant."

"There's no way I can get warrants for that many suspects by tonight."

"Hell, we don't need warrants, we're just bringing em in for questioning. We don't need to tell them anything. The more scared they are the better, it'll help em tell the truth for a change." Dan added, his mouth forming a sneer.

"All right, I'll see to it. Just get this taken care of, you hear me? I don't want to be reading about a New Surrey lynch mob in the Richmond and D.C. papers, is that clear?"

"Yes sir. We're on it." The detectives stood, walked across the room, paused to raise the shade from the stenciled glass window of the office door and departed.

Upon their arrival in Riverton, the detectives immediately checked in with the local police to inform them of their business and intentions at the fiber plant. The act served as professional courtesy and an acknowledgement of jurisdiction. As such, the lieutenant on duty sent a Riverton patrolman to accompany the detectives to the factory.

Two men in well-worn suits and a uniformed police officer entered the business office of American Synthetic Fibers. The two secretaries seated at large wooden desks and separated from the waiting area by a three-foot tall wood-paneled partition, stopped typing barely able to mask their astonishment.

"Can I help you?" Asked the older of the two women.

"Yes ma'am you can. I'm Detective Hopkins and this is Detective Little, we're from the New Surrey police department and we'd like to speak with the plant manager."

"Is he expecting you?" The woman's face reddened realizing she sounded impertinent. The men were, after all, officers of the law.

"No ma'am, he's not, but I can assure you we're here on a matter of the utmost importance."

"Of course. I'll tell him you're here." The secretary replied in a conciliatory tone. The other woman continued to stare at the threesome, wondering what ill wind had blown them in the front door.

A moment later, a heavy set balding man, his loud tie loosened and shirt sleeves rolled up, stood in front of the three officials. "I'm Paul Harper, plant manager, what can I do you gentlemen for?"

After brief introductions all around Dan Hopkins asked, "Mr Harper, could we have a word with you in your office?"

"Certainly." Harper turned and lead the trio into his office, shutting the door behind him to the chagrin of the two women.

"Mr. Harper, how many colored boys have you got working in this plant?"

The manager replied, "Hmm, let me see." He lifted his eyes towards the ceiling and began ticking off names to himself and counting on his fingers. "Well, sir, near as I can figure, there are six."

"Are they all working on the plant floor right now?" Detective Little inquired.

"Yes sir, I believe they are. What's this all about Detective?" Mr. Harper said, justifiably curious.

"Police business." Dan Hopkins crisply answered. "Could you please send for them?"

"Now? They're in the middle of a shift . . . er, yes of course." Harper opened the door, "Mary Pat, please tell Bob to send all the colored boys to the office right away." Turning to the detectives, "Bob Cooper is the plant foreman, he'll have 'em here on the double."

"Thank you."

The plant manger was as good as his word and in short order Bob Cooper lead the six men into the now crowded reception area. The men deflated visibly upon seeing the uniformed police officer and began shuffling nervously. Two of the men were wringing their cloth caps in their hands. The oldest of the men stepped forward and in a deprecating voice asked. "Excuse me, suh, but what's this all about? None of us have done anything wrong, we jus' been working the plant."

"Didn't do anything wrong, huh? We'll see about that boy." It was the first time the uniformed officer spoke. Both detectives turned and gave him a sharp look.

"It's police business men, now, I need to ask a question." Dan spoke in a calming manner. "Do any of you boys live in New Surrey?"

Enoch's stomach lurched and he felt his bowels begin to churn. The men began to murmur, four of them shaking there heads and mumbling "No suh." Enoch and another man looked up and swallowed, each of them answering in the affirmative. The first droplets of sweat appearing on their brows.

"You two stay, the rest of you can go back to work." The weight of the world lifted from the shoulders of the four men as they headed back to work. "What are your names and addresses?" Both men answered the question, their voices all but audible as the detective licked the point of his eraser-less pencil and wrote the information in a pocket notebook.

"You two come with us. You won't cause any trouble will you? Because we can handcuff you if need be."

"No suh, we won't be any trouble, but excuse me suh, are we under arrest or somethin'?"

"Never mind now, you'll see soon enough." Detective Little smiled with cold eyes.

The secretaries and general manager were already huddled and whispering as the two men were lead out of the office. It was three in the afternoon and beads of sweat were forming on Enoch Baker's upper lip and forehead.

CHAPTER 19

"It's Him."

Chief Delaney opened his office door. Then, his eyes darting around the room and with the set jaw of a bulldog growled, "Roscoe, find Hopkins and Little and send them in here on the double." He stepped back into his office forcefully shutting the door behind him. The action achieved the dramatic effect he desired; Roscoe was up and away from the sergeant's desk before the shade on the chief's door stopped swaying.

Delaney sat back down at his desk, shuffled some papers, stacked some reports and sharpened a pencil. The glass encased pendulum of the Regulator clock swung apathetically, mocking the chief's rising ire. The portrait of George Washington, a print of Gilbert Stuart's unfinished study, watched the chief with patrician indifference, while from the opposite wall Robert E. Lee's tired gaze stared past Delaney into the troubled distance. Delaney stood yet again, circled the spacious office yet again, sitting back down and for the third time in fifteen minutes, read the article in this evening's New Surrey Dispatch.

As was their habit, the two detectives, in rolled up shirtsleeves and loosened neckties entered the chief's office without knocking. "You want to see us?"

"Damn right I want to see you." He tossed the folded paper across the desk towards the two men. "Are you responsible for this?"

"What's that Chief?"

"Don't play dumb with me Dan, it doesn't suit you. Just tell me one thing. How the hell did the paper get a hold of this story before we even started questioning the nigras?"

Police Search for Assailant of Mrs. Norma Gabriel

UNKNOWN COLORED MAN ENTERED HOUSE ARMED WITH VICIOUS KNIFE

BULLETIN A suspect was arrested by Police late this afternoon. They refused to divulge the man's name or where he was being held.

Staging one of the most intensive man hunts in the history of local law enforcement, officers today were leaving no clue uninvestigated in their effort to apprehend a colored man who broke into the home of Mrs. Dorothy Gabriel, 224 Pritchard Street, last night and grappled with her daughter-in-law, Mrs. Norma Gabriel.

Mrs. Gabriel, wife of Pfc Thomas Gabriel, was at home alone when the incident occurred. Members of the family today denied that the 26-year-old girl had been criminally attacked.

Mrs. Gehrhardt P. Bittner, mother of the young lady, and Mrs. Dorothy Gabriel, her mother-in-law, gave a member of The Dispatch staff this afternoon the following account of what happened:

Washing Out Clothes

Mrs. Dorothy Gabriel had just gone out, leaving her daughter-in-law alone. The the latter made a telephone call call and then went upstairs where she removed her dress and prepared to wash some clothes in the bathroom. It was stated she was doing this when she heard the front door open, but thinking that it was her mother-in-law did no investigate. She became suspicious, Mrs. Bittner stated, when a pet cat, "Spunky," start-

ed to mew in a strange fashion. She threw the bathroom door back to call to the cat and saw the colored man on the stairs.

Threatened With Knife

He sprang at her, placing a sharp knife at her throat. Mrs. Gabriel described the Police Search man as having gray, bulging eyes. His face was covered with a mask, he was about 5 feet 11 inches tall and weighed between 175 and 185 pounds it was said.

Members of the family stated that she pleaded with her assailant, and also pointed out money which was in another room, but refused to loosen his grasp. It was said that she asked the negro, "You wouldn't want to kill me?" They said he answered, "No."

Gains Advantage

It was then reported that the victim suddenly wrenched loose loose from the man's grasp gaining hold of the wrist of the hand in which the knife was was held, They said that he dropped the knife and apparently losing his nerve, rushed from the house. A few minutes later her mother-in-law returned, but Mrs. Gabriel, not wishing to worry the older woman, was said to have gone next door to the home of Walter Wolfe where she described what had occurred. They notified the police who immediately launched an investigation.

Knife Is Clue

Chief clue at the moment seems

to be the knife, which the attacker dropped. This was described as a short, wicked-looking weapon with a hook on the end ordinarily used for cutting leather. The handle was taped and the blade was only a few inches long. was stated, police will bring Mrs. Gabriel to the station house where a number of local colored people will be brought in for questioning and examination as to identification. Mrs. Gabriel who is employed at the McDermott Woolen Company, estimated the age of the intruder at about 26. PFC Gabriel is stationed somewhere in France or Germany.

Chief of Police H.P. Delaney had no statement to make this afternoon, except that the case was being investigated from every angle.

Jim Little slouched into the worn leather chair opposite the Chief, slid the overfilled ashtray over and lit an Old Gold cigarette. "Come on, you know how things work around here. Not to mention it's probably a slow news day, and this has all the makings of a really big story. Young white gal, hubby serving overseas, colored man, rape, their going to have a field day with this, boss."

"Jim's right, boss, I'll bet you dollars to donuts that somebody who knows somebody who knows somebody heard something or other and whispered it to somebody else down at the city desk and so old Bobby Hudson had a reporter lying in wait for the day's police reports." Dan Hopkins pontificated.

"That or the planets aligned and some reporter happened by at the right time and place, doesn't much matter now, cat's out of the bag." Jim tapped the ash off of his Old Gold.

"Aw, hell, this is going to be a big mess, ain't it? I only got 3 months to retirement and now this. Don't hardly seem fair does it?" The Chief sighed.

"Yeah well, I don't imagine this Norma Gabriel thinks it too fair either."

"You got that right, Jim, you got that right." Dan grunted.

"Well, y'all know what I mean. Anyway, I had'em round up all the colored boys they could find. Had about thirty of em', not including the two you brought from the plant. Based on the Gabriel woman's description, we sent most of them home. Too fat, too thin, too tall, too short, you know the drill. That left us with nine that matched the description more or less. One thing's for sure, they got the message loud and clear, and'll take it home to their mammies and pappies."

"What message is that chief?"

"That we mean business, and we will catch the black son-of-a-bitch that raped that white girl and see that he gets what's coming to him. Or as you high falootin' detectives like to say, he'll be punished to the full extent of the law." The chief stood and walked to the door, opening it he called, "Roscoe, but on a fresh pot of joe, it's gonna be a long night. Excuse me boys, but police business is police business and coffee is coffee."

"And always the twain shall meet." Dan smiled without mirth.

Jim Little lit another cigarette from the glowing stub of the first, "Of course, the paper said Mrs. Gabriel drove off the assailant, so then, there was no rape."

"The preliminary report I filed didn't say one way or the other about her being raped. I was purposely vague about that, and naturally when the paper interviewed the two mothers, they're sure not going to mention rape. Don't want the scandal, and they don't want the girl to be damaged goods." Dan Hopkins scratched at a place on his leg.

"Well, that can be the official line for now, but this is a small town and word travels fast. No secrets in a small town, and besides those black boys we sent home sure know there was a rape. I figured scaring the hell out of 'em might get 'em to fess up. You know how it is with these coloreds, the truth isn't in 'em."

"Know what you mean, chief." Jim intoned, avoiding Dan's sharp glance. "Have you sent a patrol car for Mrs. Gabriel?"

"She should be here any minute, sent my own Packard and Billy-Bob in his street clothes over to pick her up. He's going to bring her in around back. I figure the paper will have a reporter camped out front. No use throwing more fuel on the fire. It's going to get hot enough around here once the word spreads 'round the white folks."

As if it were scripted, there was a soft knock on the office door. The chief answered and into the room came Norma Gabriel followed by Billy-Bob Harmon. The three men scrambled to stand as she entered the room and an awkward silence ensued. The detectives had questioned her that morning, but this was the first time the chief had laid eyes on her. He thought her a little plain, but not wholly unattractive, she seemed sweet and in his eye's an innocent. In fact, she somewhat reminded him of his own daughter. The sight of her forged his resolve. There would be justice.

"Hello again, Mrs. Gabriel, we're so sorry to have to put you through this. This is Chief of Police Delaney, and you remember Detective Little."

The Chief came out from behind his desk and took Norma's moist, limp hand in his. "We'll try to make this as easy for you as we can, but we're going to need you to be brave, and no matter what happens, rest assured we will catch the man who did this, and until then, we'll keep you safe."

Norma demurely removed her hand from the chief's and looking down at the floor, whispered. "Thank you."

"Now Norma . . . May I call you Norma?" Dan checked himself in mid-sentence.

"Yes."

"Good. Now, Norma according to my notes from this morning," Dan flipped the small leather covered note-pad open, "You were assaulted by a colored man between the ages of twenty-five and thirty, wearing a black fedora pulled down low, a dark brown jacket, and a white handkerchief tied across the lower half of his face. Is that correct?"

"Yes." Norma had still not made eye contact with anyone in the room.

"Mrs. Gabriel," The chief interjected, "the reason we brought you down here, of course, is we hope to have you give us a positive identification on the animal that violated you in this way. Pardon my strong language ma'am, but this is serious business and we mean to treat it as such."

Dan continued. "Norma, we're going to take you downstairs to a room where we usually do our questioning. We're going to bring in the suspects one at a time, dressed in a manner similar to your description and have them say a few words. Detective Little and myself will be in there with you, so you'll be perfectly safe."

The Chief broke in again, "Take your time, we want you to be sure, and if you need to see anyone of them more than once just let us know. There's no hurry." Norma nodded.

Jim stood and said, "Well, then, let's get to it." The three men tripped over themselves in deference to the unfortunate young woman, in a clumsy mix of pity and good manners.

The room downstairs was a windowless cube, the cement floor and blank walls painted institutional green. A single bright light bulb hung from the ceiling, it's acute brightness casting unpredictable shadows. On one side of the room, opposite the single door, a thick-topped metal table and three chairs were in position. A pitcher of water, three glasses, and a clean ashtray was centered on it. The air was stale and redolent of fear and sweat.

"Norma, you sit yourself down here between Dan and me." Jim pulled the center chair away from the table. As Norma sat down, Dan found his seat and poured three glasses of water. Jim set his silver Ronson on the table and slid his pack of Old Golds towards the ashtray. "Care for a smoke?"

"Yes, I would, but I brought my own. Thank you." Norma opened her small purse and retrieved a pack of Chesterfields, tapping one out and placing the near empty pack on the table. Jim flipped open the lighter, its flame lighting her cigarette and then his own. Their combined smoke billowed up through the harsh light like a thunderhead.

The door opened and a uniformed man asked if everything was ready. Dan nodded. Norma's hands trembled. The officer walked into the room followed by one of the detainees and another policeman. The alleged assailant was dressed according to Norma's description: black fedora, brown jacket, white handkerchief tied over the lower portion of his face. His head was tilted down and he was staring at the floor, he didn't seem to know what to do with his hands. The officer to his right gave the dejected man's arm a shake. "Say it."

Without looking up, the man mumbled a few words into the bandit-style handkerchief tied across his face. The officer shook the man harder, "I said, say it boy, look up and speak up, you're already in enough trouble, we may just keep you here no matter what this lady says, now say it."

The man straightened up, looked at Norma, and softly, but clearly said, "No, I'm not going to kill you."

"One more time boy, and this time say it like you mean it." The uniform on the right snarled.

"No . . . I'm not gonna kill you." Rivulets of sweat ran down the masked man's temples. Norma could not take her eyes off of the man. She was lost in pity and shame.

The same officer then looked at Detective Little who gave a slight nod of his head and the hint of a smile. The officer's smile was not as subtle. "Okay boy, drop your pants."

The man's eyes widened above the mask, and with an imperceptible shake of his head said, "Suh, you can't mean that suh, I didn't do nothin' to no white woman, this ain't right sir. Please, I'm a married man."

At the same time, Norma, not taking notice of the man's protestations, turned with her hand over her mouth and made to stand up. "I . . .I can't, I feel sick. I'm sorry. I can't do this . . . this is too much."

Dan took her hand and squeezed it firmly and whispered into her ear, "Mrs. Gabriel, Norma, this is why the chief told you to be brave. This was his idea, not mine, he said that since the man was masked, we needed to do everything we could to ensure you could identify him, please understand, I know how difficult this is for you." Norma sat back down, took a sip of water, removed a handkerchief from her purse, wiped her mouth and lit another cigarette.

"Boy, you deaf or somethin'? I said drop your pants and shorts too, I wanna see you hangin' out there in the wind."

In resignation and humiliation the man complied. Norma stared straight ahead and pulled deeply on her cigarette. A moment later the man pulled his pants back up, was turned around and lead from the room.

"Well, Norma, was that him?" asked Jim Little.

"No, I don't think so."

"Don't think so? Come on now, either he was or wasn't."

"Give her a break here, will ya Jim?" Dan hissed. "This is going to be hard enough for her, got it?"

"I don't think that was him, the eyes were wrong, and his hands . . . his hands were too small." Norma said ignoring Little.

"Too small, huh?" Jim leered.

"Detective Little, you lookin' for a fat lip? How about we be a little professional here?" Dan's expression left no room for doubt.

"I'm sorry, Norma, Dan's right, of course, I'm sorry Dan, it won't happen again. It's been a long day for all of us." Jim was suitably chastised.

"And it's going to get longer, let's move on to the next suspect." Dan stood and walked to the door to let the guards know they were ready for the next one.

Over the next ninety minutes six more detainees were paraded into the room one at a time, each costumed as the assailant of Dorothy and Norma's perilous and expedient imaginations. Each of the men carried on their shoulders the weight of helplessness. Around their necks hung the millstone of four hundred years of American Southern culture. None of them were willing to gamble their innocence for the short-lived satisfaction of righteous indignation. Each man did as he was told with habitual acquiescence, but each man did not suffer the humiliation with the same bearing. One was cowed to the point of urinating, a puddle forming at his feet before he was told to drop his pants. The man's degradation was made complete by the escorting officer's rebuke and then derisive laughter. Three of the men suffered their ordeal with the pragmatism that came with growing up in New Surrey. Get it over with and go home, bearing all things, believing all things, hoping all things and enduring all things, just getting it over with. Two of the men stood tall and looked directly into Norma's eyes. She couldn't hold their gaze and each time had to look away. They refused to give those present the satisfaction of their discomfiture, speaking the phrases loud and clear and dropping their pants without the slightest hesitation. Each of the two earned the sobriquet of "Uppity Nigger" from Jim Little. Each man, no matter how hard he would try, would never forget this night, and each man upon seeing Norma, knew Enoch Baker was not long for this world. That's just the way things were.

For Norma the atmosphere in the room rapidly became intolerable. The closeness, the tobacco smoke, the smell of fear, perspiration, unwashed bodies, unwashed clothes, urine, the bright harsh light, the hard metal chair and the reaped whirlwind of emotions took a collective toll on the young woman. After each man was brought in, she asked for and received permission for a short break out into the fresh air. Accompanied by the detectives, the three of them stood out back under a light pole and smoked their cigarettes. Not a word passed between them and after the last smoke was stubbed out, they silently went back down into the basement of the police station. The breaks became progressively longer and each time it was more difficult to return to the interrogation room.

In her silence, her mind raced and wrestled with the permutations, ramifications and justifications of what was happening here, this night, in this place. It was halfway through the ordeal, while she was still hoping against hope that Enoch would not be one of the men paraded into the room, when something inside of her changed. She didn't see it coming, and when the thought came to rest, she realized it was right. It brought with it an uneasy resolve. It was what she needed to do.

She knew, of course, that one of the men yet to come would be Enoch, it had to be, fate would not spare them that. She now knew one other thing: she would have to do what was right. The right thing. She would have to do whatever it took to spare Gabe, her family, his family, the entire town of New Surrey for that matter the pain of scandal. Her marriage was probably beyond saving, at least that was what she had convinced herself of when she was with Enoch. But who could say, and with a scandal, there would be no chance at all. It would be difficult, but one day, everything would be just fine. She would do whatever it would take, pay any price, and bury anyone who would stand in her way. She was doing the right thing.

Norma turned her face away from the seventh man and she found it hard to breathe while he stood before her. After the man had been lead out of the room, Norma did not ask for a cigarette break. With tears tracking down her cheek, she gripped the edge of the table, and softly said, "It's him."

Dan snapped shut his notebook, and said, "Well, that's it then. Let's get you out of here Mrs. Gabriel."

CHAPTER 20

Some Kind of Mistake

As Enoch was lead to a small solitary cell, he began to understand what he had known in his heart of hearts all along. Since being taken from the plant office, his questions were answered by "Shut up, boy" or ignored with deliberate stone-faced silence. Sitting on the dirty cotton mattress he leaned forward, rested his elbows on his knees and covered his face with his hands. He had to think, and think fast.

What's goin' on here? What's happened? Somethin' else musta happened to Norma. This gotta be some miss-understandin. She'll straighten 'em out, she'll do it, I know she will. How the hell did the police find out what happened? Can't figure that out, surely the old Missus Gabriel didn't tell, and Norma can't have much to say 'bout it. Somethin' else musta happened, maybe some other man got her. She'll straighten it out, she surely will. Ain't no piece of tail worth this kinda trouble, white, black, purple or green, No sir.

Enoch straightened up and the too bright light from the single bulb hanging high above him hurt his eyes. It was the same harsh light that illuminated Norma in the other room, but in the confines of the cell, it's brightness devoured shadows. Rubbing at his stinging eyes, a stray thought ran through his mind: God is light and in Him is no darkness at all. However, it brought him little comfort.

The sound of a door opening and closing, and the hollow sound of stiff leather soles on concrete pulled Enoch to the door. He gripped an iron crossbar and placed his face sideways against the bars to see who and what was coming. Of course, it was a guard.

Enoch Baker Held For Action Of Grand Jury

NEGRO CHARGED WITH RAPE, IS GIVEN HEARING BEFORE JUDGE FLAGLER

Enoch Baker, colored, 26 who resides at 17 West Ogden Street and was employed at the American Synthetic Fiber plant at Riverton, has been held for action of a Corporation Court grand jury charged with rape (criminal assault with force). The announcement was made by Commonwealth's Attorney Newton P. Vann who stated that he would request an early trial.

The arrest followed the alleged attack about 8:45 Tuesday night of Mrs. Norma Gabriel at the home of her mother-in-law, Mrs. Dorothy Gabriel, 427 Pritchard Street.

Enoch Baker was taken into custody yesterday afternoon by city police and his arraignment this morning before Judge JanFlagler followed intensive questioning and investigation last night and this morning by city police officers.

The charge carries a maximum penalty of death in the electric chair.

Police Act Swiftly

Today's swift action followed 24 hours of intense police work on the part of the city police force, starting Tuesday night when they were notified by telephone from the Walter Wolfe residence of what had occurred.

Launching an immediate investigation it was learned that Mrs. Norma Gabriel 26, whose husband, Pfc Thomas Gabriel is stationed somewhere in Germany, had been home alone when the negro, his face covered by a mask entered the house.

Washing out some clothes in the bathroom at the time. It was said that she became suspicious when her pet cat, "Spunky" started mewing in a strange manner.

Opening the door to investigate it was said that the negro sprang at her, placing a knife at her throat.

Officers rounded up several colored people on Tuesday evening, but they were released when Mrs. Gabriel failed to identify then.

Arrest At Riverton

Yesterday afternoon at 3 pm detectives of the city police department drove to Riverton to endeavor to question negro employees of the American Synthetic Fiber plant living in New Surrey.

Upon questioning it was discovered that Enoch Baker's cutting knife was missing. He was placed under arrest and later identified by Mrs. Gabriel as the attacker. The court has appointed R. J. Harrington and Ernest Oakes, Riverton, attorneys for Baker.

"Excuse me, excuse me suh?" Enoch's voice made the guard slow his step, but not stop.

"Suh, suh, please tell me why they're holdin' me here? What're they chargin' me with? Suh, what's gonna happen next? Please tell me why I'm in jail. Ain't nobody told me anything"

The policeman stopped and faced Enoch, rocking back and forth on his heels. A malignant grin spread over his face. In the hard light emitting from the cell, the grinning visage looked like a cruel Halloween mask. "Boy, you don't know what you done? You take me for a fool, boy? Well, don't matter none, the judge is going to tell you what you done before too long, and if he don't, there's a bunch of them ol' county boys who'll tell you what you done. First the detectives are going to have a talk with you

174

boy, and I'd tell 'em the truth if I was you." The man gave a slight shake of his head and walked away.

Enoch sat back down on the bunk, leaned over and returned to holding his head in his hands. He was tired, hungry, thirsty, confused and terrified. He was losing the ability to keep events of the last twenty-four hours in a logical and chronological order. Random details repeatedly interjected themselves into his inner conversation and with each detail a convoluted analysis ensued. Each thought unleashed a torrent of others until it was impossible to return to his original line of reasoning. All of this infected by the uncertainty of not knowing why he was being detained. Perhaps he knew. He did know. But the truth was simply too horrible to contemplate. Enoch stood up again, and deeply inhaled through flared nostrils, the air in the cell was stale, but there was something else. For the first time in his life, he realized he could smell fear. His own.

His stomach growled repeatedly. The sound all but echoed in the small cell. Enoch's mouth was so dry that his tongue stuck to his palette and cheeks each time it swept around trying to induce saliva. His throat burned and ached as if he had smoked three packs of cigarettes out on a bender. He also had to use the toilet soon. His physical discomforts multiplied his anxiety. Had anyone told his mother? Was she coming to the station to get him out? What was Norma thinking? Was she telling the police it was all a mistake? His mind circled and circled like a mule turning a millstone.

Enoch Baker had never owned a wristwatch or even worn one. Time was measured by light, the steam whistle at the plant, the church bell and an old alarm clock he shared with his mother. In the silent, windowless bowels of the station-house, it was impossible to judge the passing of time; at best he could measure time by the increasing urgency of his bladder and gut. But even his body functions betrayed him by appearing and disappearing. He was lost in time and place.

It was shortly after eleven o'clock before the leering guard returned and led him to the green interrogation room. Norma was gone. The table had been moved to the center of the room, one chair across the table from two others, a pitcher of water, two glasses and a metal cup rested on it. Enoch imagined it to be three or four in the morning.

"So knock-knock, you don't mind if I call you Knock-knock, do ya boy? You know why you're here don't ya?" Jim Little fell into the natural role of being the antagonist. Good-cop-bad-cop was tried and true methodology.

"Suh, I don't know why I'm here, I truly don't. But suh, I need to use the toilet real bad, I'm 'bout to mess myself suh, please, can I use the toilet?" Enoch was sweating heavily and on the edge of panicking.

"You better not mess yourself boy, you're already stinking this place up, and I'll be damned if we're gonna have nigger shit all over the place." Little snarled.

Dan Hopkins turned to the guard at the door, "Gardner, get a slop bucket and some paper and take the prisoner to his cell and let him do his business." The wash rooms in the station-house were all clearly marked "Whites Only".

Enoch was lead away, the word "prisoner" ringing in his ears. Dan sat silently the entire time Enoch was gone, tired and disgusted. The thought of a powerful black man raping a married white woman made him physically ill, and his partner's cracker attitude, real or imagined, was wearing on him. It would be a long night.

After he had relieved himself and been returned to the room, the guard pushed him down forcefully into the chair across from the detectives. Jim Little launched into a diatribe berating the skin color, education, personal hygiene and the sexual predilections of the man sitting helplessly across from him. Enoch Baker did not appear to have heard a word of it. He sat motionless, staring at the pitcher of water and swallowing repeatedly.

Dan watched Enoch's eyes and followed their stare. He filled the metal cup with water and slid it towards the younger man. Enoch took his eyes off of the pitcher and looked into Dan's eyes. Dan nodded and Enoch emptied the cup in one swallow, wiping his face on his sleeve. Jim continued his rant. Dan poured him a second, nodded, and again the water disappeared in a single swallow. Dan went to pour a third time when Jim took the cup and threw it across the room.

"Jesus H. Christ, you plan on drownin' this nigger before the state has a crack at him? Boy, might as well get used to it, 'cause you're gonna be awful thirsty where you're going."

The interrogation went on into the small hours of the morning. The same handful of questions was asked over and over. They were asked in various permutations and random order trying to catch Enoch in a lie. Jim did most of the questioning, with Dan only asking an occasional clarification, and seeing that Enoch was given cups of water throughout the interrogation. They never once allowed the prisoner to tell his version of the previous evening's events, nor did they allow him to elaborate on any of his answers. There was never a break, and Enoch's stomach growled and protested in hunger.

"How long have you known Mrs. Gabriel?"

"How long you been working in the Gabriel house?"

"You have a set of keys to the house?"

"You rape that girl?"

"You use a knife, then lose it there?"

"You think you wouldn't get caught?"

"How come you didn't run off, get out of town?"

"How long you been bird-dogging that white woman, sniffing at her skirts?"

After the first hour, when Enoch gave up on trying to explain things, his answers lapsed into monotonic monosyllabic utterances. The interrogation lasted five hours. Enoch was broken, but he never wavered from the truth while an elaborate web of lies wove around him and eventually ensnared him. He was finally taken back to the cell, the light was blazing and the stench of the slop bucket, sweat, and dirty mattress was oppressive. The guard scowled, cursed and held one hand covered his nose as he pushed Enoch into the cell.

It was impossible to recognize whether Enoch had noticed or not. His eyes were fixed on the floor and face was expressionless. Enoch had surrendered to the darkness within. He had become what in penitentiary parlance was known as a "Dead Man Walking"; tried and sentenced before any court proceedings had begun, "Dead Man Walking" in the minds of the white men around him, and, now, in his own mind as well.

Enoch removed his shirt and bunched it into a pillow, curled on his side and turned his back to the light. There was a certain release in the abandonment of hope. It was like loosening your grip on floating debris and slipping beneath the waves. It was like finally straightening out your fingers and letting go of the ledge, plummeting through space with four-seconds to contemplate impact. He lay there in newfound apathy and for the moment, the random tumbling thoughts ceased. The desertion of his inner voice from his body and circumstances would help get him through this one way or another. He fell asleep. Sleep is the refuge of the despondent.

CHAPTER **21**

Guilty Minds

Peace visits not the guilty mind
(Nemo Malus Felix)
JUVENAL (55AD – 127AD)

Norma: Norma languished in the tepid water; it was the second bath she had drawn in as many hours. She had given up on any hope of scrubbing herself clean; she knew that after the night's events she could never be clean again. Sitting still and silent in the dark bathroom, Norma watched the weak, mottled light from the streetlamp out front undulating on the wall each time a small breeze rustled the leaves. The repressive guilt was crushing her, changing her, molding her into something or someone she could no longer recognize. The guilt pressed down on her so that she wanted to just slip under the bathwater and drown herself. As she prepared to submerge, a cold analytical voice came to her, just as it had during every crisis she had endured since childhood. She knew that it would be physically impossible for her to inhale the water. She would explode to the surface greedily filling her lungs once she felt the tiniest trickle of water streaming into her windpipe. This was the rationalization she used to avoid the terror and pain she anticipated with death by drowning. She could simply not face the unknown with the possibility of being held accountable for her betrayal. How could she face God and His ensuing judgement? In her despondent state she dwelled on murderers, assassins, and traitors. In self-recrimination she reflected on John Wilkes Booth, Benedict Arnold, Brutus, Judas Iscariot.

Ah, yes, Judas. You betrayed an innocent man, so did I. Poor innocent, simple Knock-knock, I was hungry, needed a man, curious . . . and in total control. You didn't stand a chance. How could I believe we could get away with it, doing it in Gabe's family home, in Gabe's childhood bed . . . I must be crazy. And so, where are the thirty pieces of silver? No silver, it's not that simple. Just a chance to spare Gabe the pain of my mistake, of my adultery, to carry on and have a normal life, either with me or somebody else. I may not be in love with him anymore, but he deserves better than this. Judas betrayed a man who was willing, who was expecting, to die for the greater good. I've betrayed a man who's being forced to die for the greater good, the greater good of the Gabriel family.

She absently took the safety razor off of the edge of the tub and began twisting the handle. The top slowly opened, like tiny casement doors leading to a storm cellar. She tilted the razor, and tapped the blade into her hand.

Judas, you took that silver, threw it back and killed yourself. What's the Bible say? Go thou and do likewise?

Norma took the razor blade gingerly between her thumb and index finger. She pressed the corner into the flesh of her wrist just below her thumb. In the semi-darkness a small bead of thick jet black blood welled from the tiny cut and trailed down her forearm. The pain was instant and her sense of anticipation amplified it all out of proportion to the size of the cut. She dropped the blade into the water and stood grabbing the bath towel pressing it hard against her wrist.

I'm such a goddamned coward . . . but I can't stand the pain . . . I can't face whatever comes next . . . can't face God . . . can't face living . . . can't face dying . . .can't face Gabe . . . can't face Knock-knock . . . again . . .I'm nothing but a goddamned coward . . .goddamned is right. Judas Iscariot.

In less than a minute, the bleeding stopped; she dried herself and slipped on a dressing gown. She walked into the master bedroom and climbed into the large bed.

She would never sleep in Gabe's room again; it was now occupied by the ghost of a dead man walking.

Gabe: The orders stood unchanged. The regiment was still slated to invade Japan, the battalions trained incessantly, with each of the companies drilling until their skills and duties were instinctual. Each man was convinced he was headed for the Pacific and each man was convinced death would find him there. That butcher's bill would be high-er than anything they had seen so far, and these men had witnessed the unimaginable. The Japanese would defend their homeland yard by yard with suicidal ferocity. It was because of this that the veterans of second platoon, D Company trained with a sense of urgency and foreboding.

Likewise, it was with urgency and foreboding that Gabe continued to love and obtain solace from Irmgard. He found himself thinking less and less frequently about Norma. But when he did ruminate on what was quickly becoming a failed marriage, a mistake, his thoughts were resolutely marching from soul searching to deepening resentment. It was not like Gabe to grow churlish or spiteful, but with what he had been through and was going through now, the burden of Norma and her silence was difficult to endure. With the impending return to com-bat, the rigors of training maneuvers, the mixed emotions of day-to-day life among the enemy and the immediacy of a beautiful woman, Gabe resolved to not write a word to Norma until he received a letter from her. He had even ceased to ask about her in letters to his mother, which had become less and less frequent these past months, and his mother had correspondingly ceased to mention her as well. He sec-ond-guessed himself and wondered if this was the right course of action to take with Norma. In the end, he didn't know, but at least it was a course of action.

Ten days had passed since he had last climbed into Irmgard's bed. He had returned from field exercises that afternoon, showered, changed into a clean uniform and immediately made his way the sev-eral blocks to her apartment. He had almost decided to wait a day and get some rest, but he couldn't. The ten-day separation infused their lovemaking with an energy he didn't think possible.

He was lying on his back and she had fallen asleep in the fold of his shoulder, with her back to his side, and her head resting on his upper arm. Usually he was the one to drift off, but tonight he was hav-ing trouble falling asleep. Perhaps he was too tired to sleep. He endured the pins and needles in his arm as the weight of her head cut off the circulation. Finally, he gently shifted his arm from under her head, her hair fell away from across his chest and he sat up on the side of the bed.

He padded across the wooden floor, went to the row of pegs on the opposite wall and fished a pack of Camels from his shirt pocket. Crossing to the open window he lit a cigarette and watched the smoke curl away into the night air.

God, she's beautiful. Beautiful, sexy, smart, and funny . . . and she wants me. What the hell does she see in a sad sack like me? Wonder if she feels sorry for me? Or sorry for herself? Maybe she sees me as her ticket outta here, a better life for her and the boy. Shit, it doesn't matter, all that matters is here, here and now, we'll work the other stuff out later, when the time comes. If it comes.

That's it then. I'm done with Norma, I don't care what she does, it's over, whether she writes me or not, If and when, God, that's a big if, if and when, I get back from Japan I'm coming to get her, take her home, divorce Norma, and marry her. I've got to convince her to wait for me.

CHAPTER **2 2**

Ensnared and Entangled

T he machine-like rapping of a billy-stick passing back and forth across the bars of the cell jolted Enoch into consciousness. The shock of passing from a bottomless, dreamless sleep to his current circumstance was both physical and psychological. He scrambled from his bunk and fell to the floor. It served to further debilitate him.

"Rise and shine, boy, there's a man wants to see you, and I hear-tell he's not too happy. Mr. Vann wants you brought to his office, boy, and he's gonna tell you how it is." The guard had changed, but the attitude and sneer had not.

"Suh, jus' a minute, I need to make water."

"Go ahead, and be quick about it, that's one man you don't want to keep waiting."

Enoch stood, walked to the chamber pot in the corner and emptied his bladder. When he was finished, he buttoned his pants and turned to the guard. "Suh, I'm really hungry, suh, I haven't had anything to eat since breakfast yesterday. Could I have a bite to eat afore we go?"

"You deaf or somethin', or you just stupid? Boy didn't I just tell you that man don't like to be kept waitin'? Being hungry is the least of your problems." As the officer spat out the words two more guards appeared at the cell door. One carried a shotgun resting across his forearms and the other a set of manacles, the chains tumbling and trying to free themselves from the man's grip.

Baker Waives Grand Jury; No Trial Date Set

Newton P. Vann, Commonwealth's attorney said this morning that Enoch Baker had waived a hearing before the grand jury. No date has been set for the trial.

Baker, colored, aged 26 is charged with criminal assault with force.

He was taken into custody Wednesday afternoon at the American Synthetic Fiber plant, Riverton where he was employed. The case was sent to the grand jury yesterday morning by Judge Jan Flagler.

The commonwealth attorney has stated that he is desirous of an early trial.

Ernest E.Oakes, appointed by the court along with R. J. Harrington to defend Baker, represented the prisoner yesterday when he waived grand jury hearing.

Oakes stated that he wished to discuss the matter further with his partner R. J. Harrington, before stating how soon his case in the defense of the accused would be ready.

While no date has been set, it is thought that the case will be heard within the next week.

The two men opened the cell, stepped inside and ordered Enoch to stand in front of the bunk; the armed policeman stood in the hall. They fastened a length of chain around his waist and secured it with a lock, so that a foot long length dangled down from his side. Through a large ring centered at his belt buckle they passed two more chains attached to manacles, which were then clamped and locked onto his wrists and ankles. Enoch's trembling vibrated through the chains.

"Listen you black piece of shit, you keep your head down and don't look at anything but your feet. People in town are already getttin' hopped up about you, and we don't need no uppity-nigger bullshit spurrin' 'em on." The guard pushed Enoch forward. He shuffled along like Marley's ghost and was led to a waiting vehicle around the back of the station. Unaware of his surroundings he climbed into the windowless back of a patrol wagon, lost in fear and despair, and concentrating not to fall.

The ride to city hall, where the Commonwealth's Attorney's office occupied three spacious rooms on the Southeast corner of the building, was uneventful. Enoch shuffled and clattered from the paddy wagon to a freight elevator at the back of the building. Flanked by guards he was lead down a hall, through a glass paned door and into a small reception area. The secretary stood, saying she would go and tell Mr. Vann they had arrived.

She returned immediately. "Mr. Vann is ready to see you now." She led the men into the spacious many-windowed office.

Newton P. Vann sat at his desk backlit by the morning sun. The effect was ethereal and added to the cherubic appearance of the rotund little man. The yellow-white hair combed over his shiny bald crown shimmered in the light like tinsel. His crisp white shirt, its sleeves rolled up, glowed, starkly contrasting with the dark suspenders and matching bowtie. He removed his gold-rimmed spectacles and allowed his small porcine eyes to evaluate the prisoner from head to toe.

"Well, well, well, Knock-knock Baker, it's been a coon's age, uh, pardon the pun, since I've laid eyes on you." The officers dutifully chuckled at their boss' witticism.

"Boys, remove the chains from the prisoner, and then leave us all by our lonesome." Vann continued.

"But sir, that's, uh, against regulations." The older policeman blurted out, immediately regretting he had spoken.

"What did you say, Kelly? It is Kelly, isn't it?"

"Yes sir, it is. I just meant that . . . "

"Officer Kelly, are you deaf or just stupid? I said unchain the prisoner and clear the room. NOW." The little man's veined bulbous nose darkened. Under different circumstances Enoch might have gained some satisfaction from the scene, but not today. The men did as they were told, the chains falling to the carpet with a muffled clink. They filed past the secretary, who stood stock-still and wide-eyed.

"Miss Stickley, is there something I can do for you?" Mr. Vann asked as pleasant now as he was angry a moment ago.

The woman was startled back into the present and with her eyes never leaving Enoch Baker, uttered, "Yes sir, I mean, no sir, sorry Mr. Vann, I'll be right outside if there's anything you need."

"Of course you will, dear." Vann smiled sincerely, as she turned and left the room, soundly closing the door behind her. "Now, Knock-

knock, let's you and I get down to business. You know, I usually don't have prisoners brought up to my office, and especially colored prisoners at that. But, you and I, well, you and I go way back don't we, Knock?"

Enoch answered dully, "Yes suh, we surely do."

"Do you remember your mama used to cook and clean for my mamma? You might not remember that, you were just a little nappy-headed piccaninny. You remember that, Knock-knock? How is your mama these days, she still bake a mean pecan pie, does she?"

Enoch again answered quietly, "Yes suh, I remember, and yes, she still bakes pies."

"Pecan pies?"

"Yes suh, pecan pies. Uh, Mister Vann, suh, may I say somethin' here, suh?"

"Why sure Knock-knock, long as you're not here to argue with me, I can't brook no arguing today, got a touch of indigestion. What do you have to say?"

"Well, suh, I haven't had anything to eat since breakfast yesterday, and nothing to drink since last night, I'm powerfully hungry and thirsty, suh, I'm feelin' weak from the hunger, suh."

Vann looked at Enoch with an expression of exaggerated concern, "Why, Knock-knock, that's terrible, I think I might have something around here, let me have a look-see." He opened a lower drawer in his desk and began fishing around. "You're in luck, boy, I knew I hadn't finished lunch yesterday. How about half a ham sandwich and a pear, sound good?"

"It does suh, it surely does. Thank you, Mr. Vann, suh.

Enoch devoured the half sandwich in two bites, and was polishing the pear to green brilliance when Vann raised his voice and called out, "Miss Stickley, come in here please." There must have been an edge to his voice, because Kelly burst into the room his revolver drawn and at the ready. Both men jumped, the pear flipping out of Enoch's hand and rolling across the carpet and under the desk.

"Everything all right in here?" Kelly felt the heat rising in his face as he stood before the two seated men.

"Hell's bells, Kelly, it's you again. What are you workin' on a hat trick of dumb-assedness? Third time's the charm, Kelly, one more screw-up and you'll be pulling the graveyard shift for the rest of your. . .dull... dimwitted . . . life. NOW, GET OUT OF HERE AND DON'T COME BACK 'TIL I CALL FOR YOU." While Vann vented his displeasure, Enoch got down on his hands and knees to retrieve the pear. By the time he was back in his seat, Kelly was gone and the mercurial Vann was smiling at him benignly. "Miss Stickley? Miss Stickley, could you come in here, please? Alone."

The woman came into the room and stood behind Enoch facing Vann. "Yes, sir?"

"Miss Stickley, would you please bring us a couple of mugs of your excellent coffee, black, if you will." Vann's secretary stood there with arched eyebrows in mild surprise. Vann nodded to her and she left. She returned in short order with two steaming mugs of coffee.

Enoch cupped his hands around the mug, blew across the top and sipped. Vann didn't touch his. The steam danced and swirled in the sunlight. He looked at Enoch and his eyes and voice hardened. "Knock-knock, you're in a lotta trouble, a whole lot of trouble."

"But, but, suh, I didn't . . ."

"Boy, you here to argue? I already told you once I ain't arguing today, your job is to shut-up and listen. That's it, boy, shut up and listen. You understand what I'm sayin'?"

"Yes."

"Good, now listen, you got to tell me the truth. Jus' go ahead and tell me you did it. Because we know you did. Believe you me, it'll go a lot easier on you if you just go ahead and tell me you did it. You understand, boy?"

"Yes, suh, I do."

"So, are you saying you did it, you raped that white girl Norma Gabriel?"

"No suh, I meant I understands, that's all I mean."

"Now lookee here, Knock-knock, we have proof you did it, we have your knife, we have sheets and clothes with, uh, body fluids on it, we got some other things. Any jury in the country, white or nigra is going to convict you of rape, you know that, don't you?" Enoch sat looking at Vann without answering. Vann continued, "And another thing, boy, you and I both know you don't got the money to hire a mouthpiece, you can't afford a lawyer, boy, you're as good as fried already, you know that?" Enoch sat mute. Vann continued his harangue working into the pitch and rhythm of a Pentecostal preacher. "Of course, it could go the other way, the way it went with that colored fella a couple of years ago. You remember that, don't you? County boys took him out and strung him up. People are gettin' up about this Knock-knock, raping a niggress, that's one thing, but raping a married white woman, well, that's a whole different kettle of fish. Now, I don't want that to happen to you, we go back, we do. Now, if you jus' go ahead and tell me you did it, I can promise those county boys won't get a hold of you. I give you my solid gold word on that Knock-knock. I surely do. You don't want to get strung up do you?"

"No suh, I don't, I don't want to go to no 'lectric chair neither."

"Well, that's just what I mean, you play ball with me and you won't get the chair." Vann stood and walked to large wooden bookshelf and lifted one of its glass doors. "You know what these books are Knock-knock?"

"Books 'bout law I suppose."

"That's right, these books here have all the laws of the Commonwealth of Virginia written in them. Let me show you somethin' here." Here took one of the cream colored volumes from the shelf and opened it to a page marked by a ribbon. " Here read this to me, read what it says, this is the law, boy." Vann handed the open book to Enoch.

Just as quickly Enoch handed it back to him, "Suh, I'm not too good at readin', maybe you should jus' go ahead and read it to me."

"All right then, I will." And with an officious courtroom voice Vann began reading paragraph after paragraph, pacing back and forth across the carpeted floor with Shakespearean deliberation. The effect was not lost on Enoch, who understood virtually none of the verbiage; but with each Latin phrase, twist of syntax and turn of circular logic his plight became more clear to him. "Knock-knock, you understand what this says?"

"Uh, yes, suh, I think so."

"Well, then, boy, why don't you go ahead and put it in your own words and tell me what it says."

Enoch took a deep pull on his tepid coffee. "Suh, maybe it'd jus' be better if you told me what it says in your words. I might get a little confused."

"I thought so. Well, it says that if you're found guilty of rape the penalty is death. In the Commonwealth of Virginia, that means death by electric chair. You ever seen somebody electrocuted Knock-knock? It's not a pretty sight, not pretty at all." Enoch wiped the beads of sweat from his upper lip and his left leg began bobbing up and down as if he imagined the current coursing through his body. "But you know what else it says? It says here, that the judge, at his discretion, that is, if he's so inclined, can change the sentence to prison time. A long, long stretch of prison time, but that beats being electrocuted by the state or strung up by the white folks of New Surrey by a long shot, don't it?"

Enoch stared ahead blankly, his leg bouncing in palsied frenzy and his torso beginning to sway back and forth like a temple monk in prayer. "I said, it beats it by a long shot, don't it?" Enoch's gyrations halted for a second as he slowly nodded in affirmation.

Vann sat back down at his desk, rolled his chair back and opened the wide center drawer. He withdrew a several sheets of paper and slid them to the center of the desk. Next he removed a fountain pen from his shirt pocket, unscrewed its cap and placed it across the bottom of the paper. "Now Enoch, I'm only gonna say this one more time. If you tell me you did it, you attacked and raped that girl, and sign this here piece of paper, I'll make sure you get, not one, but two attorneys, lawyers, appointed to defend you in court. I'll also make sure you don't get thrown to an angry mob for a lynching, and, most important of all, I'll speak to the judge for you and tell him not to give you the electric chair because you cooperated with an officer of the court. We won't need to bother puttin' you in front of a jury, cause we know what they'll do, so this paper also says you want to be tried by the judge, not a jury." The little man picked up the pen in his pink hand and held it out to Enoch.

Enoch sat back, drained the last of his coffee and quietly spoke. "No disrespect Mr. Vann, but I believe I'd like my mama and the Reverend Crenshaw to read that paper afore I sign it."

"No disrespect to your mother or to Reverend Crenshaw, but we don't have the time for that, and besides it's too dangerous for them to come here, we tryin' not to let the good citizens of New Surrey and the county know where you're being held, you know, jus' in case. I'm thinking of your safety boy, I truly am. Now, this here's a one time deal, you sign it now, or you take your chances, it's up to you, you know I didn't have to bring you here to my office, but we go way back, Knock-knock, we surely do."

Enoch studied the paper and pen on the desk and then looked into Vann's eyes. In that instant the full weight of his circumstance collapsed upon him and he began to sob. A forlorn and inconsolable weeping, he repeatedly wiped the tears and mucous from his face, trying to dry his hands on the front of his shirt, his shoulders heaved and he rolled forward trying to place his head between his knees to compose himself.

Vann sat silently, trying in vain to appear sympathetic and not self congratulatory.

Watching Enoch wiping his eyes and nose, he discreetly replaced his fountain pen in his pocket, opened the drawer and from it placed a pencil across the document.

If Enoch noticed the switch he did not acknowledge it, he picked up the pencil, and as tears streamed down his face he laboriously signed his full name to the document and set the pencil down.

"You did the right thing boy, the smart thing, surely you did."

Enoch stared past Vann, looking out of the window, he watched the light change, clouds were passing in front of the sun.

"Miss Stickley, you can inform the officers we're through here and they can return the prisoner to his cell." Two of the officers entered the room, each taking one of Enoch's arms and lead him out. Through the closed door, Vann could hear the shackles being put back on Enoch and he smiled ever so slightly. With his thumb and index finger he gingerly picked up the pencil by its end and dropped it into the wastepaper basket.

He called out, "Miss Stickley, could you come in here please?"

As his secretary stepped into his office, he was wiping his hands with a handkerchief. He pointed to the coffee mug that Enoch had drained, "Throw that away, will ya?" She picked it up and left the room.

CHAPTER 23

Good
Old Boys

"**W**ell, Newt, you did it again. You cleaned my clock, don't have a penny left to my name." Jack Cheever sighed, relighting the thick remains of his King Edward cigar.

"Yeah, well, that's a first. You must be the only banker in Virginia without a red cent to your name. It grieves me, Jack, truly. Ever notice how bankers are always the first ones to cry poor mouth? Ain't that the truth, boys?" Newton Vann chuckled as he raked silver coins into a mountainous pile on the green surfaced gaming table, a shining island on the deep green sea.

"Ever notice how lawyers are always asking if something's the truth? Know why? It's 'cause they have such a hard time recognizing it. The truth's not in 'em." Jack said mock-punching Newt in the arm. They all had a good laugh at the Commonwealth attorney's expense.

Vann let his glasses slide down his nose and glowered at the banker. "Jack, you still have that stack of unpaid parking tickets? Maybe our most esteemed Chief of Police sittin' right here might like to hear about that."

"Aw hell, Newt, you got at least as many as Jack does, maybe more. Fact is, I'm thinking of launching an investigation, it's been reported that a prominent lawyer in town is running a gamblin' parlor." Hiram Delaney, still in his disheveled work clothes, tapped his gold badge for emphasis.

It was, without a doubt, the finest gambling parlor in town. During the warm months Newt held the Friday night poker games on his sizable

Baker Moved to Another Jail

Chief of Police H. Delaney announced this morning that Enoch Baker, 26, colored, charged with rape, has been removed from the jail here and incarcerated elsewhere for safe keeping.

Police would not disclose where he was being held. He was removed from the jail here yesterday evening. No official reason was given by officers for his removal. But it is supposed that the action was taken to forestall any possible demonstration.

Baker, who played on a colored football team here some seasons ago is awaiting trial charged with the attack of a young married woman whose husband is in the army.

Police stated that the only person Baker had asked to see was his mother.

---

screened-in porch, where light breezes periodically cooled the men and cleared the fog bank of tobacco smoke. A Tiffany lamp was elegantly suspended over a round, green baize-covered table that occupied the center of the porch. Bottles of beer lounged on and against an oversized block of ice in a galvanized washtub while bottles of excellent bourbon, decent scotch and modest gin rested on a teacart. With its cut-crystal whiskey tumblers, tall pilsner glasses and brimming ice bucket, Newt's veranda compared favorably with any New York, Richmond or for that matter, London, private club.

Once the evenings turned cool, the Friday night poker ritual would move to the barroom in Vann's basement, a less comfortable, but no less well appointed gentlemen's preserve. The five friends had been playing poker almost every week for more than twenty years. Yes, indeed, the finest gambling parlor in town.

Pat Whitney was the next to push away from the table. Draining the last of his bourbon and branch, he stood unsteadily. The high school principal slurred his words slightly. "Home again, home again, jiggety-jig. Well, another fine evening of fun and fellowship, my hearties. As always, thanks Newt for the excellent hospitality, although one must suspect you turn a tidy profit at it, you lucky S.O.B., even so, I'm still going home with a few bucks in my pocket. In spite of you, my friend."

Max Goodwin, the Commissioner of Revenue stood along with the others. "All I can say to you two smart-alecks is I hope you plan on reporting those ill-gotten gains on your tax forms." This began another round of guffaws and back slapping as the men made their way to the screened door. Suicidal moths strafed the porch light, Newt's dog, Mr. Hoover, began barking and stars watched indifferently as another Friday night drew to a close.

Vann sidled next to Hiram Delaney and mumbled into his ear. The Chief backed away from the door, sat heavily into a deep cushioned rattan chair and waved to Jack, Pat and Max as they left. "Y'all be careful driving home boys, don't want to see any of you in the drunk tank tomorrow."

As the three men disappeared down the dimly lit brick walk, Newt pulled the other cushioned chair next to Hiram. "Thanks for staying, another scotch and soda?"

"Sure, why not, I never turn down good scotch, especially, free good scotch."

"Why, Hiram, I'm surprised at you, don't you know nothing's free in this here life?" Newt unfurled his winning smile like a battle standard.

"I do know that. How's about I just go ahead and give you a sawbuck for tonight's booze?" The chief grinned with mirthless eyes.

"That won't be necessary, chief. I believe you're trying to break my poor tender heart with a comment like that."

"You'd have to have a heart for that to happen, Newt."

"I suppose you're right. Anyway, I expect you heard I got that colored boy to sign a confession today, or at least make his mark, you know, X marks the spot." Newt poured two fingers of scotch into fresh glasses and sprayed soda water from a silver topped bottle.

"Well, then, I guess that's all she wrote for ol' Knock-knock Baker. It's a crying shame all around, I've known that boy all his life, hell, I used to have him shine my brogans back in the day. Always thought he was a good egg. You know, I got it on the Q.T. that there 's a little more to this here story than meets the eye."

"Do tell, Chief, do tell." Newt answered as he rose and walked over to his seersucker jacket hanging on a chair. He fished into its inner pocket and brought out a long leather cigar case, then sat back down. He flipped it open and held it out to Hiram. "Try one of these, it's a Romeo y Julieta Presidente, it's not every day you get to smoke one of these dusky beauties, no indeed. You were saying?"

"Don't mind if I do. Can't help but notice you don't pass these around the poker table."

"No sir, not at five dollars a pop, I don't."

"Good God Newt, a five dollar cigar? Now you got me really worried. A five-dollar cigar? That's just burning money ain't it? What are you buttering me up for?

"I would burn money if it was as smooth and sweet as fine Cuban tobacco. You know what they say about these cigars?"

"What's that?"

"They're so smooth because they're hand rolled on the thighs of virgins."

Hiram let loose a laugh as he clipped off the end of the cigar. "I like that, I'll have to remember that one."

"Enjoy it chief, a good cigar, good whiskey and a cool breeze, doesn't get much better than this, does it? Now tell me, what do you know about this black rapist son-of-a-bitch that I don't already know about?"

"The operative word here is rapist." Delaney lit his Presidente, slowly rolling it over the match flame so that it would light and burn evenly; the cigar smoker's sacrament. He then allowed the smoke to slowly billow out of his open mouth and blew some into his glass of whiskey.

"How's that?" Newt moved to the edge of his chair.

"I've heard from more than one person that, well, he didn't exactly 'force' himself on her."

"What are you trying to say, Hi?"

"No tryin' about it. I'm sayin', that rumor has it: Norma may have been carrying on with Knock-knock." Delaney's face was stone still as his cheeks became florid.

"That's ridiculous. Who told you that? Not that it matters a goddamn. He's signed a confession, so, as you so aptly put it, 'that's all she wrote.'"

"I know, I know. But I just thought you might want to know what some people are saying around town." Delaney drew on the cigar, tilted his head back and exhaled thick smoke into the porch's cross breeze.

"You think there's anything to it?"

"Well, you know, 'where there's smoke there's fire." Delaney released another tobacco thunderhead into the air and blew it away with a second breath, impressed with his own wit.

"Maybe so, and that gives all the more impetus to what I wanted to chat with you about."

"Oh Lord, here it comes, you sure I can't just go ahead and pay you for the scotch and cigar?"

Vann ignored the chief's comment. " Chief, I'm not going to beat around the bush here. Man to man, I believe it will be in everyone's best interest to move that nigger to a different jail."

"Really? Why's that, Newt?" Hiram asked suspecting he already knew the answers and that he was giving the seasoned courtroom attorney free reign.

"First of all, to keep that Negro boy safe, hell, a lynch mob could be whipped up in two shakes of a lamb's tail."

"C'mon counselor, remember who you're talking to. That would take a little discreet help from the Dispatch news desk and a little seed money and hootch to the local rabble-rousers."

"Well, it's been known to happen, there are, of course, other considerations."

"Go on."

Vann leaned back into the chair, uncrossed and re-crossed his legs and sipped his scotch and soda. "Look we both know this case is a done deal, what with a signed confession and all. It always comes back to that, it's like money in the bank. But here's the thing, this is the kind of case that can get good press coverage, Washington, Richmond, Baltimore, to name a few, hell, maybe even New York and Chicago."

"I think I now where your going with this, but go ahead anyway."

"Well, let's face it, Hi, winning a case with a little higher profile looks awfully good on the old resume. It may come as a surprise to you, but I might not want to spend my entire career here in New Surrey, it's been what you might call a great steppin' stone. And after twenty plus years here, I'm getting ready for a little change of scenery"

"Doesn't surprise me."

"Then of course, there's Judge Colson. I may be talkin' out of school here, but I hear-tell that the Judge plans on running for Congress."

"State or federal?"

"Federal."

"Oh, I see." Delaney shifted uncomfortably in his chair. "So I guess a case with a little higher profile would do the Judge some good as well."

"No moss growin' on you. No siree."

"Yeah, well, a man needs to know which side his bread is buttered on." The Chief conceded.

"Well said, my friend, well said. I took the liberty of calling Chief Stinson down in Harmonsville to begin making the arrangements, he owes me a favor or two."

"You did what?" Delaney's voice hardened and his eyes grew sharp. "You arrogant, self-inflated son-of-a-bitch, you've stepped over the line, Newt. Don't you think you might have asked me first? I'm the fucking Chief of Police, and Knock-knock Baker is my fucking prisoner."

"Whoa, whoa, whoa, Hi, no disrespect meant, no disrespect at all. It's just that time is of the essence here, and I wanted to expedite things, that's all. I had a marker I could call in, so I was trying to make your job easier, plain and simple."

"Bullshit, you rationalize it, justify it, and twist and turn it anyway you want, but you stepped way out of bounds here." Delaney drained his glass and sat back in his chair. "And I promise you Newt, if you ever try something like this again I'll make your life so miserable you'll wish you had never heard of New Surrey."

"You're right Chief, you're right, absolutely one hundred and fifty percent right. But hell, you know how things work; now I owe you. I owe you in a big way, and it never hurts to have a little leverage, never hurts at all. And of course, I'll let the Judge know what a big help you've been in this here matter."

"And I suppose that keeping that boy hidden away somewhere will make it all that much harder for anybody to question that signed confession. It'll also make it harder for anyone who believes it was consensual sex to raise any questions."

Newt extracted a white handkerchief out his pocket and wiped his brow. "Well, you yourself said it's a rumor. If it started in the colored community, well, then, who gives a damn? You know sure as I'm sittin' here they sure as hell aren't going to stir up some Jim Crowe wasp's nest of trouble. And if any white people believe it, well, you know what'll happen then . . ." Vann continued, twisting his voice into a high pitched parody of Southern womanhood, "Why yes, Betty-Jo, I heard about those two carryin' on for months . . . But you know, it's really . . . none . . . of . . . . my . . . business." Newt's voice returned to normal, "Not to worry Chief, I've seen it happen time and time again and it'll happen here as well. Besides, people have mighty short memories."

Chief Delaney stood; firmly planted his quarter smoked Presidente firmly between his lips and wordlessly turned to leave.

"Chief?" Newt asked, standing as well.

Delaney walked to the screen door, place his hand on the brass handle and turned, "It'll be taken care of. I'll call Stinson in the morning and arrange transport for the prisoner by three p.m."

"Thanks Hi, I appreciate it, I surely do, and I know for-a-fact Judge Colson appreciates it too." Vann grinned widely and proffered Delaney his right hand.

Hiram Delaney ignored the hand, twisted the brass door handle and stepped into the night. He began walking down the bricked path, but after four steps paused and turned. "Newt, I don't think I'll be back for Poker." He turned and again began walking away.

Newton Vann in a practiced hail-fellow voice called out, "Now Chief, don't be that way, no hard feelin's, y'hear? You'll be back." Newt took a puff of his cigar; the tip glowed bright in the lowlight of the porch steps. "You'll be back, I've seen it happen time and time again."

CHAPTER 24

Angel
Moses

Enoch's mind had become a hornet's nest. Malevolent thoughts buzzed through his waking hours with little reprieve. The deep rasping and malignant humming of several thoughts over and over, only increasing and decreasing in volume as they approached and retreated. Some would sting him repeatedly causing actual physical pain, thoughts of his mother, his innocence, a life gone unfulfilled. Other thoughts would use their sharp mandibles to chew away at any remnant of hope or peace of mind. Chewing them into so much paper for the expansion of the nest. As each hour passed, there was less Enoch Baker and more of a dangerous cacophony of disconnected thoughts. Enoch was letting go, one by one of the things that kept him anchored to life and reality.

I need to get to sleep, need to get to sleep, only peace I got, only quiet I get, help me Angel Moses, help me dream, got to dream, got to dream, got to dream, got to fly, got to dream, got to fly, got to dream, got to fly. Help me Angel Moses.

Surprisingly, in his sleep, just when one would expect the hornets to be more hideous than ever, they disappeared. It was because Enoch had been able to manipulate dreams since childhood; Angel Moses had taught him. He thought of her often in recent days.

Angel Moses was well into her nineties when Enoch was a boy. Her skin was paper-thin; her hands and throat a lesson in anatomy. Her white hair was pulled back tightly and tied with a piece of string. Her face was tan and crisscrossed by a crackle of fine lines like the cover of an ancient

Baker Enters Guilty Plea

B U L L E T I N

Enoch Baker entered a plea of guilty when arraigned at 3:30 o'clock this afternoon on a criminal attack charge, before Judge Byron T. Colson, in Corporation Court.

At the request of attorneys for the accused, Tuesday, June 26 was set to hear testimony of Mrs. Norma Gabriel, victim of the alleged attack, would be heard in closed court, other testimony in open court.

The crime carries a maximum penalty of death in the electric chair.

Enoch Baker, 26-year-old colored man accused of rape was expected to be arraigned about 3:30 this afternoon.

Baker, charged with the criminal attack on a young married woman here on the night of June 13, waived a hearing before the grand jury after the case had been sent to that body by Police Justice R. Jan Flagler.

Baker was taken into custody on June 13 at the American Synthetic Fiber plant near Riverton where he was employed.

Pending his arraignment he was transferred from the jail here to one at Harmonsville last week.

The decision to arraign Baker late this afternoon came as a surprise and with hardly anyone aware of what was taking place.

To Hear Evidence In Enoch Baker Case Saturday

PRISONER APPEARED COMPOSED AT HIS ARRAIGNMENT YESTERDAY

Judge Byron T. Colson will hear testimony in Corporation Court in the Baker case on Saturday afternoon instead of next Tuesday as first decided.

Following the arraignment yesterday at which time Baker pled guilty to the charge of criminal assault force and arms. It was ordered that the court "shall proceed to hear evidence relating to the circumstances on Saturday June 23, 1945, at 1 o'clock."

The prisoner appeared unmoved yesterday when arraigned before Judge Colson in Corporation Court.

Attired in a gray pencil striped suit he sat in a chair flanked by his attorneys, R. J. Harrington and Ernest Oakes. He wore a striped shirt without a necktie; his shoes had been white ones, now dyed black.

He sat facing the Judge turning his head neither to the right or left, but his eyes looked up to the judge's bench from time to time.

He stood, his hands folded in front of him without any noticeable emotion on his face as City Clerk Sam Burns read off the charges of criminal assault by force and armed.

Asked what his plea was he answered "Guilty." His words were audible to the few who were in the court room at the time.

Remanded to jail, City Sergeant Lester Jones snapped handcuffs on the prisoner.

Baker is the son of Melissa Baker of 17 West Ogden Street. He has always lived in the city holding various odd jobs about New Surrey before his employment at the American Synthetic Fibers plant, Riverton. Several seasons ago he was a member of a local colored football team. He is 26 years of age.

The city sergeant said that Baker would be held elsewhere until his trial.

book. Her teeth were still strong, her eyes had gray circles edging her black irises. She always wore the same faded blue housedress, a stained gray cardigan and men's shoes. Her voice was low and calm as if it could quiet a storm.

She had spent the first third of her life as a slave on a tobacco plantation in Tidewater Virginia. After the war, she came north to New Surrey at the behest of a long dead sister. She married Aaron Moses, partly because he was handsome and treated her kindly and partly because he had a job with the railroad and would always be able to put food on the table. He worked for the railroad for fifty-five years. She buried him two weeks after he received a gold pocket-watch and a small pension. She made do selling potions and tinctures and treating sick children and animals for people who didn't trust doctors and hospitals.

She had been a healer and a visionary. Angel knew about plants and animals, could charm bees and understood the unseen world of dreams. Many of the adults in New Surrey's colored community feared her or appraised her with a skeptical eye. Not so the children. They loved her, her stories, her endless wealth of knowledge, her magic.

The children came to her singly, in pairs or in groups of threes and fours. They would bring her biscuits, baskets of fruit and vegetables, fried chicken, eggs, cast off clothing and twice repaired shoes. Anything the kinder families of New Surrey could spare. Once there, the children would stay as long as possible. There would be stories, often Angel would teach them about the medicinal plants in her garden, how to talk to animals, and when available, give them a spoonful of honey, honey that tasted especially good because she had charmed it from the bees. Best of all, they loved when she would interpret their dreams. Whenever she did this she would also teach them some small facet of the dream world.

The first time Enoch heard her explain that it was possible to fly in dreams, he was captivated by the idea. Not only could one fly in dreams, but the dreamer could control flight, like a crow, or a nighthawk, or like one of those aero planes out on Stockton's field. Enoch listened closely to her instruction and began practicing immediately, and from then on, each time he saw her he asked about dream flying. It took Enoch years of practice and concentration, repeating a mantra before falling asleep so that his subconscious would be pliable.

This was how Enoch Baker was able to escape as he lay on his cell bunk. During the past week of madness he had determined that perhaps there were other ways to manipulate his subconscious, perhaps there was some way to meld the real world with the dream world. If only he could speak with Angel Moses one more time, even for just five minutes. It took incredible focus and concentration, far beyond that of dream flying. He could only do it when there was some kind of distraction that kept his waking mind occupied and thus fending off his tormentors.

In those moments he was able to step out of his body and observe himself and his surroundings like watching a motion picture show. He tried it as he sat dressed in an old suit waiting to be taken to court, but to no avail. The guards shackling him and leading him out to the back lot where a paddy wagon awaited broke his concentration.

"Get in there boy, and don't even think of causing any trouble, y'hear?" Enoch climbed into the back of the police van without saying a word. The door closed and he was seated opposite a uniformed man holding a shotgun. Dim light filtered into the space, dust motes careened along unseen paths of wind as the van drove off.

"Enoch, I'm going to go ahead and remove those cuffs and shackles. You've never given me a lick of trouble, so please don't think about it now, cause I'll shoot you, I swear I will." Mike O'Toole had spent more time with Enoch than any other officer in Harmonsville jail. It was not in his nature to be unnecessarily cruel. He believed the prisoners were better behaved when treated with a little respect and consideration. Generally he was right. Mike was the exception, not the rule.

Enoch nodded to O'toole in appreciation as the chains clattered to the floor. Once loosened, he bent forward and rested his head in his hands, trying to focus and concentrate. Soon he was free.

Look at your sorry ass, boy, bet you wish you could walk around with me. O'Toole is keepin' a good watch on you, he keeps fingerin' the safety on the sawed off shotgun of his. I never knew how bad that suit looks on us, and those piss poor shoes painted black. Enoch studied the inside of the van closely, even peering through the small window at the driver in the cab.

The hour-long ride did not provide much in the way of distraction and Enoch was pulled back into himself almost before he started. For the rest of the ride the hornets harassed him mercilessly.

Shortly before his arrival in New Surrey, the guard set his shotgun aside and put Enoch back in chains. Once at the courthouse he was placed into a small room with his guard and told to wait. Again he tried to focus and wander out of body, but again there were not enough distractions to quiet his thoughts. The hornets buzzed.

After what seemed like hours, he was taken into court. He shuffled down the left aisle of the courtroom. Except for the metallic clink of his chains and the sound of his shoes skidding along the wooden floor the room was silent. He was lead through the small gate in the wooden balustrade that separated the players from the audience. He was seated at a table flanked by Mr. Oakes and Mr. Harrington, and as the judge, lawyers and court officers began to confer he closed his eyes.

He hovered in the air and watched the proceedings from above. He saw himself staring straight ahead, looking, but not seeing. He watched the Judge and the other men around him remove their glasses, replace them, remove them again, scribble notes and talk to one another in low murmurs. He looked out into the courtroom. There were only a handful of people present, none of which he recognized. In the front row a bald man in a white linen suit was scribbling furiously in a notepad. After a moment he was drawn back to the front of the court. A tall man dressed in a brown serge suit and sporting a bowtie stood and shuffled some papers in his hands. He began to speak and he watched himself turn his head towards the man, and expression of otherworldly indifference on his face.

"Enoch Franklin Baker, you are charged with criminal assault with force, you are also charged with armed criminal assault. How do you plead?"

He watched as his body was nudged to stand by his attorneys. He faced the Clerk of the Court and answered in a clear monotone.

"Guilty."

He watched the corporeal Enoch continue to stand there with a blank look on his face as the Judge announced he would be remanded back to jail. His ethereal self followed at a small distance as the escorted prisoner shuffled down the middle aisle of the courtroom. As the shackled man left the room, Enoch looked down at two men sitting on the aisle near the double doors, they were veteran court watchers.

"You ever see anybody cool as a cucumber like that after being charged with rape?"

"Cool as a cucumber nothing, he's just plain cold-blooded. That nigger is guilty as sin."

"You can say that again."

CHAPTER 25

Legal
Treachery

Newton P. Vann was drawn to blood sports. He hunted and fished with near religious fervor. But his lust for blood ran further afield. The summer before entering law school at the University of Virginia, his father sent him abroad. After a single summer's evening in Seville at the Maestranza an avid devotee of the matador's cape and sword was born; a lifelong *corrida de toros*. He's followed the sport and pageantry ever since.

He is also drawn to the cockpit, but his high profile and reputation precludes him from indulging in local cockfighting. Vann, however, takes the moral high ground with regards to dog fighting, bear baiting and bull baiting, his utter love and devotion to dog flesh trumping his intrigue with blood sports.

The great irony in all of this was that he was denied the opportunity to participate in the definitive blood sport. During the Great War, while doughboys went over the top and fought hand-to-hand using rifle butts and entrenching tools, Vann sat at a desk requisitioning grain and fodder at the remount station in Front Royal, Virginia. Thanks to the auspices of his influential father he found himself searching for another outlet and settled upon the next best thing to combat, the penultimate blood sport, he became a prosecuting attorney for the Commonwealth of Virginia. It is a vocation that helps to satisfy his gladiatorial needs.

Every bullring, every cockpit, every coliseum, every courtroom has and requires its spectators. Some few are there to see the artistry, the talent and finesse of the combatants, their strength, courage and bravery, but most are there to see blood, in one form or another. But this was not true in the balcony where the spectators watched with sympathy and fear. Their concern was for the prey. They were the colored community of New Surrey.

The courtroom was filled to capacity, raising the ambient temperature by another ten to fifteen degrees. The obsolete belt-driven ceiling fans were not up to the task, their long wooden paddles thrashing the air uselessly. In gray hats and uniforms, Virginia State Police were posted liberally around the room and outside it, looking bored, their presence adding to the spectacle. An occasional individual word or phrase would rise above the susurrus hovering in the room, particularly when there was some change or addition to the cast of characters inhabiting the front of the court. The downstairs crowd was mostly male and all adult. It was a cross-section of New Surrey and the surrounding counties' population. Dressed in suits and overalls, house dresses and church-going finery, they sat, perspiring and whispering, gossiping and speculating, men and women alike. In the balcony, women outnumbered men, church clothes were more common than work clothes and the atmosphere was considerably more quiet. Except for prayer, they were all but helpless, three hundred years of subjugation bearing down on them more oppressive than the heat.

Shortly before one o'clock, before the principals arrived, Sam Burns, Clerk of the Court surveyed the courtroom as he always did before legal proceedings. He was a bit surprised to see a packed house, especially since this was a done deal. A guilty plea, a signed confession, "wham, bam, thank you ma'am, should be all over but the shouting" before it starts.

This bunch is here to see the sentencing, to see if Ol' Knock-knock, uh, Enoch, will faint, or shriek and cry, or piss-his-pants, or if his mother and sister will. They'll be disappointed if he just sags with relief one way or the other. Look at this place. Sharks and buzzards, the lot of 'em, circling for some poor nigger boy who's got whatever good sense he might have had scared out of him. 'Wonder if those stories are true? My Daddy used to say they all wanted a white one on the side. Look at those troopers, Colson and Vann got a full heada steam goin' on this one. Judge even asked the bailiff to make sure there were plenty of seats for the press. Shit.

BAKER DOOMED TO DEATH CHAIR

Confessed Man Sentenced at Hearing Before Judge; August 10 is Fateful Date

COLSON HEARS TESTIMONY OF ACCUSER IN CLOSED SESSION— ACCUSED OFFERS NO EVIDENCE—APPEARS SHAKEN

Enoch Franklin Baker, who became 27 years of age last month, was sentenced by Judge Byron T. Colson at 1:45 o'clock this afternoon to pay with his life for the crime of criminal assault by force and armed committed against Mrs. Norma Gabriel on the night of June 13, 1945.

Ordering the prisoner to be remanded to the state penitentiary in Richmond, Judge Colson fixed Friday, August 10, as the date for Baker to be electrocuted. Before passing sentence the judge announced that he would tolerate no demonstration of approval or disapproval from the spectators, warning that any such offenders would be subject to heavy imprisonment and fine.

Over in 45 Minutes

Just 45 minutes after the court had opened, Judge Colson called the prisoner to face the bar. Asking him if he had anything to say in his behalf, he shook his head. Baker's words were not audible to the first row of spectators. The judge then declared that in accordance with his plea of guilty and in evidence of his guilt, he was guilty of rape and passed the death sentence. Ernest Oakes in pleading the prisoner's case before the judge, sought mercy on the grounds that Baker had voluntarily confessed, waived grand jury hearing and had plead guilty when arraigned, saving his victim the added embarrassment of a public trial. He also sought leniency on the grounds that the commonwealth's attorney had not demanded the death sentence.

Extra Officers Present

Starting promptly at 1 o'clock Baker was ushered into a packed courtroom. He was between two state officers and there were a dozen or more others stationed at every exit and in the corridors of the Rourke City Hall. Baker, dressed in the same gray suit that he wore when arraigned earlier in the week appeared more nervous than on his last appearance. He wore a white shirt, a bow tie, and brown slippers. He sat in the same chair; his face, the muscles of which twitched from time to time, was sunk in the palm of his left hand. He showed no other outward sign of emotion.

Dr. Mallone Testified

Mayor T. C. Mallone who attended Mrs. Gabriel, was called first. Questioned by Mr. Vann, he stated that he had been called to the home and and had made an examination. He also stated that he had taken young woman to the hospital where further laboratory tests were made. Dr. Mallone said that he could not ascertain whether or not due to precautionary measures which the victim had immediately taken. He said she was not physically injured.The attorney for the defense waived any questions.

Sgt. Elam on Stand

Sgt. Frances Elam of the city police force was called next. He was questioned by Mr. Vann concerning a confession which Baker had signed. Identified by Sgt. Elam as the confession which the prisoner had signed in

the presence, along with the Commonwealth Attorney and a stenographer, was offered as evidence. Again the defense waived any questions. The Commonwealth Attorney then called for the evidence of Mrs Gabriel. The judge and the parties involved retired to the Judge's chambers at 1:10 where this was given in private.

The Judge returned to the court room at approximately 1:30. The prisoner appeared to stumble slightly as he walked back to his chair. He slumped back in his same position looking at the floor. His legs were crossed He brought his hand back to his face again as if to steady it.

Mr. Vann's Address

The Commonwealth's Attorney, all evidence apparently completed in the closed chambers, then addressed the Judge.

He stated that he left the matter of the sentence in the Judge's hand well aware of the import and with the hope that he would not be called upon again to pass sentence in such a case.

Mr. Vann stated that the city officials were appreciative of the cooperation and attitude which citizens had taken in the matter, showing that they had confidence in the justice of the court.

He also praised the attitude of Mrs. Gabriel, which enabled the officers to solve the problem. He gave credit too, to the police force.

(Continued on Page 2. Col. 7)

208

Baker Doomed To Death Chair *(Continued from Page 1.)*

He made no recommendation for punishment, stating that he left that entirely to the court. He said the man had made a confession also pleading guilty of the crime.

Attorney R. J. Harrington assisting Oakes in defending the prisoner requested that Mr. Vann explain what brought about the confession of the prisoner. Mr. Vann said that the prisoner, who had been on the defensive when first brought to his office, finally hung his head and said: "Yes I did it."

A large crowd filed into the court room at 1 o'clock this after noon awaiting the judge's decision. The court room was filled to capacity and many people had to remain in the hall outside. Before time for the case to start, officers cleared the room of all minors.

There seemed to be quite a definite feeling of tenseness as the people sat waiting for the case to begin. Most of the spectators were men and there were only 10 or 15 women present. When the prisoner was brought into court, he appeared nervous but not giving vent to his emotions. He appeared to be sleepy. While Dr. Mallone was giving his testimony, he sat very still twiddling his thumbs.

When Judge Colson stated that he sentenced the prisoner to death in the electric chair Baker's body quivered and beads of perspiration broke out on his forehead. He was twitching his hands but did not break down. The spectators were asked to remain seated while the prisoner left the court room. When it was announced that everyone could leave, one man in the audience said "Didn't I tell you?" in a rather loud tone of voice and

one of the officers on duty quickly seated him and told to remain quiet.

Baker was taken into custody in less than a day after his crime was committed and had admitted his guilt within thirty-six hours of when the alarm was first sounded.

The police were advised of what had occurred by Walter Wolfe, a neighbor to whose house Mrs. Gabriel went after the attack. Officers dispatched to the scene were given an account of what happened, along with a description of the assailant.

Description Was Helpful

The man was described as weighing 155 to 165 pounds. His age was estimated at about 25, and police were advised of the color of the clothes he wore. Mrs. Gabriel said the man wore a mask, but she was able to tell officers the color of his eyes.

Mrs. Gabriel was said to have cleaned and burned trash in the back yard of her mother-in-law's home on Pritchard Street until about dusk on the night of the attack.

She was alone in the house upstairs washing out some linens in the bathroom about 8:45 when the front door opened, but didn't feel alarmed thinking it was a girlfriend who often stopped by entered without knocking.

No Time To Give Alarm

She became suspicious when a pet cat "Spunky" started to mew strangely, and when Mrs. Gabriel opened the bathroom door police state she was confronted by a Negro on the stairs.

It was said the attacker armed with a knife, sprang at her; placing the weapon at her throat. Threatening to kill her, and refusing to be moved by her

pleas or offer of money, he was said to have forced her into a near bedroom. Later she was able to push some bed clothes over the knife and he left without it.

Net About City

With the description and using all available officers, a net was quickly thrown about the city. A number of men answering the description were rounded-up, including one that the police had had complaints of for looking in windows. However, when Mrs. Gabriel appeared at the police station later in the night, accompanied by Dr. T.C. Mallone, police stated that she did not identify any of the men and they were released.

In checking in the city Tuesday night Baker was seen in the gallery of a city theatre.

The chief clue, in spite of the fact that the handle was taped and contained no fingerprints, was the knife with which the attacker was armed. It was a short unusual looking knife, small and with a hook on the end, and the next morning was identified by Officer Loy as being used for cutting fabric.

Knife Used At American Synthetic Fibers Plant

Loy, who had worked at the American Synthetic Fibers plant at Riverton, spotted it as a tool used there for working in fabric.

Aware that a number of New Surrey colored laborers were employed at the Riverton plant. Chief Delaney dispatched detectives to check there. As a result of the visit Baker was taken into custody and returned here.

Mrs. Gabriel was asked to return to police headquarters. Upon her arrival a handkerchief was tied around his face as the *(Continued on Page 3. Col. 1)*

Baker Doomed To Death Chair *(Continued from Page 2.)*

attacker was stated to have worn and he was confronted by Mrs. Gabriel. According to police she said he looked and talked like the man.

Confesses to Vann

He was questioned late into the night by Detectives Hopkins and Little of the New Surrey Police force., but it was not until about 10 o'clock Thursday morning that he confessed privately to Commonwealth's Attorney Newton P. Vann. He repeated his confession before Mr. Vann, his secretary and Sgt. Loy.

Enoch Franklin Baker, known as Knock-knock was born in the city on July 2 1918, and is the son of Melissa Baker, 17 W. Ogden Street.

He worked at various jobs about New Surrey before going to Riverton and several seasons ago was an outstanding member of a colored football team organized in the city and playing in the city and playing in the area.

Had Police Record

He has a police record, first coming to the attention of local police on March 15, 1933 on a disorderly conduct charge. This was dismissed, but two years later on March 19, 1935, he received 10 days for petty larceny. Two months later he drew several months on a similar charge.

His next notation on city police records was for disturbing the peace on February 14, 1939 for which he was fined.

In November 1942 he was sent to the grand jury along with three other colored men charged with assault with intent to maim or kill. The charges grew out of a cutting scrap at the colored recreation hall on E. Ogden Street. The case against Baker was finally dismissed.

Moved To Quick Finish

After his conference last Thursday morning to Mr. Vann, Baker was sent to the Grand Jury by Judge Jan Flagler. Later the same day, represented by Ernest Oakes and R. J. Harrington, Riverton, who were appointed by the court to defend him, he waived a grand jury and indictment.

Arraigned Tuesday in Corporation Court he pleaded guilty to the charges of criminal assault with force and armed, placing himself entirely upon the mercy of Judge Colson.

The court set this afternoon to hear the evidence from every angle.

What a damned circus, just to see a poor dumb black boy get his comeuppance. Yup, there's Frank and Maurice in their usual spot, most consistent damn court watchers we got here. Bet the bench over there is worn to the shape of their fat asses. Hey, boys. Sam nodded to them in response to their friendly hi sign.

"That Sam Burns, he's a right good fella' aint he?" Frank leaned into Maurice.

"Sure is, you know Dorcas had him in school, she thinks the world of him. Says he was always a helpful and responsible boy." Maurice beamed. "What'd you make of all them troopers? You think the there's gonna be trouble with the niggras?"

"Might be, just might be. But don't you worry none Maurice, any trouble, you just stay close to me. I don't go anywhere, 'specially a place like this without my little pistolo here." Frank patted his pants pocket.

"You know, I can't remember the last time we saw something like this, you know, a nigger and a white gal. Can you?" Maurice scratched his chin plying the depths of his memory.

"That's because we didn't. Don't you remember back in'38 when that colored fella was brought in for raping that Hollis girl?"

"Now that you mention it."

"And those Hollis and Atkins boys broke him out of jail the night before trial and strung him up."

"And doused his poor skinny ass with gasoline and lit him up afterwards." Maurice added.

"Just goes to show ya." Frank nodded in exaggerated solemnity.

"What's that?"

"You don't mess with them Hollis girls. Don't much matter if'n you're black or white."

"I know what you're thinkin' Frank. Who would? Right? Hell they're so ugly their mothers have to tie pork chop bones around their necks just to get the dog to play with them." Maurice chuckled, and Frank joined in.

The people around them turned to look at them, curious and disdainful; suddenly everyone's attention was drawn to the front of the court. The door to the right of the bench opened and the Bailiff, ramrod straight and in a deep officious voice boomed out.

"Oyez, Oyez, Oyez. All persons having business before the honorable, the Corporation Court of New Surrey are admonished to draw near and give their attention, for the court is now sitting. God save the United States and this honorable court. All rise."

When Judge Colson entered, his black robe fluttering, the entire courtroom rose as one body and sat when the Judge settled into his chair. As the Judge and the other men conferred, making last minute preparations and adjustments in low voices, the spectators continued to whisper. The murmuring came to an abrupt halt when the Judge spoke to the bailiff, who then signaled to the back of the court.

The door at the back left side of the court opened and Enoch, escorted by a State Trooper before and behind, entered the court.. He walked tall, but his head was bent forward and he was looking at the floor. Appearing to be in deep thought, it looked as if he were altogether somewhere else. Every set of eyes in the room was locked on the slow procession making its way forward. Every neck craned and turned with clockwork precision as they passed. The only sound was the soft beating of the loose leather belts turning a ceiling fans. There were a hundred emotions in the room distilled down to a communal sense of anticipation and tension, but the subtle nuances of all the other feelings were there as well. It hung thick in the humid air, and a thousand ceiling fans could not have blown it away. The air was redolent with something else, the smell of blood and fear. Newton P. Vann was in his element.

Off to the judge's left, in a single row of chairs, sat the cast of characters for the day's drama: Dr. Mallone, Norma Gabriel, Sgt. Elam, Walter Wolfe, Detective Little and Detective Hopkins, each sitting up attentive, with hands folded in their laps as if they were waiting to see the headmaster for a switching.

Enoch was made to stand while the charges were read and other legal formalities were dispensed with. For the first time since entering the court he turned his head to the right. For an instant his eyes locked with Norma's and in that instant a dozen questions, but no answers passed between them. As quickly, Norma looked down, her face flushed and her eyes welled with tears. Anyone quick enough to have observed this briefest of exchanges would have assumed she was filled with fear and loathing. They would have been wrong.

The first witness to be called was Dr. Mallone. He took the stand. Directly in front of him in the first row of spectators sat Marjorie Clemmons and Daisy Rodgers, friends since childhood. They brandished matching lacquered fans, with which they cooled themselves, coquettishly using them to hide comments and expressions, and to indicate various points of interest around the crowded venue. The two of them looked like they had just breezed in from an ice cream social. In fact, they were there on a whim, or more accurately, on a dare. They had egged each other into attending over gin and tonics one afternoon several days before. Having been discussing Norma and Knock-knock when the challenge arose.

Marjorie and Daisy found Dr. Mallone's testimony extremely interesting, different statements making them catch their breaths, caus-

ing them to make eye contact and exchanging signals with their penciled eyebrows or occasionally tapping each other with folded fans to
emphasize a point. They were bursting at the seams to discuss what
they had just heard. Daisy considered excusing themselves to the lady's
room and would have, if propriety had allowed.

Sergeant Elam was called to stand next and his testimony was mercifully short. Even so, the two women fidgeted in their seats like school-
girls barely able to contain themselves. This was turning into something
far different and far better than expected.

After the City Sergeant's brief exposition there was a pause in the
proceedings as the Judge conferred with the bailiff and Commonwealth's
attorney.

"Oh ... my . . . God, oh, my God. Did you hear what I heard?"
Marjorie wheezed into Daisy's ear.

"I know, I know, I told you it was true, didn't I tell you it was true?"
Daisy countered.

"It's so exciting . . . and interesting. Don't you think it's interesting?
Aren't you glad I talked you into coming?" Marjorie tapped Daisy on the
wrist with her fan.

"Talked me into coming? I was the one that talked you into coming,
practically had to twist your arm."

Both women jumped at the banging of the gavel. The Judge was
staring directly at them, a no-nonsense expression on his face and said,
"The Court will now hear evidence from Mrs. Gabriel. It will be heard in
my chambers. Court will remain in session until we return, please remain
seated and Bailiff, see that order is maintained. Mrs. Gabriel, Gentlemen,
to chambers, please."

The bailiff intoned, "All rise." and the Judge, Norma, Enoch, and
the attorneys passed through a door behind the bench.

"I can't believe it, you almost got us thrown in jail, I swear you did."
Daisy said with theatrical flare.

"Me? You were the one who almost got us put in the pokey. What
would we tell the boys when they came to bail us out?" Marjorie giggled.

"If they'd bail us out." Daisy flipped open her fan and looked over it at Marjorie.

"Oh, they will, don't you know we can be very persuasive . . . or failing that we can simply clamp our legs shut." Marjorie fluttered her fan trying her best to portray a courtesan.

"Oh, you're so bad. One hundred percent correct, but sooo bad." Daisy cracked her fan over Marjorie's knuckles. "And speaking of bad, see . . . see, it's true, she didn't have a scratch on her. You heard the Doctor, no evidence of physical violence, and for that matter, no evidence of rape."

"Shhh, lower your voice will you?"

"Oh, sorry, I got carried away." Daisy whispered hoarsely, looking around her guiltily; no one seemed to have noticed them.

"So then, she was carryin' on with him, well, I'll be, it's true. Just imagine, a married white woman bedding a nigger while her husband is serving overseas. That's low, really low."

"Well, you know what they say, while the cat's away the mice will play." Daisy tittered.

"Mouse nothing, you mean big black rat don't you?" Marjorie hissed.

"Hey c,mon now, we've known Knock-knock all our lives, he's a nice boy, always has been. He shouldn't have to go to prison for being stupid, Lordy, half the men in this town would be in prison. No, all the men. If anyone's to blame it's Norma Gabriel, she should know better, she's the one with that persuasive little piece of real estate you mentioned earlier." There was no longer any humor in Daisy's voice.

"Your mind's in the gutter again." Marjorie smiled trying to lighten things up.

"This whole town, this whole courtroom is in the gutter as far as I'm concerned."

"You're right, Norma Gabriel is finished in this town, and what about when Gabe gets home? Wouldn't you like to be a fly on the wall when they have that conversation? And they will, trust me, someone's bound to tell him what was going on, if they haven't already." Marjorie gave up on trying to bring humor back into the conversation.

"All I can say is she better speak up and set things straight." Daisy sighed.

"How can she do that? It's too late to do that. She'll never change her story now, it's snowballed far beyond that."

"Well, I guess you're right, but somebody ought to say something, I mean all those people aren't going to just stand by and watch. Are they?" Daisy's eyes questioned Marjorie.

"Don't know."

"Well, maybe you and I should say something, maybe we ought to say hey, wait a minute here. Don't ya think?" Daisy's eyes flashed.

"Not me, I'm not. I have to live in this town, remember? Fred owns a store downtown, we have to provide for our children, and that's not the only reason."

"Oh really? What's the other reason Marj?

"Easy. It's simply, none . . . of . . . my . . . business, and if you had any sense in that pretty little head of yours you'd realize it's none of your business either. We don't know what really happened, it has nothing to do with us."

Marjorie's words struck Daisy like a brick falling out of the sky. They derailed her train of thought and she sat there in complete silence for several minutes. Finally, removing her hat and gloves, she straightened her hair and checked her lipstick in her compact and sighed. "I suppose you're right, when you get right down to it, it really isn't any of our business. Is it?"

With ringing familiarity the voice of the bailiff called out. "All rise."

The upper gallery of the New Surrey courthouse wrapped around the three walls facing the judge's bench; it was about twelve feet wide with three rows of seats on risers and a narrow walkway. The heat and the ordure of humanity rose from below, and with the sun streaming in the large mullioned windows, three to a side, the balcony was a hellish perch from which to observe the trial below. Its saving grace was that it was closer to the antiquated ceiling fans. Also that by some twist of unintended physics, the acoustics of the room were such that nearly every word spoken from the front could be heard, even those words not intended to be heard by spectators. Situated above, the balcony provided a better view of the proceedings than seventy-five percent of the seats on the floor below.

Negroes solely populated the gallery on this and most days when trials pertinent to their community took place. They were required to sit there by signs posted in the entranceway of the courthouse. It had always been that way and not one of them gave it a second thought. Occasionally a white face could be seen up there, but it was nearly always an eccentric or a troublemaker.

Halfway down the right side of the balcony sat Missy Baker. She was flanked by her sister Luella and the Reverend Crenshaw, with his wife Ivy and Ivy's sister Lily sitting directly behind. As the Judge and the others rose and left the room to hear Norma's testimony, Lily leaning forward and in a stage whisper said, "You hear that? You hear what that Doctor said? That Jezebel, she the whore of Babylon, that's what she is. She jus' gonna sit there and lie, lie like a rug."

"Vengeance is mine, saith the Lord." Reverend Crenshaw intoned quietly.

"Good Lord John, not now, you're not gonna start preaching now of all times are you? Please." Lily retorted.

"Mind yourself, don't you go disrespectin' my husband, I won't stand for it." Ivy glared at her sister.

"Sorry, didn't mean no disrespect, John. It's jus' that, well, you know."

"Jus' what? Jus' that I'm speaking the truth? It's God's Word and it's the only truth we gonna hear in this room today. We all know that." John said, his lips twisted into a peculiar smile.

"You're right about that." It was the first time Missy had spoken since climbing the gallery stairs.

"You think they still gonna 'vict him after what that doctor had to say?" Ivy asked innocently.

"Course they are, he pleaded guilty and signed that 'fession, and besides you think that Judge Colson and that ol'slippery Newt Vann are gonna take the word of a colored boy 'gainst a white woman? 'Course they won't." Lily rasped.

"Las' time, no, the only time I saw him, he was so scared and tired he'd a signed anything and said anything. Doesn't matter much though, my Enoch can't read a lick. Never could." Missy's voice remained calm and steady.

"The details don't matter, who done what to whom don't matter either. Only thing matters is the truth and the only truth bein' God's Word. Apostle Paul wrote 'The wages of sin is death.' And nothing we can say or do gonna change that."

"John Crenshaw, you shut your mouth, this ain't the time or the place to be talkin' like that." Lily snarled in righteous indignation.

"Let me finish, and 'sides, when is the time? If not now, when? All sin have consequence, the bigger the sin, the bigger consequence, that's all, that's the way it is, and that's the way it gotta be, ever since Adam and Eve bit into that apple."

"Well, if that be true, what about that whore of Babylon down there? When she gonna get her consequences?" Lily asked, still outraged.

"Don't know, that none of our business, that why the Book say 'Vengeance is mine saith the Lord.' That's what I meant before when I said it."

"Reverend, you leavin' out the second half of that scripture. It say 'The wages of sin is death; but the gift of God is eternal life through Jesus Christ our Lord.' That the only hope we got, I'm grabbin' on to that, my boy been saved, I know that, you know that too." Missy Baker's eyes never left the door to the judge's chambers.

"Amen, Missy, amen." Crenshaw said, taking Missy's hand.

"All rise." Rang out from below.

After everyone had settled back into their respective places, the Judge asked, "Mr. Vann do you have any further evidence to put before the court?"

"No further evidence, your Honor, however I would like to read Mr.Baker's confession to the court before beginning my summation."

"You may proceed."

"Thank you your Honor, to wit:

Question: What is your name?

Answer: Enoch Franklin Baker

Question: You are willing to make this statement of your own free will?

Answer: Yes, sir.

Question: Nobody has threatened you or promised you anything?

Answer: No, sir.

Question: Enoch, are you the young man who on the night of June 13, 1945 assaulted Mrs. Norma Gabriel?

Answer: Yes, sir.

Question: You went into her home on Pritchard Street, did you?

Answer: Yes, sir.

Question: You found her in the hall or bedroom, did you?

Answer: Yes, sir.

Question: You assaulted her there against her will?

Answer: Yes, sir.

Question: On the bed?

Answer: Yes, sir.

Question: After you accomplished your purpose you then came out the front door?

Answer: Yes, sir.

Question: You saw her go in her home a short time before that?

Answer: Yes, sir.

Question: You want to make this confession to be submitted to Judge Colson of the Corporation Court, for such consid eration as he can give you?

Answer: Yes.

Thank you Judge, that's all." Vann was satisfied, he had thrust the matador's sword deep and true.

"Mr. Vann are you ready to begin your summation?"

"Yes, your Honor, I am."

"You may proceed."

"Excuse me your Honor, but before my esteemed colleague begins, I would like to ask him one final question." Ernest Oakes stood addressing Judge Colson.

"Go ahead Mr. Oakes."

"Thank you, your Honor. Mr. Vann could you explain what brought about the confession of the prisoner, what were the circumstances, sir, that caused this man to sign such an incriminating document?"

"The Judge interjected, "Mr. Oakes, Mr. Harrington, let me just say this, the confession is neither the key nor the only instrument in establishing the prisoner's guilt. There are other irrefutable pieces of evidence, as you are well aware. Mr. Vann you may continue."

"I had the prisoner brought to my office the morning after his arrest. He appeared nervous, and understandably was quite defensive at the beginning of the interview. In our conversation, I laid out the facts as I knew them. I told him what I believed would be the outcome of the case against him, and finally offered my opinion as to what he should do, based on what I would do if I were in his shoes. No threats were made nor were any promises, the facts were simply laid out as I understood them at the time. Finally, Enoch just hung his head and said 'I did it.' I had the stenographer record the confession you just heard and he made his mark on it."

For the first time during the hearing, Enoch began to shift in his seat and his crossed leg began to bounce quickly, though he never raised his head from his left palm. It was the only sign of agitation he had displayed thus far.

"Anything further questions, Mr. Oakes? Mr. Vann?" The Judge asked, mildly exasperated.

The two men indicated 'no' in unison.

Newton Vann's summation was brief and to the point, resting mainly on the confession and the knife found at the scene. His summation lasted all of three minutes. He returned to his seat and began shuffling papers on the table in front of him.

The defense's summation was similarly brief, attempting to refute the irrefutable, and relying heavily on Dr. Mallone's testimony of no signs of physical violence or rape.

The Judge looked up, removed his glasses, and spoke evenly, "Enoch Franklin Baker, please stand . . . In view of the evidence presented before me, the plea of guilty, and lastly, the signed confession, this court finds you guilty as charged of criminal assault with force and armed. You may be seated."

Enoch deflated as he heard the words, it came as no surprise, but the reality of hearing the Judge's verdict sliced down on him like the fall of a guillotine blade.

Judge Colson continued. "Mr. Vann, Mr. Oakes, you may each address the court before sentencing."

Newton Vann stood tall and proud, like a heroic matador presenting the bull's ear as a prize. He spoke continuously turning from the audience to the judge as he addressed each in turn. "Let me begin by thanking the citizens of New Surrey for their attitudes and help in this case. The city officials truly appreciated it, they surely do. I would also like to commend the City Police force, especially our two detectives Dan Hopkins and Jim Little, and of course Police Chief Hiram Delaney. Thank you, men. I'd also like to mention at this time Mrs. Norma Gabriel, for her bravery, cooperation, attitude and forthrightness in bringing this man to justice."

Vann, turning to the Judge, continued, "Your Honor, the State makes no recommendation as to sentencing of the prisoner, the State has full confidence that your Honor appreciates the import of this sentence and will make the right decision. On a personal note, let me say I sincerely hope, your Honor, that you are never asked to pass sentence on a case like this again." Vann returned to his seat at the long table in front of the judge's bench, being careful not to look at Enoch.

Ernest Oakes stood, buttoned his coat and approached the bench. In a strong, clear voice he addressed the judge, never once turning to acknowledge the spectators. "Your Honor, We sincerely believe that Enoch Baker deserves to be shown mercy when sentenced for the crime he has been found guilty of committing. The State has clearly not requested the death penalty, your Honor, it is because he is an illiterate, benighted Negro and is deeply remorseful of his crime. It is indicative, I believe, of the state's desire to see mercy bestowed. Your Honor, this convicted man, has the mind of a child locked in the body of an adult. He has been fully cooperative with the police and this court, he voluntarily confessed, he waived a grand jury hearing, and plead guilty when arraigned. Not only did these actions save the court time and money, but these acts also spared Mrs. Gabriel the added embarrassment and humiliation of a public trial. Your Honor, these are the acts of a contrite man, please take them into consideration as you pass sentence. Thank you, your Honor."

The Judge banged the gavel several times to get everyone's attention. "Before passing sentence, I would like to make one thing absolutely clear. I will tolerate no demonstration of approval or disapproval from anyone in this courtroom. If I hear so much as a groan or snicker I will throw that person in jail so fast and for so long their head will spin and I will impose a fine that will bring tears to their eyes. Please do not doubt me on this." He paused for a moment and studied the audience for emphasis, the State Troopers coming to attention under his basilisk stare.

"Enoch Franklin Baker, approach the bench." Enoch shuffled over to a spot several feet in front of the judge, keeping his head down as he approached, but looking up at the judge once he came to a stop. "Enoch Baker, do you have anything to say before this court passes sentence on you for the crime you have been convicted of?"

Enoch shook his head no and mumbled a few inaudible words.

"Enoch Franklin Baker for the crime of criminal assault with force and armed I sentence you to be remanded to the State Penitentiary in Richmond, where you will be held until Friday August 10th on which day you will be electrocuted until you are dead. May God have mercy on your soul."

Enoch swayed a little as if being caught by a gust of ill wind. He began to perspire heavily, his hands trembled, but not so anyone could notice and the pupils in his brown-black eyes dilated wildly. He turned his head slightly to look at Vann who was busying himself with papers and briefcase as to not acknowledge Enoch or any of his friends and family. The matador stowing his cape and sword until his next fight. Enoch saw Vann with sightless eyes, he had been witnessing this entire drama from above, carefully watching Norma throughout, with her mother-in-law, Vann, the Judge and his own mother. He hoped he could find some way to not reenter his body, but that was to happen on August 10th.

Help me Angel Moses, help your boy Enoch, I can't do this, I can't.

The Judge ordered everyone to remain seated as Enoch was handcuffed and led out of the court by the same door he had entered by. The Bailiff one last time bade everyone to rise, the Judge left and they were dismissed.

The first man to stand was the attorney Ira Day, who was a long time friend of Gabe and wanted to see the trial first hand. It was certain that Gabe would one day ask him about it. He made a point of making eye contact with Sam Burns. Both men nodded an understanding that they would talk later. As Ira stood motionless, he felt disoriented by the previous hour's events. He was not a man that liked being taken by surprise and Judge Colson had completely astounded him. He left the courtroom with an uneasy smoldering anger.

Behind Ira, people began filing out in near silence. Most people felt drained and empty, others didn't know what they felt. Not knowing if their bloodlust had been satisfied or not.

Upstairs in the balcony not a person moved or spoke. Missy's shoulders heaved as she cried silently into a lace handkerchief. She wept soundlessly due partly to pride, she didn't want those people down below to hear her crying, and partly out of having taken the Judge's warning to heart. The Reverend and the two women around her rubbed her shoulders and hands and pressed their cheeks against her, joining in her mourning and sharing her grief. She was inconsolable. All eyes were on Missy, some openly weeping, others praying while staring at her.

In the courtroom below the bailiff and a couple of State Troopers gathered and kept looking up at the balcony waiting for them to leave. Finally, the Bailiff lost his patience. "Hey, y'all up there, go on, get out of here. It's finished, show's over, go on, git." The three men downstairs continued to talk, they lit cigarettes, opened a couple of the windows to help air out the place, the windows had been kept closed during the trial as a matter of custom. Occasionally one of them burst into laughter at something one of the others said. They were doing their best to ignore the people up in the gallery, not wanting to have a confrontation and not wanting to acknowledge they cared one way or the other.

Finally, however, it became clear no one was moving, and this time the Bailiff raised his voice to a higher pitch, sounding more shrill than he intended to. "Hey, I thought I told y'all to leave, now go, or we'll get some more troopers and come up there and pitch you outta there. You hear me? Now go. We're done here. Go home, unless you want some real trouble, ya hear?"

The Deacon Williams was the first to stand. He was directly across the gallery from Missy Baker and Reverend Crenshaw. A look of satisfaction, triumph and enlightenment came over the faces of the men down below. Deacon Williams didn't move from his place. Instead, he stood straight as a cedar of Lebanon and in a sonorous baritone began to sing:

> *"Mine eyes have seen the glory of the coming of the Lord:*
>
> *He is trampling out the vintage where the grapes of wrath are stored;*
>
> *He hath loosed the fateful lightening of His terrible swift sword:*
>
> *His truth is marching on"*

As the deacon began to sing the chorus, John Crenshaw marveled at the Deacon Williams' strange choice of song. He didn't really know why, but it just seemed right, it seemed to speak to them there in that overheated, crowded courthouse in which Missy Baker's boy had just been martyred.

On the main floor, Sam Burns, Clerk of the Court, had reentered the room when he heard the singing. He made his way over to where the Bailiff and the troopers stood slack jawed and gazing upward.

The Bailiff broke the trance that held them transfixed for the past minute or two. "Well, if that don't beat all, a nigger standing up there in my courthouse, singing a Yankee song. C'mon, let's go out and get some more boys and drown 'em out with Dixie."

Sam stepped in front of the Bailiff, "Hold on Roy, you damn fool, that's not why they're singing, they're singing for Missy Baker, they're singing for Enoch. Leave 'em be."

As the Deacon finished the chorus another woman, at the end of the row where Missy sat, stood and added her voice.

> *"I have seen Him in the watch-fires of a hundred circling camps,*
>
> *They have builded Him an altar in the evening dews and damps;*
>
> *I can read His righteous sentence by the dim and flaring lamps:*
>
> *His day is marching on."*

Again, during the chorus two more men and another woman stood, and began to sing.

> *"I have read a fiery gospel writ in burnished rows of steel:*
>
> *'As ye deal with my condemners, so with you my grace shall deal;*
>
> *Let the Hero, born of woman, crush the serpent with His heel.*
>
> *While God is marching on."*

Now a dozen more stood as the pitch and fervor of the chorus grew and grew.

> *"In the beauty of the lilies Christ was born across the sea,*
>
> *With a glory in His bosom that transfigures you and me:*
>
> *As He died to make men holy, let us die to make men free,*
>
> *While God is marching on."*

They continued to stand and sing, singly and in pairs. John Crenshaw looked at the Bailiff and Troopers standing dumbstruck. He nudged Missy and motioned her to look down. Off to the side, standing away from the others, stood Sam Burns. He was singing.

> *"He is coming like the glory of the morning on the wave,*
> *He is wisdom to the mighty, He is succor to the brave,*
> *So the world shall be His footstool, and the soul of Time His slave,*
> *Our God is marching on.*

When Missy Baker saw Sam Burns singing, and looked around, seeing every person in the gallery on their feet and in full voice, she too, stood and began to sing. When the others saw her, they raised their voices to a greater pitch until the windowpanes began to vibrate.

Down below, the Bailiff and troopers shook their heads in bemusement both at the colored people singing upstairs and at that nigger loving Sam Burns, and with that they simply left the building.

> *"Glory, glory, hallelujah!*
> *Glory, glory, hallelujah!*
> *Glory, glory, hallelujah!*
> *His truth is marching on."*

Out on the street people stopped, listened, and wondered. Standing entranced at the magnificent singing flowing from the courtroom windows, not knowing why, or what it meant, but simply appreciating its beauty.

Inside, as the last notes of the last chorus echoed off the walls, the people began moving from their seats towards the stairs. No one spoke a word. Silently they made their way home, lost in their thoughts, adrift in their sorrow.

CHAPTER 26

A Twist
of Fate

Zeus does not bring all men's plans to fulfillment.
HOMER, *The Illiad*

The baker's boy delivered a paper sack of warm Brötchen, the small hard-rolls Gabe adored, to the back stairs of Irmgard's apartment. He placed the bag further than usual inside the doorway to keep it from getting wet. It was a breezy, gray day and the rain came in sheets, making the delivery boy's job thoroughly miserable. However, for most of Munich it was an unexpected respite from the unseasonable July heat and humidity.

Irmgard had climbed out of bed, trying not to disturb Gabe. She was successful. Gabe continued to lie on his stomach, his left arm hanging off the bed, his head turned in the same direction and snoring softly. She put on a dressing gown, walked to the window and assessed the day, stormy weather. She rubbed her arms and closed the window three-quarters of the way. She went downstairs and retrieved the bag of warm rolls, something she had taken for granted before the war and now accepted with renewed gratitude. She put water on for coffee, strong, real coffee, American coffee, compliments of the Marshall Plan, another exercise in new-found appreciation. She sliced cheese and smoked ham and sausage and arranged them on a plate.

Her heart soared in joyful anticipation as she saw the day play out in her mind. Her son was away at her parent's farm in the Schwarzwald, and there was absolutely nothing that needed doing, the shop was closed, it being Sunday. She and Gabe would spend a rainy day in and out of bed, reading, playing rummy, listening to jazz records on the gramophone he had bought her, eating leisurely meals and simply enjoying one another's minds and bodies. Ach, wie herrlich

It was close to nine o'clock when Gabe awoke to the smell of hot coffee and warm bread. He smiled, yawned and stretched. Irmgard was not the only person in the apartment that morning with a profound sense of gratitude; it was as if the two of them had been given an undeserved second chance at life. Gabe drew on his shorts, walked to the small bathroom and emptied his bladder for an inordinately long time. He then washed his hands, splashed water on his face, brushed his teeth, and stood there just staring at himself in the mirror. Life seemed so much better since he had cut the tie that binds, since realizing once and for all he would never go back to the way things were. His marriage and dead-end jobs had all been stupid mistakes. The war had opened his eyes. What was it the old soldiers used to say? Oh yeah, I have seen the elephant. He continued to stare in the mirror and then grinned. Wonder what the poor people are doing today? It was an odd expression his father used to say whenever he was having an exceptional day and all was right with world.

"Gabe, are you all right in there?"

"Finer than frog's hair? Why do you ask?"

"I thought maybe you fell in. Come have breakfast. You with your frogs hairs."

Gabe padded into the tiny kitchen, wrapped Irmgard in his arms and gave her a soft, lingering kiss. They sat down at the small kitchen table, poured coffee and began to breakfast.

"Well, tomorrow's the big day, are you sure you won't change your mind? Bitte sehr, meine Liebchen?"

"Stop, Gabriel, your German is not so good as my Englisch, and I told you, no, I simply can not go with you."

"C'mon, it's not every day a guy gets a ten day pass to London, it'll be so much more fun with you. I don't see why you can't or won't come with me." Gabe absently stirred his coffee.

"First of all, Reich Minister Goebbels, and Feldmarschall Goering assured us there was no more London." Her face darkened as a sardonic cloud passed over it. "Karl is coming home in three days, and who will run the shop? Everything is so easy for you Amerikanern."

"Irmie, you're being silly. You can write your parents to keep him an extra two weeks, he'd probably jump for joy and you could just close the store. Put a sign on the door saying family emergency, nobody will give it a second thought, or hire Mrs. Pilz to mind it."

"Mrs. Pilz? She can't add two plus two. I'll be ruined. No, I can not close the shop, what will I do for money? I won't have two pfennigs left. Nein, nein, nein. Absolut nichts."

"I'll take care of it." Gabe said with an air of growing defeat.

"Ja, ja, now you're rich, so you are rich and handsome, how wonderful." She laughed not without kindness.

"I said, I'll take care of it."

"Yes, I'm sure you can, but there's more problems. I'm a German, you think I can simply go to England? I have no papers. What will the people there say to me, what will they do to me? What will they do to you? It will never work."

"Listen, with this crazy black market, anything can be arranged, and believe me, there are a lot of guys out there that owe me favors and once we get to London we could leave immediately and rent a cottage in the Cotswold. Ride bicycles and have picnics all day, and at night, well, I'm sure we'll think of something to do. It'll all work out, you'll see."

"Ach, Gabe, please let's change the subject. I'm not comfortable leaving my son and my work. I could not enjoy myself, and you would not enjoy having me there, now please, maybe some other time."

"All right, I understand, I'm disappointed, but I understand. I won't mention it again."

Gabe was as good as his word. They passed the day in delicious, decadent laziness. Morning passed to afternoon, afternoon to evening. On the Gramophone, Benny Goodman passed to Harry James, Harry James passed to Tommy Dorsey, Tommy Dorsey passed to Artie Shaw throughout the day. As the time to leave approached, Gabe wondered if he shouldn't ask Irmgard to accompany him one more time, but then thought better of it. He dressed, thanked her, kissed her goodbye, kissed her again and promised to bring her something nice from London, promised to be back in two weeks and took his leave.

In the darkness Gabe began to make his way back to his billet. The rain had stopped. He strolled at a leisurely pace, light hearted, reflecting on the day and savoring the anticipation of ten days in England. If his happiness was at all tempered it was because Irmgard wouldn't be coming along. He had never really expected her to, but the fantasies it evoked brought him endless enjoyment.

He was in no hurry, wandering streets he rarely traveled. Passing darkened shops, picking his way around rubble-strewn sidewalks, having to walk on the street a good part of the time. It was slow, but pleasant going. Dim lights filtered from apartment windows and the lights from an occasional passing vehicle helped guide his way, although sometimes a passing truck or car would have the opposite effect, sabotaging his night vision. To preserve it he soon learned to close his eyes at just the right instant. Moving through the nocturnal ruined streets and parks with feline grace became a game to him, he moved along envisioning himself as a commando or a second-story man.

He exited a pitch-dark alley, climbing over a substantial pile of bricks and stone shot through with long spears of steel reinforcing. When he reached its summit, turning the alley corner, Gabe carefully began to descend the mound.

He heard the howl of a motorcycle engine at full throttle in the distance, but was preoccupied. His right foot was lodged in a crevasse of building stone. He gripped a steel bar to keep from falling and began maneuvering his leg to free it from the accidental mantrap. Gabe extricated his foot with some small effort, but at the cost of a scraped ankle and torn trouser leg.

Stepping off of the pile and onto the street, the scream of a flat twin-cylinder engine wide open, and the hoots and Indian war cries of drunken boys filled his ears and vibrated his heart and lungs. He turned to the right looking for the source of the noise and saw nothing, no headlights or moving shadows. He spun to the left in time to see the black silhouette of a German motorcycle with sidecar and several men hanging on to it hurtling towards him. He could hear their drunken laughter as the sidecar caught him mid-torso. He heard the crunch of bones as his left arm snapped just above the wrist and then felt the pain of the broken arm as the sidecar fender caved in his ribs. His breath exploded from him as he was lifted off his feet. His right boot came off and flew into the road. He was thrown back onto the pile of rubble he had just climbed with the force of an artillery blast. His head snapped back and made the first jarring contact with the stone, lacerating his scalp and concussing him. As his body slammed down he felt a white-hot tearing sensation through his body that robbed him of consciousness. The BMW kept driving at full speed with intoxicated indifference.

When he came to, it was still dark. He had no idea how long he had been lying there and was hopelessly trying to piece together what had happened. In his semi-consciousness he was sentient enough to know he was cold, which meant he was going into shock. He looked down at his left arm and saw his hand and wrist bent at a ninety-degree angle to his forearm. He was able to slowly and painfully bring his right hand to the back of his head; his hand came away bloody. He tried to sit up and couldn't. He summoned whatever strength and determination he had left and tried again, and again he failed. It was as if something was pinning him down, but he couldn't feel the weight of anything lying on him. The pain radiating from the left side of his chest and the shortness of breath from the exertion nearly made him blackout again.

With his right hand he began gingerly patting down his body in the darkness. Halfway down his body, on the right side, six inches below his ribs he felt it. He was impaled on the steel bar he had held climbing off the debris. The discovery of the steel bar piercing through his side caused him to lie back and remain absolutely still.

He now began to concentrate on thinking instead of moving. His lucidity came intermittently between the rushing tides of pain. He tried to list what he knew. He was cold. He was in shock. His arm was broken and probably some ribs. The steel bar had most likely not hit any vital organs or major vessels because he was still alive. He knew if he moved and the bar was holding something in place he would bleed out in a couple of minutes. He knew he was going to die. He had survived the war to be killed by a couple of fucking drunks, American drunks. Blackness.

The next time he came to the sky had turned silver. The blurred shadows of men stood over him. Two were holding bottles of plasma running through rubber tubing into both arms. He turned his head slightly and realized it was resting on something soft and had been bandaged.

He saw that his left arm was straightened and splinted, and detected someone moving rocks and digging below his right side.

One of the medics knelt down close to Gabe's face having noticed the flutter of eyelids. "Hey, Buddy. You're hurt pretty bad, but we're going to get you through this. Okay? So just hold on."

"I was . . ."

"Shhh, just lie there. You were hit by some drunk G.I.'s from the Quartermaster corps, those Service of Supply sons-a-bitchs. Out joyriding on a Kraut motorcycle."

"How . . . did . . . you find me?

"Easy now, guy, that's the best part, seemed when they were pulled over by the MP's your garrison cap was found on the floor of the sidecar. When they were questioned about it, one of them broke down crying and said they hit somebody, but were too drunk to stop. Too drunk to stop, imagine that. Anyway they told us about where they thought it happened, and we didn't have any problem finding you. You are one lucky bastard, that's all I can say. By the way, you are T.J. Gabriel, right?

"Yeah . . . lucky."

"Good, 'cause that's the name on the lining of the cap."

"O.k., lucky T.J., you still hanging in there? Here's what we're going to do, we've cleared below that rod. We're going to saw it off and transport you to regimental, they'll remove it there under more controlled conditions. Understand?"

"Yeah . . .understand . . . It's Gabe."

"What's that?"

"My name . . .my name is . . . Gabe."

"O.k. Gabe. Listen closely, we're going to try and cut this without giving you any morphine. So hang tough. Your blood pressure is already pretty low. I'll give you a little if you need it. But let's give it a try without first. O.k. Don, slow and steady with the hacksaw."

Gabe felt the strange sensation of the hacksaw teeth biting into the steel rod. It wasn't painful but it vibrated every bone in his body, and he thought his fillings were going to shake loose.

"You're doing great Gabe, almost done, hold on just another minute." There was an audible crack as the rod broke in two. Gabes body shifted violently as the snapping bar caught the medic unprepared. He screamed in blinding, searing pain.

Blackness.

CHAPTER 27

A Lifeline
for Enoch

The knock at the hooked screen door was amplified by its banging against the ill-fitting door jam. Through the screen the evening's visitors were able to see soft light spilling from the kitchen into the center hall. The house was silent. John Crenshaw knocked harder the second time, the clacking of the hooked screen door announcing a determined presence at the front entrance of 17 W. Ogden Street. John's wife gave him a look chiding his impatience.

"Hello the house, anybody in there?" John called out through the screen into the hall.

"Hold your horses. John Crenshaw, you ever read that Book of Job? That ol' Job's got a thing or two to teach you 'bout patience." John's sister-in-law, Lily, called back at him as she turned the corner into the entry hall and walked to the front door.

"I was jus' takin' a peach pie out of the oven, you wouldn't want to burn a real nice peach pie would ya?"

"No, indeed sister Lily, no indeed. I smelt it clear out to the street, that's why Ivy and me are here." John smiled broadly.

"I swear." Ivy slapped John on his arm. "We've come by to see how Missy an' you are holdin' up."

"Well, come on in, and have some lemonade while the pie cools. It's been a hard couple of weeks. I can tell you that." Lily lead them back to the sweltering kitchen, reached through a window that opened to the

Judge To Hear Counsel For Baker Tuesday

Judge Byron T. Colson will hear counsel for Enoch Baker, local negro, now confined at the state penitentiary in Richmond on Tuesday, August 7 at 1 o'clock in Corporation Court here.

Baker, confessed rapist, who was sentenced to die on August 11, was given a 30 day reprieve Monday by Governor Darden.

The reprieve was granted, it was stated in order that counsel for Baker could make an appeal to Judge Colson.

It is supposed that the condemned man's attorney will ask the court to entertain a petition, the contents of which have not been made public and will likely not be known until it is presented to the court or filed.

What action can or may be taken in the matter is not known.

---

back porch and lifted a small fan, placing it in the window and switching it on. "That's better."

John placed his well worn leather Bible on the table, loosened his necktie and rolled up his sleeves. "Lordy, it's hotter than the gates of you know where in here." Ivy had retrieved a small fan from her purse, supplementing the meager electric fan.

"What'd the ol' folks say? If'n you can't stand the heat, stay outta the kitchen." Lily smiled, taking a pitcher of lemonade out of the ice box. "She ain't eatin' enough to keep a bird alive, so I'm makin' a pie to see if I can tempt her."

"Yes, ma'am. You got an answer for everything." He said the smile never leaving his eyes. But, after a moment of bantering and small talk, John sipped his lemonade and became serious. "I'm sorry to hear that. She hasn't been to church, I hear tell she hasn't been to work or doing anything at all. That true? Ivy says nobody's seen her since the trial, ain't that right Ivy?"

"Deed, it is. She's got to get out of the house and clear them cobwebs." Ivy agreed.

"Well, what you expect? Her baby boy's in the state pen, goin' to be electrocuted for something he didn't do, and ain't nothin' us colored folks gonna be able to do about it." Lily replied more harshly than she had meant to.

234

"We can pray." John said quietly, ignoring the edge in Lily's voice.

"That's true, but I'm startin' to wonder if God doesn't hear white people's prayers better than he does ours. We been prayin' for things for a long time, and doesn't seem like much ever changes for us." Lily's voice softened.

"I don't 'spect God cares much 'bout our color, I 'spect he looks at a person's heart. God only got three answers to prayer, you know that? Yes, no and wait. We been in an extra special long waiting time. Maybe cause He loves us all the more, He gonna give somethin' worth waiting for. We ain't nobody, black or white that be able to tell God what to do, He 's gonna work in his own good time." John finished his lemonade and poured himself another glass.

"Well, if that's true John Crenshaw, I sure wish jus' this one time, He work a little faster, 'cause Enoch is runnin outta time."

"You be careful there, sister, you soundin' a little disrespectful to God." Ivy said, breaking her silence.

"You jus' said there was nothin' we could do about it. That's why I'm here, I think jus' maybe there is something else we can do." John pulled a handkerchief from his pocket and mopped his brow.

"What's that, have all the cooks and housekeepers poison the food and then burn down the city?" Lily answered only half joking.

"Sister, you jus' full of yourself tonight, ain't ya?" Ivy spoke up again.

"Well, I have a safer plan for now. Could you kindly ask Missy to come down for some lemonade, and I'll be able to tell you both at the same time."

"She surely knows you're here, you knocked on that ol' screen door, like'n to raise the dead and she still hasn't come down to say hello. So I don't know if'n I can coax her down or not." Lily stated the fact pure and simple.

"You go ahead an' tell her I got an idea maybe help to save Enoch, she'll come down then, I know she will."

"I'll try." Lily said sliding her chair across the timeworn linoleum, wiped her hands on a dishrag and disappeared through the door.

John stood to stretch his legs, walked over to the counter and sniffed at the fresh-baked pie. He tested the pie pan with his finger, pulling it away quickly. The pie had stopped bubbling, but was still too hot to eat.

"Pardon my language sweetie, but that sister of mine is full of piss and vinegar, always has been, always will be. She's somethin' else, that 's what she is." Ivy continued working her fan.

"That she is, but I think jus' maybe that's jus' what Missy needs right now. I'm glad she's stayin' with her." John sat down again and drank some more lemonade from the sweating glass.

Missy Baker entered the kitchen followed by Lily. She was wrapped in a worn blue chenille robe, and from behind dull sunken eyes murmured "Hello John, hello Ivy, I understand you have an idea."

John and Ivy were taken aback by the change in Missy since seeing her last, only a week ago. She seemed to age before their eyes. "Yes, that's right."

Missy sat down heavily in a kitchen chair. "John, you think you could say a prayer first, we need all the prayers we can get."

"I'll be glad to, let us bow our heads and pray." John led the three women in prayer. He asked for Godly wisdom, he asked for God to comfort Enoch and all the other people touched by this, he asked for God to preserve Enoch's life and finally he asked for God to forgive Norma Gabriel and for Him to open her eyes and pierce her heart with the truth. The last part of the prayer elicited a snort from Lily. They pronounced in unison "Amen and Amen" when he finished.

"Thank you." Missy whispered.

"Last Sunday, Hobbles Jackson, over in Milltown had me over to preach the Sunday night revival service at his church. Well, we went over in the afternoon to visit a while and have supper together before the preachin'." Missy Bakers eyes were hard and fixed on John has he continued. "Hobbles allowed as he didn't think much of them two lawyers Enoch got given to him by Newton Vann. Did you know those lawyers work for that American Synthetic? Anyway, he said Enoch should have better lawyers, he should have Negro lawyers who understand him and what happened to him. Missy, you ever hear of the N-double A-CP?"

"The N double what?" She asked with a blank look on her face.

"The N-A-A-C-P, that stand for the National Association for the Advancement of Colored People. Hobbles say they been around for a long time, but are mostly in the big cities, that's why we never heard of them. They help colored folks when they got problems. Any kind of problems, but 'specially problems with the law. They have colored lawyers that will work on something for free. Jus' to help, that's what they do. I don't know how they do it, but that don't matter, we don't need to know why or how, only when. So this N-double A-CP they have an office in Richmond, and Hobbles, he have the telephone exchange number for them." John paused for another sip of lemonade. "You think that peach pie cooled enough yet?"

"Never mind that pie, what are you sayin'?" Lily interjected.

"I'm sayin' that on Monday morning I went over to see my cousin Rooney, he has a dry goods store in Bordentown and he's got a telephone in the store. I went there 'cause I didn't want any 'spicious ears listening in on the party line here in town. I took money from the church emergency fund, I figure this is a bad 'nough emergency, and I used it, I gave it to Rooney so I could call the long distant operator and she put me through to the N-Double A-CP office. Say, you sure that pie ain't ready to eat?"

"You tryin' to be funny John Crenshaw?, 'Cause if you are, you ain't. This is serious business, what happen next?" Ivy interrupted giving him her all-too-familiar evil eye.

"Course I know this is serious, I'm jus' tryin to ease things up a little. Anyway, the man on the phone said they was very interested and he asked me to hold on why he got somebody from the legal department, 'magine that, a legal department for colored people, right bout then I got pretty excited. Here the best part. They sendin' lawyers up here to New Surrey to look at the court records, and then they sendin' lawyers to talk with Enoch in that prison. This Friday they'll be here lookin' around in the courthouse.

How 'bout that?" John grinned like the cat that swallowed a mouse.

The three women sat there awestruck, he had not told Ivy before this. He didn't want anyone to know before Missy. Missy bent over and hid her face in her hands. After a long pause, Lily stood and kissed John on the cheek. "I believe that pie is ready to eat now."

When Missy Baker looked up at John, tears were freely flowing down her cheeks. "John Crenshaw, you're a good man, a fine man. Thank you."

John's voice caught in his throat, "You know Missy, it's not me, you know that don't you?" He wiped his eyes.

CHAPTER 28

Lost

In the middle of our journey of life I came to myself within a dark wood where the straight way was lost.
DANTE ALIGHIERI, *The Devine Comedy*

Gabe passed in and out of fevered delirium. He slept for days on end, only to explode in rage and terror, causing the orderlies to wrestle him into restraints. Neither the doctors nor the sisters were able to determine if his screams were from pain or nightmarish visions. Mercifully he was unaware of the stench that enveloped him like a burial shroud. The fetid, purulent discharge from the drains inserted near the angry black and wine-colored wound in his side, and the mucous discharge from his empty bowels demanded nearly constant attention from the nurses. The roughly sutured incision running down the midline of his abdomen looked like a pockmarked and cratered entrenchment, more like the Somme than a man's abdomen.

The nurses frequently called for the sister that ran the ward, who in turn would summon the doctor, all of them gathering around Gabe's bed not putting voice to their thoughts. When was this Yank going to let go and die?

It was mid-afternoon of the sixteenth day when Gabe's fever began its retreat. The rapid movement behind his eyelids ceased and they slowly opened and brought the room into flawed focus. For the past twenty-four hours the rivulet of pus running from his side had all but stopped and the penicillin and sulfa drug induced diarrhea had begun to subside.

Gabe's first awareness came as a great thirst, his throat felt as dry and cracked as a drought ravaged river bottom. Next came the throbbing in his left arm, the pain keeping time with his pulse. His chest ached and would periodically be stabbed with sharp jabs as he sighed in the course of normal respiration. Any movement at all, just a subtle shift of his weight would unleash a blazing torrent in his side, it seemed he could not lie still enough to keep the demonic pain at bay.

The first to notice his return from the abyss was a freckled, redheaded nursing volunteer. She had been changing the foul bandages on the stumps of a double amputee in the bed next to Gabe's. The girl, in her khaki uniform and red-cross-emblazoned-white apron turned in the direction of the strange sound she only half heard.

The sound Gabe emitted was a combination of a croak, a hiss, and rattling expiration. He was unable to form the word "water", and gesturing was too painful to contemplate.

The volunteer hurriedly finished bandaging the amputee, promising to be back in a few minutes to chat. She turned again to Gabe. "Oh dear, oh dear." And ran down the length of the ward. "Sister, oh, oh, Sister!" The ward supervisor wanted to know immediately if there was any change in Private Gabriel's condition. "I believe he's regaining consciousness."

The commotion at the end of the sepsis ward was outside of Gabe's field of vision, although his ears detected the increase of activity.

The sister, as head of the ward, delegated one nurse and another nursing volunteer to find the doctor on duty for the day. "Eleanor, would you please look for Dr. Howard in the canteen, Maureen, would you please check the medical offices, if either of you see him, inform him that the peritonitis patient has just now regained consciousness."

A staff nurse filled a small pitcher with water, placed a glass and drinking straw on a tray and began walking quickly towards Gabe. She placed the tray on his bedside table, turned abruptly and returned in a moment, arms loaded with two pillows and a rolled blanket. Gabe sensed what she was going to do, and painfully rocked his head from side to side silently forming the word "No" through cracked lips. She patently ignored him, knowing better than he what was needed.

"Now ducky, we're going to sit you up, get you all comfy and give you a nice drink of water. Here we go. There's a good fellow." She grabbed his emaciated frame under the armpits and lifted the upper part of his torso off the bed.

Gabe's eyes grew huge in their sockets, he instantaneously broke out in cold sweat, the corded, wasted muscles of his neck tightened and his arteries and veins rose in rigid anger. It felt as if every wound, internal and external were being ripped asunder. He let out an unearthly, unnatural groan sounding like the Golem of Prague, and then, he lapsed back into unconsciousness.

Nurse Avery was committed to her course of action, realizing that stopping halfway, would be worse than completing the act of sitting him up. She listened to his chest and took his pulse. Satisfied, she went back to her station and waited for the arrival of Dr. Howard. She did not have long to wait.

The doctor nodded to the sister in the direction of Gabe. Arriving at his bed, he unclipped the chart from the iron rail of the footboard and began flipping through the pages. "I thought you said he had regained consciousness? Did he awake and slip back under?"

"Nurse Hopgood, could you please come over here for a moment?" said the Sister, exercising her authority over the ward. The nurse made her way over to where the sister and doctor were standing. "Dr. Howard wants to know if the patient was awake and then lost consciousness again"

"Yes doctor, he was awake and trying to communicate, but seemed quite delusional. I tried to sit him up and he struggled so frightfully, that he simply passed out. I checked his vitals, and though his heart rate and respiration are somewhat elevated they are quite strong."

Doctor Howard removed his wire-rimmed glasses, extracted a handkerchief from his coat pocket and began polishing them. "You shifted this patient on you own, did you?"

"Yes, doctor, I thought . . . ?"

"You thought? You thought what? You thought that perhaps you would kill him? Throw him into shock? Tear adhesions in his abdomen? Good Lord, Nurse, it was the pain you caused this man, what is his name?" Checking the Chart, "It was the pain that caused Private First Class T. J. Gabriel to faint, little wonder his pulse and respiration are elevated."

The Sister flushed deep red, subconsciously taking a step back from the doctor, "I was only doing what I thought best for the patient, nothing more, nothing less."

The doctor's eyes flashed, interpreting the disclaimer as something akin to disrespect. He clenched his jaw, "Bloody hell Nurse Avery, are you or are you not familiar with this man's condition? You're not some rank amateur; you're a well-seasoned, experienced professional working the sepsis ward, one of the most difficult assignments in hospital. You may have bloody well killed this man. Let me bloody remind you that peritonitis is one of the most painful conditions you are likely to encounter is this ward or any ward in this bleeding hospital. Every nerve ending lining his vital organs and investing the peritoneum is inflamed and firing off; all without the benefit of morphia. You have no idea, do you?"

The attention of the ward nurses, volunteers and patients were drawn to the row at the foot of Gabe's bed. Some of the nurses were enjoying Nurse Hopgood's dressing down, while others were in high dudgeon that a doctor could treat a dedicated nurse so badly.

The doctor's voice quieted and turned steely, "If there wasn't such a bloody labor shortage, I'd have you bloody sacked on the spot. Now listen, and listen closely, you are not to move, not so much as touch this man without notifying me first. Is that crystal clear to you Nurse? Sister?"

The Nurse did not meet the doctor's grim eyes. Looking down, and trembling with an admixture of emotions answered, "Yes, I understand, and may I say Doctor How . . ."

"No, you may not say. You are the one most emphatically wrong here. Increase the patient's intravenous fluids for 30 minutes and administer one-sixty-fourth grain morphine intramuscularly and call me the instant his eyelids so much as flicker. Now I'm off to have a word with Matron Thorpe. I suggest you watch this man very closely sister. Your career may depend on it." Doctor Howard quick-stepped away and out of the ward with military precision.

"Mama, when is Herr Gabe coming back to see me? Will he bring me a toy? Don't you miss him too?" Karl asked, chewing on a piece of coarse bread slathered with thick, black, sugar beet syrup.

"Don't speak with your mouth full." Irmgard replied hiding her exasperation. Her son had been asking the same questions repeatedly over the past few days. It was the third time he asked her today. "Ja, of course I miss him too. And I don't know if he's going to bring you anything. If he does, wonderful, if not, that should be all right too. You understand, don't you Karl?"

"Ja, Mama, I know. But I still would like him to bring me something."

"Natürlich Schätzchen, we'll have to wait and see."

Irmgard was growing increasingly concerned, and her son's innocent questions deepened her anxiety. Gabe should have been back from England four or five days ago. She could understand not hearing from him for a day or two. She was sure he had duties to catch up with, and extra work that had piled up while he was away.

But now, the second-guessing had begun. Had there been some change in the war and had he been transferred to the Pacific? So quickly, so much of an emergency he couldn't get word to her? Had he met another woman in England, someone who stole his heart away from her? Did he receive word from his wife and they have reconciled? Had his wife come to England to meet him? Had he been hurt? Had there been an airplane crash? Perhaps he was just angry. Perhaps she had upset him more than she thought by refusing his invitation to accompany him. Maybe he was just tired of her.

Over the last forty-eight hours, the questions haunted her. They stalked Irmgard's every waking hour, only to then invade her dreams. Each question spawned a dozen more, and when she had finished analyzing her way through the maze of doubt, she would move on to the next one. Over and over her mind worked various permutations as she followed her daily routine, and felt her soul growing cold and empty.

"Now hurry little one, we have to get dressed and get to work. Opa said he would come by this morning and take you with him for the day, won't that be fun?"

"Opa said I could give Tristan and Isolde carrots, and if they liked me he'll teach me to drive the wagon."

"I think they'll like you."

"Me too. And Mutti, maybe tonight Herr Gabe will be back."

"Ja, ja, maybe."

Irmgard had no one she could share her burden of concern with. Most of her friends and family would not understand. It was common for people to look with disdain at women who became involved with occupation troops. They were either prostitutes or gold diggers practicing the worst kind of fraternization with the enemy. It was for this same reason she couldn't go to the American authorities. How would it look? Would she get Gabe in trouble? And even if she could summon the courage to ask, she had no idea how to begin going about it. Worst of all, she was terrified of the answer she might find.

The longer Irmgard pondered her dilemma, the more she realized just how little she knew about Gabe, and how little he knew about her. She knew he was from Virginia, but not from which city. She knew he was married, unhappily, but not his wife's name. She had no idea the name or number of his outfit, or the name of his commanding officer. These mundane facts seemed unimportant in the heat of the moment, and she assumed she would learn these things in time. She also realized that for his part, he did not know where her parent's Bauernhof, farmstead, was, only that it was in the Black Forest somewhere.

When Gabe was fourteen days overdue, Irmgard decided to follow through with a plan she had conceived the week before Gabe left. It was part of the reason she could not travel with him, and it was a secret. She had arranged to sell her business, inventory and favorable lease to Mrs. Pilz's nephew Dieter. Dieter was a bachelor who had been severely wounded in Russia, where he had lost a leg. He had saved every pfennig of his military pay including his pension for being wounded. The shop was just the sort of thing he was looking for.

Irmgard had planned to put the proceeds of the sale towards the travel expenses of accompanying Gabe to the United States. She had conspired a thousand different ways to surprise him and now in bitter irony, the surprise was on her. It would be impossible for her to stay on. Wondering each time the tinkling of bells announced the front door opening, only to be disappointed, and that, for years on end. And so the sale was put into motion, the final price agreed upon, the papers to be drawn up and then signed, finalizing the transaction. The date for the signing was the first of August.

On that hot and humid day, two of her father's farmhands loaded her meager belongings into the wagon while Tristan and Isolde stood patiently in their traces, being fed an endless supply of carrots by Karl. Irmgard and then Dieter Pilz signed the agreement. Account records, a signed lease and a ring of keys were exchanged for a bank draft. Hands were shaken all around and the two of them left together.

Out on the street, Irmgard placed her hand on Dieter's arm, "I have a favor to ask of you." Dieter stopped and rested on his crutch.

"Of course. Anything. What can I do for you?"

Irmgard undid the strings of her leather folder and withdrew a sealed envelope from it. On the brown paper in her precise script was written a single word, 'Gabriel.'

"Dieter, would you please put this in a safe place, and if someone with this name ever comes looking for me, will you please give this to him."

"Of course, I will, of course." Dieter slid the envelope into a similar folder that he carried.

"Vielen Dank. Grüss Gott."

"Grüss Gott."

Dieter turned out to be an astute merchant. Business, if anything, increased. He began carrying a wider range of merchandise, and after a few months began considering renting the shop next door to expand his operation. He also turned out to be an extremely hard worker, the epitome of the German work ethic. He would collapse into bed each night exhausted, falling into deep dreamless sleep in short order.

On one such night, he drifted off with a lit cigarette in his hand. He was overcome by smoke before he could feel the flames. It was a humane twist of fate. He died in the ensuing fire, burned beyond recognition, his charred bones identified only with dental records. The shop, as well as the one next door burned to the ground and were a total loss.

Not a timber or crossbeam, piece of furniture, or item of merchandise survived. And neither did Irmgard's envelope for Gabe.

CHAPTER 29

The Forlorn Hope

It was the third time in as many nights that the four men had met to finalize their plans. In the impossible heat of Richmond in August, they sat in shirtsleeves and loosened neckties, suit jackets hanging on one hundred and twenty-five year old wooden pegs mounted on the wall of the converted tobacco warehouse. Damp handkerchiefs mopped brows and sweating bottles of Coca-Cola were constantly being shifted around to keep from wrinkling and staining the documents they were studying.

It had been more than a week since the long distance phone call had come into the office of the N.A.A.C.P. of Richmond, Virginia. The details of which had been meticulously recorded by Elijah Tobias, a law student volunteer who helped with legal matters several days a week. The message was then passed on to the chapter president Royston Maxwell, who deemed it of sufficient import to contact his team of lawyers, each of whom had his own law practice and worked for the association pro bono.

They spent the first forty-eight hours performing their due diligence, checking on the veracity of the tale Elijah had so carefully recorded. Satisfied, the four then met to compare notes and to strategically plan the appeal that would spare Enoch Baker's life.

Clarence Smith, the oldest and most experienced of the attorneys, was made chief counsel by general assent. He would assign tasks, collate material and ultimately decide which direction Enoch's defense should take. All of this needed to be done with the utmost urgency. Enoch had

Counsel for Baker to Ask Judge for Writ of Error

Judge Byron T. Colson will hear counsel for Enoch Baker, confessed rapist, sentenced to the death penalty, tomorrow afternoon in Corporation Court.

Baker, to have died in the electric chair this Friday, was recently given a 30-day reprieve by Governor Darden in order that his counsel might direct an appeal to Judge Colson.

Counsel for Enoch Baker this afternoon filed with the clerk of Corporation Court a petition addressed to Judge B. T. Colson for a writ of error *coram nobis* and motion for reversal of judgment under section 6329 Code of Virginia 1942.

In support of the petition they also offered a number of signed affidavits most of which were offered in evidence of Baker's "exceedingly low mentality."

Among those signing petitions were Mrs. Melissa Baker, Bessie Tyler, Andrew Tomblin, Marshall Manning, Floyd Carlin, Francine Sanborne, George D. Hoover, Roscoe B. Jones, B. Forrest Bowen, Bernard C. Ludwig, Reba M. Barley, Porter H. Cooper, Sally Warren, John K. Flowers, Kenneth Corley, Florence S, Marr Canfield A, Morton, Margaret Berry, John T. Fremont, Lester M. Perry and T.C. Barnes.

Attorneys for Baker according to the petition are Rockwell W. Robertson III, Landry Q. Ambrose, and W. Bennet Hopgood, Jr., all of Richmond and Clarence P. Smith, Jr. of Petersburg, Va.

The petition in part is as follows :

" * * * assign as error rendering said judgment and sentence null and void (1) action of the court convicting, adjudging, and ordering your petitioner and movant guilty of the crime upon basis of the confession and plea of guilty involuntarily procured from him and (2) the action of the court in convicting, adjudging and ordered your petitioner and movant guilty of the crime herein before set forth and imposing the aforesaid sentence upon him notwithstanding his insane condition, each of which was in violation of his rights under the law * * * "

---

a grim appointment to keep, and time had almost run out. The lawyers were willing, no, enthusiastic, to set everything in their lives aside for Enoch Baker.

At the initial meeting, in the relative cool of the evening, with the large warehouse windows tilted open and under a row of tin-hooded ceiling lights, Clarence summed up the case and gave each man an assignment needing to be done in no more than three days. Turning to Landry Ambrose he pushed a set of notes across the table towards him.

"Land, you know your way around the prison system." There were chuckles around the table. "You go and interview this Enoch Baker. We need to know everything that happened and size him up, and you have a mighty good sense of when somebody's trying to pull the wool over your eyes."

He pushed two more sheaves of paper to Ben Hopgood and Rockwell Robertson. "You two are going to be the backbone of this team.

I need you to begin researching this case, no holds barred, grasp any straw, turn over every rock. Concentrate on a writ of error, see which one fits this situation the best, once you have it, gather briefs, citations, anything we might need. I've given you two a thankless job, but I thank you, and I'm sure Mr. Baker will as well."

Clarence slid his own set of documents into his brief case. "I'll be traveling up to New Surrey to talk to the boy's mother, his pastor, and anyone else who'll talk to me. I'm hoping to speak with the Commonwealth's Attorney, but I'm not holding my breath on that one. I'll be calling each of you long distance at home every night to hear what you've found. We'll meet again Thursday night to organize our work. Good night." The four men stood together and left, each deep in his thoughts.

The next three days consisted of long hours and little sleep. The frenzied activity, the debates and counter debates, the reports by phone and in person served to nurture and bring to fruition a strategy. The hard work and sense of purpose in the task at hand, a task for which they had been trained, was an aphrodisiac stoking their ardor for the law. In unanimity the lawyers agreed that another two good days of work were needed, with the stipulation that the appeal be essentially completed. They continued to be in close communication those two days, as iron sharpens iron, they worked in one accord.

The strobe effect of summer lightening on the walls of the makeshift boardroom and the pregnant moments before the thunder's corresponding answer came gave a Shakespearean finality to their brain-storming. The first oversized drops of rain began beating a ragged tattoo on the tilted windows and a welcome cool breeze crossed the room, stirring the papers and bringing relief to the men in several ways. The tension was carried away with the breeze and discussion became easier.

As usual, an initial period of social intercourse ensued. Anecdotal insights and small triumphs and defeats were shared, each somehow related to the current case. Clarence eventually navigated the conversation to relevancy, and from that point on held as true as a compass needle to the mission: saving the life of Enoch Franklin Baker.

"All right now, here's what we're going to do. I'll read the writ through one last time. You listen carefully, go over it in your mind with a fine-toothed comb, if you hear anything problematic or have any ideas scribble them down and we'll get back to it when I'm done. Here we go." Clarence sat up straight, cleared his thought and by force of habit instilled an officious tone to his voice.

"PETITION FOR WRIT OF ERROR CORAM NOBIS AND MOTION FOR REVERSAL OF JUDGEMENT UNDER SECTION 6329, CODE OF VIRGINIA 1942. TO THE HONORABLE BYRON T. COLSON, JUDGE OF THE CORPORATION COURT OF THE CITY OF NEW SURREY:

The petition and motion of Enoch Franklin Baker respectfully represents:

One.) That your petitioner and movant is a citizen of the United States; that, prior to the twenty-third day of June, 1945, he was a resident of the City of New Surrey, Virginia; that since that date he was and is now confined at the Virginia State Penitentiary in Richmond, Virginia;

Two.) That on the fifteenth day of June, 1945, he was arrested and taken into custody by the police authorities of the City of New Surrey, Virginia, and was and has been held in their custody from that date until he was by them delivered to the custody of the Superintendent of the Virginia State Penitentiary; that on the fifteenth day of June, 1945, he was charged upon a warrant issued by R. Jan Flagler, Police Justice of the City of New Surrey, Virginia, with having, on the thirteenth day of June, 1945, committed the crime of rape upon one Norma Gabriel; that on the fifteenth day of June 1945, he waived, in writing, the finding of an indictment by a grand jury and consented to be placed on trial in Corporation Court of the City of New Surrey, Virginia, upon the warrant and charge made therein as aforesaid; that on the fifteenth day of June 1945, two attorneys were appointed by said Court to represent him; that on the twentieth day of June, 1945, he was arraigned is said Court upon said warrant and charge, whereupon he entered a plea of guilty; that on the twenty-third day of June, 1945, he was by said Court adjudged guilty of the crime of rape as charged in said warrant and sentenced to death by electrocution, all of which appears more fully from the records of this Court in the case of Commonwealth of Virginia versus Enoch Baker, and prayed to be read and considered as a part of this petition and motion;

Three.) That the sole claim and authority, by virtue of which your petitioner and movant is now restrained of his liberty and is now about to be executed, is the judgment and sentence aforesaid;

Four.) That the said judgment and sentence were obtained in the following manner, to-wit: That your petitioner and movant was on the fourteenth day of June, 1945, suddenly arrested without a warrant and without information as to the causes and reasons therefore, or the nature or cause of his accusation; that he was one of a large number of persons arrested and taken into custody by the police officials of the City of New Surrey, Virginia, in an effort to ascertain the identity of the perpetrator of the crime aforesaid, he was forced by police officers of the City of New Surrey, Virginia to dress himself in certain clothing and in a certain manner and exhibit himself before the said Norma Gabriel, and was immediately thereafter incarcerated in a cell in the police station of the City of New Surrey, Virginia; that he was there for the first time advised that he was being detained for the rape of said Norma Gabriel; that on the evening of the day aforesaid, he was, for several hours, continuously and persistently questioned by police officers of the City of New Surrey, Virginia, and an agent of the Federal Bureau of Investigation, concerning his whereabouts and activities on the night of June thirteenth, 1945; that during said period of interrogation he was told by the persons aforesaid that they believed and knew that he was guilty of the crime aforesaid; that they possessed evidence sufficient to convict him of said crime; that certain evidence had been by them discovered at the home of the said Norma Gabriel which conclusively demonstrated and established his guilt of the crime aforesaid; that a large number of persons had been arrested on the night before by police of the City of New Surrey, Virginia, and that none was the person who committed the crime aforesaid; that when he was placed on his trial his guilt would be established; that the people of the City of New Surrey, Virginia were aroused by said crime, and that a number of them would possibly assume the matter of inflicting punishment upon the guilty party; that he 'had better tell the truth' and 'had better confess' that he was guilty of the crime aforesaid; that it would be 'easier' if he confessed that he committed said crime; that if he did not so confess, he would be abandoned to the mob but that if he did confess, they would lend him assistance and protection; that he was abused and called vile names, and threatened with physical injury and violence; that despite his statement of hunger and request for food, he was denied the same; that early on the morning of the day following, to-wit the fifteenth day of June 1945, he was taken into the office of the Commonwealth's Attorney of the City of New Surrey, Virginia who then and there stated to him that he was in serious difficulty; that if he would 'play ball' with said Commonwealth's Attorney and 'tell the truth,' he, the said Commonwealth's Attorney, would assist him, but that if he did not do so, he would be seized by a mob and hanged; that your petitioner and movant had no funds with which to privately employ counsel in his behalf, and could not hope for an outcome of the case other than conviction and a sentence of death; that if your petitioner and movant confessed, attorneys for his defense would be procured; that it would be better for him to confess that he committed the crime, and that if he did, he, the said Commonwealth's Attorney, would assist in the avoidance of an imposition of the death sentence; that the said Commonwealth's Attorney read from a book in demonstration of the fact that under the law of the State of Virginia, it was possible to avoid the death penalty in cases of rape; that he, the said Commonwealth's Attorney, would confer with the Judge of the Corporation Court of the City of New Surrey, Virginia, in an effort to save your petitioner and movant from a penalty of death; that in consequence of these events and activities, and the nature and character of the crime with which he was charged, your petitioner and movant was highly excited, greatly apprehensive of bodily harm, worn, strained, and exhausted; was bewildered, confused and unable to think; was in great fear; that as a consequence of the facts and circumstances aforesaid, and because of his ignorance, lack of education, illiteracy, state of mentality, his unfamiliarity with and lack of understanding or comprehension of legal procedures and technicalities, his lack of opportunity to confer with counsel, his friends, or anyone else, your petitioner and movant believed that the evidence in the hands of the police officials of the City of New Surrey, Virginia pointed to his guilt and was sufficient to cause a jury or Court to believe that he was guilty, that he could not successfully sustain a defense to his prosecution for said crime, that the death penalty would be inflicted upon him, that if he did not state that he committed said crime, a mob would seize his person and subject him to violence, injury and death, that only by stating he committed said crime could he expect to save his life, and that the Commonwealth's Attorney, aforesaid would assist him, and would keep and perform his promise to request leniency of the Judge of the Corporation Court of the City of New Surrey, Virginia; that these circumstances engendered in his mind a feeling of despair and futility, and overpowered his will to continue to assert and insist upon his innocence of the crime alleged, and induced and required him to sign a statement , consisting of questions asked by the said Commonwealth's Attorney and answers by your petitioner and movant, to the effect that he was guilty of the crime aforesaid, and these and other further advices, indications and evidences of the gathering of a mob to injure or kill him, caused him to waive in writing the finding of an indictment by a grand jury and to be placed on trial upon a warrant charging said crime, all on the date aforesaid, to-wit, the fourteenth day of June, 1945 and caused him, on the twentieth day of June, 1945, to enter a plea of guilty, and caused him to refrain from offering evidence in his behalf upon his trial on the twenty-third day of June, 1945, and caused him to refrain from calling the attention of the Judge of the Corporation Court of the City of New Surrey, Virginia, to the facts and circumstances thereof; that no such confession, plea of guilty, waiver of indictment or failure to present evidence in his behalf would have occurred save for the causes and inducements aforesaid; that the judgment and sentence of the said Court, aforementioned, were imposed in consequence of his confession, plea of guilty, and failure to present evidence in his defense.

Five.) That your petitioner and movant was, on the thirteenth day of June, 1945, and was since that date continuously to the present, and consequently upon the dates of the confession, plea of guilty, judgment and sentence, aforesaid suffering from a disease affecting his mental faculties to the extent that he was, at all times hereinbefore stated, incapable of distinguishing between right and wrong, and incapable of resisting insane impulses flowing from his diseased mind, and incapable of committing the crime of rape, and legally disabled from being tried, convicted, sentenced or punished therefore;

Six.) That none of the matters, hereinbefore stated in paragraph four and five, was, for the reasons and causes aforesaid, brought to the attention of the Corporation Court of the City of New Surrey, Virginia, upon the trial, conviction, and sentence of your petitioner and movant, and consequently none was considered by said Court in connection with the issue of his guilt or innocence or in mitigation of the punishment inflicted; that either of these matters, if known, would have legally prevented the judgment rendered and sentence imposed;

Seven.) That, as hereinbefore set forth, your petitioner and movant had and still has a meritorious, full and sufficient defense to the charge upon which he was tried;

Eight.) That for the reasons aforesaid, your petitioner and movant is now actually, unjustly and unlawfully imprisoned and restrained of his liberty, and detained under sentence of death under authority of the Commonwealth of Virginia, in violation of his rights under the Constitution and laws of the Commonwealth of Virginia;

Nine.) That since your petitioner and movant was, as hereinbefore set forth, prevented from utilizing remedies available at his trial, and is now prevented from taking an appeal or applying a writ of error from the Supreme Court of Appeals because the record is fair on its face and the matters herein complained of do not appear therein and no errors of this Court can be shown in said record as it now stands, and is now prevented from applying for a new trial by reason of the expiration of the term of this Court at which such judgment was rendered and such sentence was imposed, and is now prevented from moving in arrest of said judgment by reason of the fact that the face of the record is fair and in appearance all the precedings are regular, he is now remediless, save in this proceeding in this Court;

Ten.) That your petitioner and movant assigns as error rendering said judgment and sentence null and void (one) the action of the Court in convicting, adjudging and ordering your petitioner and movant guilty of the crime hereinbefore set forth and in imposing the aforesaid sentnence upon him, upon the basis of the confession and plea of guilty involuntarily procured from him, as aforesaid, and (two) the action of the Court in convicting, adjudging and ordering your petitioner and movant guilty of the crime hereinbefore set forth and in imposing the aforesaid sentence upon him, notwithstanding his insane condition; each of which was in violation of his rights under the Constitution and laws of the United States and the Constitution and laws of the State of Virginia, and more specifically, the Fourteenth Amendment of said Constitution of the United States and Article one, section eight and eleven of the Constitution of Virginia;

Eleven.) Wherefore, to prevent a further miscarriage of justice and to relieve your petitioner and movant from additional punishment on a judgment which is null and void, your petitioner and movant prays for an order and judgment setting aside and quashing the judgment rendered against him on his confession and plea aforesaid, and declaring said judgment null and void, and that this Court make such further orders deemed and found necessary to obtain your petitioner and movant complete discharge from said judgment and sentence."

Clarence sat back and emptied half of his bottle of Coca-Cola. The others sat in silence; none of them had scribbled a single note or question. The sound of the rain blowing over the windows filled the vacuum caused by the contemplative silence. After a time the slow rhythmic smack of a clapping hand dispelled the reverie. Landry Ambrose was momentarily speechless and found himself expressing his sentiments with simple applause. Clarence smiled and joined in, which in turn inspired Ben Hopgood to clap as well. The clapping accelerated and increased in intensity, Rockwell didn't know how to react. He looked down and allowed a small smile to cross his lips. The smile widened and soon he and everyone else were laughing in congratulatory good humor.

"Hot damn, boy, you outdid yourself this time." Landry blurted out and then gave a contrite look at Clarence. The men had a tacit agreement to not use coarse language amongst them. "Sorry. Brilliant, absolutely brilliant."

"I agree. You've covered every base, crossed every T and dotted every I. Excellent work, Rock, you've outdone yourself." Clarence waxed effusive.

Landry asked the all-important question. "What about the rumors and unsubstantiated fact that their sexual union may have been consensual and not rape at all? Are we going to mention that? Point out the old cliché 'it takes two to tango'?"

"Ben and I discussed that and we feel that it's too emotionally charged. You know as well as I do that it never ends well once the so-called honor of Southern womanhood enters the picture. It would simply come down to a ' he-said, she-said' type argument, and who are they going to believe?"

"What about witnesses? It seems all the coloreds knew what was going on, you know how things like that get around, and I'm sure there are more than one gossiping old biddy in among the whites that knew about the affair." Landry continued.

"Yes, we discussed that as well, but here's the problem, you know what it's like in those small towns, the colored folks are just plain scared and the whites too proud or apathetic to stand up for some poor ignorant colored boy." Rockwell replied.

"I think you made the right choice, that's a dangerous road we don't want to go down." Clarence interjected.

"Dangerous or not, it's the truth and as my Grandmother used to say, the truth will stand when everything else falls." Landry replied, with a slight edge to his voice.

"And my Grand-daddy used to say, ' son, pick your battles, is this really the hill you want to die on? Clarence answered with continued calmness. "I think the writ takes the wisest course under the circum-stances, maybe the consensual affair angle would work in New York or Detroit, but I think it's too dangerous anywhere below the Mason-Dixon line. Rock, I'm very impressed, I think you and Ben put together an excellent document. Thank you."

"Let's just hope the Judge is as impressed as we are." Rockwell intoned, as a reminder of the solemn nature the work.

"How can he not, it's as obvious as the nose on his face. Enoch Baker was railroaded." Ben interjected.

"It seems everyone but the Judge and Commonwealth's Attorney knows that, but it's a different matter getting them to admit they were wrong." Clarence acknowledged the obvious doubt occupying the extra seat at the table.

"Especially with the judge running for congress." Ben added.

"You got that right." Landry agreed.

"Well, gentleman, let's have the briefs done citing precedent, and the affidavits I brought back, including the Wasserman test results, positive for syphilis, so that we're ready to go the first part of next week." Clarence was tired and intent on wrapping up their meeting.

Ben interrupted them. "Well, no matter what happens, at least we know we have done everything in our limited power to save this man. That's something we can be proud of, and Lord willing, may just work." Ben Hopgood then stood, walked to a wall cabinet and removed four scratched and chipped coffee mugs. He rooted around in his overstuffed satchel and extracted a fifth of bourbon, pouring a small tot in each cup. He passed them around, stood at the head of the table next to Clarence and offered a toast. "Gentlemen, we are 'The Forlorn Hope'. I give you The Forlorn Hope, one for all, all for one."

The four attorneys tapped their mugs together and drank. The look on their faces was mild bewilderment. "All right then, what's this all about?" Clarence asked.

"Yes, I'm afraid I don't understand either, doesn't sound very promising." Rockwell added in his typically melancholic fashion.

Landry sat quietly, waiting for the explanation. "And you call your-selves educated men? Elijah dubbed us that, you know how much he loves history. Well, the Forlorn Hope was a group of strictly volunteers who would be the first to carry a ladder to the wall of a besieged fortress or enter the breech. It was considered suicidal and generally was. However if successful, the rewards and promotions could be great." Ben smiled broadly and poured another sip into each cup. "Gentleman, to The Forlorn Hope."

"To The Forlorn Hope." The men agreed, and drank the second toast.

CHAPTER 30

Not a
Prayer

Shortly after one o'clock the sky darkened to a gray-green. The thunder served as Mosaic background over the lone voice of Clarence Smith and the studied silence of the spectators filling the courtroom. Everyone turned their heads in unison towards the mullioned windows as the deluge began with its attendant roar. It was as if the pressure of the falling rain was sucking the air from the building, as if the profound drop in barometric pressure could ripple the Confederate battle flag that hung framed over the mantle of the court room's obsolete fireplace

By anyone's standard, the presentation of the writ of error coram nobis was a tedious exercise in complex and archaic jurisprudence. Clarence Smith served up a word salad of legal terms that few in the audience, or for that matter the bench, found appetizing or digestible, presenting arguments and counterarguments that only legal minds could follow. The spectators, mostly colored seated in the balcony, were there as a moral presence. They sat silent and grim and mostly bored, but sit they did, in affirmation of a miscarriage of justice that had been perpetrated on their neighbor and kin Enoch Franklin Baker.

Mercifully the afternoon drew to a close. Judge Colson expressed perfunctory gratitude to all parties, announced he would render his decision in several days after due consideration and left the courtroom as all stood. His professional demeanor did not break until he entered chambers. He stalked over to his desk, raised the stack of papers to chest level and let them drop onto the blotter, loose papers escaping the pile and drifting to the floor like autumn leaves. He tore his robe over his head,

Counsel For Baker Claim Judgment Is Null And Void

SAY CONSTITUTIONAL RIGHTS VIOLATED

Counsel for Enoch Baker convicted of rape and sentenced to die in the electric chair appeared before Judge Byron T. Colson this afternoon requesting by petition a writ of *error coram nobis* and motion for reversal of judgment under section 6329, Code of Virginia.

They based their requests for relief on the grounds that Enoch Baker's confession was involuntarily and improperly procured, that an involuntary plea of guilty was used in obtaining his conviction and that by reason of his mental condition he could not legally have been tried.

The hearing was set by Judge Colson for 1 o'clock, but before that hour the Corporation Courtroom was crowded—with spectators—mostly colored people.

At 12:50 all the seats on one side of the room were filled with negro spectators and 15 or 20 more stood about the entrance. They continued to arrive until by court time the seats at both sides were filled mostly with colored people and they crowded both entrances. There was no disorder.

Attorneys for Baker sat at the right of the judge, their table covered with legal documents and books.

Newton P. Vann, commonwealth's attorney arrived a few minutes after 1 o'clock and Judge Colson entered at 1:05.

Clarence P. Smith, Jr., Petersburg, admitted to practice in the New Surrey court subscribed to the oath and then introduced the remaining attorneys for Baker. They were Rockwell W. Robertson III, Bennet Hopgood, Jr., and Landry Q. Ambrose, all of the Richmond bar. Their oaths were also administered.

Smith presented papers in the case to the court and to Mr. Vann and immediately launched into a long discussion of Baker's rights in seeking remedy in the fashion presented before the court.

He explained at great length the procedure under which action was being sought citing numerous cases in which action similar to that sought by Baker had been given.

Smith stated that the council would show the court certain matters not existing in the records, information outside the scope of the records that would be sufficient for a reversal of judgment.

Indicating that the matter of Baker's sanity and mental condition would be a factor in the case. Smith stated that the counsel had requested the superintendent of the state penitentiary to have Baker examined and that he had refused on the grounds that such request would have to come from the governor.

Smith said that he through the judge, could request such a procedure but insisted that they wished to proceed under judicial rights rather than legislative.

The matter of procedure was still being presented at 2:45 with none of the new information having been presented.

---

bunched it up and hurled it into a leather chair. He muttered a litany of obscenities worthy of the mule skinner's art. He clipped the string of curses, opened the door, heavily placed his old copper ice bucket on his secretary's desk and bellowed to no one in particular, "Fill this damn thing with ice, I don't care if you have to go to Alaska to get it."

The stars pierced the heavenly firmament with brilliance that no man-made light could diminish. The afternoon's storm cleared and cooled the air; a light breeze carried the first divination of the end of summer.

It was the kind of night that Newt Vann loved. He had spent most of the evening sipping bourbon and branch and rereading a Dashiel Hammet mystery. At eleven thirty he was not only wide-awake, but also slightly invigorated by the change in weather. He marked his place, stood, checked his pockets for a cigar and lighter and walked to the coat tree standing next to the door. When Mr. Hoover heard the jangle of his collar and leash he was besides himself with joy. The middle aged Scottish terrier transformed into a puppy at the familiar sound.

"Settle down, Herbert, settle down, let's go for a stroll."

Mr. Hoover and Mr. Vann walked the empty streetlamp-dappled streets in excellent fettle, enjoying a glimpse into private lives revealed by lighted windows. The pair of middle-aged politicians also enjoyed the long stretches of starlit darkness, and at each corner, Hoover took a contrary turn leading them farther from home. Soon they found themselves walking a block off main street. Between the trees Vann could see the shadow form of the old municipal courthouse rising toward the stars, it's four-sided clock dimly backlit. Halfway up the black edifice, well below the clock face, a lone window shone bright with light.

"Well, lookee here, Herbert, the Judge is burning the midnight oil. I'll bet he's madder than a wet hen that those colored boys dared to challenge his judgment. What ya say we go over and see if we can cheer him up? You being a Republican and all." Vann laughed out loud.

Vann let himself into the building. As Commonwealth's Attorney, his office was on the second floor. Vann led Mr. Hoover to the fifth floor where the Judge had his office and knocked lightly on the door.

The Judge opened the door. His eyes were sunken, carrying dark baggage beneath them. His steel gray hair looked as if clumsy fingers had raked through it a hundred times. "Newt, what brings you out so late? Anything I can do for you?"

"Well, we wouldn't refuse a drink. Herbert and I were out taking the air and saw your light shining out like a beacon of justice."

"You ever run out of bullshit? All right, come in, I need a little break anyway. That mangy mutt of yours isn't going to piss on my carpet is he?" The Judge scowled.

"He just might, you know Mr. Hoover is a Republican." Vann's retort was made to the Judge's back having turned to retrieve a bottle and some glasses.

"You know, Newt, I'm not so sure it's entirely appropriate for you to be here." The Judge sat heavily in a leather chair, as he motioned for Vann to toss the robe off the other and have a seat.

"Well, it's just two old friends having a drink, and I'm sure Mr. Hoover won't say anything, even though he belongs on the other side of the aisle."

"Did you think that nigger, er, worthy negro attorney, would ever finish? Good Lord, I had to piss like a race horse, another five minutes of that torture and I'd a sent him to the chair, too." The Judge pronounced without a trace of humor in his voice.

"My, my, Judge, a little testy are we?"

"Yes, I'm testy, I'm exhausted and feel like I've been ridden hard and put up wet. I'm surprised you're so cheery, hell, they disparaged you even more than they did me."

"Ridden hard and put up wet, huh? Well then, an old war horse like yourself shouldn't take it so hard, hell, it's just water off a duck, if you pardon all the critter metaphors." Vann reflected with an outward lightness of heart. "It's just those black boys doing their job and can't say I blame 'em. I'd do the same if I were in their shoes. It's the law, Judge, nothing personal in it."

"Maybe so, but I'll be damned to have my judgment questioned by some uppity colored lawyers from some Dogpatch law school. The more I think about it the madder it makes me. Trying to get that rapist son-of-a-bitch off scot-free."

"Aw Judge, forget about that, it's not about the rape, if that's what it was, it's about the writ of error, and a masterful piece of work it is, if I do say so myself." Vann sipped his drink and clipped the end off his cigar.

"Masterful nothing, it's a damned pain in my ass. Wish I had a big rubber stamp and pad of red ink. Know what that stamp would say?" The Judge didn't wait for an answer, "It'd be one word, NO. With red ink. That's what it would say."

Vann started laughing, "I thought you surely had one of those, Judge, I surely did. So besides rubber stamping those papers, how are you handling it.?"

"Why the hell do you think I'm still here? I have to refute the damn briefs case by case and then cite other precedents to support my decision." The Judge pulled the brass ashtray stand over next to Vann.

"So you've already made your decision?" Newt leered.

"Hell, I had my decision made before those boys left Richmond. Don't you remember, Newt, I made a decision back in June, seems nobody but me respects that though. Now, it's just research."

"Don't you have some law clerks to do that?" Vann raised his eyebrows as he spoke.

"I do, but this is too important for amateurs, you and that damned Republican dog of yours ought to know that."

"True, true, ain't that right Herbert?" Vann bent down and scratched Hoover's head.

"Well then, Judge, we better let you get back to it. Thanks for the drink, keep up the good work." Vann stood, shook the Judge's hand and unsteadily made his way to the door.

"Oh, by the way, you'll be receiving a request for a witnessed and signed affidavit refuting the allocations point by point. There are a few more of those going out as well. You will do a good job, won't you Newt." The Judge spoke in the imperative.

"You know I will, Judge, you know I will. I'd say goodnight, but seeing as I've never been here seems kind of pointless." Vann closed the door lightly behind him.

CHAPTER 31

An Address

Ｉt wasn't until Sam Burns had run out of excuses and petty tasks that he finally set out for Ogden Street. His duties as Clerk of the Court had played out for the day, although he did manage to stay a full hour later than usual catching up his files. He lingered over supper chatting with his wife and children until their patience began to fray. He stopped for cigarettes, an evening paper and a pack of Beemans gum, each at a different shop and exchanged prolonged pleasantries with folks he knew in the stores and along the way.

The sun was setting noticeably earlier as summer drew to a close. Streetlights came alive with an audible click; something that not everyone could hear, but Sam had always had good ears, poor eyes, but good ears. The call of mothers beckoning their children in from their post-supper adventures rang through the neighborhoods. Vehicular traffic was light as he turned onto Ogden Street and made his way to number seventeen. The house had a forlorn look to it that Sam never noticed before. The shades were drawn and only a distant light shone through the transom window above the door. He knocked loudly, and then regretted it as having sounded too much like the demanding knock of the police.

From the other side of the door a female voice asked, "Who is it?" There was no hostility in the voice, neither was there any note of greeting.

"It's Sam, Sam Burns, here to see Missy."

"What do you want with her?" The voice sharpened slightly.

"I've got something for her. She asked me to bring it over."

264

"Let me see if'n she wants to see you." The voice said heading away from the door.

"All right then, she'll talk with you." came the reply several long moments later. The door opened to reveal Lily, the Reverend Crenshaw's sister-in-law, standing squarely in the doorway like Cerberus guarding the gates of Hades.

Sam stepped forward and offered his right hand to the woman. "How do you do, my name is Sam Burns, are you staying with Missy?"

"Yes I am, I'm Lily, an old friend of Missy's. She needs as many friends as she can get right now, and you mind what you say to her. You upset her any more than she 'ready is you going to have to answer to me." The woman turned abruptly and began walking back to the kitchen. Sam stood for a moment, his right hand still extended. She expected Sam to follow her, and he did.

They entered the kitchen and without offering Sam a chair, Lily went to get her charge. Sam looked around the shabby room and wondered at how often Enoch had eaten here, how many good times and bad had occurred here. It was inconceivable to think that Enoch would never see this place again. Lily soon returned and asked him to follow her to the parlor.

The sole lamp with its rose colored globe weakly illuminated the room in pink light. Sam's eyes took a moment to adjust to the strangely tinted and shadowed surroundings. Missy Baker was seated in a tufted upholstered chair, and she did not rise or make any obvious acknowledgement of Sam's presence in the room. Lily motioned for him to be seated on the tired sofa. It was only then that Missy's eyes seemed to focus and she spoke quietly. "Hello, Sam, thank you for coming." Her voice was flat with resignation.

Sam, like the others, was shocked by Missy's appearance. She had aged considerably since he seen her last. Even in the odd lighting he could see that her usual nut-brown skin had a grayish hue. Her hair appeared coarse and shot through with streaks of dull metallic gray as it was drawn back from her forehead. She gave the perception of having shrunk in on herself. Sam tried very hard not to drown in the pity rising in and around him like a flood, the sense of hopelessness and despair

Petition And Motion For Baker Dismissed By Court

Court Rules Petition Was Without Merit

Judge Byron T. Colson has declared that the petition for a writ of *error coram nobis* and motion for reversal of judgment, argued yesterday by counsel for Enoch Baker, convicted rapist who has been sentenced to die for his crime, were without merit and as such were denied and dismissed.

The counsel took exception to the ruling of the court, indicating they will now, probably by means of habeas corpus seek to carry their appeal to the Supreme Court.

Judge Colson requested that the exception be noted today as his mind was made up in the matter.

Smaller Crowd

Not as many people were present today as were on hand yesterday, but still the majority of spectators were negroes. There was no demonstration upon the court's decision.

Opening court a few minutes after 10 o'clock, Judge Colson immediately delivered his 14-page opinion. There were no interruptions.

First of all, in the course of his statement, Judge Colson reviewed the history of the case declaring that on June 23 at Baker's trial, these facts were proved:

Reviews Facts

Until dusk on the evening of June 13, Baker's victim was occupied with some activities on the lawn, and at dusk she went to an upstairs bedroom and bathroom with the purpose of washing linen. She turned on the lights in these rooms which were the only lights on in the house. Fully clothed, she neglected to draw the blinds.

While in the bathroom she heard the front door open and thinking it was her mother-in-law, she closed the bathroom door. Some minutes later attracted by an unusual noise from her cat she opened the door. A man whose face was masked, a handkerchief under his eyes, confronted her. He was attired in a tan gabardine jacket, brown pants and hat. In his hand he held an instrument leveled at her, which she mistook for a pistol but some time later discovered to be a knife.

Taking hold of her, Baker pulled her into the hall. She offered money but he said that was not he wanted. Whereupon she attempted to free herself and opened her mouth to scream. As she did so, he assaulted her with the knife which he placed on her throat and said, "Better not do that."

Acted To Save Life

At this time she became fearful that in addition to ravishing her it was Baker's intention to kill her. Throughout the ordeal she was possessed by this thought. She testified that all her actions were for the purpose of saving her life.

It was the opinion of the court that from the type of weapon used, from the promptness with which it was brandished she endeavored to cry for help, that her fears was supported by reasonable grounds.

After the ravishment had been completed she pleaded with Baker for her life, assuring him that if he would leave she would make no report to the authorities. This he accepted and immediately departed, leaving forgotten in the bed the knife and other evidence.

As soon as she had undergone such precautions as she could to protect herself, the crime was reported to the police. They were given an exact description of the physical appearance of the rapist and the clothing which he wore. The evidence left by Baker was identified by the police as being used only by laborers at the plant of The American Synthetic Fibers Corporation at Riverton.

Investigation Established Facts

In the establishment of these facts at the trial, the commonwealth was not indebted to any statement of the accused, Baker. Armed with the information that the assailant was a colored man and an employee of the American Synthetic Fiber Corporation, police officers rounded up and confronted a number of negro employees and city residents that evening. In each instance she positively stated it was the wrong man. When confronted by Baker, she made a spontaneous and immediate identification, and in her testimony at the trial she stated that she had no doubt that he was the man.

Jones, the police officer, testified that her identification was accompanied by an immediate shriek and a loss of composure.

(Continued on Page 2. Col. 3)

Petition And Motion Dismissed (Continued from Page 1.)

Evidence In Every Detail

The victim's testimony was corroborated by irrefutable evidence in every essential detail. That force was used was established by the discovery of Baker's knife; that Baker is the guilty man was established by the discovery in his home of every article of clothing worn by the rapist at the time of the assault, and by proof of the fact that after the rapist left her home, Baker, garbed in these very clothes returned to his home and changed to other clothing. Particularly impressive was the description of and discovery in the possession and ownership of Baker of the gabardine jacket, which is described as being of unusual design. Police Officer Jones testified that of 26 New Surrey colored men employed at the American Synthetic Fibers plant, Baker was the only one who possessed a jacket.

The fact that carnal connection was had and completed is established by the finding in the chemical laboratory of the F. B. I.

Appoint Capable Counsel

Before discussing the motion now before the court, the judge deemed it advisable to review the actions taken by the court to protect the rights of the accused.

Upon being informed by the commonwealth's attorney of the nature of the charge against Baker, and that he was without means to employ counsel, this court designated counsel to represent him. Such counsel were carefully selected and consisted of Ernest Oakes Esq. and R.J. Harrington of Riverton.

That the counsel for Baker was capable, Judge Colson pointed out by reciting their 15 year record of active practice in federal and state courts in both civil and criminal cases.

Their integrity and capacity deserved respect, he stated, and continued:

It is significant that neither in the petition in this case, nor in any of the affidavits is there any intimation that in the defense of this cause they acted improperly or negligently or without full consideration of their duties to the accused.

Relied On Mercy Of Court

They could have opposed the commonwealth at all stages of the proceedings, but had they elected to submit the fate of their client to a jury, in evidence of the guilt against him heretofore outlined, it is difficult to see what defense they could have prepared on his behalf.

Had they gone before a jury on a plea of not guilty, they faced what appears to be conclusive evidence in the possession of the commonwealth, establishing the guilt of their client.

In this situation, and having obtained concession from the commonwealth that he would make no recommendation as to the death penalty, they adopted the strategy of full cooperation with the commonwealth by waiver of indictment and plea of guilty. At the trial they argued earnestly and with ability that their client was entitled to the mercy of the court.

Explained To Baker

It was pointed out that before Baker was permitted to waive indictment, the court made a detailed explanation to him of his rights.

With this background established, Judge Colson then took up the petition: their contention that at the time of the crime and at the time of the trial Baker was insane, and that his confession and pleas of guilty were obtained by the fraud of the commonwealth's attorney and other officers and were made as a result of fear, duress and fraud.

No Insanity Proof

It is not only the inadequacy of the evidence offered that fails to make the case of insanity, it is the omissions that are most striking, the judge declared. He pointed out that an affidavit of Baker's mother, his brothers and sisters and a statement of a New Surrey physician who treated him for eight years did not say he was insane. In the doctor's statement he pointed out that there was not a line stating that he had observed anything unusual in Baker's conduct, or even that Baker was not of average mentality.

Most significant, the judge pointed out is the absence of any statement from the counsel of Baker as to their investigation of sanity before the trial. "It is not to be assumed that competent counsel would permit a client to plead guilty to an offense punishable by death without satisfying themselves that a motion under code section 4909 would be of value." he said, and added that if there be any doubt as to sanity, the provisions of code section 5007 are available.

Discounts Baker's Charges

Declaring that the charges of fraud, duress and fear should be considered first upon the facts, the judge took up each of Baker's accusations. He pointed out that there was no mob violence exhibited at any time; that when (Continued on Page 3. Col. 2)

267

Petition And Motion Dismissed *(Continued from Page 2.)*

Baker was brought before open court on several occasions, in no instance did the court observe any large and hostile crowds as charged. Nor was any condition of nervousness, strained apprehension and confusion on the part of the prisoner observed by the court.

Charges Termed Ludicrous

As to certain interviews alleged to have taken place between the accused and police officers, and the charge made against the commonwealth's attorney, Judge Colson said:

"It is noted that the affidavit fails to name the officers in question, and as for charges against the the commonwealth's attorney, the court finds these to be inherently incredible, against an experienced lawyer who, is rounding out 25 years service as attorney of the commonwealth of this court. No possible motive can be assigned for a man of his experience and standing to be guilty of the lawless and high-handed conduct which Baker charges. The accusation that this official threatened Baker with murder and deceived him into false confession without any assigned motive appears to the court to be ludicrous and unbelievable.

In the picture of fear, fraud and oppression which is painted, the effort is made to obliterate Baker's former counsel. But they can not be removed from the scene. Thoroughly capable and completely honest, they were there through it all.

Where were they when the mob formed? Where is their motion for a change of venue? In their numerous interviews with Baker, some of which were held alone in the office of the judge, did they fail to note the alleged low mentality of their client? Is the court to assume they learned of threats and false promises to him, and failed to act thereon? Were they afraid? Were they deluded?" he asked.

Contention Without Merit

It is contended that in spite of the foregoing, the statements of Baker, for the purposes of this motion, must be considered as upon a demurrer to the evidence. Under section 6329, it is conceded the court has the authority to weigh the evidence to determine whether or not a case is made, but, it is argued, that the common law writ is not abborgated, but merely supplemented by the statute. It is not necessary to decide this to reach the conclusion that this contention is without merit.

The clear facts before the court are that the plea of guilty was deliberately and freely interpreted under the advice of counsel in hopes of attaining mercy of this court. The case was argued fully from that view. That one may voluntarily enter such a plea and being disappointed in the results, by the simple expedient of obtaining new counsel, and making uncorroborated reckless charges against responsible public officials, he may thereby overturn the former judgment and obtain a new hearing, is not, and could not, be sound law. If such were the law, there could be no finality to any legal proceeding.

Therefore the court finds the facts averred in this petition do not make out a case for issuance of a writ. The objection of the commonwealth appearing in its motion to strike are also well taken. This court at the trial made full inquiry into the circumstances of the confession and ruled it admissible. The plea of guilty was made in open court and under the considerate advice of competent counsel. Hence these matters have been adjudicated. All of the facts alleged if true were known to Baker prior to waiver of indictment and confession in open court. Protection of the law was around him and there is no conceivable reason why he could have presented such contention at the trial."

Declaring that by present motion Baker sought to take advantage of his design or negligence, Judge Colson declared the petition and motion as being without merit and "are denied and dismissed."

---

siphoned off the air around him. He had trouble filling his lungs with the air needed to speak.

"Missy, I'm so sorry about all of this, and I'm ashamed. I'm ashamed of being an officer of that court and how wrong . . . "

"Thank you Mr. Sam, we all know it's not your fault, not your fault at all."

"I just wish to God that there was something I could do to change things, that there was something anyone could do."

"We do too." Lily's voice rose out of the shadows.

"He in God's hands now, everybody tells me that, and I believe it. Got to believe it, else wise . . . else wise, don't know what'd I do."

"All them other people in God's hand too, and He gonna pay 'em back for this, He surely will. Bible say 'vengeance is Mine, saith the Lord.' He gonna catch up with that woman and that Judge and that Newton Vann. Maybe not today, maybe not tomorrow either, maybe at Judgment Day, but He gonna catch up with 'em, believe you me." Lily's hard voice filled the dim room.

"Amen." came Sam's simple answer.

"Maybe we should pray for them." Missy's words came with a catch in her throat.

"I can't, not now. I know it's the Christian thing to do, but, I can't, not right now, maybe someday, but not now, not here." Lily replied.

"Me neither." Missy whispered.

"Nor I." Sam joined in.

"Mr. Sam, you got something for me?"

Sam reached into the inner pocket of his linen jacket and extracted an envelope. The envelope was unsealed and in it was a single sheet of paper, and on the paper was written a single address. Handing it to Missy, he said, "Remember what I told you, my Uncle Walt is a big shot with the Red Cross, so you give it to me and I can get it there in a couple of days, instead of a couple of months."

"Yes, I remember. I will. Thank you, Sam, thank you for everything, you're a good man Sam Burns, a good man." Missy stood and beckoned Sam to her, she wrapped her arms around him and pressed her head to his chest. Sam in his surprise brought his arms up around her and returned the hug. "Now I got a letter to write."

Lily walked Sam to the door, thanked him and said good night. She returned to the living room to find it dark and empty. She shrugged and returned to her work in the kitchen.

CHAPTER 32

Battle
Fatigue

Oh, that way madness lies; let me shun that.
WILLIAM SHAKESPEARE

Gabe's recuperation was a slow, grinding process. There were numerous setbacks and minimal measured improvement. Each day Gabe's frustration and impatience grew, their tendrils enveloping his mind. He projected his distorted emotions and perceptions onto the staff with belligerent obstinacy. While the workers recognized his conduct as an expected sequelae to the recovery process, the care of Private First Class Gabriel stretched their patience to the breaking point.

There were several reasons for the behavior, which was so out of character for Gabe. While his body was slowly, steadily healing, his mind spiraled into darkness. He could not adjust to becoming a care receiver instead of a caregiver, and this, due to sheer stupidity and a handful of drunken G.I.s. In the haze of pain and opioid induced confusion he lost track of time, never knowing the date or time of the day. He also lost track of the only people that mattered to him. His marriage had died on the vine, its roots being shallow and the separation of time and distance not allowing it to be cultivated and nurtured. There had been no word from her in months, and his mother's occasional letters were only banal chitchat. When first regaining consciousness after the accident, he was asked if his wife should be notified. "No" was his monosyllabic answer. His later queries about Irmgard also proved fruitless. Returned letters and, more disturbing, reports from his platoon buddies that the shop no longer existed, pushed him closer to the edge. Thoughts of losing Irmgard multiplied his suffering ten-fold.

There was one more thing. Doctor Howard had begun to wean him off of the morphine that had sustained him for almost two months. The dosage was gradually being decreased and the intervals between administrations of the drug were lengthened. Gabe would break into a sweat, grow nauseous, tremble and become disoriented long before it was time for his next dose. Sleep eluded him, allowing ample time to contemplate the darkness and grow acutely aware of his body's yearning for the poppy. He was denied the sanctuary of sleep and the results were deeply telling. His nights were filled with the faces of Irmgard and Norma, his father and a hundred dead and dying soldiers, named and unnamed. When sleep did finally arrive, it was no sanctuary, but a repository of ever more terrible dreams.

The sun angling into the atrium atop the military hospital formed miniature Jacob's ladders for the dust motes to ascend and descend. The light had a perfect clarity, more characteristic of Florence than of London. The newly glazed windows, courtesy of a nearby German V-2 explosion, had not yet been coated with industrial grime, giving the daylight a jewel-like radiance. It would be one of the last truly sunny days before the damp grayness of autumn settled over London. Gabe neither appreciated it, nor cared, nor noticed.

His wheelchair was parked in a pool of sunlight. A blanket covered his legs and a threadbare cardigan sweater enveloped his thin upper body. He sat there with the hopeless resignation of an invalid, old before his time. A small dose of morphine recently administered was easing his discomfiture. On his lap rested a copy of Great Expectations, open, but unread.

Gabe looked up as a cheery female voice addressed him from behind, "Good morning, Private Gabriel, and how are we this lovely morning?"

Slowly spinning his chair around to face Maureen, a nurse volunteer who had managed to make occasional connections with him, he looked at her through glassy eyes, "How are we?" I don't know how 'we' are, but I'm more fucking dead than alive, that's how 'we' are."

"Now Gabe, there's no need for that kind of language. It was just a friendly question."

"You're right. How about I'm more bloody dead than bloody alive. How's that? Better?"

Maureen's eyes pierced Gabe's as she rose to the challenge, smiling sweetly and saying, "Why yes, as a matter of fact it is. But not by much."

Gabe made no reply, his stare passing through her. She continued nonplussed, "I see you're reading Great Expectations, one of my very favorites, and if I may say so, one of Mr. Dickens' very best. Pip. Mrs. Haversham, what a sad, wonderful story."

"Sad . . . wonderful . . . " Gabe repeated with a blank expression.

"While I'm here, is there anything I can get you?"

"Sure, how about a bottle of cognac, a couple of morphine syrettes and a loaded forty-five?" Gabe replied with a bitterness in his voice.

Again she rose to his sarcasm. "Actually, I was thinking more along the lines of some tea and biscuits. Gabe, if tea and bikkies don't cheer you up, how about these?" and with that, she produced two letters from the pocket of her apron. She made to hand them to Gabe and reaching toward her the book toppled to the floor. His sluggish reflexes allowed the letters to fall as well. "Here, let me help you with that." Maureen squatted to pick up the letters and book.

Gabe lashed out at her, his words venomous. "Stop it. Just stop it. Can't you just leave me the fuck alone? Get out of here and just leave me the fuck alone. Nobody asked you to come up here," with that, Gabe stood up. The blood rushed from his head causing the room to spin. He tried to steady himself on the arm of the wheel chair. The chair rolled away with slapstick timing, crashing Gabe to the tiles. As Maureen stepped back and watched in amazement, Gabe scrambled to sweep up the letters and book, and then righted himself into a sitting position. He looked up at the young woman not understanding how his life could have been reduced to this. In his mind some great dam gave way and released a flood of despair and self pity. He wept. Weeping for the dead and the living. Weeping for his loss, knowing that nothing would ever be the same again. He wept, unable to see beyond the blackness, knowing life would never be any better than this.

Maureen sat down on the floor, wrapped her arms around him and gently rocked him back and forth, not saying a word. Eventually she stood and taking his hand helped him to his feet. She lead him over to an upholstered couch, the flowered pattern and potted palms lending a sense of the absurd to the scene. She sat him down heavily on the sofa and as he wiped his face with his sleeve, she looked down at him, "Sit here a moment, that's it, I'll fetch us a nice cup of tea." He straightened up and as his lips parted to speak, she took her index finger and sealed his lips. "Don't say a word, Gabe, just this one time, don't say a word." He didn't, and with that she went for the tea.

By the time she returned he had collected himself and approached his previous state of apathetic despondency. The two letters rested on the padded arm of the couch, unopened. "There now, nothing like a nice cup of tea to set things right. That's better isn't it?" Maureen smiled. He could not bring himself to agree with her and simply looked away, a sarcastic reply writhing behind his eyes.

She reached across him and grasped the letters, "Why don't you read your letters? A letter from home is bound to cheer you up." She passed them to Gabe.

He became exasperated fumbling with the letter and trying to still his shaky hands. Worried that he would become enraged and tear them in half, Maureen gently took them from his hands and opened the first one. "Shall I read it to you?" He nodded.

Maureen settled back into the couch, angled the letter to take full advantage of the sunlight, cleared her throat and read:

Dear Private Gabriel:

My name is Frank Artucci and I am writing to you on behalf of myself and my wife Melba, to thank you for your kind letter of December fourth of last year. I apologize for taking so long to write you, but as you can well imagine, this is very difficult. In that letter you told us the manner in which our son, Frank, Jr., died. We took great comfort in knowing that Frank did not face the end alone. As a retired U.S. Army lieutenant, I know that typically the platoon leader or company commander writes to the next of kin, and so we were particularly touched that you, being there during Frank's last minutes, took the time to write us yourself. You will never know how much that means to us.

In your letter you stated that Frank died well, and was brave to the end. These were words my wife needed to hear. Private Gabriel, during the first war, I served with Company A, First Battalion, Three hundred Eighth Infantry Regiment, Seventy-seventh Division, we were cut off in the Argonne for six days, you may have heard of us. Some people called us the 'lost battalion', I only mention this to assure you that I fully understand what you have been through. I have seen many men die in combat, on both sides. In the end it doesn't matter, each of them, in all the wars, made the ultimate sacrifice. There is no such thing as dying well. But I do appreciate the kind words that brought such comfort to my wife.

In your letter you gave us the impression that you were the one responsible for our son's death. Again, I must rely on my own experience to say that only the enemy was responsible for his death. Things happen so blindingly fast and with such violence in combat, that for the platoon medic to take responsibility makes no sense at all. I have the utmost respect for what you have done and continue to do. Where the infantryman can go to ground when things get too hot, you must run into harm's way to try and save a wounded man. I have seen the dedication and compassion of medical men and litter-bearers and know that beyond a shadow of a doubt you are much the same.

So please accept our eternal gratitude for helping our Frank, Melba and I always knew this could happen. We are so very proud of him, and now, we are proud of you.

God Bless You.

Frank and Melba Artucci

Gabe gazed at the clouds through the opposite windows. Maureen watched as he worked through the catalogue of the dead hidden deep in his brain. Finally, he turned and looked at Maureen.

"I remember that kid. I killed him. As sure as the shrapnel from the kraut eighty-one millimeter, I killed him."

"Oh Gabe, please, don't." Maureen placed her hand on his arm.

"I couldn't find the severed artery, a simple clamp and he would have lived. Then, I couldn't hit a vein, couldn't get a line into him for plasma. I blew it, I failed that man, and now he's dead, and his parents think I'm some kind of hero. It was a mortar barrage. We shouldn't have been there. We had no reason to be there."

"You can't do this to yourself, it was war, he was killed by the Germans just like the letter said, you'll drive yourself crazy. You are a hero Gabe, a bloody great hero."

As Maureen turned to face him more squarely a thin shaft of sunlight struck the nursing pin she wore on the strap of her apron. She saw the tiny circle of jeweled light flash and race across Gabe's eyes. "Gabe, you have to understand it's no one's fault . . ."

The words hung in the air, filling the empty space of the solarium. Gabe had begun to sweat and tremble. His eyes were fixed hundreds of miles away and his lips moved, speaking barely audible words. Maureen leaned forward to hear.

Gabe whispered the same word over and over, "Incoming . . . incoming . . . incoming . . .

Gabe regained consciousness to the familiar sensation of a drug-induced hangover. The diminution of sensory perception, being lost in time and place, the dry mouth and fetid breath were all symptoms he had experienced with some frequency over the last few months.

He was surprised to find himself the lone patient in the small-whitewashed room. The gray light from the window gave no clue what time of day it was and he had long ago surrendered to not knowing what day or date. He willed his mind towards clarity and rallied his strength to sit up in the bed. It was then that he noticed the leather straps restrain-ing his wrists and ankles. Instead of righteous indignation or primeval panic he was placid, simply relaxing his body and closing his eyes almost relieved. Almost. His serenity was short-lived.

"Nurse! Nurse! Sister! Anybody!" His throat rasped and burned until the shouts ended in a fit of coughing.

He heard the unexpected mechanical sound of locks being opened. A nurse he did not recognize entered the room. "Ah, Private Gabriel, I see you've awakened. Are you feeling any better?"

"Was I feeling bad? Worse than usual?"

"Why yes, yes you were. Don't you remember?" She stepped over to the bedside stand and poured him a glass of water and helped him take small sips through a straw.

"Thank you nurse, uh . . . nurse?"

"Donovan, Anne Donovan."

"Nurse Donovan, I can't remember much of what happened to land me here. Why am I alone in a locked room, and why the hell am I strapped down?" Gabe's voice moved between agitation and calmness.

"Yes, well, let me go for the doctor, he'll explain it to you ever so well. He will want to have a chat with you in any case." She turned and left the room. Several moments later she returned followed by a short, fine boned man. He, in turn was followed by a heavily muscled mountain of a man, dressed all in white and arms festooned with tattoos.

The white-coated little man looked down at the clipboard in his hands and then appraised Gabe. "Private Gabriel, my name is Doctor Canfield-Smythe and this is Seamus, late of His Majesty's Royal Marines. Seamus O'Hara, he's an Irishmen you know, he's normally quite a mild mannered sort, but he has, after all, an Irish temper. So, having said that, I'm going to have Seamus undo the restraints; I trust you'll behave yourself."

Gabe nodded and with a soft lucid voice asked, "Where am I and why am I here?"

"Ah, yes, a bit complicated that. Well, let's take those questions one at a time, shall we? First, you're still in the hospital, same hospital you've been in since your accident, Military Hospital number 17, but I suppose it'll revert to Saint Sebastian's now that the war is over, it was a R.C. hospital, and a damned fine one at that." The doctor tittered at the witticism. "You're on the fifth floor, the psychiatric floor. It seems you had a psychotic episode yesterday and Dr. Howard would like me to have a look at you, so to speak. You, see Thomas, may I call you Thomas? I'm a psychiatrist; the Victorians called us alienists. I want to help put your mind at ease."

"I'm in the loony bin." Gabe bristled.

"Now, now, we've come a long way since the days of Bedlam, or should I say, Saint Mary of Bethlehem Hospital."

"Why am I here?"

"Well, Thomas, as I said, you had an episode yesterday while speaking with a nurse volunteer in the sun room. You became incoherent, and then catatonic, completely unresponsive, even to painful stimuli. To put it plainly, you just weren't there."

"I remember the sun room, I remember Maureen, she read a letter to me, than it becomes fuzzy, I don't remember anything past the letter."

"Yes, Maureen, a very observant young lady. I questioned her about what happened and she indicated that you seemed to become anxious, that is, full of anxiety after she read you a letter. I've read the letter, I can see how it might bring on an anxiety attack in someone in your condition."

"My condition?" Gabe asked.

"Well, Tom, may I call you Tom? Well, Tom, in my professional opinion you have a fairly severe case of Battle Neurosis, sometimes it's called 'shell shock', sometimes 'battle fatigue'

"Battle fatigue? It's not battle fatigue, Doc. Battle fatigue is how chicken-shits, slackers, cowards get off the line. No, I'm sure it's not battle fatigue. It was probably just something I ate, or maybe some kind of vitamin deficiency or something."

"Yes, well, that's just the kind of Philistine ignorance we doctors are trying to overcome. Battle Neurosis is nothing to be ashamed of, under certain conditions it can happen to anyone."

"Bullshit."

"Yes, well, Tom, something happened, let's spend a few days together and see if we can get to the bottom of it, say what?"

"Yeah, sure, just so you know it's not battle fatigue. If that gets out, I'll never be able to face my buddies again."

"Not to worry Tom, mum's the word, all of the fifth floor records are strictly confidential, in fact, they're not even passed on to your Company Commander or anyone else."

"Good, and by the way, it's Gabe."

"Excuse me?"

"My name, it's Gabe. Not Tom, not Thomas . . . Gabe."

"Oh I see. Well, Gabe, we won't replace the straps, the window is barred and the door locked, I'm sure you understand," with that, Dr. Canfield-Smythe, Seamus and Nurse Donovan took their leave.

Gabe slowly and clumsily swung his legs to the floor and sat on the edge of the bed, allowing a moment or two for the dizziness to pass. He massaged his ankles and wrists and then stood. After a few tentative steps he began to pace around the room, surprised at how well he felt. He moved the small table and chair and began some easy exercises. Again, he was surprised at how little pain he felt. He would not have been able to do this just a week ago.

Shit. Maybe I am going to get better. Maybe I'll be able to get back to Munich and find out what happened to Irmgard and Karl. I can't believe it. Here I am in the loony bin for battle fatigue, ain't that something. Well, it's not battle fatigue, that's for sure. I'll show them. Battle fatigue, the loony bin, what a crock of shit.

Gabe began to laugh, first in small bursts, but then in waves. He laughed all the harder when he realized that the nurses on the other side of the door were probably shaking their heads and twirling fingers at their temples. It was the first time Gabe had laughed in months. It was a manic laughter, and would be the last time he'd laugh for years to come.

The following afternoon, after a morning of Freudian bantering with Dr. Canfield-Smythe, Gabe was awakened from an uneasy nap by a tentative, somehow feminine knock on the door. Clearing his head and dismissing the dream specters lingering from his sleep, he bade "Come in."

Maureen entered the room, walked to the bed and bent over Gabe. She hugged him tightly, kissed him on the cheek and whispered, "Oh Gabe, Gabe, how are you? I'm so sorry about the other day."

"There's nothing to be sorry about, it wasn't your fault. I don't know what happened, I don't understand what's happening to me. I'm just so damned unhappy, sad and unhappy."

"It's melancholia, depression, Gabe. It's just from being in hospital for so long. It'll get better once you are released, you'll see. Just keep a stiff upper lip and all that rot." She smiled.

"If you say so. But I feel like I'm being torn apart inside, you see I've always believed in hard work. If I work hard enough, I can get out of this place, but then . . . how the hell did this happen to me . . . so many things beyond my control that I work to correct but can't . . . and then? Why does it matter? Why should it matter? Because my long dead father said so?"

"Why are you so hard on yourself? What makes you so driven and obsessed about hard work and achievement? About getting it right? Even when things happen that are beyond your control you get upset, as if it was your fault that accidents happen. Gabe you need to let go of that idea, if you don't it'll destroy your life. You're a fine upright man Thomas Gabriel, you're just too hard on yourself, that's all."

As Maureen spoke, Gabe looked at her as if he was gazing through her and into the distance. As if he was peering into long past events or the distant future. When Maureen finished, Gabe swung himself out of bed and walked to the window purposely turning his back on Maureen to gaze on the bright outdoors. He placed his hand on the window frame and leaned his forehead against it, the glass fogging with his breath as he spoke.

Gabe spoke quietly, Maureen had to step closer to him to hear what he was saying and then closer again for clarity. "The year I turned thirteen, the summer of 1931, it was hard times for everyone. Well, that year, that summer, on the day school got out, my father came to me and said he was giving me a job, that it was a good job and one that would teach me something about life. I got really excited about it. I knew we were in the depression, like I said, hard times, and I knew there were plenty of grown men who didn't have jobs. So I felt pretty special. I had me a job for the summer and not just any job, but a good job where I'd learn something. In my excitement I asked my father how much I'd be paid. You know what he said? He said 'We'll see.' Not the best answer for a thirteen year old boy. But I swallowed it, figuring it was a job and he'd pay me when he could."

"So what was the job?" Mauren said posing the question to Gabe's back.

"He took me to his Uncle Rupert's farm, not mentioning the job the whole way there. At the farm, we walked to the far end of the south forty where a thirty foot section of stone wall stood, or I should say, used to stand. In front of me was a thirty-foot long pile of stones running along a stream and then turning away from it. The wall was a total ruin, like the tumbled-down walls of Jericho. My old man told me it would be my job to rebuild the wall. He said he didn't care how long it took me, as long as I did a good job and did it right."

"And did you do it right?"

"That first day I wore myself out and rebuilt the entire length of the wall, placing the biggest stones at the base, and working my way up the wall with smaller and smaller stones. I worked like a demon to impress my father, stopping only to take a drink of water from the stream. I was exhausted, had scraped knuckles and scraped knees, I was exhausted, but proud of myself. I thought that damn wall looked pretty good. At least good to a thirteen year old boy.

"Was he impressed?" Ann asked.

"Impressed? Yeah, he was impressed all right. So impressed that I had to stand there for better than an hour as he kicked over and tore every stone down on that wall, the whole time telling me what I did wrong, or asking me 'what were you thinking when you placed this one?' It was pretty humiliating, he made me feel about two inches tall. And that's when he told me I'd be back the next day and the day after that and everyday until I got it right."

"Oh, you poor dear, what a terrible thing to do to a young boy. Especially at that age, when boys are just coming into themselves and are so fragile." Maureen said, lightly placing her hand on Gabe's shoulder, and then quickly removing it, forgetting herself in the moment.

"Yeah, I guess. Well, that went on for about two weeks or so, same thing each day. Dropping me off at six-thirty in the morning and picking me up at seven thirty or eight and then making me watch for an hour as he tore the whole thing down. The whole time telling me what I did wrong, but never once telling me how to do it right. Hell, I never knew a wall could go back together so many different ways. Finally, I had it. I couldn't take it anymore, the hard work, the frustration, but more than that. The isolation, spending the day there by myself, day after day, eating my packed lunch alone, with nothing to do but wonder how I would screw up the wall this time.

"So what did you do?"

"One day I just quit. Spent the day taking dips in the stream, catching crayfish, resting, exploring, you know, all the things thirteen-year-old boys do."

"Little wonder, I'd have quit as well. What did your father say about that?"

"Not much at first. He just kind of stood there in disbelief. And it might have been all right if I hadn't opened my big mouth." Gabe paused for a long moment, looking out of the window raising his head as if he was following the flight of a bird. "But I did, yeah, I sure did. All the frustration of the previous couple weeks exploded out of me, him tearing the wall down, my humiliation, inadequacy, the loneliness, missing out on summer vacation, but it was more than that. I was crying, shouting at him through the tears. It embarrassed me that I couldn't keep from crying, but I couldn't, hell, I was thirteen years old. The dam inside of me had broke and every unfair thing and mistake he and I ever made flooded out of me. It was my own personal Johnstown flood. You know, for a long time after that I flattered myself thinking the outburst, standing up to him made me a man. He had told me the job would make a man out of me."

"Oh, Gabe, what a horrible story. What a burden to put on a thirteen year old." Maureen said, her voice growing thick.

"Yeah, well, I'm not done. The whole time I was shouting at him, he didn't say a word. Just stood there silent as the grave looking at me. When I finally couldn't shout anymore, I collapsed in on a pile of stones, sniffling and doing that hiccup that comes after you cry really hard. I can remember this like it was yesterday. He walked over to me and very calmly said 'Son, I guess I can understand where you're coming from. Now stand up, I have a few things to say to you.' Well, I thought maybe, just maybe he was going to say he was sorry, he was so calm, almost pleasant, maybe he was going to tell me he loved me, or maybe he was going to tell me how to build a goddamned stone wall."

"Did he?" Maureen asked in a whisper.

"He stood in front of me, as I got up. It seemed like it took forever before he said anything, but then he spoke. The first thing he said was: 'Don't ever speak to me like that again.' He raised his arm and backhanded me across the face. The next thing I knew I was on the ground on the other side of the pile of stones. I had never been hit so hard in my life, my legs were scraped up from falling over the rocks and I could feel the right side of my face starting to swell. Looking back, I think it might have been the first time I had been truly afraid of my father."

"Who wouldn't be afraid?" Maureen asked, her head slowly, unconsciously shaking from side to side.

"He walked around the other side of the stone pile and calmly told me to stand up. I was afraid to, but even more afraid not to. When I stood in front of him, he took his thumb and wiped the tears off my cheeks. I think I might even have smiled. Then he said 'Son, don't you ever, ever again quit a job. You can suffer the shame of being fired, but don't ever up and quit like this.' Then he knocked me down again, backhanding me with his left this time. Then he stepped over to where I was on the ground. I'll never forget the look on his face, and I'll never forget what he said to me."

Maureen stood silently behind him as tears began tracking down her cheeks.

"His face was blank and his eyes were empty, and calmly and slowly he told me that I was a quitter, dumber than a sack of hammers and he was ashamed of me and embarrassed to call me his son. Then he just turned around went to his truck and drove away. I spent the night sitting on that pile of stones, hating my father and swearing to myself I would prove him wrong."

"Dear God, why didn't you run away? I've never heard anything so cruel."

"You know I don't think it ever crossed my mind, I guess I'm my father's son and decided then and there I would build a perfect wall. He picked me up the next night and we drove home in stone cold silence. I could tell my mother had been worrying about me, but she wasn't about to go against my father. That night I collected all the camping gear I could find and piled it on the front porch. The next day at breakfast I announced I was going to pitch a tent and finish the wall, and that I'd appreciate it if someone could bring me food every two or three days, you know, stuff I could cook over a campfire. I built that wall for the next seven weeks, from first light until it was too dark to make out the stones. I spent an entire week sorting and getting to know individual stones, and then I began to place them. Once that started my father began to come by daily and tear down sections he didn't think were right. But as the summer wore on and I carefully laid the stone in small sections at a time, he tore down less and less and his visits came further apart. I finished the wall three days before school started. When my father did his final inspection he didn't say a word one way or the other. But he didn't touch a single stone either. He helped me strike my tent and clean up the campsite and drove me home. He never mentioned the wall again."

"Oh Gabe, what a story. I don't know what to say, or even what to think. I can't decide if your father was a monster or a saint. I suppose a bit of both, I really don't know what to think." Maureen took Gabe's hand turned him towards her and lightly kissed him on the cheek.

"Yeah, me either. It's funny, I don't remember anything about being thirteen, but I remember that summer, that beating, and the wall. I can still remember individual stones. I lived and breathed that wall and dreamt about it almost every night and continued to for years. I still dream about it sometimes. But you know something?"

"What's that?"

"Looking back, I think he was right."

"About what?" Maureen asked.

"About teaching me to be a man. What it takes to be one."

"What does it take, Gabe, what does it take to be a man?" Maureen's words sounding more harsh than she intended.

"It takes perseverance, it takes working hard, knowing there's nothing you can't do if you work hard enough, it means never giving up once you've started something."

"Rubbish. That's a bunch of poppycock. Of course, the sentiment and idea is noble. But who could measure up to that standard? How could anyone live like that?"

Maureen was becoming angry, not at Gabe, but at his father once again. "Don't get me wrong, it's a fine ideal, just not terribly practical, no one can live like that."

"I do."

"How can you say that? What about when things happen beyond your control, my God, you're a medico in an infantry company at war. Random events happen all around you all the time. What happens then? What about the accident that put you in hospital?"

"You don't understand. You just don't get it, you couldn't. Just think about it, most of those so-called random events could have been predicted and prevented. Why wasn't I more careful stepping out into the street, I heard that motorcycle coming. I could give you a thousand examples. Why did I let Lieutenant Brownlee and Menendez stand in that tower window making perfect targets? I know there are true random events, but not as many as you might think, and even those are arguable. When something like that happens, well, it's because somebody dropped the ball, and lots of times it's me who dropped it. It's a matter of perception, and my perception is from the top of that wall."

"Have you told this story to Doctor Canfield-Smythe?" Maureen knew the answer before she asked the question.

"No, I haven't told that head-shrinker that story, and I'd appreciate it if you didn't tell him about it either. It's very personal. I've never told anyone that story before, not even my wife."

"I'm honored, but I have to ask. Why did you tell me?"

"I don't know. Maybe I just needed to get it off my chest, maybe I just needed someone in here to try and understand me." Gabe walked over and sat on the bed.

"Gabe, you can't blame yourself for things like that, it almost sounds arrogant. Its an impossible position to put yourself in. You need to work this through with someone, if not Canfield-Smythe than maybe the chaplain, but it's not a healthy way to look at things."

"Says you. Now I have a favor to ask of you."

"Yes?"

"I know it's against hospital regulations, but since I can't leave this room, may I have one of your cigarettes?"

Maureen smiled, fished down into an apron pocket and took out a pack of Woodbines, lit two on one match and handed one to Gabe.

CHAPTER 33

Too Late

The following day Gabe moved back to the psychiatric ward, to a room with three other beds, only one of which was occupied. Gabe was worried the other patient would be a screamer or raving lunatic, but he proved to be just a young soldier who babbled and cried in the night.

Gabe soon realized the room change was something of a mixed blessing. He liked the relative freedom of the ward, yet had enjoyed the isolation of the locked white room. But the stillness and solitude of that place had exasperated his inability to measure time. What he thought were days had been weeks, but in the end, it mattered little. Once the darkness had descended upon him and since the first mention of "shell shock" and "battle fatigue", he wanted to just be left alone. He withdrew into himself, caring neither about time or place. The nurse volunteer Maureen was the only person he allowed limited entry, to everyone else he had slammed the doors shut. Limited entry, at best.

The morning session with Canfield-Smythe was more of a struggle than usual. When he could bring himself to speak, the words were couched into what Gabe imagined the doctor wanted to hear. The effort had taken a toll, and he returned to his bed, pulling the privacy curtain around three sides and burrowing into the khaki military-issue blankets. Lying on his side, he faced the window with its heavy locked grillwork. The steel mesh and lock had been painted over in dark green so often it could no longer be opened. Gabe watched the gray sky, gazing through the screen meant to keep him from jumping. The thought of jumping had not crossed his mind until he noticed the screen. It was an irony that brought him little satisfaction. But jumping was a fleeting thought as the clouds passed before his eyes. Instead he wondered how he could have ended up here. How could things have spun so out of control?

"Gabe? Hello, Gabe? May I visit with you a bit?"

Gabe drew back the curtain to see Maureen at the door. He nodded and she made her way over to the bed.

"I'm so glad to see you've finally been moved out of that awful isolation room. I imagine you're much relieved. You are relieved aren't you?"

"I won't be relieved until I'm out of this place. I have some unfinished business in Germany." Gabe said.

"Oh, Gabe. The war is over, don't you think everyone, including the Germans, have suffered quite enough? I should think you would be happy to never lay eyes on Germany again."

"It's not like that. It's not what you think. It's personal."

"I see. Well, then, maybe you shall go back one day. I don't have to tell you life is full of surprises." Maureen reached into her apron pocket, shook two cigarettes from the pack of Woodbines and lit them, handing one to Gabe. "Oh, by the way, I have something for you. I'm not sure if you remember, and this is the first chance I've had to bring it to you. There was a second letter for you. Here it is."

Maureen handed Gabe the letter. He examined it front and back, shaking it and sniffing at the sealed flap. "It's from my hometown, but the name and address don't mean anything to me."

"Perhaps it's a secret admirer. Open it and let's have a look, shall we?"

"No not now. I'm sorry, but I think I need to be alone to read it. I have a funny feeling about it. Besides, I'm not fit for human company right now, and it would be better if you left. I don't mean to be rude, I'm just so tired, and I don't think I can stand any news from home right now. I'll see you tomorrow if you want."

The nurse-volunteer stood up from the edge of the bed and trying to mask the hurt said, "Of course, of course I understand. So sorry to have intruded, I'll come back tomorrow. Is there anything I can bring you next time?"

Gabe shook his head and answered her with his eyes. She turned and left the room in silence. Gabe spent the rest of the afternoon and most of the early evening in half-sleep, unable to escape the demons, interrupted only by a small supper of potato soup and a bacon sandwich. When the hour arrived that most people retired for the night, Gabe resigned himself to another long night of the "big eye", insomnia of his own brand, of his own manufacture. He no longer had the concentration to read the books and newspapers provided him, nor could he write letters. He just didn't have it in him; despair robbed him of motivation. Halfheartedly trying to name state capitals and doing multiplication tables, allowed him no escape. He wasn't all that sure he desired to escape any longer. There is emotional familiarity with the darkness. Finding it difficult to get comfortable he rolled onto his side. He spotted the letter and reached over for it. Sitting up and switching on the hooded reading lamp, Gabe tore the envelope open along one edge, leaving the flap intact. He shook out the lined composition paper and began to read the shaky, child-like script.

Dear Mr. Gabriel,

My name is Missy Baker. I don't think we have ever met, am a cook and housekeeper and have worked for different white folks around town for many years. I believe you may know my only son, Enoch, most folks call him "Knock-knock". Before he got his job at the plant, he did a lot of odd jobs around town. He also made a name for hisself playing football on the colored football team in town, the New Surrey Browns. Mr. Gabriel, he's a fine boy, with a big heart and don't have a mean bone in his body.

He's in a lot of trouble and you are his last chance for saving his life. I'm asking you as a mother trying to save her son to please help him. I'm sorry to write you like this, but I don't know where else to turn, and I hope you will do the right thing.

Mr. Gabriel, this is very hard and I'm ashamed of Enoch to be telling you this. I'm sure you were very upset and are coming home when you heard what happened, and I'm sure you heard your wife's side of the story. No disrespect, but I want to tell you the truth of the matter. Enoch and your wife have been carrying on and sinning in adultery. All the colored folks in town know about this and been telling him it is wrong, and a lot of white folks know about it too. I know this must be a shock for you, but you can ask folks and they will tell you. Norma and Enoch played together when they were little children and then met again as grown-ups and one thing lead to another. I'm not making excuses for my boy, just explaining what happened.

You know what they said happened, but what you don't know is that your mother is the one who caught them in bed sinning in your house. Enoch ran away, and the next day your wife and mother told the police she was raped. They arrested him at work and put him right in jail. Mr. Gabriel, my boy was never very good in school and he can't hardly read or write, so Mr.Vann told him to confess and not have a trial, and Enoch was too scared and confused to not listen to him. Judge Colson is running for the U.S. Congress, and he wants to be famous, so he lied and gave Enoch the electric chair. They are going to kill my boy on August 11th and I believe you are the only one who can stop it. The Judge and Mr.Vann won't listen to any of the lawyers. The colored folks are too scared to speak up to the judge and the white folks too busy or just don't care.

Mr Gabriel, I'm not saying my boy did nothing wrong and don't deserve punishment, but I don't believe he deserve the electric chair. It take two people for that kind of sinning. Mr. Gabriel I'm asking you to please come home right away now that the war is over and see for yourself what happened and then talk to the judge, Mr. Vann and even the governor if needs be. Please Mr.Gabriel, don't let my boy die

for something that's not all his fault. It's just plain wrong
and you can save him as Norma's husband. I will be praying
for you and for Enoch.

I don't always write very good, so Reverend Crenshaw
has helped me some with this letter, he sends his best and
agrees with everything I have written you.

Sincerely,

Missy Baker.

Gabe lowered the letter to his lap and squeezed his eyes shut,
allowing the words to run roughshod through his mind. Picking up the
letter again, he reread it, slowly taking measure of each word. Oh God,
this is just what I need right now. Just what I need.

He ground the palms of his hands into his eyes as if trying to
obliterate the sentences piercing him. First came the betrayal, Norma
cheating on him this whole time, and if that isn't bad enough, cheating
with a goddamn nigger. Then came the guilt, how could he feel
betrayed when he had done the same with Irmgard? But betrayed he
felt nonetheless. There was the truth of the letter itself, that boy didn't
deserve to die, the pain in his mother's words, death once again doing
its *Danse Macabre* all around. The faces of a hundred dead began flashing through his brain squeezing themselves in between Norma, Missy
Baker and Irmgard. No, goddamn it, not this time, I can stop them, I
can save him. I can get out of here and save him. Thoughts and emotions began forming an inescapable repetitive pattern in his mind.
Swirling ever faster, Gabe felt as if he was standing in the eye of a
storm, paralyzed, unable to break the cycle, about to abandon all to the
tempest.

Gabe willed his legs to swing out of bed and stand, staggering a
few steps. It was as if all of the nerves in his body were unable to escape
the whirling chaos of his mind and perform their normal functions. His
breathing and heartbeat changed in unexpected and unexplainable
ways. His pulse and respiration racing and slowing, waxing and wan-

ing, Gabe thought he might die. Regaining his balance, he made his way into the hall and slowly walked over to the nurse's station.

A stern faced woman in a starched nurse's uniform looked up from her paperwork. The desk lamp reflected in her glasses made her eyes impossible to see. Gabe did not recognize her as he stood before the counter staring down at her with empty eyes.

"Young man, you know the regulations. Patients are not allowed out of their rooms once the lights have been turned off. Now, shall I call one of the orderlies, or will you go back like a good fellow?" It wasn't until she finished speaking that she noticed the look on Gabe's face. "Young man, is everything all right? What's wrong?"

"Nurse, what day is it?"

"Why, it's Thursday, why do you ask?"

"No, the date, what is today's date?" Gabe said, his voice barely above a whisper.

"It's the twenty-third of September. Is everything all right?"

Gabe stepped back from the counter and squeezed his eyes tightly shut against the enormity of the nurse's answer. The buckling of his knees was the last thing he felt. His head made an audible crack as it hit the floor tiles, as the nurse knocked over her chair rushing to his aid.

CHAPTER 34

Off of the
Row

Courage is resistance to fear, mastery of fear—
not absence of fear.
MARK TWAIN

"**W**hat time you got?" Harry Manning asked, stretching his long legs and repositioning himself forty-five degrees to his chair more like a plank of oak flooring than a man. "That damned wall clock still ten minutes fast?"

" 'Course it's fast, all the damn clocks around here are ten minutes fast. Warden does that on purpose. You know that well as I do. So, if you know that, you know what time it is. So why the hell are you asking me what time it is?" Bill Riddick reached round his chair and pulled a new pack of Camels out of his uniform jacket and began hammering it against the palm of his left hand with undo ferocity.

"Don't get your shorts in a twist. I'm just passing the time while we wait. But just as long as we're talking 'bout time, why the hell you think the old man bothers having the clocks set that way?" Harvey said, vaguely pointing in the direction of the dinner plate sized clock on the rough green-gray wall.

"Simple. Everybody will be ready to go ten minutes early, so nobody's ever late."

Harry helped himself to the pack of Camels sitting in front of Bill and extracted a cigarette. "Yeah, but that's just it. Everybody knows the clocks are ten minutes fast. So we all ignore the extra ten minutes and usually get there just in the knick of time anyhow."

"Listen to yourself will ya? Sure you know about the ten minutes, but the old man has got you talkin' and thinking about it don't he? Sure he does." Bill stood and walked over to the hotplate on the counter and poured himself another mug of mature coffee. "He's dumb as a fox, the old man is, dumb as a fox all right."

"You know, I never thought of it that way, but you're exactly right. Guess that's why he's the Warden and we're just a couple of screws." Harry chuckled.

"Knock it off. I hate that word. I can't do nothin' about those son-of-a-bitch cons, but to you, we're Correctional Officers of the Commonwealth of Virginia. Prison guards for the Old Dominion, got it?"

"Boy, oh boy, you sure got up on the wrong side of the bed this mornin' didn't ya? What's the matter with you anyway?" Harry glanced at the clock again. " You cursing your luck for drawing the short straw for duty on the row?"

Bill struggled to remain patient. He could barely stand breathing the same air as Harry, but wasn't sure why. "Curse my luck? Damn, are you crazy or something? All we got to do is take that shine from the row to the death house. What were you hoping for? Takin' him from the holding cell and strapping him into 'Ol' Sparky' yourself and throwin' the switch . . . so's he can ride that bolt of lightning? Nooo . . . we got the easy job, a bunch of goons, spooks and wise guys yellin' at us, then we're outta here. We're done once we get him in the holding cell."

"Guess you're right again. I was just a little pissed in general for getting called in for special duty." Harry conceded.

"Of course I'm right. You know the deal, all hands on deck when it's time to fry a bad guy. At least we're gettin' some good o.t., could be worse." Bill stood up, checked the clock and drained the stained white mug, grimacing. "Well, it's about that time, we better get going." He removed his uniform jacket from the back of his chair and slipped it on, buttoned it, straightened it, and adjusted his tie. Then he removed his hat from one of the wooden pegs on the opposite wall, adjusting it on his head just so.

Harry pulled himself together as well and the two of them left the break room, and crossed the hall into an anteroom. Before them were steel bars forming a cage, much like the drunk tank in a small town jail, only that behind the bars there was a counter and a seated guard. He looked up from his newspaper, " You boys are cuttin' it a little close aren't ya? Rogers and Haney were here ten minutes ago."

"See what I mean?" Riddick said giving Harry a knowing glance.

The guard behind the bars stood and walked to the back of the room, unlocked a metal cabinet and rooted around inside, returning with two small boxes of shotgun shells, one twelve-gauge double-O buck and the other twelve-gauge pumpkin-ball slugs. He then retraced his steps and unlocked a bar spanning a wall rack and retrieved two short-barreled pistol-gripped shotguns. Placing them on the counter next to the shells, he unlocked the cell door and beckoned the two tardy guards in. Signing their names on a clipboard, they picked up the tools of the trade. They loaded the guns, alternating buckshot and slugs, pocketing a handful of shells into coat pockets.

Harry grinned, ratcheting a round into the chamber. "I love the feel of a good riot gun, don't you? Makes my pecker feel longer." Bill shook his head and gave him a look that said "You're an asshole."

They hurried down the hall to find the Warden and the two other armed guards waiting on the other side of the double doors. The Warden made a point of looking at his watch. "Let's go, it's time." The Warden surrounded by the guards, set off briskly, passing through several more sets of doors, each more secure than the last until reaching the entrance to death row itself.

Before entering, the Warden turned to the escorting guards, took a deep breath and spoke. "Gentlemen, I just want you to know, that no matter how many times I've done this, it never gets any easier, and you never get used to it. Are you ready?" The men nodded yes in one accord. The Warden pressed a buzzer next to the heavy door.

There was an answering buzz and the men passed through the door and stood next to another barred enclosure that stored additional weapons, contained levers and switches and protected the guards in the event of a riot or some other act of violence. One of the two guards opened a sliding drawer, deposited a full set of manacles and chains, and with metallic finality, pushed the drawer through its opening

The cellblock designated as death row was a long high-ceilinged room, an acoustic nightmare harshly lit by metal-hooded lights suspended from above. The left wall rose unadorned, the brick painted dull green like the rest of the prison with no windows to ease its monotony. To the right were two stories of cells, ten above, ten below. Metal stairs led up to a catwalk allowing egress to the upper row of cells. The air was thick with sweat, fear, urine and hatred, the ordure of society's detritus.

It was six o'clock in the evening, Friday, the tenth of August. The five men stepped onto the main floor and began to walk towards the stairs. For a moment there was only the low masculine murmur and dull clanging sounds of any prison block. As the first foot falls echoed across the block, the atmosphere was rent with a sound like that of many waters. A roar of voices seemed to warp the very air, like the shimmering ripples of a heat mirage, sweeping over the five men. They faltered for a second and bent into the sound like men advancing into a tempest. They instinctively picked up their pace, wading into a flash-flood of sound and fury.

Officer Riddick was no longer convinced of his good fortune in drawing the escort duty from death row to the death house. It was an exercise in self-discipline for the men not to scream back or break the arms and hands protruding through the bars in impotent rage. It would be easy enough, using the bars as fulcrums snapping the bones cleanly. It had been done before.

The men could only recognize occasional words and phrases escaping through malignant din. There were curses and encouragements, sympathy and schadenfreude, but mainly, there was hopelessness, desolation and all-consuming wrath. It was hell without the flames and darkness. Abandon hope all ye that enter here.

The Warden and his detail reached the next to last cell on the upper tier with grim determination. A series of arcane bars and levers shifted, strained and slid open the cell door with complicated medieval grinding and grating. The Warden and two guards entered the cell, the other two guards stood on the gangway facing different directions, patiently enduring the auditory assault.

The Warden stood to his full height and with a raised voice addressed the prisoner: "Enoch Franklin Baker, by order of the court of the Commonwealth of Virginia you are to be transferred to a holding cell where you will remain until such time that the sentence of death is to be carried out. May God have mercy on your soul."

The two guards each took Enoch by an elbow and raised him from the bunk to a standing position. The Warden nodded and Officer Haney fastened the manacles and shackles to the prisoner's wrists and ankles. He passed the heavy chain through the iron ring on the chain locked around Enoch's waist. The Warden sighed with quiet satisfaction.

There was no real need for the chains; there was no place for the prisoner to escape to. He stood no chance of resisting the practiced nightsticks, brass knuckles and gun grips of the guards. The chains were the punctuation to the sentence being carried out. They were a reminder to the prisoner and all the other convicts on the row that they had ceased to be men in the worldly sense. Dead man walking.

Enoch made his way through the row with mincing steps. His shoulders were not hunched over, and he held his head up, staring forward. He was inured to the cacophony swirling around him like flocks of ravens and howling wolves, never acknowledging the arms reaching out from the bars to touch him with encouragement or malediction. Enoch was escorted from death row. He never turned to look back. Being led through the warren of halls and passageways, the ringing of his chains was the only sound to be heard. It was not until they stepped out into the August heat that his eyes moved and blinked in the hazy white-hot brightness.

He moved along in the trance-like state of a steer in an abattoir chute. The shouts of the inmates spotting him from the exercise yard did not penetrate his contemplation. He climbed the stairs and passed through the doors never to see the sun or feel its warmth again.

CHAPTER 35

The Big
House

Cell 'C', Building Nine
Virginia State Penitentiary
RICHMOND, VIRGINIA

C ell 'C' measured a full eight by twelve feet, luxurious by Virginia prison standards. Except for the fact that it was located in Building Nine, the Death House, it would have been a considerable improvement in Enoch's circumstance. There was a bunk, porcelain sink and seat-less commode along with a small shelf bearing a Bible, a dog-eared tablet of writing paper and a pencil. The latter items were of no use to Enoch, reading and writing had been as unattainable in his childhood as his freedom was now.

The cell would be illuminated for the next twenty-four hours and a guard posted immediately outside of the cell on suicide watch. From the holding cell he would be taken to eat his last meal, bid good-bye to any final visitors and make a single phone call. Then one hour before his appointed time his head and left calf would be shaved for the electrodes to make better contact and a prison chaplain summoned.

But that was still nearly twenty-four hours in the future. Once his chains had been removed and the guards retreated, Enoch sat on the bunk, performed the ritual massage of his wrists and ankles and then stretched out, closing his eyes to the harsh light.

Lying there, he was not afraid to die, he had never been afraid to die; he had spent too many years in church to his mother's everlasting credit and comfort. But he was afraid of pain, as all sane men are. A dread heightened by the boundless cruelty of fellow prisoners and the patho-logical sadism of some of the guards, who whispered to him anecdotes about death by electrocution in gruesome detail. His sole consolation was that if performed properly, he would lose consciousness with the initial jolt and the pain would be over almost before it began. A humanitarian insight shared with him by the prison chaplain.

Stretched out on the bunk it was not the fear of pain or the agonizing whether he would shame himself at the last minute, messing his pants and unable to make his legs work. What bedeviled him was that for the past seventy-two hours each time he closed his eyes his mother and sister's last visit ran through his brain. Appearing in minute detail, like watching a Pathé newsreel at the Saturday matinee.

Enoch recalled his mother and sister seated within arm's reach on the other side of a wire-mesh screen. Guards were posted on either side of the barrier ensuring that mother, son and daughter would not so much as touch finger-tips through the wire. The women were dressed in their Sunday finest, including pillbox hats, white gloves and small patent-leather purses crammed with tissues. Their expressions were of benevolent nonchalance as if they were visiting a distant cousin, but their eyes belied the look on their faces. They were as fragile as spun glass.

Enoch spoke first: "Hello Mama, glad you could come and visit, what time you have to catch the bus this mornin'?" Lord, she look bad, musta been cryin' all night, Naomi don't look like herself either. Why they got to be the ones punished, why they gettin' punished for my stupid-ass doin's? Ain't right, it ain't right, I oughta send 'em home this very minute.

Naomi perked up visibly at the sound of Enoch's voice. "We didn't have to take the bus, Pastor Crenshaw put the word out to the congregation and 'Sloe-eyed' Putnam done volunteered and drove us all the way here."

"Yes it was very kind of Mr. Putnam, what with gas and rubber rationing and all." Missy spoke softly and calmly.

The hint of a misplaced smile passed across Enoch's face. " 'Sloe-eyed' Putnam? Lordy, he mus' be a hunert years old, blind and deaf too, you got driven to Richmond by a mole, that's what you did." Despite the dire surroundings, Naomi brought her white-gloved hand to her face to stifle a smile.

"Mr. Putnam is a good man and Deacon of the church, don't you go disrespectin' him like that." Missy gently chided, naturally asserting her maternal authority.

"Don't mean no disrespect Mama, I know Deacon Putnam is a good man, knowed him since I was a boy. I just don't want you getting killed, that's all." Enoch knew it was the wrong thing to say before the words left his mouth. The change in his mother's dark eyes confirmed it. Why I go and say something like that for? Why I go and talk 'bout getting killed? Just slipped out, I know that, but if'n I ever learned to keep my great big dum' ass mouth shut I wouldn't be here now.

Missy deftly changed the subject. She and Naomi took turns telling Enoch the hometown news and gossip. They chose the topics carefully as if they had rehearsed on the way there. The time passed and for isolated moments the threesome slipped into places of comfort in the small talk, reminiscences and reflections.

Jack Peterson, the guard on Enoch's side of the wire, quietly cleared his throat to catch Enoch's attention. As Enoch looked at him, Guard Peterson moved his eyes to the clock on the wall and Enoch understood there was not much time left.

"Mama, they going to take me away soon. I got to ask you some things. You going to be all right, you know, afterwards? Who gonna take care of you?"

"Don't you worry 'bout me. I got a good job, and Naomi is being courted by Kenneth Tipton's son Johnny." Missy looked into her son's eyes for a moment and a single tear rolled down her cheek. "They going to take care of me. Are you eating and sleeping? Taking care of yourself?"

"Oh, Mama, what does that matter now? I don't have much appetite and don't sleep much, you know, plenty of time for that later."

"Stop talkin' like that boy. You have to be strong and alert, you need to be strong and alert to be prayin'. Prayin' like Jesus in the Garden of Gethsemane, you got your time in the garden right now, you'll see, you'll see God gonna respect your prayers, he gonna walk and be with you, you jus' keep prayin, prayin' strong and alert."

"Yes, Mama."

"Enoch, there one other thing."

"What's that, Mama?"

"That woman."

"Norma?"

Missy's face hardened and her tears seemed to evaporate. "That's the one. I fixed her wagon."

"What'd you mean Mama? What'd you mean you fixed her wagon? What did you do? She already caused us enough trouble an' all."

"I wrote her man, I wrote Mr. Gabriel in the Army and told him what happened, told him everything, 'bout you and his wife, 'bout them crooked dumb lawyers, about them politickin' judges and Commonwealth Attorney and that you was sorry and made a bad mistake, but it takes two people and you don't deserve to die 'cause it wasn't no rape."

"Oh, Mama."

"Oh Mama, what? You know me son, you know I try and be a good and godly woman, but that woman, that whore of Babylon, she took my son from me forever, now I need to take her man away from her. I'm not gonna standby while nothin' happens to her cause she white. I wrote her man and asked him if'n he would write the Governor and whoever else important. Letters telling them what happened and to set you free. I had to do it, was all that was left, nothin' else worked. So, there's still time, you still got three days, that why you need to be down on your hands and knees, prayin in that lonely Garden Gethsemane." Enoch couldn't remember ever seeing this side of his mother.

Enoch then shared the results of weeks and weeks of contemplation and self-examination, thoughts about Norma that were distilled down to their basic essence. "You can't jus' blame her. We got caught by old Mrs. Gabriel, what she gonna do? She stuck. She jus' traded one man for another, some poor black no-account nigger she was carryin' on with while the big dog away, tradin' for her husband she gonna live with and have babies with and be with 'til death do them part. And that old lady, imagine how she feel, a colored man with her son's wife? What she gonna do?"

"How can you say that, son? There's more here than you just going to jail, there's more here than even the death penalty. There's honor, there's your good name, there's your Daddy's good name too. You listen to me now boy: you did not rape that woman, no sir, you did not rape her and there's plenty of folks that knows that, and now that Mr. Gabriel, well, he knows it too. And if nobody in town brave enough or cares enough to stand up, well then, maybe he will, maybe Mr. Gabriel do the right thing. I got his Army address from Sam Burns, he said Mr. Gabriel is a good man and surely he do the right thing."

Jack Peterson placed his hand on Enoch's shoulder and wordlessly nodded at the wall clock. "Mama, Guard here, he a good one, he says it's time to go. Mama, I love you, you the best mother a boy could ever had." Enoch's voice finally broke and tears flooded his eyes as the realization of what was happening washed over him. "Don't worry 'bout me Mama, we be together again someday, don't you worry none."

With Enoch's first and final show of emotion the two women lost any last shred of dignity and self-control. As one the two of them hurled themselves at the wire mesh barrier, locking their fingers through the evenly spaced holes and pressing their cheeks against the wire. Enoch lunged for the mesh at the same time, pressing his fingers against the women's and his face against his mother's.

While the guards had witnessed this scene many times, no one with an ounce of humanity in their bones could fail to be moved. They gave the family a moment in a tacit and flagrant breach of regulations, rules trumped by a rare opportunity to show kindness.

The guard posted outside of cell 'C' on suicide watch looked up from the racing form he studied. Prisoner Baker was stretched out on his back, his eyes tightly closed and weeping. He went back to his form, looking at 'Cindy's Charm' in the fifth race as the horse to beat.

CHAPTER 36

Unexpected Visit

When Pilate saw that he could prevail nothing, but rather a tumult was made, he took water, and washed his hands before the multitude, saying, I am innocent of the blood of this just person; see ye to it.
MATTHEW 27:24

Enoch did not attempt to fight sleep. Instead, he embraced the somnolence besieging the embattled citadel of his mind. He willingly threw open the gates and raised the portcullis in abject surrender. Any man cursed and privileged by knowing the time and manner of his death must come to terms in his own way. Many cling on to every waking moment in compensation for the long sleep that awaited them. They mostly fail. It is like trying to hold the wind. Enoch greeted sleep as a respite, a weapon against the waiting. It is the waiting that drives the condemned mad. Slowly sleep made short cautious advances into his mind. It was sleep that was dreamless and restful.

With no window and no clock, morning caught Enoch unaware, when a guard awoke him from half-sleep. His first thought was why had they bothered? He sat up on the bunk and rubbed his face with his hands. For one last morning he opened his eyes and hoped that something had changed. He was not so naïve as to imagine this had all been a bad dream, yet he hoped that someone, anyone, had realized the magnitude of the mistake. It was a fleeting thought, having become more elusive with each passing morning.

A guard with a metal tray appeared and opened the small door in the bars. On the narrow shelf at the opening he sat a mug of hot black coffee, a pressed-metal spoon and a tin plate with an egg and two pieces of dry toast. "Here ya go, boy, breakfast time." The guard said without malice. The death house guards had been hand-picked and trained to be calm and considerate, or at the very least, apathetic. Enoch ate mechanically.

An hour later Enoch opened his eyes at the sound of the barred door opening. He turned over and sat up to see Don Morton, the prison chaplain, entering his cell. The older man was Abe-Lincoln tall and thin, with a shock of white hair, an aquiline nose and razor sharp chin. Laugh-lines and crow's feet worked the corners of his kind brown eyes. His tan suit was still crisp; the day being young.

"Hello, Enoch." The chaplain sat down on the edge of the bunk.

"Hello, Reverend Don, sir."

"How are you feeling?"

Enoch was helpless against the numerous disrespectful answers that flooded his mind, but knew it would serve no purpose to alienate this good-hearted man. "I'm feelin' 'bout as well as can be expected, sir."

"I understand, son. I just stopped by to let you know I'll be here all day, anytime you want to see me, you just go ahead and tell the guard."

"Yes, sir. Thank you kindly, sir."

"Enoch, there's a couple of other things."

"What's that, sir?"

"Well, for one, I've been asked to see what you would like for your, uh, your dinner."

"You mean my last meal, sir?"

"Yes. That's right." The chaplain answered, troubled by the simple, yet difficult question.

"It's all right, you can call it the last meal, the boys over on the row told me 'bout it, said next to gettin' outta this here prison, it's the only good thing about going to the death house, yes sir, only good thing. So I've been giving it some thought."

With two fingers Don Morton fished a fountain pen and small note-book from his shirt pocket. "Well that's good Enoch, so then you know the warden will do his best to give you anything you want, within reason, of course. You know what I mean. So what'll you have? Fried chicken and mashed potatoes?"

"No, sir. I've had enough fried chicken in this here lifetime, every Sunday long's I remember." Enoch met the chaplain's eyes, "No, sir, no more chicken for me. I want me a thick juicy steak. Ain't had near enough steak in my life, so's I'd sure like one for my last meal; thick, black on the outside and blood-red on the inside. I'd like home fries, cooked with lot'sa chopped onions, and I'll need catsup to go with that."

The chaplain was taking careful notes, scribbling in the pad resting on his angular bony knee, interrupting the young man's reverie, "Is that it, Enoch?"

"No, sir, there's still a little more. I'd like snap-beans cooked in bacon grease, and collared-greens cooked in butter, lot's salt an' pepper ons both. And if'n you think it's all right, I'd like some of them little fancy white dinner rolls, warm, with butter and honey to slather on 'em. My mama used to bring them to me when she served a big fancy dinner somewhere. Mama always got the best leftovers. I loved it when she had to cook big doin's."

Don read back the list to Enoch, checking each detail. "So that's it then? Sounds like quite a meal."

"Well, sir, not 'xactly, if'n you don't mind, there's still dessert and one or two other things. I'd like two or three bottles of ice cold Coca-cola, and then hot coffee with cream and sugar. For dessert, I want a couple of big ol' over-ripe peaches and vanilla ice cream, lotsa vanilla ice cream, if you please, sir."

"I see you have been giving it some thought. You going to be able to eat all this, sounds like it'd feed an army. I'll bet you're Mama had a dickens of a time keeping you fed."

"Yes. sir, if it be my last meal, may's well be a big one. You think the warden will give me that meal?"

The old man patted Enoch on the knee in a fatherly manner. "Well, son, I can't promise anything, but he usually does his best, so we'll see, there's nothing here that seems unreasonable to me."

"Good." Enoch said mirthlessly.

"Are you expecting any visitors today?"

"None's I know of, my mama and sister came to say good-bye four days ago, they allowed as they didn't want to be here today. Mr. Smith, my lawyer from the N.,double C., P. came to see me yesterday. He told me they's was tryin' to get word to the Governor, but he tol' me not to put too much hope in that. Anyhow, he said he and the other N.-double C. P. lawyers will be there tonight as witnesses. I heard there's got to be witnesses."

"I see. Enoch, you're also allowed to make a telephone call. Is there anyone you would like to call?"

"No, sir, I don't think so, nobody I would want to talk to has a telephone."

"I see. All right then. Well, I'll go let the kitchen know about your meal, and then I'll be by to see you a little later, maybe before dinner. But, remember, if you need me before that, you just go ahead and tell the guards. Now is there anything else you need before I go?"

"Yes, sir. Yes sir, there is."

The old man stood, unfolding his long body like a carpenter's rule. "What's that, son?"

"I was wonderin' sir, if'n you wouldn't mind prayin.'"

"I have been praying, I pray for you and all the men on the row everyday, I do it during my quiet time with the Lord, just at sunrise. And I'll be especially praying for you today."

"Thank you sir, you're a good man, but that's not what I had in mind by askin'."

Reverend Don sat back down on the bunk, his knees pointing skyward as he turned to Enoch. "Well, then, Enoch, why don't you tell me what's on your mind."

"Well, sir, I was hoping you might pray for my Mama and sister. There's no need to be wastin' prayers on me, sir. I'm heaven bound, and I know the Lord be taking care some folks for what they done to me. But that's all right, I heard the preacher say in church revengence is mine says the Lord. But, this goin' to be mighty hard on my Mama and Naomi, could you please pray for them, please, sir?"

For the first time since entering the cell, Don noticed Enoch's eyes moistening and felt his own voice thickening, "Of course, of course, I will, you can count on it."

As he stood to leave, the chaplain felt as if he had received a sledge-hammer blow to the abdomen. He couldn't remember the last time, or any time for that matter, that a death house inmate had made such a request. These men were self-absorbed, that was generally how they ended up on death row, particularly when they reach this point of the journey. Walking from the cell, the chaplain waded through a desolate swamp of emotions, sadness clung to him like black mud, and one thought harassed him like biting flies: most of the men here deserved to die for what they had done. But Enoch? Enoch was different, from the first day he met him; Enoch was out of place here. As the hairs on the back of his neck stood, he believed it more than ever. And there was nothing he could do about it.

The hours passed and by a small act of grace, Enoch was able to grab snatches of sleep. However, the ever more persistent growl in his stomach began to interfere with his rest. He was mildly relieved when a guard lightly tapped the bars with a billy-stick to get his attention.

"Baker, you have a visitor."

"I do?" He answered so surprised he forgot the obligatory "sir."

"That's what I just said. I'm going to take you to the visitors room and I'm not going to chain or cuff you. But I will crack your skull a good one if you even think about causing me any trouble. Got it?"

"Yes sir, I got it, no trouble at all sir. Sir, can you tell me who my visitor is?"

"Have no idea. All I know is I was told to escort you to the visitation."

The two men made there way through corridors and locked doors until they reached the visiting room. The cubicle he was lead to was identical to the one on death row where he had said goodbye to his mother and sister. He sat on a metal stool bolted to the floor next to a wire-mesh screen. The guard positioned himself several feet behind and off to the side.

On the other side a door opened and a guard followed by a small man entered. The visitor, short and slight was dressed in a seersucker suit, sported a navy blue bowtie and held a panama-straw hat in his hands.

Enoch recognized him immediately from the New Surrey courtroom, but could not retrieve his name. The harder he tried, the more impossible the task became.

The visitor, sitting on a matching stool, immediately read the look on Enoch's face and introduced himself. "Hey there, Knock-knock. I wasn't sure if you'd remember me, I'm Sam Burns, clerk of the court back home."

"'Course I remember you, Mr. Burns, I was jus' havin' trouble puttin' a name to the face. Thank you for comin' to visit. But I need to ask you, and don't mean no disrespect, but why're you here, sir?"

Sam spoke the words without meeting Enoch's gaze. "No disrespect taken. It's a fair question and I'm not sure I know why I'm here myself. All I do know is that I'm afraid if I didn't visit, I'd regret it for the rest of my life."

"How's that?"

"I don't know. I guess I just wanted to let you know I think you got a raw deal. I . . . this is hard to talk about . . . I don't think you raped that woman anymore than I believe in the man on the moon. And while I'm at it, I think the Judge and Vann did you dirty, don't know why, but I have my suspicions."

"Thank you for that, Mr. Burns, sir, but that still don't explain why you come all the way to see me."

"I told you I didn't fully understand it myself. I guess I wanted you to know that not everyone believes you're guilty, and not everybody thinks you deserved what you got."

"Thanks again, but I guess it don't matter much anymore. What's done is done. I ain't the first nigger killed for bein' stupid and doubt I'll be the last."

Sam took a folded white handkerchief from his pocket and mopped his brow. "Whew, this is as harder than I thought it would be. There's one more thing."

"What's that?"

"I just want to say I'm sorry."

"What you got to be sorry about? You didn't do nothin'. This ain't your fault, this is all my own doin'. I been told my whole life not to mess with white people, 'specially white women. So what you got to be sorry about? You gonna get up from here and go home free as a bird." Enoch's eyes flashed.

"You're right. You didn't let me finish. I'm sorry I didn't do more to keep this from happening. You know the Gospel stories?"

"'Course I do."

"Well, I may not be Judas, but I sure feel like Pontius Pilate. I feel like I just washed my hands of the whole thing, and now I can barely take it. That's why I'm here Enoch, to ask your forgiveness."

"You the one gave Mama Mr. Gabriel's 'dress overseas?"

"Yes, I did."

"Well then, you done plenty. But I got to tell you, Mr. Burns, I got to say I wish you hadn't done that. I know you meant well, but I wish you hadn't give Mama that 'dress."

"Knock-knock, she asked me to find it for her, I couldn't say no. She was so desperate and it was the last shred of hope she had."

"She also wanted to do something to get back at Norma. I wish she hadn't. It didn't do any good and that man overseas, well, he didn't need to know right now. It's hard enough to be a soldier, he done seen enough pain an' sufferin' Didn't feel like that right away, but now I do."

"I'm sorry."

"Please stop sayin' that, Mr. Burns. I already tol' you there's nothin' you need to be sorry 'bout."

Sam turned as he received a signal unseen by Enoch that his time was almost over. "Thank you."

"Mr. Burns, would you mind lookin' in on my Mama from time to time."

"You know I will." Sam stood looking at Enoch trying to fix his face into his memory.

"Well then, guess I'll see you later, and if I don't see you later, then I'll see you later." Enoch spoke the words as a blessing, and Sam looked down not being able to meet his eyes.

Sam turned and began to walk towards the door. Enoch stood and called out, "Mr. Burns?"

Sam stopped and faced Enoch from across the room. "Yes?"

"Sam Burns, you're a good man."

Sam stood motionless. "So are you, Enoch Baker, so are you."

CHAPTER 37

Wrongful Death

It is the cause, not the death, that makes the martyr.
NAPOLEON BONAPARTE

The last meal is a rite of passage condemned men pass through. Its finality in name and function are either a horror or a comfort. Usually both. Enoch was surprised to have found his appetite. He had not expected to eat much of the requested meal in its sumptuous splendor. He had looked forward to it only because it marked passing time. The hours and minutes were drawing to a close and soon it would all be over.

However, as he sat down to the meal, his hunger transcended the physical and ascended to the spiritual. With the food before him he tried to fill the empty places in his being. The Warden and Chaplain had been as good as their word. The meal was exactly as Enoch had ordered, except perhaps for the small white dinner rolls which weren't quite right. The prison cooks had done a creditable job with the side dishes, but they were up against stiff competition in the culinary expertise of Missy Baker. But the steaks, the steaks were as near works of art as anything Enoch had ever seen. Two steaks, thick, cooked to blood-rare perfection just as he had desired them to be. He ate them with near-religious fervor, like an archbishop taking the host during mass.

When he first sat down on the hard metal stool at the equally hard metal table he swore he would think of nothing but the food. No memories, no inner conversation, no more regrets, just the physical sensations, tastes moving over his tongue and the pleasant fullness of his stomach. But it was difficult.

Food is the liturgy of the family, especially for the working poor. Precious, but obtainable, it is the true tie that binds. Recipes and traditions passed from generation to generation until the line is blurred whether the celebration is the reason for the meal, or the meal the reason for the celebration. There was no celebration in this meal, no twelve seated around the table, no communion, no doing this in remembrance of me and no betrayer to dash out and hang himself. There would be the Gethsemane his mother had spoken of, and Enoch would enter it as soon as the meal ended; the final hours perspiring blood in prayers of resignation, then to walk his own Via Dolorosa.

It was all of this that Enoch brought to the table. It was a Sisyphean task to concentrate on only the physical. He counted the chews, he closed his eyes to experience tastes and textures and contemplated the wonders of the body's functions, at least as he understood them. Odd thoughts meandered through his intentionally cleared mind. There was one he couldn't shake. It was a conversation he had with "Popeye" Johnson, his neighbor on the row. "Popeye" derived sadistic pleasure in repeatedly describing death by electrocution in graphic detail to the other prisoners. A literal captive audience, unable to escape his terrible imagery. Smoke and the smell of burning flesh, eyeballs popping out of sockets and blue flames erupting from the ears, multiple jolts of current if the first one or two didn't do the job, and the evacuation of the bladder and bowels. Of all the horrors he foretold, the latter was the one that most often haunted the walking dead. Most recoiled at the shame of it, but for some, it seemed a fitting final revenge. On contemplation, so it was with Enoch Baker, he was beyond shame and the thought of revenge gave reason to eat all the food he could.

Back in Cell "C" Enoch laid down in uncomfortable repose, having to undo the button at his waist. He was dancing around the edges of half-sleep. He didn't dwell on the future, he didn't dwell on the "could-have-beens", but his mind was unable to escape the past. He tried to envision the faces of the people he loved and . . . hated. He made lists: the best Christmases he had ever had, the best birthdays, the best presents, the best dogs, the best liquor, and with trepidation, the best women. He continued until the self-hypnosis was complete. It was interrupted by the sound of hard-soled shoes on the cement and the metallic sounds of lock and key.

"Enoch, Enoch Baker, it's almost time boy." The guard announced calmly.

Enoch's eyes snapped open at the words. Rolling over, he slowly sat up. Before him stood two officers and a small cart on which sat scissors, hand clippers, a straight razor, bowl of steaming water, bar of soap and a nappy white towel.

"We're going to have to shave your head and leg boy, you're not going to give us any trouble are you? 'Cause we can do this the hard way or the easy way, it's up to you." The guard rested his hand on his night-stick as he spoke.

"No, sir. I don't want no trouble, I'm ready, I been waitin' on ya."

The man who pushed the cart removed the scissors, bent down and cut up along the outer seam of prisoner's left pants leg. He then soaped and shaved the fine curly hair from Enoch's leg, and dried the area gently. Next he took the hand clippers and cut the tight curled hair on top of Enoch's head. Finally shaving top of his head down to the skin with smooth, deft swipes of the straight razor, wiping it on the towel between passes and then drying the scalp with the same towel, creating a perfect tonsure.

Enoch opened his eyes and looked at the two men, their faces were blurred by the tears pooling in his eyes. The men turned and left the room wordlessly.

The final hour passed. Enoch repeatedly rubbed his hand over the smooth skin on the top of his head, the movements becoming a nervous habit under the duress of the moment. He was understandably nauseous and wondered if his deliberate gluttony had been ill conceived. He sat in cold sweat and struggled unsuccessfully to quell the trembling. The tremors rippled across him like wind on the water foretelling a storm; cat's paws before the gale. His mind raged and pleaded with God at the same time. Then he heard the door at the end of the hall open and the tattoo of numerous shoes walking towards him. He lowered his head into his hands and began a chant that would take him through to the end. Over and over he whispered an improvised mixture of the Twenty-third

Psalm and the Lord's Prayer, jumbling the words and ideas in any way they occurred to him.

He looked up to see five men standing outside of the cell. Warden Radford, Chaplain Morton and three guards, the two who had shaved him and one other, grown familiar in the past twenty-four hours standing silently. Two guards stepped forward and unlocked the cell, the Warden and Chaplain entered and stood before the condemned man.

"Enoch Baker, you have been sentenced to death by a court of the Commonwealth of Virginia. It is our duty to carry out that sentence. Your cooperation has been noteworthy and I have decided not to take you in chains. Please do not make me regret that decision."

Enoch was unable to answer, his throat constricting and the panic trying to claw its way out of his chest. He could barely manage short pant-like breaths.

Oh God . . .Oh God . . . Oh God . . .

The chair was positioned at the front of a long, wide room. Workshop lights hung from its high ceiling and the brick walls were unpainted and unadorned. Thick cables covered in black woven material ran from the chair to a small room off to the left, from which a tiny window could observe the proceedings. Leather straps, electrodes and a slender rod holding the headpiece festooned the square oaken chair. Ten chairs, in two rows of five sat out fifteen feet in front of the death seat, more like petitioners to the a king on his throne than witnesses to an execution.

As Enoch entered the chamber he looked at the ten witnesses seated before him. He did not recognize the six witnesses required by the law, but derived some small comfort in seeing three of the four N.A.A.C.P. lawyers seated in the second row. But it was Sam Burns seated in the front row on whom Enoch focused. Their eyes locked on one another's and Sam nodded to him.

Enoch was lead to and seated into the chair. His legs and arms were strapped down, a thick belt placed across his chest and made snug. The Warden and Chaplain stood off to the right side of the chair. In front of him stood one of the guards.

The guard stared straight ahead at attention and began to speak: "Enoch Franklin Baker. You have been sentenced to death by the Corporation Court of New Surrey, Virginia for the crime of criminal attack and rape. Electrical current shall now be passed through your body until you are dead. Do you have any last words?"

Enoch never took his eyes off of Sam. He was now visibly shaking and spoke so that he could be plainly heard despite his unsteady voice. "I just wanna say one thing. I'm not being put to death for rapin' that women, it was no rape. I'm bein' put to death for bein' stupid. Sam . . . watch out for Mama and Naomi. I'm bein' put to death for bein' stupid . . . and I guess that's enough of a reason . . . must be."

A black canvas hood was placed over his head. A hole cut in the top for the seating of the electrodes and another in the front through which only his nose was visible. The witnesses could see Enoch's chest heaving as a sponge soaked in saline was positioned on top of his head and the metal headpiece set in place and secured with a chinstrap. A second guard fastened the cabling to the electrode strapped to Enoch's left calf. They then stood back and waited.

The Lord is my Shepherd . . . He leadeth me to the power and kingdom and the glory . . .though I walk through the shadow of the valley of death I will fear no evil . . hallowed be thy Name . . . forgive us our trespasses as we for. . .

Enoch never heard the command to throw the switch.

CHAPTER 38

Insult to
Injury

Talk sense to a fool and he calls you foolish.
EURIPIDES

Above all things Sam Burns wanted to leave the room. He needed to vomit. He needed to get away from the hideous stench of death. The ozone mix of fear, sweat, burning flesh, and feces suffocated him and in some respects robbed him of the will to go on. It was a smell he would never forget.

He did not want to return to New Surrey. He did not want to enter that or any other courtroom ever again. He did not want to see Judge Colson or any of the officers of the court ever again, not in the courthouse, not on the street, not anywhere. He did not want to see Norma or Dorothy Gabriel, or for that matter, Missy Baker ever again.

He wanted to take his wife and children somewhere far away, maybe California, maybe Spain. He wanted to work with his hands, or work the land, or teach, anything but be a cog in a system whose corrupt and murderous machinery could masticate the innocent. Enoch Baker had changed Sam forever. He wanted out of the room. He wanted to bathe, change his clothes and burn them, anything to erase the stench.

Enoch's body would not be unmasked, removed and cleaned until after the witnesses had filtered out through the reinforced metal door on the opposite side of the room. The Warden and the Chaplain remained standing off to the side in hushed conversation. As Sam made his way past them he stopped, looked at them and made an instant decision to talk to them. As he approached, the men they looked up from their discussion and watched Sam with benign curiosity.

Sam stretched out his hand to the Warden. "Hello Warden, I'm Sam Burns. I was wondering if I could have a word with you?"

Taking the proffered hand the Warden said, "Hello. I'm Gene Radford and this is Don Morton." It was the Chaplain's turn to shake Sam's hand. "What can I do for you Mr. Burns?"

"Warden, can we go somewhere else? I need to get out of this room."

"Oh, of course, sorry, I should have realized." He said briefly glancing at the slumped, oozing body several feet away from them. "Let's just go back to my office, in all honesty I could use a stiff drink."

The office was further away than Sam had supposed. The trio left the death house, crossed the yard, made their way through fenced-in walkways and into a low brick structure that looked more like a school than a prison. Once in the office and seated comfortably, all three men loosened their ties and unbuttoned their collars, each cued by the other to do so. Cigarettes were broken out and lit, the smell of rich Virginia tobacco was a pleasant diversion. The warden walked over to a cabinet, retrieved three crystal tumblers and poured a generous splash of George Dickel into each.

Handing the drinks to the two men he sat behind his desk, raised a the glass and said, "To Justice."

To which Sam Burns bristled and answered "And to those who are denied it." before lifting the glass to his lips.

The Warden allowed the counter-toast to go unchallenged. "Now, Mr. Burns, you wanted a word with me? Do you mind if Don listens in?"

"Not at all. You see, I'm a friend of the Baker family."

"Yes, of course, I assumed that, or you were a friend of his victim's family."

Sam felt his cheeks redden, the two other men assumed it was the bourbon. "Victim? That's a poor choice of words, Enoch was the victim here."

"Excuse me?" The Warden stiffened slightly in his chair.

"I apologize. I'm not here to discuss the case. It really doesn't matter much at this point. Does it? Anyway, I'm here on behalf of Melissa Baker, the deceased's mother. I understand she requested her son's body be returned to New Surrey for burial in the family plot. I told her if it was possible I would accompany Enoch's body home."

The Warden pursed his lips with counterfeit sincerity. "I'm afraid that won't be possible Mr. Burns. I sent a letter to that effect to Mrs. Baker the day after she made the request, you must have crossed paths with it on your way here today or yesterday."

"A letter?" Sam took a long pull of bourbon, grimacing to swallow it down.

"Yes, a letter. In it I explained to her that in the Commonwealth certain crimes mandate that the corpse be turned over to an anatomical lab at one of the medical schools for dissection. Rape is one of the crimes listed. So you see, there's nothing any of us can do about it. It's the law."

"You put that in the letter?"

"Yes."

"In those terms?" Sam leaned forward in his chair.

"Basically, yes."

Sam's eyes flared and drew his hands into fists, speaking slow and coldly. "You wrote that dead boy's mother a letter like that? You are one cold-hearted son-of-a-bitch. Do you have an ounce of compassion or decency in that bleak soul of yours?"

The Warden rose to his feet. "I ought to take you outside and punch you in the mouth for that. And I would . . ." Radford sat back down and drained his glass. "If it weren't true. I'm not going to show compassion to these bastards, they deserved what they got. If you want to be compassionate, how about thinking about the poor woman he raped. What about her mother? What about her husband? Ever think about that Mr. Burns, that ever cross your nigger-loving sympathetic mind?"

"How the hell do you sleep at night?" Sam hissed through clenched teeth.

"Sometimes I do and sometimes I don't, but if I don't it's usually because of indigestion Mr. Burns."

Sam stood and walked to the door, nodded to the Chaplain and looked at the Warden. "Warden, you are a prick." He opened the door and stepped out into the hall.

The warden's voice followed him out of the office door. "And you, Mr. Burns, are a fool."

CHAPTER 39

Hearing
the Truth

*When you gaze long into the abyss,
the abyss also gazes into you.*
FRIEDRICH NIETSZCHE

It would be years before the stigmata borne by a soldier suffering "Battle Fatigue" or "Shell Shock" would cease to bleed. The condition would one day be known as Post Traumatic Stress Disorder and be readily forgiven, and effectively treated. But that was in the unimaginable future.

Gabe made his way down the gangplank of the Liberty Ship turned commercial freighter, Lucretia Mott, so christened after an early suffragette. Gabe was glad to be off the ship. Early March is not a good time to cross the North Atlantic, and the March of nineteen forty-six was worse than most. Standing on Pier sixty-seven, dressed in an ill-fitting suit of English wool and holding a leather suitcase secured with straps, Gabe made his way out of the freight terminal and onto West 28th Street. The tall undamaged buildings of Manhattan took his breath away and brought tears to his eyes. Gabe cried easily these days.

A stoker aboard the Lucretia had given him an address and directions to a flophouse in Chelsea, not far from the pier. Once Gabe had settled into the fleabag accommodations the next order of business was to find a Western Union office. The toothless man behind the desk directed him to the freight depot three blocks away. The smells and sounds, sights and pace of lower Manhattan swirled round him, catching him up in a dizzying whirlwind. It was as if there had never been a war at all. He was the stranger in a strange land.

Standing at a tall wooden desk, Gabe fished into an inner jacket pocket and pulled out a fountain pen. Unscrewing the cap, he took a Western Union form from its cubbyhole and began to write out a message:

To: IRA DAY, ESQ.   MARCH 19,1946

TAVIS, HEINEMAN, AND DAY, LAW OFFICE.

NEW SURREY, VIRGINIA

GREETINGS IKE—STOP—WILL BE ARRIVING NEW SURREY SAT. 3/23—STOP—WILL COME TO YOUR HOUSE SAME DAY 12 MIDNIGHT—STOP—DO NOT-REPEAT-DO NOT TELL ANYONE OF MY ARRIVAL— STOP—NEED TO DISCUSS MATTERS—STOP— DISCRETION OF THE UTMOST IMPORTANCE—STOP— LEAVE PORCH LIGHT ON IF THIS SUITS—STOP—GABE

Taking the form, Gabe stood in line for several minutes before wordlessly passing the message and then the fee through the trough under the barred window. He left the office and flagged down a cab.

"Where to buddy?"

"Grand Central Station."

"No problem this time of day, be there in no time." Pulling away from the curb, the cabbie continued, "So, Bub, you from outta town?"

There was no answer from the back seat of the cab. Turning halfway in his seat the driver saw Gabe staring blankly out of the window. The cabby turned forward and tried again, "Follow baseball, Buddy? Won't be long now. How about them Dodgers, think those Brooklyn bums'll do any better this season? I doubt it, you?"

Silence.

"Oh, the silent type, huh? Well, suit yourself, just trying to be friendly, that's all."

The cab deposited Gabe at the bustling train station. He nodded to the driver, paid his fare and added a generous tip. The driver nodded back in deliberate silence and drove off. Gabe entered the terminal, found a ticket window and bought a ticket for Cedar Spring, Virginia. He would have to switch trains in Martinsburg, West Virginia and take a south-bound up the Shenandoah Valley to Cedar Spring, the first stop past New Surrey. He would sequester there in the small railroad hotel until he was ready to see his childhood friend turned successful attorney.

The train ride south was uneventful, although Gabe's memories stirred as the landscape became more familiar. When the train stopped in New Surrey, Gabe drew his hat down over his face and feigned sleep until it left the station. It was late morning, Saturday, March twenty-third when he arrived in Cedar Springs. He stepped off the train to the famil-iar smells and sounds of small-town Virginia and was acutely aware that he had been gone a long time. It was the "Whites only" sign next to the depot restroom that confirmed he was home, or at least what was once home. Growing up, such signage was all but invisible, now it made bile rise in his throat. He reached into his jacket pocket and ran his fingers over the crease of Missy Baker's letter.

He checked into the railway hotel and spent the rest of the day tracking down and hiring a car for the evening. He expended a great deal of energy fending off inquiries and avoiding small talk. It made finding a suitable automobile all the more difficult. The sole car he could find to hire cost him an exorbitant five dollars, but at least it was a dependable 1938 Ford coupe. Gabe was a Ford man. That night around nine P.M. he confirmed the most direct route to New Surrey with the studious young man behind the desk. It hadn't changed. Gabe thanked him, abruptly turning away before there was any chance of being engaged in conversa-tion. Day by day it was becoming more difficult to converse and tonight he would have no surplus words to spare.

The late night drive to New Surrey proved easier than Gabe expect-ed. He had not driven a vehicle in almost two years, but once he adjust-ed to the Ford coupe's idiosyncrasies everything went well. Even in the dark, the road became more familiar with each passing mile. He arrived in New Surrey at eleven-thirty P.M.

Gabe noted that the porch was illuminated as he turned on to London Street and was relieved to know Ike was waiting for him.

Knocking lightly, Gabe had not removed his hand from the door when it opened, spilling light and warmth into the night. Ike had been waiting for him.

"Man, are you ever a sight for sore eyes. I can't believe you're actually standing here. You're not going to believe the scuttlebutt around here. You're like Mark Twain, the rumors of your demise have been greatly exaggerated." Ike said, his cheek pressed against Gabe's, holding him in a great bear hug.

"Let go of me ya damned weepy Black Irish." Gabe smiled sideways as he extracted himself from Ike's grip. "That's part of why I'm here. To set the record straight, at least with you."

"Well, come on in, let's have a look at you." The attorney maintained his game face as he surveyed the gaunt, pain ravaged face and body of his friend. He had aged considerably and Ike wondered if he would have recognized him on the street. "My friend, looks like you've had a time of it, glad you're back home."

"I'm not home, this isn't home anymore."

"Don't be ridiculous Gabe, this will always be your home, and I'll always be your friend." Ike said in his best 'hail-fellow-well-met' voice, his concern for his friend tucked far behind his blue eyes.

Gabe didn't answer and changed the subject. "Hell, wish I was smart enough to have landed a cushy office job in the Pentagon, bad enough you joined the squids to be a swabby, but then to end up behind a desk at the Department of the Navy, you oughtta be ashamed of yourself." Gabe's mouth smiled, but his eyes did not.

"Hey you dog-faced son-of-a-bitch, you're not going to make me feel bad for having an education. I graduated law school in the spring of '41 and joined up the Wednesday after Pearl Harbor. I got assigned to the Judge Advocate General's Corps, what the hell else are they going to do with a lawyer except send 'em to J.A.G.? Listen, I put on some coffee and have a bottle of Bushmill's that hasn't been touched since before the war." Ike disappeared into the kitchen to the thumping of cabinet doors and clatter of china.

Gabe visually explored the old Victorian parlor, it hadn't changed since they were kids and Ike's parents were still alive. Ike returned with a laden tray, carefully placing it on the low table between them. Gabe reached for a cup, "I love what you've done with the place."

"Still a smart-ass. Put down the damned cup and pour us each a Bushmill's will ya?"

After several toasts, and each man preparing heavily sugared and creamed coffee between libations, they settled back into the soft chairs, both lighting a cigarette in turn with the silver clam-shaped lighter on the table. The Irish whiskey, the smoke, the comfortable familiar room and the presence of an old and dear friend allowed Gabe to lower his guard for a time, to invest his emotions in the telling of his experiences. Something he had never done in one sitting. No one person had heard the complete unabridged tale. Gabe spoke nonstop for nearly three hours. In those hours he spilled out more words than his combined total spoken in the previous six months. A torrential downpour of much tragedy and occasional triumph, bravery and cowardice, helplessness and guilt, of love found and then lost, of the overwhelming weight he had failed to shoulder, of the recurring dreams and the slow slipping away of his sanity, losing the desire to make a connection with anyone, anyone at all. And then there was the letter from Missy Baker. Ike sat quietly allowing Gabe to get it all off of his chest. Gabe opened and unpacked story after story, exploring dim corners and unlocking rooms like someone clearing out a dead relative's house. "My God." Ike thought to himself over and over again when he was not thanking his lucky stars for having worked in the Pentagon. When Gabe finished, the two men sat exhausted looking at one another.

Ike broke the spell. "Gabe, I don't know wha . . ."

Gabe interrupted him. "Don't, just don't."

"But . . ."

"Listen, I never meant to burden you with this stuff, it's just that, well, it's just that once I got started I couldn't stop. Just forget about it, okay? Just forget it."

Gabe's friend ran his fingers through his thick jet-black hair, his cyan eyes studying Gabe's face for further clues. "Jesus, Mary and

Joseph," whispered Ike reaching back to his Irish Catholic roots to help navigate Gabe's troubled waters.

Gabe drained his glass, stood, stretched and walked over to the fireplace. He studied the family photos in their gilded frames. "There are a couple of more things."

"Mother of God, Gabriel, don't you think you've said enough for one night? Let's finish in the morning, you can have the guest room. A good night's sleep will help both of us put this all in perspective."

"No. I have to get through this while I still can, and there's no way I can stay in this town." Gabe shook his head slowly as he spoke.

"Well, then, let's have it, what else is on your mind?"

"This." Gabe handed Ike a worn, stained envelope from his coat pocket.

"What is it?"

"Just read it, I'm gonna step outside for a little fresh air and take a piss."

"Faith and begoren, me boy, ya surely know we have indoor plumbing now, not like over on the old sod." Ike proclaimed in a thick faux brogue.

"And you've forgotten, I'm a red-blooded American man; the world is my urinal." Gabe commented flatly as he left the room. Gabe gave Ike a good ten minutes to read Missy Baker's letter, taking a stroll around the block. It was unlikely anyone would see him in the darkness. He was a stranger walking the familiar streets of his childhood.

When Gabe returned Ike was sitting as if carved in stone, the letter splayed open on his lap and the smoke of a cigarette with an inch-long ash rising towards the ceiling.

Ike looked up from his reverie, "I was wondering when we were going to get around to this. In fact, I assumed this was why you wanted to see me tonight."

"It was. It is. The war stories, well, I haven't, I mean you're the first person, the only person I've told them too. And you're the last. I don't have it in me to put words to it again. They come to me every night, Ike, every night, the dead and the wounded. And talking about them, it's like calling to them, it's like inviting them into my brain, into my dreams. And you know, there are so many of them, that there's a different bunch of 'em every night. Except for one, one of 'em comes to me every night."

"Knock-knock Baker?"

"Yeah." Gabe massaged his eyes and forehead.

"So, what do you know about the whole thing?"

Gabe took his hands away from his face, "Not much, just what that letter says."

"What did Norma and your mother have to say about it?"

"Nothing."

"Nothing?" Ike refolded Missy's letter and replaced it in its envelope.

"Nothing. I haven't heard from Norma in close to a year. The letters came less and less often and said less and less until they just finally stopped. That's when I realized we really didn't know each other and just didn't have much to talk about. I guess that's why she turned to Knock-knock. Wouldn't have happened if I was a better husband."

"C'mon Gabe, that's a bunch of bull. It happened to lots of guys. It's the war. It's the separation. It's not your fault. What about your mother?"

"Yeah, she wrote for a while, but then I stopped reading them, once Norma's letters stopped I didn't want to hear anything about her. I wanted ed a clean break."

"Guess I can understand that." Ike stood and stretched, poured another two fingers each of Bushmill's and sat back down.

"Is it true she was fucking him? Fucking a nigger?" Gabe asked.

"Well, I can't say for certain, but there's a number of people out there who believe she was." Ike answered.

"Hell, black, white, guess it doesn't really matter much if she's out there spreading her legs around town." Gabes eyes flashed.

"Maybe not, but this is still the South, and that makes her having a colored lover harder to swallow."

"You know, I can almost understand how something like this could happen. We were practically strangers when we got married, and she's a woman, she's got needs and I wasn't around to take care of her. Yeah, it's understandable, doesn't make it right, but it's understandable, almost forgivable. What I can't forgive, what I can't forgive is if Knock-knock Baker was her lover, how could she then go ahead and accuse him of rape. She's not stupid, she knew what would happen to him."

Ike raised his glass while finishing Gabe's sentence. "A lynching, the electric chair, or life in prison without parole."

"I just don't get it. How could anybody be that hard-hearted? That cold? I guess I really don't know her at all. I'd have done anything to save the lives of my men, anything, given up my own life, willingly, for those guys. It's what you do when you sign on as medic. Hell, it's what you do as a decent person. And here she deliberately sends the guy she's having a fling with to his death. How could she do that? How could anyone? Hell, she murdered that poor stupid nigger. How could she do that?"

"You may not believe me, but I've spent a great deal of time contemplating that very question." Gabe stared at Ike intently as he continued. "Gabe this is going to get a little hard. Are you sure you want me to go on?"

"Go on."

"Well, I've run this thing through my head seven ways to Sunday. And when I toss in some of the scuttlebutt around town, with a grain of salt, mind you, I can only come to one conclusion."

Gabe lit a cigarette, tilted his head back and blew the smoke straight up. "Go on."

"I don't think it was Norma's decision."

"What are ya saying?"

"I'm saying, I think she was caught between a rock and a hard place." Ike took a long pull on his Bushmill's, stood and walked across the room to the piano, pulled out the bench and sat down heavily on it.

"Stop beating around the goddamn bush and tell me what happened."

"Okay, okay, here it is. I think the two of them were caught in bed by your mother and she was the one who put Norma up to charging him." Ike stared at the floor for a long moment before looking up and meeting Gabe's eyes.

"Good God."

"Yeah."

"Good God, that explains it, sure as shit that explains it." Gabe ran his hands through his hair.

"It's the only way this makes any sense to me. Your mother gave her an ultimatum, expose her as a whore of the worst kind, or charge Knock-knock with rape and save face, her son's honor and hopefully his marriage. Not to mention a little bit of sweet revenge."

"So you're saying she did this for me? You're saying Knock-knock Baker went to the electric chair for me?" Ike sat mute, watching Gabe as he came to the terrible conclusion. "If I'd have been here I could have stopped it. If I'd have been here that boy would still be alive."

"That's why his mother wrote you." Ike said very softly.

"Too little, too late." Gabe whispered half to himself.

"Yeah."

Gabe stood abruptly as if some spring operated mechanism had ejected him from the chair. "I gotta get some air, I gotta go." He grabbed his coat off the sofa and made for the door.

"Gabe, wait. I told you this was hard. Don't go. Please."

"It's all right, I'm just going out for some air, I'll be back, I just need to get out of here for a little while." Gabe walked the cold dark streets of New Surrey for almost an hour.

When Gabe returned, he entered the house without knocking to find Ike sitting in his chair, coffee in hand and smoke curling from a cigarette in the ashtray. Ike had lit a fire while Gabe was gone, its yellow orange shadows danced around the room.

"I'm glad you came back."

"My mother . . . That's a bitter pill to swallow."

"They did it because they love you."

Gabe spoke with a voice like still water. "They did it to save their reputations. They did it as damage control, and my mother, well, my mother needed to get back at the two of them."

"Maybe that was part of it, but not all of it. There are no easy answers here."

Gabe continued in the same calm tone. "What about the trial? Didn't anyone speak up for him? Anyone?"

"The trial? What a fucking sham that was. I was there. But, you know, I wasn't sure I could believe my ears, so thanks to Sam Burns I finagled a look at the transcripts. Then later I went to the appeal hearings filed by the NAACP lawyers, and again Sam provided me copies of everything. Unbelievable, what a miscarriage of justice, no worse, it was an abortion of justice."

"So then why didn't you do something to stop it?" Gabe's voice developed an edge to it.

"Aw, Gabe, come on. I wasn't a counsel of record, I wasn't anything. What was I going to do that those negro lawyers hadn't?"

"Too little, too late."

"Something like that, I guess."

"So what happened at the trial?" Gabe's voice softened again.

"All right, here's my take on it. To begin with, they arrested him without a warrant, it wasn't issued until two days later. They questioned him and scared the shit out of him throughout that first night, and then the next morning they took him to see Newt Vann, the Commonwealth's attorney."

"Bastards."

"It gets worse, a whole lot worse. It seems Vann told Knock-knock he wouldn't be able to afford a lawyer and that if he confessed Vann told him he would see to it that he wouldn't get the electric chair, only prison time."

"So he did it?" Gabe shook his head.

"Of course, he was scared and confused. Hell, wouldn't you have done the same thing? I would have."

"Yeah, you're right. "

Ike continued, "So they appointed him two corporate attorneys from Riverton. I bet those two sons-a-bitches hadn't seen the inside if a courtroom in twenty years. They weren't worth a couple of dead flies. They allowed Knock-knock to waive a trial by jury."

"Why?"

"Who knows? Maybe Knock-knock insisted, having taken Vann's words to heart, maybe they wanted to get it over with as soon as possible. Maybe those two idiots just didn't know any better. Well, you know the rest, Colson threw the book at him, wham, bam, thank you ma'am, gave him the electric chair without a second thought."

"Son-of-a-bitch." Gabe muttered under his breath.

"Yeah, well, Colson is going to run for congress, and you know, there's no such thing as bad publicity."

"Son-of-a-bitch."

"Yeah, well, there's more. Somebody in the colored community contacted the N.A.A.C.P. in Richmond and they sent up a team of colored lawyers. They filed a writ of *error coram noblis*."

"What's that?" Gabe arched his eyebrows.

"It's something like an appeal, where they ask the court to reverse its decision. But Colson shot it down, denied it without compunction. I read the writ and that's where most of what I'm telling you comes from. They did a creditable job putting it together considering the short amount of time they had. Knock-knock was given a thirty-day stay of execution until a decision was made. You know the rest."

Gabe stood. "I gotta go. I need some time to think all of this through. I wasn't going to come back, but there's still some things we need to talk about, and I can't take anymore tonight. I'm tired and it feels like my head is about to explode. What have I done? I'll be back tomorrow night, if that's okay."

"Of course it is. The light will be on, just come on in, the door will be unlocked. Gabe, be careful driving home. Don't do anything stupid, this is not your fault."

"Yeah." Gabe turned, retrieved his coat and left the room. He walked out to the Ford, climbed in and started the engine. As the motor came to life, Gabe was overcome by an irresistible urge. He opened the door and vomited.

CHAPTER 40

A Plan

He who abandons the field is beaten.
VICTOR HUGO

The drive back to Cedar Springs proved difficult. Through mental turmoil and the sting of tears Gabe made several wrong turns and found himself lost in the Virginia countryside. Each time, by following basic compass points he navigated his way back to a familiar road or landmark. But it took immense concentration to unravel functional ability from the Gordian knot of his psyche. It was as if he was driving by pure muscle memory.

When he finally arrived at the hotel he was exhausted. Exhausted and angry, frustrated, outraged, hopeless, and despairing, he struggled to maintain a tenuous grip on reality. His mind was slipping away faster than he could grasp for it.

Having reached his room, he mechanically undressed and climbed under the covers. When he finally fell into troubled sleep the dreams began, the dreams of the shell-shocked, the dreams of the battle fatigued. They were more vivid, horrendous and real than any experienced to date. The war dead and maimed came to him in accusation. Enoch Baker came to him in pitiful silence, only staring at him with baleful empty eyes, while Norma and his mother choreographed the dance macabre that consumed the rest he desperately needed.

Gabe awoke to the dim glow of dawn moving through the window, more zephyr than light. The twilight transition from half sleep to half wakefulness had always been Gabe's favorite time of the day. Now it was a dark passage through which he passed wondering if this was how the rest of his life was going to be.

He grew aware of a stinging sensation on his face and palms of his hands. Clenching his fists, sharp pain shot up his arm and a warm sticky sensation ran across his fingertips. Sitting up, in the soft light he saw bloodstains all across the pillowcase and bedding. Looking down at his hands he realized he had driven his fingernails into the hard flesh of his palms. He would not have thought it possible, except there it was, a self-inflicted stigmata. He touched his fingers to his face and felt the sting of more cuts. He padded across the floor, switched on the light and stared at himself in the dresser mirror. His face bore several parallel scratches clearly inflicted by his own hands, manifesting his own private brand of self-loathing. Embracing the pain he washed his face and hands with hot soapy water and then dried himself, patting the trickle of blood resulting from vigorous scrubbing of the wounds.

Walking to the door, he cracked it open and hung the "Do Not Disturb" sign on the door knob. He would spend the day in his room, trying to recoup some sleep. Gabe heard people say they were too tired to sleep and dismissed it as idiocy. He was not too tired to sleep, he was too afraid. He wondered again, if killing himself might not be the only way to escape his night terrors. From the outland reaches of his sanity it occurred to him that with suicide he might become a permanent denizen of his dreams; a private hell as just reward for taking his own life. So despite suffering the physical and psychological ravages of sleep deprivation, Gabe fought long and as fiercely as he could. Fear fueled his resistance, but there was something more. On some deep psychic plane he hoped that when finally overwhelmed, his sleep would be dreamless. It was.

It was late in the afternoon when the deep rumble and vibration of a German armor assault shocked him into consciousness. A wedge formation of Panzer Kampfwagen fives and sixes, Tigers and Panthers, were approaching somewhere in the distance. The illusion dissolved with the shrill howl of a steam whistle. The grinding of steel treads gave way to the roar of giant drive-wheels as the last of the great steam locomotives, heavily burdened with freight tore through town. The juggernaut of a Waffen SS panzer abteilung was the Baltimore and Ohio Mikado making the four o'clock express run to Memphis. Realization brought no relief to Gabe, only frustration, as he wondered what kind of armistice could end his personal war.

Gabe descended the stairs to the lobby scrubbed and in a fresh set of clothes. He stopped at the desk and requested a sheet of writing paper and an envelope. He scribbled a note to Vernon Clagget that he would need the Ford a second night, inserted a five dollar bill and sealed the envelope. Writing "V. Clagget" on the outside he handed the envelope to the desk clerk asking if he could see that it was delivered to the proprietor of the feed store across town. The clerk assured him it would be taken care of. If the man noticed the scratches down the side of Gabe's face he didn't mention them. Gabe took an evening paper from the stack on the desk, slid the man a nickel and made his way across the street to Myrtle's Café. He was ravenous; it was his first meal in twenty-four hours.

That evening, driving through the profound darkness of rural Virginia, Gabe wondered what tonight's consultation might bring. He had never intended to extend the visit beyond one evening. And while he long expected it to be difficult hearing about the events of last summer, he had been blindsided. It had never crossed his mind that Norma might have been coerced into making the accusation, that she had done it to save their marriage. That she had sent Enoch Baker to his death for him. Or that she may have been coerced into it by his mother. He gripped the steering wheel forcefully to steady his trembling hands as he considered the implications.

He assured himself repeatedly that tonight would be different. There would be no more delving into the events of the past two and a half years. Tonight he would talk about the future. Over the past six months he thought through the arrangements he needed to make and how Ira Day, Esq. attorney-at-law would carry them out. The crucible he endured the night before had convinced him. He was taking the right course of action and forged his resolution to make it so.

As expected, the porch light on Ike's London Street home shone brightly a second night. It was the lone beacon on an otherwise dark street. Gabe parked the car, walked up to the front door and entered without knocking. He was greeted with traces of cigar smoke, the warm inviting smell of brandy, a flickering fire and a melodious offering from Benny Goodman's clarinet.

"I didn't think you were going to show up." Ike said with a voice a little too jovial.

"I told you I'd be back."

"I know you told me you would be back, but saying it and doing it are two different things."

"Not for me they're not."

"Okay . . . point well taken. Drink?"

"Sure." Gabe removed his jacket and tossed it on the sofa, taking the other chair next to the fireplace.

"Well, how are you doing?" Ike asked, pouring a cognac into a snifter, admiring the rich amber color in the waver of firelight. If he noticed the scratches on Gabe's face he, too, didn't mention them.

"I've been better."

"Yeah, it was a pretty rough night, wasn't it?"

"It's been a pretty rough couple of years, and last night was the icing on the cake." Gabe frowned with the first sip of brandy.

"I can understand that."

"No . . . you probably can't." The second sip of brandy going down easier.

There was a long void filled only by the sound of the fire. "Sorry . . . you're right." Ike changed the subject. "You said you wanted to make some arrangements and conduct a little lawyerly business between friends. What did you have in mind?"

"I can't stay here. I don't want to stay here. New Surrey holds nothing for me now, only bad memories to add to the collection. As far as I'm concerned, the quicker I get out of here, the better."

Ike nodded in affirmation. "I'm sorry to hear that. I can't help but feel you're making a mistake, and I'd be lying if I didn't say I'm disappointed and saddened. I guess I'm selfish, hoping you'd be back and we could just pick up where we left off, you know, just like old times."

"Sorry. Maybe someday, but truth is, I'm not the man that left New Surrey in nineteen forty-three. It wouldn't be the same."

"So what about Norma and your mother?"

"Apparently they're not the same people either. I can't face my mother right now. Can't face her and can't forgive her. And the same goes for Norma."

"C'mon, Gabe. Give it some time. Time heals all wounds."

"What makes you think I want to be healed? I don't want to be healed. I want to put the ghosts to rest. I want them to forgive me, I want to make it up to them somehow. That's what I want."

"You want redemption."

"Yes." Gabe's voice was barely audible.

"I wish there was something I could do to make it happen. I wish to God I could."

"That's assuming there is a God. And after the Huertgen I find it highly unlikely. If He's there, He didn't do much to help Knock-knock, either." Gabe pressed his hands to his temples and closed his eyes.

"Where are you going to go?" Ira asked.

"I don't know, have no idea. Head north or west. I'm not too worried about that right now." Gabe answered.

"You'll let me know?"

"Yes and no. That's what I'm here to talk about. I'll contact you on the first, every six months and you'll let me know if there's anything that needs my attention. I'll assign you power of attorney and I will wire you money to open a bank account under your name. Ike, unless I tell you different, you're to tell absolutely no one that we're in contact."

"What about Norma and your mother?"

"No one."

"But Gabe, she's your wife, there are legal ramifications."

"She'll file for divorce after an appropriate amount of time, claiming abandonment, or desertion, whatever you want to call it."

"And your mother? You're just going to abandon your mother as well?" Ike asked.

"For now, yeah. I couldn't face her. She's got innocent blood on her hands just like me. The difference is, though, she dipped her hands into it deliberately, while my hands were covered in it because I failed to save their lives. If she should die before I return, if I return, I'll trust you to handle the estate with my best interests at heart. Will you do that much for me, Ike? I'll send you a yearly retainer."

"Don't worry about that, I'll do as you ask. I just wish you'd reconsider this course of action."

"I've considered and reconsidered it, and this is what I want to do. This is what I have to do. At least 'til I resolve some things, at least until I feel better, but I'm not too optimistic about that. If I could find a cave, I'd become a hermit, or maybe a Bowery bum or a hobo. But I'd still have to connect with people, carry on conversations, invest myself in some kind of relationship, and that's exactly what I can't do. I can't risk losing anyone else that way, not now, not ever. So the only way I can keep that from happening is to not put myself there."

"That's not a reasonable position to take. You're not being rational here. Stay and I'll get you help, Hell, I'll help you. You can't see things clearly while you're in the middle of it." Ike pleaded.

"I've arranged for a copy of my birth certificate to be sent to you and I'm leaving you my discharge papers for what they're worth. They're likely to do me more harm than good."

"What do you mean?"

Gabe lit a cigarette and leaned back in his chair swirling the cognac in its snifter. "You know the service. They diagnosed me with Battle Fatigue, and there went my honorable discharge."

"You were given a dishonorable discharge?"

Gabe tilted his head back and blew smoke towards the ceiling. "Not quite, it's called an 'other than honorable' discharge. That's some bullshit isn't it?"

"Yeah, you're right about that." Ira shook his head.

"It's not exactly going to work in my favor looking for a job."

"Listen, Gabe, this isn't what I was expecting to hear from you when you wired me. You've kind of blind-sided me with this whole disappearing act. Listen, I've got an idea."

With a dubious expression on his face Gabe answered, "I given this a lot of thought, and I've decided this is what I want to do and there's nothing you or anyone else is going to say to make me change my mind."

Ike leaned forward in his chair. "I know, I know, and I also know how you are once you've made up your mind. I'll do whatever you want. But just hear me out, for what it's worth. See, I have this cousin Danny. My cousin Danny on my mother's side from County Donegal, well, let's just say he marches to the beat of a different drummer. Anyway, he became a Trappist monk."

Gabe smirked. "I'm not becoming a Trappist monk, if that's what you're thinking. Hell, I'm not even Catholic."

"It's not. You know anything about Cistercian Orders, about the Rules of St. Benedict?"

Gabe interrupted. "Forget it. It's not an option."

"Will you let me finish?"

Gabe nodded, inhaling the golden fumes from his warm snifter of Cognac.

Ike continued. "As I was saying, Trappist, or Benedictine monks . . ."

"Why are they called Trappist?" Gabe asked interrupting again.

"Jesus, Mary and Joseph, I'm about to tell you. It has something to do with the location of their first monastery in France. But what's more important are the Rules of St. Benedict. It's what guides their day-to-day living and just about every other aspect of their lives. Especially what he had to say about speaking, actually, more like not speaking."

"A vow of silence?" Gabe asked.

"No, not really. They believe that words should be spoken only when absolutely necessary. Benedict thought that frivolous speech would take away from contemplating God. So as you can imagine, it's a pretty quiet place. Benedict also said that they should work with their hands, so every monastery produces something to support itself. Some bake bread, some raise crops, keep bees, brew beer, distill brandy."

"Beer and Brandy? Monks?" Gabe arched his eyebrows in mock skepticism.

"Apparently Benedict never said anything about abstaining from alcohol. Anyway, people, uh, men go there from time to time and stay with them. Helping around the place to earn their keep. Listen Gabe, I can't think of a better place for you to go and start getting over the past. You won't be alone, but you won't have to talk to anyone. You can allow passing time to exorcise the ghosts, for you to heal."

"How the hell do you know so much about goddamn Trappist monks?" Gabe's face flushed at his choice of words.

"I'm a lawyer, remember. So when I heard about Danny joining a monastery I did a little due diligence to see what he was getting himself into. And you know what?"

"No, what?"

Ike continued, "It doesn't sound half bad. In fact, there are some days I seriously consider joining him. Law practice can be pretty tough and ugly. You know what they say, 'the screwing you take isn't worth the screwing you get." Ike raised his glass towards Gabe in a mock toast.

"So, where is it?"

"Utah."

"Utah? What was Benedict a Mormon? How many wives are monks allowed to keep?"

"Smart ass. Why don't you go and find out."

"I'll have to think about it."

"There's nothing to think about, just go. Hell, if you don't like it or whatever, you can leave. No harm, no foul." Ike stood and went over to the tall cherry-wood secretary and opened the desktop. Rifling around in one of the drawers he removed paper and an envelope and began writing a note. He sealed it in the envelope and on the outside wrote: Brother

Hubertus, Abbey of Christ the Redeemer, Grantville, Utah. He handed the envelope to Gabe.

"I thought you said his name was Danny." Gabe said looking up from the envelope.

"It is, uh, it was, now he's Brother Hubertus. I wrote in the letter that you were a man of good character, that you were a good friend of mine, and that I would consider it a personal favor if he would help you in every way possible."

"Gabe found it difficult to find his voice. "Thank you."

"You need to go there, my friend."

"I'll give it some serious thought. Ike, thanks for everything, I need to go."

"Before you go, I need to have you sign a couple of papers and a couple of blank sheets down in the corner. It'll save me a bunch of work later on."

"No problem." Gabe nodded and followed Ike to the secretary where the papers were in a manila folder. He signed them, and wordlessly walked to the door, followed closely by Ike. Gabe turned and faced his friend. They hugged one another for a long moment, neither man speaking a word. Gabe turned and left.

It would be thirty years before they'd lay eyes on one another again.

A Beginning

Vigils, the first of the Hours.

Gabe stared into the imperfect darkness of his room, the graduated shades of gray of unadorned walls giving way to blackness. The brothers referred to it as a cell, but that was a term he preferred not to use. The feather pillow was doubled under his head, then it was wrapped around an arm as he rolled onto his side. He threw the covers off and then pulled them on, performing the frustrating gymnastics of insomnia. Gabe cursed his inability to sleep. Bone weary after a day of putting up hay for the abbey's livestock, he couldn't understand why sleep eluded him. Yawning repeatedly, despite the comfortable bed and cool night air, sleeplessness tormented him like some neighbor's barking dog.

His mind wandered in and out of box canyons and patrolled dead end streets. Repetitive thoughts and ideas plagued him. He half hoped and prayed, and half knew all would be tempered by the light of day. For the moment however, sunrise seemed a century away.

Damn it, why can't I fall asleep? I'm going to be worthless by tomorrow afternoon. What the hell is going on? What am I doing here? I don't want to be and can't be a monk. Am I going to just live here like an orphan left in a basket at the front door? God, please let me get some sleep. If I could just get some sleep, I could figure the rest out in the morning.

It had been a month since Gabe arrived and gave the Abbott, Fr. Hubertus, Ike Day's letter of introduction, four weeks since entering the sanctuary. Until a few days ago he had no problem with falling asleep. Now for the fourth time in as many nights Gabe switched on the light, dressed, brushed his teeth and wished he had a cup of coffee. Any hope of sleep had been completely abandoned. Switching off the light, and sitting on the straight backed chair, he debated whether he should pack his bag and leave. Deciding it would be the ungrateful act of a coward, he made his way outside and stood on the gravel path as he had the night before and the night before that.

For a moment he gazed up at the clear, moonless sky in awe, the pale band of the Milky Way and a thousand constellations never failing to humble him. In an instant he was the boy camped out during the summer of the stone wall, then he was the soldier on combat patrol having just crossed the Rhine. The unchanging night sky was one of the few consistencies in his life and because of that, he loved it. Gabe lit a cigarette, carefully cupping his hand over the flame to not compromise his night vision or alert enemy snipers. Some habits died hard.

He began climbing the half mile towards the knoll that overlooked most of the monastery buildings, the crunch of gravel measuring his progress. After a hundred yards he paused and began to search the night up ahead of him. Then he saw it. Faintly flickering in the darkness were six multicolored flecks of light. Walking another hundred yards, the six stained glass windows of the abbey's chapel appeared like poorly lit paintings in a darkened gallery. A slight shift in the direction of the breeze brought the sonorous murmur of men's voices. Although he did not understand why, the sound brought him comfort. Perhaps the healing had begun.

Arriving at the chapel, he sat down against the cool brick wall just below the inscribed corner stone. He leaned his head back against the brick and allowed himself to be filled with the sound of the monk's chanting. The sound washed over him like a gentle cleansing tide, flooding away the questions and struggles. The lilting melodies served as a lullaby, and in moments Gabe was asleep.

He awoke with a start, as one of the brothers placed his hand on Gabe's shoulder and gently squeezed. Gabe scrambled to his feet looking like a marionette taken up by a puppeteer. The monk also stood, offering his hand.

"We haven't met. I'm Brother Ambrose, and you of course, are Mr. Gabriel."

"Please call me Gabe."

"All right then, Gabe, how long have you been asleep here?"

"I guess since right after you began your singing in the dark." Gabe said.

"Singing in the dark?" Ambrose chuckled."Oh. You must mean Vigils. But that begins at three. And now we've just finished Lauds and have taken the Eucharist, that means you've been sleeping there for about four hours. You surely must be cold and stiff, come breakfast with me."

Gabe nodded yes and the two set off down the trail for the dining room in companionable silence. In the dining hall there was strict adherence to the rule of St. Benedict, no one speaking a word unless it was absolutely necessary. They shared a simple breakfast of tea, oats and an apple, sitting across from one another on unadorned wooden benches. When they had finished, Brother Ambrose quietly said to Gabe, "Come with me."

The monk lead him outside where the sun had risen sufficiently to warm their faces and signify the start of a summer day in the highlands. Ambrose lead the way ascending across an alpine meadow towards a copse of trees crowning the Southeast ridge. The monastery's main buildings sat in a small valley, so that it was a climb to reach any of the working places of the abbey. The pasture was nearly ready for a second cutting and Gabe marveled at the array of flowers, blue cornflowers, yellow Indian paintbrush and whole ranges of white field daisies that interspersed in the tall grass. The men walked in silence, the sound of insects, birds, and the hiss of grass moving in the breeze displaced their silence.

"So where are you taking me?" Gabe said, wondering if he had broken Benedict's rule.

"You'll see soon enough. We're almost there." Brother Ambrose said, turning and taking a few steps backward, looking like an excited school boy.

They entered the copse of quaking aspen and towering Colorado spruce, the minimal undergrowth lending the wood the appearance of a well tended hunting preserve. The men walked through mottled patches, and it was much cooler in the trees. The light and the air changed as they approached the far side of the small alpine forest. Leaving the trees again, Gabe and Brother Ambrose stood on a ridge line. A thousand feet below them a second valley stretched into the distance, snow capped mountains forming a spectacular and distant back drop to the scene before them. Below, in the valley, a river snaked between a patch work quilt of cultivated fields, and small stands of timber floated like islands in the sea of green. A barn and several outbuildings stood next to the river. A dirt road ran past the structures and followed the course of the river. Some distance beyond the barn, a cemetery stood half hidden by trees. The collection of white and gray stones haphazardly dispersed and miniaturized by the distance.

"You know, this may be my favorite spot in the whole world," the monk said absently.

"Not hard to understand why," Gabe agreed.

"So Gabe, tell me. Are you lost?"

Gabe looked at Brother Ambrose, his eyes questioning his companion. "No. I don't think so. I mean, it's a straight shot through the woods and down the pasture."

Brother Ambrose smiled. "That's not what I mean. I mean in the greater sense. Is that why you've come to us? Have you come to us because you've lost your way in life? Through the years we've had a number of men that have come to Holy Redeemer lost to themselves. Some have stayed and found themselves, others have moved on, perhaps continuing to search."

Gabe hesitated. "I'm not sure."

"Fair enough."

"I mean, it's not like I want to become a monk, if that's what you're thinking." Gabe continued.

"No one is expecting you to become one, nor asking you to. I just want you to know you're welcome to stay here as long as you wish. I realize the monastic life is not for everyone, but so far, you seem to fit in well. You have to be very clearly called by God to become a monk. God has to make you willing to be willing, and then He gives you a peace about exchanging one life for another. You give up a great deal only to gain so much more."

"Well, I haven't been called to be a monk, I don't know what I've been called to do. You are right about one thing though."

"What's that?"

"I'm lost," Gabe said. He bent over and picked up a stone and hurled it into the valley.

"Then stay a while Gabe. The solitude and beauty of this place can help you. And by God's grace and help you may be able to find yourself, if that's what you want. Oh, and don't worry. It's not like we'll hold you prisoner. You can come and go as you please. But, please, stay for a bit."

As the weeks passed Gabe continued to assimilate. He also continued to struggle with his guilt and questions. But there was one thing that had changed. A subtle, but real camaraderie had grown between him and Brother Ambrose. It was not built on so many words, but on a nod of acknowledgement and understanding from across the chapel, or sharing a meal in companionable silence. It had been a long time since Gabe felt he had an ally.

One afternoon towards the end of August, as everyone filed out of the dining hall, Brother Ambrose sidled up to Gabe and whispered, "I'm hiking up to the ridge later, care to join me? Say, four o'clock?"

"I'd like that," Gabe nodded.

They followed the same path they had several weeks earlier. As they walked Gabe occupied his mind by observing the changes that had taken place around him. The changes in the vegetation, the feel of the soil below his feet and the near invisible changes in the trees.

Upon reaching the ridge crest the two men stood and absorbed the view in mute rapture. First exalting at the sight of the mountains and then studying each detail of the valley with elation.

"I never tire of this place. It recharges me," Brother Ambrose said.

"How could you? It's magnificent."

"Come along then, there's something else I wanted to show you up here." Brother Ambrose turned and led Gabe along the spine of the ridge, its slope to the valley below becoming steeper and finally falling off as cliffs.

Gabe never took his eyes from the view and hadn't noticed where they had stopped along the edge of the wood. The monk turned his back to the valley and faced Gabe. "This is the other thing I wanted to show you."

Gabe followed Brother Ambrose' eyes and saw a cottage of stone and logs appearing somewhat dilapidated, forlorn and neglected. It looked to have two rooms and although the boards of the front porch sagged and a shutter was off its hinge, essentially it seemed to be structurally sound. "So what's the story on this place?"

"I'm not exactly sure, it might have been the original cabin. I've heard it was a shelter for sheep herders and a groundskeeper's cottage. It's been empty for the fifteen years I have been at the abbey."

Gabe carefully stepped on the front porch and tried looking inside where the a shutter was hanging crookedly. "So why has it stood empty? Seems like a waste. It's livable enough."

"I suppose no one has shown any real interest in restoring it. And I guess maybe the right man for the job just hasn't come along." Brother Ambrose's lips quivered. Clearly he was trying to keep from smiling.

"I see," Gabe said, shaking his head slowly from side to side. He had not made up his mind yet, whether he would stay. "So were you a con man in your previous life?"

The monk laughed. "I should think Father Hubertus would be thrilled to have someone living here and keeping it in good repair. It would serve a number of purposes. If you were to decide to give it a go, it'd give you focus, allow a way for you to earn your keep -- one of Benedict's rules -- and perhaps help you find yourself."

Gabe stepped off the porch and walked over to a patch of purple flowers growing next to the steps. He squatted down and studied them closely. Brother Ambrose walked towards him. "That's Russian sage, it reseeds itself and comes back every year, it must have been planted a long time ago."

"The bees sure like it," Gabe said.

The monk then realized Gabe was not so much looking at the flowers as he was watching the bees working them. Brother Ambrose was mildly surprised at how close Gabe put his face to the bees. "So you're not intimidated by bees?"

There was a tiny hint of pride in Gabe's answer. "No, of course not. My uncle used to keep bees and he always said you had to be either really unlucky or really stupid to get stung by a honeybee. Said they were way too busy going about their business to bother with mere humans."

"Your uncle's a wise man. In which case there's another thing I need to show you."

Brother Ambrose lead Gabe around the back of the cottage. An outhouse stood at the edge of the trees, beyond that a work shed, and next to that a clearing that held twenty separate stacks of wooden boxes. "Welcome to my pet project."

Each hive stood on cinderblocks and consisted of three to five wooden boxes, known as supers. Metal covered lids sat atop the multicolored collection of supers. The uncle's supers had all been white but Gabe liked the contrast the colors provided. The air hummed with the coming and going of the worker bees on their appointed rounds.

A smile formed on Gabe's lips. "So you keep bees."

"Yes, this is the Holy Redeemer apiary. It's my destiny to keep bees."

"Why is that?" Gabe asked.

"Saint Ambrose, my namesake, is the patron saint of beekeepers."

"I see. Well, I'll admit I've always found them interesting," Gabe said slowly walking towards the hives.

"So it's settled then. Consider yourself the beekeeper's apprentice. You'll move in and fix up the cottage, and God knows what else the Prior will find for you to do. Are you all right with that?"

"Listen. Brother Ambrose. I'm not sure. Let me give it some thought," Gabe said as he surveyed the colonies.

"Please, Gabe, call me Ambrose. Just plain Ambrose," the monk said watching the bees' flight patterns.

Gabe turned and began walking towards the woods, heading in the direction of the monastery halls.

Ambrose raised his voice and called after him. "It's just like the old song then."

Gabe stopped for a moment but did not turn to face Ambrose. The monk stood just staring at him and called out. "You know. Like it says in the song, I once was lost and now am found."

Gabe just continued walking, not looking back at the monk. He thought to himself "was blind but now I see . . . Yeah right."

CHAPTER 42

A Dark
Epiphany

Sext, the Fourth of the Hours,
the hour of the Crucifixion.

For Gabe, dawn was the most important time of the day. It meant that he had made it through another night. It was also liberating, dispelling the fear of dreaming. Except for one or two periods caused by disquieting events, the night terrors had come less frequently in recent years. Still, each night Gabe laid his head on the pillow in worried anticipation.

Gabe's life had become defined by self-prescribed rituals loosely based on the monk's daily schedule: the Hours, the seven periods of prayer throughout the day. There was comfort in the routine and none of the rites were unpleasant or particularly difficult. Initially, he had attended Vigils, the first of the Hours, at three A.M., prayers and Psalms watching for the return of Christ. Eventually he settled into Lauds, the six A.M. prayer of praise that began the day for Gabe. It was the greeting of the new day that Gabe found most enjoyable. Following the routines of the monk's day had another unintended consequence, it had brought about a slow, ongoing reconciliation with God. A God that Gabe assumed had abandoned him and most of mankind.

Sitting on the wooden chair, built with his own hands, he watched the Eastern sky lighten, brighten and change color as it heralding the imminent arrival of the sun. Sipping thick honey-sweetened coffee and smoking the first of three cigarettes he allowed himself for the day, he watched for the exact instant the arc of the Sun appeared over the mountains.

Thus satisfied, having fulfilled his obligation to the new day, his eyes searched around him with practiced scrutiny. It had been almost fifteen years since he had repaired and restored the stone and log cottage.

Yet, after all that time he continued to see blemishes or time damaged items that demanded his attention. He knew that the quicker he addressed them, the less his fragile inner peace would be disturbed. Every stone in its place.

Every stone in its place, he thought. He could not remember when the daily mantra had begun. But it whispered inside his skull every morning, part of his daily ritual, like watching the sun, counting his allotment of cigarettes... and scanning the cottage for flaws that needed to be made right.

Watching the valley below him come alive, he finished his cigarette and drained his coffee. Before getting up, however, he ran through a quick mental checklist of the jobs he needed to do that day. Mostly there were small maintenance items that could be arranged into a schedule of his own making.

On this day, his longtime friend and mentor Ambrose would make the climb to the apiary and together they'd perform the year's final "toe nail" inspection. Gabe laughed the first time he heard the expression, so called because the hives were completely disassembled and inspected down to their "toe nails." The health of the colonies and their readiness for winter would be assessed, weak hives combined with stronger ones and chalk marks made on the lids of colonies that needed supplemental feeding to ensure winter survival. He and Ambrose would start immediately after dinner and work through the afternoon. During the warmest part of the day there would be less bees in the hives and the remaining nurse bees were always a bit more tolerant on warm, windless days.

Ambrose was now sixty years old, a thin angular man, with a shock of white hair and deep wrinkles at the corners of his lively blue eyes. Gabe had long since lifted the heavy supers filled with honey, a weak back being Ambrose's only concession to age. Together they worked quietly and efficiently, wearing veils over their heads, but little other protective gear, the result of long years of practice and understanding with their insect charges.

Half finished with the apiary and opening the eleventh hive, they calmly worked the hive from opposite sides. Suddenly Ambrose straightened up and looked out over Gabe's shoulder, a movement having caught his attention. A bemused expression passed over his face causing Gabe to replace the frame he was examining and follow Ambrose's eyes. Standing a healthy distance away and trying to gain the beekeepers' attention with a minimum of movement, hoping not to attract a swarm of stinging death, stood Timothy, the order's youngest initiate. Gabe returned to the work at hand.

"Well, I suppose I should go and see what Timothy wants." Ambrose sighed.

"Have him come over here." Gabe said with a wicked smile.

"You're very cruel, my son, that will cost you ten Hail Mary's and a Novina. I don't think I've ever seen anyone as afraid of bees as our young Timothy over there." Ambrose said matching Gabe's smile.

"All the more reason, and after all, he does like honey." Gabe said to Ambrose's back as the monk walked towards the novitiate.

Ambrose returned momentarily. "The Abbot wants to see you at the rectory."

"Right now? Can we finish our inspections?" Gabe asked rebuilding hive number eleven.

"Apparently, right now. We can finish this tomorrow, besides my back's telling me it's had enough of bending over supers and hive stands for the day. Come on, let's put our stuff away and I'll walk down with you."

"O.K., but let's have a glass of iced tea before we go." Gabe said leading the way to the tool shed, removing his veil.

Settled into the rocking chairs on the porch each man held a sweating glass of iced tea and looked out over the valley. "Why do you suppose he wants to see me?" Gabe asked. "And why right away?"

"I haven't a clue. Maybe something has broken that needs to be fixed immediately. A clogged toilet, or leaking pipe or who knows what."

"Yeah, you're probably right." Gabe said as he stood and placed his near empty glass on the table between the chairs. Ambrose did the same and the two men left in the direction of the rectory. They walked purposely in their usual comfortable silence. At the rectory Ambrose bid his farewell and Gabe walked over to the brick house, strolling through the foyer and quietly knocking on the Abbott's door.

"Come in." A muffled voice answered.

Gabe entered the room. Father Hubertus was sitting behind a large wooden desk, reading glasses resting halfway down his nose, a steaming cup of tea resting off to the side. He looked up and smiled, "Sit down. Thomas, it's good to see you. Sometimes it seems like we go weeks at a time off on separate paths."

"My mother would have said we were like ships passing in the night. And by the way, I can't believe that after all this time you still don't call me Gabe."

"Oh, that's easy, you've always been like the Apostle Thomas to me, a man without guile." Abbott Hubertus smiled.

"So, Abbott, you sent that poor boy Timothy to the Apiary to fetch me. You know, of course, he's terrified of bees."

"Yes, I know." Their eyes met, and Gabe saw the tiny gleam in the Abbott's eye.

"So what can I do for you, Father?"

"I received a letter from cousin Ira today and this was in it for you." The Abbot said, pushing across the desk a sealed envelope with "Gabe" scrawled across its front.

Gabe's stomach contacted to a fist when he saw the envelope. It was just such an envelope almost a year ago, that had announced the death of his brother in a farm accident. The news had sent Gabe's heart and mind spiraling out of control for weeks, yet another loss, yet another time he should have been there, on the farm, for his brother.

Gabe met Hubertus' eyes. "Do you know what this is about? What it says?"

"If you mean have I read the actual letter? No, it's still sealed as you can see. But I do have a fair idea of what it's about."

Gabe ran his fingers along the top edge of the envelope repeatedly, as if trying to tighten its crease. "It's not good, is it?"

"I think it would be best if you read it yourself." Hubertus said, coming from behind the desk and placing his hand on Gabe's shoulder.

"Well then, if you don't mind, I think I'll take this with me and read it up at the cottage." Gabe folded the envelope in two and slid it into his back pocket, stood, and shook the Abbott's hand.

As he was going out the door, Hubertus said, "Thomas, if there's anything I can do to help, please let me know. You will be in my prayers."

Walking out into the sunlight Gabe thought to himself: This must be pretty bad. Maybe I should just go ahead and read it here and now. He fought the temptation, knowing that he would need privacy to come to terms with whatever misfortune the envelope held.

As Gabe began his climb through the meadow, the envelope became heavier with each step. By the time he reached the tree line, each step towards the cottage required more effort than he thought he was capable of. As he walked through the stippled shade and temperature gradients of the wood old sensations came back with long dormant ferocity. The bile of impending loss rose in his throat and the shame of helplessness circled above him like a malignant raptor.

At the cottage he entered the kitchen, went to the old pie safe and poured himself a tumbler of George Dickel. He sniffed the bourbon and took a long drink, grimacing as he went out to the porch and settled into his rocker. He lit a cigarette, tore open the end of the envelope and shook out its content. He opened the crisply folded heavy stock paper and began to read its typed message:

August 3, 1961

Dear Gabe:

    I'm sorry I have to inform you this by mail, but I only do so because of the rules you established for our communications. Your mother passed away this past Tuesday morning, the first of August. Apparently she suffered a heart attack and was found by the mailman when he saw her through the front door window. She was on the floor in the foyer. The medical examiner said she had only been dead a short time when found and that she had died instantly. She did not suffer at all. Your mother had made all of her own funeral arrangements and by the time you read this she will have been laid to rest in the family plot with your father and brother.

Due to the long estrangement between the two of you, she had bequeathed her entire estate to your brother. However, she never changed her will after his demise and so the estate will pass to you in toto by default. Gabe, this would all be easier if you returned to New Surrey to take care of the details. But in the event I do not hear from you by the fifteenth of September I will dispose of the house and other assets and invest the proceeds as per your previous instructions. I hope to hear from you soon, or better yet, see you. Gabe, my old friend, please accept my deepest condolences.

As Ever,

Ike

Gabe drained his glass, returned to the pie safe and poured himself a second drink, this time mixing it with water, ice and less bourbon. Back on the porch, he lit another cigarette, suspending the three cigarette rule for the day, reading and rereading the letter. He stared out across the valley, rocking to and fro, his feelings carefully muted. Emotional numbness being the oldest and strongest of Gabe's defenses. A bastion that protected him many times through the years, but hardly impregnable, it's stone walls eventually crumbling more times than not.

Numbness soon gave way to an uncomfortable sense of relief. It was over with, no longer wondering when it would happen or how it would happen. There was also a terrible comfort in geographical distance. Alleviated of having to make the arrangements, at having to greet mourners and be the object of undeserved sympathy, or worse, pity. Then there was the deliverance from forgiving or making peace with his mother. The solace of knowing he was the last of a family that fomented discordance and pain. That with him a root of bitterness, bitterness of unknown origin would finally die.

But relief fostered guilt. The guilt gradually making a mockery of his self willed numbness. How did things ever get this bad? Unable to forgive my own flesh and blood, an old woman betrayed by me, her first born son, the fruit of her womb, whether it was deserved or not. Memories coursed through him like runaway trains. Thoughts of his mother, his father, the two together crashing through any barricade he tried to throw up against the juggernaut of feelings. Happy memories: Christmases, birthdays, times spent together. Recollections he thought long lost, rediscovered, no longer possible to utilize them as tools of reconciliation, as instruments of redemption. Gabe began to sob.

He stood, walked the short distance to the crest of the ridge and gazed down into the valley, the breeze sweeping up from below stinging his moist eyes. No longer able to control them, tears traced rivulets over his cheeks. It had been years since he had cried, not even the death of his brother had made him weep. Pondering the enormity of it, he collapsed in place. Gabe hadn't cried since the time he received another letter, some sixteen years ago. The letter from Missy Baker.

The second line of Gabe's defenses arose as his eyes fixed on something far down the valley. Within, the bastion of numbness was assaulted and breeched, it was time for his emotions to retreat deeper, into the citadel's keep. A surprisingly effective tower of fieldstone and mortar, unassuming, benign in appearance, but difficult to overwhelm.

Everyone has to go through the death of parents, the sudden realization you are now truly alone in this world; an orphan. But I've been alone for years. And everyone has unfinished business with the dead, hell, even with the living. I'm no different from anyone else. And in the long run, what does it really matter? I'll get over it, I always do. No use crying over spilled milk. No sense in worrying about what could-a-been or should-a-been. It's just the way it is.

The proverbs and clichés raced through his brain at breakneck speed. Like an army marching to relieve the siege, the rationalizations and justifications helped dispel the pain and reinforce his flagging emotional numbness. Here was a coping mechanism that rarely failed. It might continue to protect him as long as it was not examined too closely. Self analysis and circular logic were dangerous things. Locking him into a Newgate prison of his own making.

Gabe began the long descent down into the valley. He walked, mindless of his surroundings, the time of day or physical needs. It was forty-five minutes before reached the dirt road paralleling the valley's watercourse, and another before he reached the old post and beam barn. He didn't stop. Barely taking notice except recognizing it as a landmark pointing the way.

It was another half hour before he stood at the gate of the old Mormon cemetery. In his fifteen years at Holy Redeemer, he could count on one hand the number of times he had been there. Generally it had been with Ambrose, enjoying a hike and stopping to ponder the place's historicity. But not today. On this day he was lead there by an internal force he could no more describe in words than he could resist it. Death and loss. No amount of emotional anesthesia or philosophizing could quell the flames or replace the stones as he walked among the grave markers and statuary.

He didn't leave the cemetery for twenty-four hours, alternately walking among the headstones and resting against them. It was among the family plots that he had a dark epiphany. A revelation that changed his life forever.

CHAPTER 43

A Personal Sacrament

Vespers, the sixth of the Hours.

Gabe lost track of the time that morning. In the fourteen years since the day Ike's letter had arrived, fence repair had become a constant in his life. A moderately long stretch just beyond the Chapel wanted attention this week. The work was hard and tedious, but on clear hot August days, working outside in the highland air and light was not a bad thing. He needed to be in the open air and light, away from bad things.

Gabe was stretching wire between posts when he felt a presence behind him. Turning, he saw the Abbott standing behind him patiently waiting for a break in the work. Gabe locked the ratchet on the wire stretcher and stood up straight, massaging his lower back. "Hello, Father, what brings you up this way? Feel the need to repair some fencing?"

The Abbot laughed. "I don't think so, Thomas, they made me Abbott to keep me from doing any other kind of damage around here. Listen, I was wondering if I could have a word with you?"

"Sure. I was about to head back to the shed for some more wire and nails anyway, and I'm about ready for a break." Gabe nodded towards the monastery's well used pick-up. "Hop in."

"I imagine you do need a break. You've worked right through dinner." Hubertus answered climbing into the truck, his eyes never leaving Gabe's face.

"I packed a lunch. I was worried if I went in for dinner, I'd never have the motivation to get back to fencing."

Gabe started the truck, turned the wheel and made the short drive to the tool shed behind the chapel. In a moment he opened the shed door and began loading supplies into the back of the truck.

Father Hubertus climbed out, and stood looking at the churchyard. The small cemetery attached to the rear of the chapel was the final resting place for the monks of Holy Redeemer. Fourteen simple white stones stood in a row along the back wall of the yard. A weathered wooden bench rested under an old growth Elm, strategically placed to enjoy both shade and sun at various times of the day. "Come," he said to Gabe. "Take a seat with me, this is one of my favorite places to sit and think."

When they were seated together on the bench, Gabe shook out his second cigarette for the day. "Care for a smoke Father?"

"Actually, I believe I will. Thank you, Thomas. Thank God, Saint Benedict didn't forbid us to enjoy food and drink, or tobacco for that matter. Just work hard, provide for the brothers and the poor."

"Yes, fine fellow our Saint Benedict, but there is that whole celibacy thing." Gabe smiled, not meaning to.

"Yes the celibacy 'thing'. That's a tough one, maybe the toughest. But first of all, I don't think that was Benedict's idea, and second of all, God provides special grace in that department to those who are called according to His purpose."

Gabe stared out at the grave markers, "Like the Bible says, Father, 'Many are called, but few are chosen.' I'm afraid I was never one of the chosen ones. I occasionally get the itch that can't be scratched."

"I know you do and since you've taken no vows that's between you and your confessor. Or in your case, between you and God. But maybe He just winks at it since you do so much other good work around here." The priest said. He leaned back and blew smoke straight up into the air.

"Yes, maybe. I hope so anyway. So, Father, what'd you want to talk to me about?"

"Brother Ambrose."

"Oh, I see. He's gotten much worse lately, hasn't he?" Gabe said stubbing out his cigarette. "I guess I didn't want to admit it, but I knew when I didn't see him at Lauds in over a week."

"I'm sorry, Thomas, I know how close the two of you have been, but we simply can no longer provide the care for him he needs. He doesn't recognize any of us anymore and now becomes belligerent so easily. It's a terrible thing to watch the brilliant mind ravaged by Alzheimer's disease, but if there ever was a man in the palm of God's hand it is our good brother, Ambrose."

"At least his decline has been fairly gradual. You know how I've struggled with grief and loss in my life. But this has been somehow different. It's like he's been slowly saying farewell to us. It's like he's been giving us time to get used to the idea of him being gone. I don't know, it's hard to explain." Gabe said, sounding as if he were trying to convince himself.

"I understand, perhaps it's Ambrose's final gift of grace to you."

Gabe just stared into the distance, unable to answer for several seconds.

"Father, there's something I need to tell you, something I've given a great deal of thought."

"What is it?"

"It became clear to me a few years ago when he was first diagnosed with Senile Dementia. It became clear to me, that when it came time for Ambrose to leave Holy Redeemer one way or the other, I would leave as well. It appears that time has come." Gabe said, resolutely.

"Gabe . . . Thomas . . . I don't know what to say. Are you sure? What will you do?"

"Like I said, I've given this a lot of thought. Unless I do something really foolish, money shouldn't be a problem. But more than anything, years ago, after my mother died it became clear what I had to do. For all of those people, and all those times I failed, finally there is something I can do."

"I don't understand, what are you talking about?" Hubertus asked, puzzled by Gabe's sudden change in direction.

"It would be easier to show you than it would to explain it. Do you have a few minutes? Can I show you something?" Gabe said digging in his trouser pockets for his cigarettes, and lit another.

"Of course. What do you want to show me?" Hubertus pressed.

"The cemetery."

The monk looked out at the row of simple grave stones.

"Not this cemetery. Come with me."

It was a twenty minute ride winding down into the valley, arriving, they pulled off the dirt road next to the gate of the Mormon graveyard.

"Follow me." Gabe simply said as he climbed out of the truck.

In the many years that Hubertus had served as the Abbott of Holy Redeemer he had only been to the abandoned Mormon cemetery once or twice. There had been no real reason for him to go there. His calling was to serve the living, and of course the Church, both the living and the dead. The long dead now surrounding him were neither living nor Catholics. Jesus said unto him, Let the dead bury their dead: but go thou and preach the kingdom of God.

From the look on Hubertus' face, Gabe could tell the cemetery had given him an abandoned, forlorn, desolate feeling. Gabe saw it through different eyes. He had been visiting it almost daily for the last fifteen years. He led the monk past the rows of stones, varying in shape and size, all quarried from the same source. Pale gray igneous rock, hard granite etched with the last testament of the people below them. An occasional white marble marker denoted the graves of the more affluent dead.

Hubertus asked, stopping briefly to read a badly weathered stone. "This place makes me sad, all these forgotten and lost people. There are no flowers, nothing here to indicate anyone has been here in a long time. Doesn't anyone come here, family friends . . .anyone . . . to visit?"

"Just me. I've never seen anyone else here." Gabe answered.

"When the monastery acquired the land, a right-of-way was granted and permission given for anyone to visit and even continue interments here. I wonder what happened?" Hubertus mused.

"Time happened." Gabe said as he began walking deeper into the cemetery and the Abbott followed. "As far as I have seen, the most recent graves are about forty years old and most much older than that. I suspect there isn't anyone around anymore that knew these folks. Families probably started using other, maybe closer graveyards. Who knows?"

As the two men approached the rear of the cemetery the distribution of the gravestones changed. Small fenced-in or walled areas filled this part of the cemetery. Family plots. Gabe lead Hubertus to one of the larger ones, opening a rusted wrought iron gate to stand before a twenty foot tall marble obelisk marking the center of the plot. On each of its four sides the name "Taylor" was carved into the marble. Surrounding the monolith stood twenty or so tombstones, some individually, others in small clusters. The small subplots marking the final resting place of immediate family.

Father Hubertus looked up at the obelisk, shielding his eyes against the brightness of the sun. "This was a big family, and a wealthy one as well, judging by the size and quality of the markers."

"Yeah, I thought the same thing, but the most recent of the graves is more than sixty years old. Hard to imagine what happened, a rich, sizable family, surely they must still exist. Makes you wonder." Gabe said.

" . . .'As for man, his days are as grass; as a flower of the field, so he flourisheth. For the wind passeth over it, and it is gone; and the place thereof shall know it no more.' That's from the hundred and third Psalm." Hubertus repeated, his voice nearly a whisper.

"Come here, I want to show you something." Gabe said.

He walked around the other side of the marble spire, stopping in front of one of the family subplots.

"Mother of God, are those . . ." Hubertus said stopping short at Gabe's side.

"Yes."

"Good Lord, those are infants', children's head stones aren't they?" The Abbott said, struggling to get the words out.

"Twelve of them. If you look at the ones that are still readable, not one lived past the age of two. Some didn't survive one day."

"Imagine the anguish and suffering those two poor souls must have endured." Hubertus offered, gingerly stepping past the two rows of small stones, each with a carved lamb resting on top of it. He stopped before two large markers. "Joseph R. Taylor, loving husband, Huldah Ruth Taylor, loving wife. Clearly, the small markers were their children, But there's no mention of them being a father and mother. They both lived into old age . . ."

" . . . and they died within six months of each other." Gabe said, finishing the Abbott's sentence.

"What do you suppose happened?" Hubertus asked.

"I suppose all they had was each other-- all that shared pain -- and when one died, the other couldn't go on." Gabe bent down and pulled a weed from one child's grave.

"No, I mean what do you think happened to the children?" Hubertus continued.

"Oh. Well, sickness. An epidemic, influenza. Maybe they were miscarriages. Take your pick, I guess it really doesn't matter much at this point." Gabe said, pulling another weed.

"Just curious. Just wondering, that's all. Nothing on the stones mentioning anything?"

"Nothing." Gabe said. "You know, the first time I saw the children's graves all those years ago, it hit me hard. I had just returned from the war, still real shaky and then this. But, you know, it was when my mother died that I was drawn here in spite of myself. Kind of by compulsion. I couldn't resist, guess I was like a moth to the flame. All I could think of were young lives I'd seen lost. Eighteen, nineteen, twenty year olds . . .and the German dead, boys of fourteen and fifteen. Not to mention small children killed in bombings. I had to wonder which children were better off. I had to wonder about the fairness."

"We can't judge that, Gabe. Who lives and who dies -- that's God's call. There're no way to sort that out and you'll drive yourself mad trying." Hubertus intervened.

"I believe the ones who got to spend some years alive are better off. At least they are kept alive in someone's memory, at least their names are spoken from time to time. But these babies, especially the ones stillborn or dying within hours, I don't know. Maybe it was too painful to think about them." Gabe said.

"Yes, I suppose you're right." Hubertus agreed.

There was a long silent moment. The sun poured down like a benediction. Or like nothing but sunlight.

"So I take it you've come here many times." Hubertus asked, finally. "What is it you do?"

"I . . . read the names. I thought the children deserved it. I mean, I thought they deserved to be remembered. Then, there was such peace, such a sense of doing the right thing, such a redemption, that I started reading the other names as well. You know how during mass you take communion? A symbolic act representing and partaking in the sacrifice Christ made for us? Well, this is my sacrament, a way of resurrecting the dead. Speaking them out loud. See that last infant marker?" Gabe nodded towards one stone.

"It looks like it's melting, like it's made of sugar instead of stone, so it's impossible to read."

"That one's made of limestone. Rainwater dissolves it over time. To me, having a marker like that is worse than having no marker at all. That child is lost twice. So I gave them a name—a name for all the lost children." Gabe said.

"What name is that?"

Gabe knelt down next to the dissolving stone and bowed his head.

CHAPTER 44

Nineveh
Cemetery

The body was found late that afternoon by a worker making a final pass through the cemetery in preparation of an early closing due to inclement weather. It was sitting on the marble bench in section 2-B, hunched forward, frozen in rigor with both hands on the cane supporting his upper body and the man's forehead resting on top of his hands. The worker had thought the man was in prayer until he noticed the snow settled on him and then saw the skin was the same color as the marble bench legs below him.

When the police and paramedics arrived, they carefully searched the body for identification. The first article they happened upon was the spiral pocket-notebook. As gloved hands clumsily leafed through the pages, the book was passed from person to person, and each in turn looked up and wondered what it could mean. On page after page and line upon line, the same name had been written over and over again, in dull pencil, in unchanging script, the same name. The name of an innocent recorded each time another name had been resurrected, year after year, notebook after notebook quietly, gently, carefully bringing about redemption, defeating the obsession, healing a fractured life.

The younger of the two policemen thumbed through the notebook with gloveless hands and looked up at his partner. "Who the hell is Enoch Baker?"

EPILOGUE

Norma Gabriel:

It took nearly two years before Norma's status as social pariah took its toll and she left New Surrey. The negro community vilified her for seducing and then, in essence, murdering one of their own. Whenever she came across a person of color while being out and about she was greeted with stone silence and hostile glares. The molten enmity in their eyes made the hairs on the back of her neck stand and her cheeks flush, that is, until she got used to it. If, when visiting one of her contracting circle of friends, a colored servant was present, she would not be served. This would put the hostess in the awkward position of having to make up some kind of excuse. After one such uncomfortable encounter Norma generally was not invited back to the house. She was ostracized by members of the white community that cared about such things, for a far greater breech of Southern etiquette and social mores. To them, the possibility of her having consensual sex with a black man was an unforgivable sin. To those people, Enoch Baker got what he deserved, whether it was consensual or forced.

There was a much smaller group of whites that reacted with righteous indignation. Angered that she could be so cold and cruel as to allow her lover, regardless of race, go to his death. In the spirit of true twenty-twenty hind sighted oracles, they swore, had they known, they would never have let him go to his death. They were for the most part liars and hypocrites. There was only one man for whom this was the absolute truth, and he lay three thousand miles away in a London hospital bed.

Norma continued living with Dorothy for those two years. There was an unspoken tacit agreement that the matter of Enoch Baker and the disappearance of Gabe were topics not open for discussion. At first, Norma made half-hearted attempts to find her estranged husband. Half-hearted because she wasn't sure she could face him if she did find him. She was intelligent enough to know that the attorney Ira Day knew Gabe's whereabouts. However, she also knew he was duty-bound to be as silent as the Sphinx on the subject.

In the end, her only regret was giving in to her lust with a black man. Until the end of her life she believed her subsequent actions were done for the noble cause of saving her marriage. She left New Surrey and moved to Dover, Delaware where she worked as a secretary for a large chemical company. She eventually divorced Gabe on the grounds of desertion, remarried, bore two girls and made occasional surreptitious trips home to see her parents.

Dorothy Gabriel:

Dorothy, too, believed in the strength of her convictions. For the love of her son she knew she had acted in his best interests. But at the same time, with malice fed by a lifetime of injustices real and imagined, she was able to wreak vengeance on the lovers. However, the revenge for hurting her and her son and for the crime against nature of a mixed race love affair was neither sweet nor satisfying.

She was never able to understand or forgive Gabe's self imposed exile. How could a son simply abandon his mother, the flesh of his flesh? A taproot of bitterness grew deep inside of her and tainted every part of her life. She had her will changed to exclude Gabe and leave everything to his brother. When he was killed in a farm accident she was so distraught that she forgot to once again change the will. She died six months later never recovering from the death of her youngest son and never reconciling with Gabe. Gabe inherited the estate by default.

Missy Baker:

Enoch's mother became a withered old woman the night of August Eleventh, Nineteen Forty-Five. She lost the will to live that night, but live she did, to ripe old age. Her golden years were anything but golden. She gave up any hope of ever returning to work and could barely face leaving the house and rarely did. She stopped cooking; she no longer attended church nor read her Bible nor cleaned the house nor mended her clothing. Missy found a place deep in her mind where she would spend all of her time. No doctor, no pastor nor even Naomi could summon her back from that place. When she occasionally returned it was by her own volition.

Naomi Baker:

On the night of August Eleventh, Naomi was wrought into a woman of chrome-hardened steel. Her exterior was of impenetrable hardness, while her veins flowed white-hot with the molten zeal of a crusader. Her brain became a forge in which weapons and armor were hammered into existence. She held three jobs, supported and cared for her mother and earned a teaching degree attending night school. She went on to be instrumental in establishing a local chapter of the N.A.A.C.P. and was a wise and powerful voice in the community.

Newton P. Vann:

Newt Vann died of a massive coronary days before his fifty-third birthday. He was on the golf course, a silver flask of scotch in his hand and telling a dirty joke. He was dead before he hit the ground. There was a front-page obituary extolling his virtues and achievements and his funeral was well attended. But except for his immediate family, he was soon forgotten.

Judge Byron T. Colson:

The judge ran successfully as the Democratic candidate for the House of Representatives in Nineteen forty-eight. He served one lackluster term, blustering about law and order and the threat of communism. He returned to New Surrey, retiring from public life, intending to write his memoirs. He never did.

Sam Burns:

As of January first, nineteen forty-six Sam Burns resigned his position as Clerk of the Court. He sold his house and furniture and moved his family to California. A cousin of his father owned an almond grove and was only too happy to teach Sam the intricacies of growing almonds. Sam eventually bought the grove and became one of the most successful growers in the state. He never set foot in a courtroom again.

Enoch Baker:

Enoch's corpse was turned over to The Medical College of Virginia's Anatomy Department. The cadaver was carefully and not so carefully dissected by medical students, whose coarse humor and false bravado helped to ameliorate the grisly work at hand. His bones were eventually cleaned and bleached and then sold to a medical supply house. They were assembled into an articulating skeleton and sold to a chiropractor in Springfield, Illinois.

www.ingramcontent.com/pod-product-compliance
Lightning Source LLC
Chambersburg PA
CBHW020258030726
47499CB00001B/254